THE SOLOIST

OTHER BOOKS BY NICHOLAS CHRISTOPHER

FICTION
The Bestiary (2007)
Franklin Flyer (2002)
A Trip to the Stars (2000)
Veronica (1996)

POETRY
Crossing the Equator: New and Selected Poems 1972–2004 (2004)
Atomic Field: Two Poems (2000)
The Creation of the Night Sky (1998)
5° (1995)
In the Year of the Comet (1992)
Desperate Characters: A Novella in Verse & Other Poems (1988)
A Short History of the Island of Butterflies (1986)
On Tour With Rita (1982)

NONFICTION
Somewhere in the Night: Film Noir & the American City,
A New & Expanded Edition (2006)

Nicholas Christopher

THE
SOLOIST

Shoemaker S&H Hoard

Library of Congress Cataloging-in-Publication Data is available.

ISBN (10) 1-59376-122-8
ISBN (13) 978-1-59376-122-6

Cover design by Gerilyn Attebery
Printed in the United States of America

Shoemaker & Hoard

AVALON
publishing group incorporated

An Imprint of Avalon Publishing Group, Inc.
1400 65th Street, Suite 250
Emeryville, CA 94608
Distributed by Publishers Group West

10 9 8 7 6 5 4 3 2 1

This book is for Constance

Place yourself therefore in the midst of the world
as if you were alone. . . .

—*Thomas Traherne*

THE SOLOIST

I always traveled light in those days. And so it was I set up house in Boston that spring. I had my two pianos shipped up, and my books, and never one for much furniture, I liked the empty feel of the loft the real estate people found for me, half of the thirteenth floor of an old sweatshop building in an obscure neighborhood. I had floor-to-ceiling windows, high ceilings, and it was quiet day and night with good light.

It had been a hot unseasonable spring, and on June 15 the mercury hit 96, a record. I particularly remember that day for a number of reasons, but when I first sat down to work, drowsy still, there was nothing remarkable in the air to indicate this would be so. I looked out absently on the too-familiar landscape: heat haze steaming off the river and the trees beyond the river white and dusty and to the west a network of chimneys and water towers and wires beyond which was the river again. Below me, on the nearest rooftop, the two girls in matching briefs had come out again, like clockwork, to sunbathe. They were rubbing each other with oil and photographing their cat. Boston was always a deadbeat city. But nobody bothered me there and I got plenty of work done. I used to be easily distracted, a nightbird, and while New York is a nightbird's town, Boston is a tomb by one a.m. Tombs inspire discipline. And I was in training that spring, as my manager Willy liked to call it, living in Boston and trying to put myself back in shape. I had fled there when my life became unmanageable—it was my idea of a monastery—but then it seemed a good idea to stay on, so I did.

Willy was German. Bavarian, he always said. He disapproved of my methods for many years, but just then I could do no wrong for him. He thought of all his clients in the simplest terms: you trained, you performed, and you went on holiday. And then you started over again. That's the way his mind worked. But I'm not being fair to Willy. I always had a tendency to blame others for my prejudices and self-loathing. I did not like to own up to my less flattering opinions of myself, so I passed them on. Actually, Willy thought very highly of me, he was fond of me. To slur him with hints of Teutonic rigidity is not accurate either, for in fact he was far more altruistic and open-minded than I, more loyal to our "business," and probably not so obsessed with money. Over lunch he loved to talk about theater and opera and music history, and all I wanted to hear about was tax dodges. I think I disappointed him acutely at such times. But he loved to hear me play, and as with other people in my life, nearly all of them, that always made up for plenty. If you play the piano well, on the level that I played, people want to think the best of you. They'll indulge your eccentricities, and put up with a moderate amount of nonsense, but they don't want to think you're a bastard behind the scenes. It blows it for them, and I can understand that. When I used to hear my best recordings, even I had faith in myself.

That hot June day my body felt as if it had been hammered all over. My arm and shoulder muscles were burning, my left wrist was stiff, my stomach a knot. Over coffee I played the previous day's tape and it was weak, even pedestrian. It was still missing something. Missing it terribly. Like the hurricane's proverbial eye, it was this missing something that lay at the heart of the vast swirl of circumstances that were to change my life that summer. When I said I have good reasons for remembering that day, it was a slight understatement. In fact, it was the first day in a week, and a summer, of both wonder and terror, mystery and disappointment, triumph and misery, and using it as a starting reference, like a dot on a graph, I can quite distinctly chart the turning point that was to follow. At the time, of course, as is usually the case at such times, my preoccupations were mundane. I was worried about money. And I was worried about my comeback. I was thirty-three years old and I was making a comeback. Technically, mechanically, I was playing well enough, but this crucial gap in my work was killing me on the inside and threatening to ruin me in all other ways. A spark, a flame, a veneer of confidence—call it what you will—I no longer possessed that magical essential element that had enabled me to stand out as a pianist, the element that separates the swarm of technicians from the handful of true performers. Maybe you could say I had just lost my nerve. The sound was there but the juice was gone.

I had been professionally inactive (Willy's expression) for a long while. I had avoided the concert stage and the touring circuit for four years, though I recorded four new albums in that time and did not look back on it as a period of inactivity. I had also traveled widely and helped to raise my child and involved myself in more private intrigues of varying complexities than I would care to review—but I suppose those are not professional considerations. The comeback performance, in New York, was to be the beginning of a sixteen-city tour. They told me it had to be done, that I had to get back into circulation, to sell more records, make more money. Sales lag without concerts, and people like to know that you haven't ballooned to three hundred pounds, or gone bald, or palsied, that you're not in the clinker or on the funny farm. Before I start blaming Willy again, I should say that I always liked to make money and to perform. And aside from several unpleasant and at that time urgent demands, the money ensured that I would continue to eat well and travel at will and see certain people if and when I felt like it. And the kind of women I was attracted to required money as well—plenty of it, if possible. Well, it was certainly possible, but only if the records were selling, if I was performing, touring. . . . You begin to get the idea? It only took Willy a minute or two to convince me once he had adopted this sort of logic. For Willy knew my weaknesses inside out. And, though I hated to admit it, they were rather transparent weaknesses. Outside of music, I had for a long time lived entirely for and of the flesh. I don't just mean sexually, but physically, sensually . . . I was a very sensitive animal. I don't say this boastfully: it is just a fact.

And why had I stopped performing publicly except on my recordings? I know the answer now, but back then it was quite inexplicable to me. I didn't really tire suddenly, or grow bored, or think myself too good for my public—though these were the sort of obnoxious things I told obnoxious people when they asked. I just started listening one day, while practicing for an upcoming recital, and the music was dead off my fingers. There was no chemistry between me and the instrument. It was just mechanics. The recital was canceled. I feared that the rest of my life, the hurricane, had grown too chaotic, had forced me to withdraw into a darker part of myself, thus obliterating something vital, upsetting a delicate inner balance that was not to be so easily righted again. Once that happened, the floodgates opened and I realized how truly dissatisfied I had become with my performances and how masterfully I had avoided facing this by using worldly distractions, and so the chaos had intensified, the darkness had begun to feed on itself, and so on, a vicious cycle for four years. Initially, after a few months of utter inactivity, which I was sure would put things back in order, I found that whatever was missing had grown too big to camouflage further, at least onstage, and so I stopped performing completely and exiled myself.

This muddle was the explanation I offered myself for having sliced four peak years out of my career. But as I said, it was a mystery to me at the time and a deeper mystery to those around me, and after four years it had carried me to my anchorage in a deadbeat town, practicing yoga, sleeping eight hours a night when I could manage it, on the wagon, the works. And though my playing had not improved much to my satisfaction, I had finally gone out on a limb in January and told Willy to book a tour. There was no point in delaying any further. I had to find out if I could still cut it, and maybe I needed to go onstage for that, into the pressure cooker. Nothing else had worked, and I was sick of playing possum, sick of my cowardice. I was no longer under the delusion that a purely physical rehabilitation would help me, but I believe something had shifted inside me and I was finally willing to tackle (though I didn't know this yet) the moral and spiritual torpor that truly cradled the eye of that hurricane. This was something to which I had previously not given a thought. For surely, with my tendency to lassitude, to quick adjustments in the wrong directions, I had gone bad. I always had to fight my inertia—since childhood as strong a force as my discipline—and I resented the effort. My profession had spoiled me, enabling me since I was nineteen to keep the realities of the world at arm's length whenever I chose, and this is an unhealthy thing. Especially when one is constitutionally prone to unreality—with a weakness for drugs and liquor and the flesh. And especially when one is applauded, praised, and paid handsomely for a talent so interwoven with the deceptive threads of vanity. An unhealthy profession all around. Inbred, suffocating, self-righteous.

I had three months before the comeback, at Carnegie Hall, which had always been a lucky and sentimental place for me. My mother took me to my first recital there as a kid (it was Arrau), and I made my New York debut there at sixteen during a massive snowstorm. I can still remember marching out into the lights cool as ice, playing to a fine audience and playing well, and then throwing up everything but my liver and kidneys backstage. Later on I matured: I would throw up the works before I went on and then come off in a cold sweat, my head ringing. But I loved to perform. Who wouldn't? And I could never stand those people—including so many of my self-serving colleagues—who call concert musicians, especially soloists, "artists." We are performers, not artists. Artists create things from scratch; performers interpret what is already there. The public, in its adulations, tends to forget this. I never wrote a note of music in my life except when I was drunk, and that's not art. I want to set the record straight on this tedious point from the start. The days of the great composer-performers—Clementi, Mozart, Hummel, Liszt, Chopin—are long gone. Now we have Copland and Horowitz. One is an artist, the other a performer. I don't know why people mix up the two. They wouldn't confuse an architect with a carpenter or a playwright with an actor.

My first wife, Orana, whom I would see that day for the first time in six years, who had just been flown in to Massachusetts General Hospital, two miles from where I sat at my piano, was always good at cutting through these sorts of distinctions. When I first met her, she was the music critic for the *San Francisco Chronicle*. It was after one of my recitals, at a reception in a triplex penthouse overlooking the Bay, all twinkly lights and champagne and unruffled folk with gold in their pockets. I confess I used to enjoy those parties. I met women at them that I never seemed to see anywhere else, in banks or restaurants or airports. Like rare greenhouse flowers, those women; I don't know where they kept themselves the rest of the time. And all of them music lovers. In fact, this place had a greenhouse. Orana and I walked up and down the flagstone aisles, humidifiers purring overhead, past orchids of every color and calla lilies the size of a baby's face, but whiter, and two long tables of bonsai trees planted on miniature mossy hills and dales. Staring at those bonsais, I felt as if I were in a plane flying over a Japanese forest. I expected tiny birds to alight in the trees and tiny people flying kites to scurry down the hills with their tiny akita dogs. And through the greenhouse windows the lights of the harbor danced, Orana's jet hair catching the fire of those lights and her big eyes unblinking as I pulled her close behind a cluster of palms and didn't know what to say, so enraptured was I. We were married a week later in Honolulu on a Sunday morning, and I gave my recital that night and we flew on to Seattle, where I performed on Tuesday. We had our honeymoon there on Monday. I hated that city; it kept raining snails and slugs and it smelled like wet canvas everywhere.

Orana quit her job at the *Chronicle* and started writing for the New York magazines once she had settled in at our new apartment. She was originally from Avarua, one of the Cook Islands, population 4,000. She was a wonderful wife. Small, about five-one, with nut-colored skin and thick black hair and strange green eyes from her one English grandfather, named Cook but no relation to the captain. We were married for three years. And as I mentioned, she was terrific when it came to discussing music and performing. She was the only critic I could ever read seriously. The only nonmusician I trusted on the subject besides Willy and my longtime friend and bosom-buddy Amos Demeter. But Amos was eclectic, all gut-instinct, and Willy's taste was a part of his very developed business sense. In the early days when I forever tried to outdo myself, arranging programs radical, unique, and provocative that turned into virtuoso grotesques,

Willy would keep me in line with a gentle hint. That a program half Liszt and half Rachmaninoff might be indigestible . . . perhaps a touch of Scarlatti . . . That kind of thing. But Orana really understood music in her bones. She grasped the essence of technique in the most nonmechanical sense. We used to have great stimulating arguments in the shower or the kitchen or while strolling through the park. She opened me up to the visual arts, and to varieties of music, Asian and African and minimalist, of which I was ignorant. And she never let me get away with that sensitive artist crap to which I was prone in those years. When we went to the country, I chopped the wood. When we got a flat, I changed the tire—no tow-truck nonsense for her. She gave me thirty vitamins a day and made me into a vegetarian. One New Year's Eve when I bought four grams of cocaine, she flushed it. She got me to quit smoking cigarettes and introduced me to good wine instead of whiskey. She traded in my old Jaguar for a Jeep, and I never forgave her that, though I loved to tear around Manhattan in that Jeep at all hours. She went out one day to get a cat and came home with a whole litter of Siamese kittens that followed her around the house. She made me read biographies of every damn pianist and composer who ever lived. I enjoyed that, too. After two years, she had "sivilized" me, as Huck Finn said, and I was just twenty-three then. But in the third year things started to go bad, and it was my fault.

The day before my hospital visit, I saw an old and mutual friend of ours, Patty Raymond, to find out more about Orana's condition. Patty had called to tell me Orana was checking into the hospital with a complex blood disease, that her California doctors had sent her there, given up on her, because the best hematologists were supposedly in Boston. It was odd that Orana's path should recross mine in this way, that I should be in Boston at that time. Patty and I went way back, to the early days in New York, even before I had married Orana. During our marriage, she and Orana became fast friends, and they remained so, corresponding regularly when Orana returned to San Francisco after our divorce.

I saw Patty at her bookstore. She had bought the place years before when she moved to Boston. At that time it specialized in

Zen literature, but she changed the inventory completely to old and rare editions. It was a beautiful bookstore, the sort you find in London and Vienna, made for browsing, with good oak furnishings and a brass samovar in one corner and leather chairs in the alcoves. The place was always filled with poets and students and furtive types who drank tea and sometimes read whole volumes on the premises. Patty had an office in back that led onto a small garden. A fine woman, about forty, I could talk to her about nearly anything, and in years past I had often gone to her for solace and acid advice, usually concerning my romantic entanglements. Of late, though, we talked almost exclusively about books, and she was putting me on to fine writers whom I read not only for nourishment but also as a distraction from my work—Biely and Kleist and Bulgakov. I became a manic book-buyer at that time, and Patty helped me accumulate a fine collection of first editions. Willy was impressed when he visited me that spring and examined my shelves. He told me that first editions were the best investment in the world, even if that wasn't why I bought them. A better investment than diamonds, he added, flipping through my Baron Corvo. Poor Willy, I don't mean to paint him as a philistine, but that's what he said.

That day I found Patty in her office, gazing into her garden with the telephone at her ear. She looked grim and I felt grimmer, shaken still by what she had told me the night before of Orana's condition. But when she hung up the phone, she turned to me casually, as if I had been there for hours.

"You know," she said thoughtfully, "I had a dream last week which I just now remembered, about Orana. I feel as if she's often in and out of my dreams. Do you know what I mean?"

I knew exactly what she meant. I too often dreamt of Orana. She was made for dreams—and in my case, more for dreams than everyday life. She had a gauzy look about her, as if you were seeing her through the fine mist that fringes a waterfall. Maybe this had to do with her Polynesian origins and my fanciful notions thereof—but I don't think so. I believe it was more a result of her waterfall consciousness, of that inner vision with which she was gifted. She always gave me the impression that she took things in, absorbed their essences, and then exuded an aura composed of those substances her inner life had refused. Rejected substances that nonetheless glowed. I remember how startled I was on my second visit to Florence, to the Uffizi, during our marriage, when it was not the red-haired and fabled Botticelli women who excited me, but the lithe copper-colored girls in the paintings of Masaccio and Piero di Cosimo. Those Tuscan girls all reminded me of Orana. They too had that waterfall glow about them, and the dark porous unfocused eyes.

"In the dream," Patty continued, lighting a cigarette, "she and I are in a sleek little boat on this marvelous river at twilight. The river is winding through a forest of tall white trees. It twists and turns more than any real river could. We are gliding past fruit trees and ferns and the fruit is all odd shapes—geometric—pentagons and hexagons and triangles. And Orana stands up in the prow and lets down her hair and prepares to dive, waiting for a particular spot. And then suddenly it starts to rain and I glance away, and when I turn back she's gone, and now in the prow there is a curved glass vase full of pearls. Then I woke up. What do you make of it, Max?"

I sat there gloomily, my head propped against my palm. I didn't make anything of it. My former analyst, Dr. Maria Selzer, would have had a field day with it, I'm sure. I said nothing, but I did note that Patty too, in her dream-consciousness, associated, coordinated Orana in the vortices of water and rain.

Orana was still swimming through my thoughts when I finally began practicing, three cups of coffee in me, the sunbathers already reoiling themselves outside my window, and the trees beyond the river now dark blurs in the heat. But my mind was not on my work that day. And it was not just because of Orana's plight or my shakiness about my comeback—no, there were other things preying on me. After weeks of drone work, of whipping myself at the piano each day, cutting the four years of fat away from my concentration and honing the delicate connections between fingers and shoulders and ears and lungs (the latter very important), I had on June 15 been overtaken by more temporal concerns. By the courthouse ordeal I faced the next day and the mysterious disappearance of Amos Demeter (which, unknown to me, was to set in motion my first tantalizing meeting with another central character in this pivotal moment of my life, the elusive Dr. Winters). And, also, in the back of my mind I was mulling over and anticipating the bittersweet attractions of my current *amante*, Sarah. But I am outrunning myself.

Let's just say it was a pregnant time, though you wouldn't have known it to look at me. Hot, disheveled, unshaven, in need of a haircut, I shuffled about my loft in my customary work clothes, old white trousers and white shirt and sandals. I was so preoccupied I decided to break for lunch after two hours of practicing. I had been running through two sections of the Schubert Sonata in B-flat over and over again. The opening, especially, which an overwrought critic once likened to a wave cradling the major themes and then abandoning them at the pianist's feet (!)—the opening was the key. And while I felt I was putting it forth powerfully, it seemed too intellectual, lacking that underlying iciness that should imbue it with menace. At times, I feared, it was simply overly aggressive—the sort of bombast any second-rate pianist could pull off. After several weeks, I thought I had it closer to where I wanted it, but instead of providing encouragement, this further depressed me: there was a time, I reminded myself, when that quality, that ice, would just have been there, without all this methodical tedium. For my own good I knew I had to stop thinking like that or I wouldn't get anywhere.

The last time I played the piece through, my body betrayed me. My back nerves were a tangle, like crossed wires, and my left wrist had stiffened again. I was worried about that wrist because in another few weeks I wouldn't have the luxury of thinking about it in physical terms, for itself alone—as a wrist!—or the music would suffer. By then it would have to be no more than another part of the quietly functioning machine that effortlessly, faithfully served as my intermediary to the music. But that day I was still thinking about it as a wrist, and I made a mental note to visit my acupuncturist—my last resort before painkillers—as soon as possible.

I was in the habit of taking lunch at my favorite restaurant, Billy Diamond's, a short drive from my loft. I kept my car in a garage around the corner. It would never have lasted on the street. It was an old Cadillac, a 1952 eight-cylinder convertible, a boat that I picked up one step from the junkyard for a few hundred dollars. I put in a new engine and had them gut and redo the interior in leather and walnut, eleven coats of black paint and a white top made to order by a specialist in Philadelphia. It was the best car I had ever owned. I had a weakness for cars. Garaging it alone cost me two hundred dollars a month, but it was worth it. When Willy saw it, he told me to sell it, it was undignified.

But my real weakness, at least up until that time, was women. I could go on and on about my music, but I have to admit that for bigger chunks of my life I was more obsessed with women than music. They were my undoing, Willy said. But that's nonsense. Without the women I loved, and the others I tried to love, and those who loved me, my life would have been a washout, an elaborate failure. My talent had many rewards and fulfilled me in an essential way, but it never stopped the yawning gap deep down. It was my lovers who saved me there, along the vicious inner precipices that can finish you off once and for all. Before Orana, I just went crazy with girls. I was twenty-one so my range was unlimited: young women, older women, teenage fans. . . . In my business there were always plenty of available women, more than you can imagine. It overwhelmed me back then. If Willy hadn't kept me so overbooked on tour, I probably would have gone haywire. Later on, I wasn't always comfortable with those memories, with the moral equivocations of my youth that I felt I could no longer answer for. Answer to whom? you'll ask. I think that was a problem—the big problem—I had with Ellen, the mother of my only child, my daughter Daphne. Ellen was always dredging up my past. She was fixated on it, as if it were a living breathing person, and jealous of all the women I had ever known, a whole gallery in her mind that tormented her. Of course she disliked Orana, whom she had never met. And I could understand some oblique hostility toward my first wife—her predecessor, though not in marriage. I often expected this to be a sore point, but Ellen never discussed marriage, even when things were rosy. She said she didn't want it. However, in the first halcyon days of our relationship, she dragged old stories out of me, my escapades as a gay blade, my adventures with my pal Amos, and it was all great fun, and then when our little ship hit the rocks she threw that stuff back in my face. I don't know why, because it never fazed me. She thought it all a kind of retroactive betrayal. At any rate, after Ellen (we were together one year and five months) I always vaguely felt I had to answer to someone for my past. She managed what my mother, my sister, and my manager had never accomplished: she instilled me with guilt.

But guilt or no, though Willy's cure for my roving eye may not have succeeded, it did indirectly help me to cement my reputation very fast very early on. He kept me so damn busy. Of course he looked back on that time as the golden period of my career. Rave reviews and full houses and premium bookings and record sales that kept all of us in clover. In Willy's perfect world I would have gone on like that for forty years and then retired to Switzerland, to Montreux, ensconced in one of those blue-and-white four-story villas that overlook the lake through manicured elms. Numbered accounts in two or three banks. The world at bay. Like Chaplin and Nabokov, and Diaghilev—his hero, the great impresario. This was Willy's dream, his retirement plan: Lake Geneva and a few million Swiss francs, salmon and champagne for breakfast, a staff of six and two tennis courts surrounded by rose gardens. My photograph hung in his gallery of prima donnas in his study, as it did in New York, and among the shelves of glowing mementoes, the gold medals I won in various competitions, which I gave him and which he treasures. And in warm expansive moments, over a bottle of sixty-year-old brandy, when he and his favorite companions, other retired impresarios and moneymen, have settled into that room with their No. 12 Havanas, I imagine him taking a bow before that wall of serious talented faces and saying: "It is they who put me here. I worked hard for them, but in the end they are the ones who bought this brandy you are savoring right now." Et cetera, et cetera. And I hope at that moment his eye catches on my photograph, and he squirms a little, imagining the ironic glance I would toss him were I there in the flesh. But, again, I'm being too hard on Willy. It's an unhealthy reflex, to tease him so, because I love him, I owe him everything in material terms, and a lot more besides that. In the wildest days he kept me out of hock and saw to it I didn't blow the works—and I could have, plenty of times. But I always kidded him about Switzerland, his borzoi dogs and tennis whites and the rest of it.

I know he means more to me deep down than I care to admit because my first meeting with him is one of my warmest memories. I was sixteen and my mother and her sister Clarissa took me up to his offices high above Fifty-seventh Street on a rainy spring day. I had in the previous year caused a sensation, winning the Liszt and Tchaikovsky competitions—the first American since Van Cliburn to take first prize in the latter. The time had come for real professional management, my mother said. Until then, my half-dozen or so recitals a year had been arranged by one of my teacher's agents. That was all right for a sometime child pianist, but now I was ready for bigger things. After the Tchaikovsky, my mother was besieged with letters and phone calls from agents and promoters. She knew nothing about the music world, but she had taste and class, I'll say that for her, and after asking around among her society friends and hearing Willy's name come up repeatedly as the very best, and further observing that he was one of the few among the best who had *not* tried to contact us, she decided he was the man to see. And he was very pleased to have me walk through his door. He offered a generous contract, insisted we see a lawyer before signing (Mother had class, but she was impulsive, like me, and wanted to sign then and there), and three days later everything was set. He took me to lunch at "21" and made speeches to me about art and money—speeches I would hear many times over the years. My mother hoped he would play the role my father had abrogated. And when I performed at Carnegie Hall that snowy night six months later, I remember seeing Willy as I took my bows. He was standing clapping on the aisle seat in the fourth row and the tears were running down his cheeks. Usually, from the stage, there's too much going on and you're too worked up—you just don't see people that easily. But that night my eyes went right to Willy. And it was very moving, it meant a great deal to me. My mother and my aunt and my sister Stella were in the front row that night, and unknown to any of us my father was somewhere in the back, but I didn't notice any of them.

Still fretting about the Schubert, I pulled up in front of Billy

Diamond's. It was cool inside and very pretty, the lighting attractive, the tables private. Eddie behind the bar was a friend of mine. He told one of the waiters to bring a club sandwich to the bar, and he fixed me a lemonade. Because I kept my phone switched off while I practiced, and disliked answering machines, I had my calls come in to Eddie's phone at the bar, and every evening I'd go by and find a neat list of my callers in his cramped handwriting. Such were my ways that this seemed to me the more convenient method. On that day only two calls interested me: one from Margaret Demeter, Amos's wife, and the other from my lawyer, Sweeney—the crack lawyer Willy had dug up to assist me in my latest problem.

Eddie, like half the bartenders in Boston, was once a fighter. He had the obligatory flattened nose and cauliflower ear, but also the most beautifully curved Irish lips (like lyres) and a perfect set of teeth. Rare teeth for a pug, which he was very proud of. But because of the flat nose, he talked from way back in his throat, tongue on palate like sandpaper with his *t*'s and *d*'s. He was a lovely guy, with a rosy face and warm hands, and a big family in Dorchester. When he first met me, and heard what I did, he was standoffish, but when I came back the next night and got to talking and mentioned who my father was, he warmed up appreciably.

"What's the good word, Max?" he greeted me. "You know, just last night I was telling a guy about the Stimson fight. . . ."

I had heard more about this Stimson fight in the last few months than I ever cared to know. You see, my father was also a fighter, but in a different league than Eddie. He was in fact, for sixteen golden months, Welterweight Champion of the World. He won the title in January 1942, defended it in April, June, and November, and then gave it up the following May after a last vicious battle. Jackie (to my mother, John M.) Randal fought and knocked out the infamous Carl Stimson at the Boston Garden on the night of October 7, 1941—two months to the day before Pearl Harbor. He and Stimson were the top contenders, and this fight gave him his title shot. Eddie, then a local middleweight, was at ringside that night. He had enormous respect for my father, and not just because of his ring prowess. Jackie Randal was the rare prototype that fellows like Eddie dreamed of becoming. After hitting the top, he invested his ring earnings shrewdly, to the last cent, and retired early, still in his prime, to become a man of leisure. After his retirement he became truly wealthy on California real estate and gold speculating. He chased women and gambled and traveled on ocean liners—but always within his fixed income. He never touched his capital. I wish I could say the same for myself. And of course for the rest of his life people called him Champ the way they call ex-senators Senator and ex-mayors Mayor, and he liked that. He divided his time between L.A. and Key West, and in the autumn he always went to Monaco. He hated the cold. Eddie told me that of all the pugs in any division one in a thousand becomes a champion, and of all the champions one in a hundred becomes a real gentleman. So his respect for my father was unbounded. My mother might have disagreed with his being called a gentleman. But that's another story.

The old man was said to have iron discipline, and maybe what modicum I possessed as a musician I inherited from him. But aside from that and my long fingers and my good constitution, I didn't get much else. Certainly not his money, some of which went to my sister for her kids and the bulk to medical research into tropical diseases. This was something of a mystery, for as far as anyone knew, he had never set foot in the tropics himself—unless Rio qualifies.

Sweeney's call was nagging at me. On that day, when my thoughts kept revolving around Orana, and to a lesser degree around Amos, I wanted no part of it. I always had a fear of the legal system, a spiritual claustrophobia, and I didn't have the energy just then to hear what Sweeney had concocted for our day in chambers. My nerves were shot, too, from my work. I had been laboring mercilessly over Liszt's *La campanella*, his Paganini variations. The tormentor, as one of my colleagues has called it. And truly, it seemed to me at times as if Franz had machines for hands—both in strength and reach. It's that piece, I'm sure, that was killing the small of my back and stiffening my wrist. It was not a good choice after a long layoff, but I wanted my comeback to be like no other performance I had ever given—or else why bother? Without Liszt—always one of my specialties—it would have been cheating, somehow. As for my physical condition, well, there are different schools about the wrist, for example. Whether to keep it flexed, or slightly revolving, or bridged high or low. I tended to revolve and bridge low. But I also used plenty of upper arm and shoulder—I was not a stiff, close-to-the-keyboard type. Especially on a piece like that, and this is where my lack of stamina betrayed me in those early weeks. I was opening the piece well, full of fire, and then lagging into the middle—and that is deadly with Liszt. If your intensity wanes over the course of his pieces, it's much more obvious than with many other composers. There's just no room for coasting with him, and that was never my style, anyway.

The bar was filling up as I wolfed down my sandwich, the usual loud splashy crowd that favored the place at midday. My conscience finally got the better of me and I asked Eddie for the telephone. A wave of anxiety swept my gut as Sweeney's secretary put me through.

"You got my message. Listen, what kind of answering service is that?"

"It's a restaurant. I'll bring you here to lunch one day."

"A restaurant?" There was a pause. "Now, you're all set for tomorrow?"

"I guess so. What do you have for me?"

"Well, the briefs are completed, the judge—if I can measure him by our two conversations—seems sympathetic, and—"

"To me?"

"What?"

"Sympathetic to me?"

"Well, sure."

"I don't believe that, but go on."

"Look, you can't come in with that attitude, not in a session like this. It's not like being in court, you know, being in chambers. The two lawyers and the two plaintiffs and the judge—"

"Sounds cozy."

"It's more personal, that's all, and you're not going to get anywhere if you come in swinging."

"All right, don't worry."

"Let them come off as the aggressive ones. You just sit back and keep your cool."

He went into great detail about the briefs, but I lost most of it in the din. Anyway, I hadn't called him for information, I had just wanted to ease my conscience. His voice never wavered, he spoke unmincingly and with command. Though at times I sensed his impatience, I felt reassured that however careless I was, Sweeney was on the case. A stupid and expensive illusion.

"So I'll see you tomorrow at eleven," he concluded.

"You mean, at two."

"No, at two o'clock we have to be at the courthouse. But we need a few hours to go over the briefs together. Don't you remember, that's the way we arranged it?"

"But I can't take that much time for this. I've got my work. That kills the whole day."

"The whole day! You just expect to show up and waltz through this thing," he sighed.

I knew I had gone down another notch in Sweeney's estimation. That he was thinking, A guy like this, a dreamer, an arty type in a world full of people who know what makes the great ship of Society go, and who know, above all, that the careless, the dreamers, are the first to be churned under in its wake, talent or no talent. All of this was implicit in his brief, resigned silence.

"All right, look, come by my office at noon—no later—and we'll run it through over lunch. Okay? And by the way, Max, it looks pretty good from where we sit, all things considered. Just relax." And he hung up.

I left a twenty on the bar and waved goodbye to Eddie. I was restless, and Sweeney's parting note of optimism had made me truly nervous. When lawyers think things look good, watch out. That was something I'd learned from my father. I caught a glimpse of myself in one of the big mirrors that lined the walls and made a note to shave and change my clothes before I visited Orana. I passed the enormous white semicircular piano, the kind people lounge around with their drinks while the fellow in the tux plays their favorite numbers. It brought back the painful memory of a night I broke training, and with a pool of bourbon in my gut entertained Sarah and two of her friends and Eddie and the manager with a rendition of the Preludes after closing time. Usually I avoided that sort of dumbbell showboating with a passion, especially at parties where hostesses might ask you to show your stuff. It made me cringe, like seeing an athlete roll up his sleeves and arm-wrestle at dinner. Save the ham for the stage, I used to remind myself. That's when you'd better turn on the juice for dear life, not in a parlor with a bunch of stiffs.

When I got home I found a note on the door from my friend Tim. We'd had a date to go sculling at noon. I had completely forgotten about it and I felt terrible because Tim was a busy man, an architect with a thriving hectic business, and not someone like me whose time was whimsically his own. When Tim set aside two hours, it was a big deal. Our outings were my lone physical exercise, very good for the chest and arms. I left an apologetic message at his office, and then nearly returned my other phone message, to Margaret Demeter in New York, but I refrained and got myself back to the piano.

It still gnawed at me that I had missed my sculling: I had been too busy worrying about things beyond my control. It was not just the physical release—Tim was the perfect companion. He never talked business and never brought up music. This was a novelty for me. Most people felt it rude not to open the conversation with music talk. In truth, I lived and breathed my work, even during the most chaotic times. I was always caught up in whatever I was about to perform or record: rephrasing, rehashing, making notes to myself. It's a smothering profession, but with my propensity for trouble, that wasn't such a bad thing. It kept me out of scrapes and it kept me alive, in the real sense. It took me over and left no place to hide, for all the false nooks and crannies of the ego disappear rapidly when you put yourself on the line before a full house. Up there, in that empty floating space, you're more alone than you would ever want to be. And that makes you better than you thought possible, it puts fiber in your soul. This was another sensible lesson my father taught me—from his own particular angle in his very different racket. So I hated discussing music on a small-talk level; it seemed a violation of the one part of myself I kept insulated. I liked to talk shop of course with other performers, but that's something else.

Anyway, I didn't have many friends in the business. Aside from a few other soloists, I knew plenty of musicians in the Philharmonic in New York, and the Boston Symphony, but they weren't friends. In fact, having performed with both orchestras, I probably had more enemies among them than I would care to think. Accustomed to being a soloist, and so trained, I don't think I was ever very good to work with.

Finally I attacked the Schubert again, and fell into it. When I next glanced at the clock, it was past five and I was due at the hospital at six. I didn't want it to be a shock for her, seeing me again out of the blue, so I had called Orana the night before. She hadn't betrayed any emotion one way or the other. Why should she, after all those years? As I shaved, I realized how much I had been dreading this expedition. It wasn't just my aversion to hospitals, but my terrible sense of guilt toward her, and my trepidation at what I would hear from the doctors, whom I had insisted on meeting.

My gloom deepened during the drive over there. I was ruminating on what Patty had told me of Orana's life in the previous years. After our divorce, we barely stayed in touch, and I had only heard bits and pieces. Orana had traveled extensively for a year before resettling in San Francisco and getting back her old job at the *Chronicle*. She had lived alone until she remarried. Her second husband was a writer, a Czech émigré, who taught at Berkeley. He was twice her age, a quiet sort, and after only two years together he was killed in a car accident while out with another woman. Orana was devastated. She certainly had bad luck with men. But at least I, well versed in duplicity at other times in my life, had never once cheated on her. It wasn't other women that had come between us: it was my career, which I always deluded myself took a backseat to my amours. That my work should obtrude on my romantic life did not fit my heroic image of myself at that time. When Orana divorced me, it came out of nowhere. Willy, for once ignorant of my domestic troubles, had booked me a European tour for the spring, and I was in the Berkshires practicing at Amos's farm. Orana and I had steered a rocky road our last year together. I considered her an independent woman. When we married, I knew that the long hours of solitude I required, and my months on the road when she would be home alone, and my moodiness when I wasn't performing, called for a self-sufficient partner. Nevertheless, what did us in was my overestimation of her independence. Like any vivacious young woman, especially one so precocious and hungry for new experience, she wearied of the lonely nights, the waiting, the unsociable periods, the dark periods. After all, she was young— twenty-three that year—and she was always alone. The glories of being attached to a performer, to sharing the spotlight on occasion, wear thin rather quickly. Especially to someone like Orana, who was indifferent to such stuff. I was surprised she stuck it out as long as she did, but we were wildly in love the first two years, and when it's like that you can survive almost anything. Now I think perhaps she wanted to believe I was unfaithful, to make it easier for herself. Because *she* left *me* in the end, when I was out of town, and all because of those things— especially the loneliness—that I had warned her about when we were married. When her lawyer called me up at the farm, I was devastated. There I was rehearsing nine hours a day, inhaling the good winter air, reading through Amos's mother's beautiful leatherbound Dickens, expecting Orana to join me any day, hoping we could patch things up, and all the while she and the lawyer were putting together an airtight Mexican divorce in a Manhattan skyscraper. I never forgave her that, though I didn't for a moment think she intended cruelty. It was a bad business all around, a nightmare.

And now what had become of my lovely fragile Orana? After her second husband's death, she had buried herself in her job, traveled to remote places in the summers, and narrowed her circle of friends almost to nonexistence. The exotic travel was an old passion of hers, and it had betrayed her in the end, for she had contracted the germ of this blood disease while hiking through the Burmese jungle. The doctors told her it had planted itself in her bloodstream like a time bomb and then started ticking nine months later. That was five months before they had given up on her and sent her to Boston. If these hematologists couldn't help her, the next stop would be New York, a kind of last resort, at a special center for tropical diseases. First, though, they wanted to approach it conventionally, strictly as a blood disorder.

Patty had warned me about Orana's appearance, to expect the worst and all of that. She had visited her in San Francisco a year and a half before, and even then, torn apart by her husband's death, Orana looked bad. Venturing into the jungle while at such low ebb, I thought, had been a self-destructive act. I imagined a ghastly apparition and I braced myself as I parked the car. I had seen her but once in nine years, six years earlier, after a recital in Los Angeles, and she had been lovelier than ever. Though the day before I had come on like gangbusters over the telephone, lining up interviews with the doctors and offering to pay bills, now as I strode through the lobby into one of those steel elevators, I could barely keep my thoughts straight. I wanted to be strong, supportive, fearless, especially when I first saw her. For gone apparently were the girlish glowing skin and taut muscles and bright eyes I remembered so keenly, gone were the contours of her perfect compact body—and what else would be gone, I thought in terror. Her pretty low voice, that funny way she had of clucking her tongue, her beautiful fingernails—one of her few concessions to vanity.

Her door was closed, and I spent a long minute preparing myself before I entered. She had a private corner room at the end of the hall, with a nice view of the river. This had been my doing, though Orana wasn't supposed to know about it. One of the trustees of the Boston Symphony was the wife of the head surgeon at the hospital, and she had been only too happy to pull strings for me. I was pleased to see that my prestige, such as it was, still had some bite. The comfort I derived from this disappeared as soon as I glimpsed Orana. Toughened as I assumed it was by years of misuse, I thought my heart would break.

It was a high-ceilinged room, the bed abutted the wall beside the window, and she looked tiny propped up there with her eyes closed. The air was thick with late-afternoon sunlight, very yellow, and great bars of shadow. She didn't open her eyes until I was at the foot of the bed. She looked me over carefully and her expression didn't change. She was very thin, pale, her eyes hollows, and they had cut her hair short. Her skin was transparent.

Her hands were folded on the sheets, in shadow. When she spoke, her voice was as I remembered it, low and very clear.

"Hello, Max. Come closer and don't look so terrified. You always were a coward when it came to these things."

I went up and kissed her forehead.

"Remember," she said, "when Willy had his appendix out, it took me two days to get you to the hospital."

I had forgotten that. Now, for all my prepared speeches, I didn't know what to say.

"Aren't you going to ask how I am?" She wet her lips.

"Orana, I'm so sorry. I—"

"If you're going to be like this, with a hangdog face, I'm going to kick you out." She coughed. "Pull that chair over and tell me how on earth you got me this lovely room."

"How did you know?"

"You're such a baby. The nurses were talking. Don't you know that they hear everything in a hospital? Well, whom did you bribe?"

"No one." I told her about the head surgeon's wife.

"So you're a respectable citizen up here?"

"I wouldn't go that far."

"Thank you for the flowers—they're beautiful."

They were in the shadows on a metal table opposite the bed, a dozen white roses.

"Still your favorites?"

She nodded, pushing herself up a little. "Tell me about your tour, the pieces you're preparing and the cities you're playing."

This wasn't what I had expected. I didn't want to talk about myself. And certainly not about the tour!

"What's the matter? Don't you think people *with illnesses* read the newspapers?"

"It just doesn't seem very important."

"Oh, I see," she said. "You want to know all about what's going on here. Because this *is* important. This is life and death."

I glanced away, and as the shadows shifted slightly, noticed that her fingernails were bitten all the way down.

"Is that why I'm important to you suddenly?" she asked. Then she shook her head. "Forgive me, I'm not always so pitiful, but I haven't had many opportunities to feel sorry for myself with an audience. I'm glad you came."

"You don't want to talk about it," I said timidly.

"Why not, for god's sake? But there isn't much to say. I'm not one of those people with a built-in mechanism for dealing with this sort of thing. Are there such people, really? I lack the endurance, the morbid patience. I expected to die of old age, or in an accident. Lingering was not in my scenario."

She paused, and I made an effort to move, even to cross my leg, so frozen was I. Patty, in preparing me for the worst, had not prepared me enough. I had assumed avenues were still being tested, possibilities still in the air, that there was real hope. But Orana spoke with a flat calm beyond resignation, past the nights of doubt and acceptance, just waiting for the hammer to fall. I sat there dumbly as the shadows thickened around us. I was sinking.

"Even on a daily level," she said, "I'm no good at it. The nurses get on my nerves. The doctor . . . he comes in with his bag of Hope and sprinkles you, like the Sandman."

"There is hope, then?"

"For what—a cure? Don't you see, they can't even diagnose this. They just don't know," she said, and these four words rang hard, as if they had echoed in her head over and over again.

"What's awful, Max," she said without emotion, "is how ponderous you become to yourself. A weight in your own consciousness, an object, already detached from life. That's why sick people assume others must be fed up with them, and secretly resentful—because they get so fed up with themselves. You hate yourself for failing so fundamentally. At first you fix on the minutiae: white cell counts and lymph readings and kidney scans. But you quickly lose interest in that nonsense. You realize you can't even walk to the john anymore, that someone has to wipe your chin when you eat, that time means nothing, nights come and go, and the noise outside and the weather belong to another planet. None of it has anything to do with you."

Her voice dropped. "Please, don't make me talk about it. My own blood is poisoning me. I have horrible dreams. My hands and feet are numb, the feet worst of all, because the circulation is impaired." She pushed her hair back. "Now, tell me about the pieces you'll be performing. Fill me in on the last six years—anything."

I squeezed her hand. My larynx felt encased in ice, but I started talking about the Schubert and the Liszt, the Brahms Sonata in F-sharp minor and the *Diabelli* Variations. Actually, this allowed me to deflect my feelings just when I feared I would fall apart on her. She interrupted me after a moment and her voice was level again.

"I'm sorry. There's another side to this, if you're not tired of listening to me. Things I might not have discovered otherwise. My mind is still sharp and I've been reading and keeping a journal. Remember my journals?"

I remembered there was always a black one in winter and a green one in summer, and special ones for trips, filled with her neat small hand in violet ink. And I remembered the time I violated her privacy and picked one up when she was asleep and learned some things about myself that I didn't want to know.

"Oh, the books I've been able to read," she went on warmly. "The ones I had never gotten to over the years. You know, you have no time suddenly, but in some ways you have more time than ever before. Do you still read a lot? You were always so afraid people would find out you were an illiterate genius or something. Always making up for your lost schooldays, diligently plowing through an author from first book to last, and all that philosophy and psychology."

"Yes, I'm still afraid of being caught out. I even collect rare books now."

"Of course you would," she smiled faintly. "You always had the urge to collect things. Do you know what I've been reading?"

I saw editions of *The Golden Bowl* and *The Castle* on the bedside table.

"No, they are just playthings. I mean what I am *really* reading."

I had never thought of Kafka as light reading.

"Gibbon," she whispered.

"Gibbon? The history of Rome?" I was surprised.

"More than that. An enormous allegory that transforms events into the history of a man's soul. You know, he memorized each paragraph before putting it to paper. Rounded out every sentence in his head, and only when they joined into a perfect whole did he write them out." She was studying my face eagerly, animated for the first time since I'd entered the room. "Here, listen," she said breathlessly, pulling a battered paperback from under the bedclothes.

In a lilting voice, she read me a paragraph about sun-worship and pageantries under the Emperor Elagabalus, none of which impressed me except the odd bit of information that the emperor would "never eat sea-fish except at a great distance from the sea."

"That is no more about a third-century emperor," she said excitedly, "than *Macbeth* is about a mere traitor. You see, each sentence is part of a mirror in which he is examining different aspects of his life."

I nodded but she seemed disappointed. "You think it's like any other book of history—detailed and dry—but I tell you it is a diary of the soul."

Her eyes were dilated, glowing darkly, but I was grateful for that spark of life, even if it seemed slightly lunatic. But was it enthusiasm, or just desperation—a condition I could not reconcile with the Orana I remembered. The Orana for whom Angkor Wat, not Rome, might provide the raw material of spiritual inspiration. The Orana who was such a clear and graceful thinker. And such a beautiful dancer, too, as I recalled painfully, for that mention of numbness in her feet had caught in my mind. She was right: blood counts and kidney scans didn't do much for me either, didn't prod the tenderest nerves. But the fact that her feet—once so golden and tiny, crossing our bedroom on a winter's night, or stuck with sand on a Spanish beach, or curled up under her during a drive to the country—were numb, a notch closer to coldness, lifelessness, this I found terrifying.

She was prepared to read me more Gibbon, but I deflected her gently. "What else have you read?"

"Oh, odd things. Some Gnostic texts and books on stars." She fell silent and tucked the Gibbon back under the sheet. Then she examined my face carefully, almost rudely—like a child.

"You've changed, you know. And I don't mean the smudges

under your eyes or the line or two beside your mouth. Your eyes are kinder, younger than when I last saw you. You were not well then."

"It was not a good time for me."

"No?"

"I wasn't taking care of myself. My work was suffering. I played badly that night."

She shook her head impatiently. "It's typical of you to reduce it to your physical condition and the quality of your professional life, but I was referring to your unhappiness. That remote and dissolute persona you found so attractive—I can't imagine why."

"Well, I've learned a little since then," I said, fidgeting.

She was staring past me. Her voice was almost whimsical. "Of course I had heard the rumors over the years. Gossip about parties and high living, the whispers about drugs. The girls . . ."

"Gossip?"

"Don't you think people in my world talk about such things? About the private lives of the people they review and criticize?" She looked at me archly. "We're still reporters, after all, as you used to remind me."

This was an unpleasant dig, for I had only "reminded" her of that once, in the depths of a nasty argument, knowing it would sting. And she hadn't forgotten it.

"Well, six years is six years," I said vaguely. "I don't suppose it means much now."

"I suppose not. It only hurt," and she paused and glanced up into the shadows, "on the heels of our divorce. The stories I heard. I was ashamed for both of us."

This surprised me. "Ashamed of what?"

"Oh, of what people were saying about you."

"For example."

"That you were degrading yourself. Whoremongering. Running around with rich women, a frivolous crowd, pretending to be something you weren't."

"There were some foolish times, but not like that. Why would you believe such garbage?"

"I was unhappy that we had failed so miserably." She hesitated. "Do you know now, nine years later, why I divorced you, Max? Back then you thought it was because I was lonely. You probably still believe that."

"I think it was a big part of it. I was never unfaithful to you, if that's what you're getting at."

"You are still so old-fashioned and macho that you believe infidelity and loneliness the only causes for divorce. And with your vanity, you assume it was *your* infidelity and *my* loneliness," she said wryly. "But what if it was the other way around? Maybe you were the one who was lonely and I was betraying you. Maybe I left you for another man. You never considered that possibility, did you?"

I shook my head.

"Of course it's only half true. There was no other man for some time, but there was something in you—I don't know if loneliness is the word—that frightened me, that I couldn't live with anymore. Some part of yourself that you would never share—maybe out of kindness, I don't know. Forgive me for going on like this." She patted my hand. "I've had too much time to brood. Suddenly you don't think about the future and that leaves too much time to fret over the past. Would you mind pouring me some water?"

She looked at me earnestly. "Now tell me, will you open with the Liszt or the *Diabelli*?"

After that long elliptical detour, we were back where we had started. A nurse stuck her head in the door.

"Five minutes until your bath, Miss Cook. I'm afraid you'll have to leave then, Mr. Randal."

"I never did take my second husband's name," Orana said. "He's dead, you know."

"Yes, Patty told me."

There was an awkward silence. Then I said, "I'll be opening with the Schubert, I think. The Sonata No. 21 in B-flat."

"I never heard you play that."

"I never have played it publicly. But this tour has to be special. I have to wheel out all my heavy artillery." I laughed nervously. "It's my comeback performance."

"So I've heard, though I don't understand what it is you're

coming back from. I have your recent recordings, all up to par. Maybe the last one was a bit off, a little mechanical."

I jumped on her words. "You think so?"

"I just sensed your heart wasn't in it."

I grunted.

"Why the long layoff from public appearances? Surely not this nonsense of chasing young girls into your thirties? And not drugs, I hope?"

"Is that what you've heard?"

"I told you, you hear lots of things. I knew it wasn't anything physical. And even the best recording engineers can only do so much for sloppy play. I figured you'd just gotten bored with it after all those years—though that bothered me because you used to need that fix of the live audience."

"I'll tell you about it sometime."

And I thought to myself, Orana you may be a first-rate critic, but you're dead wrong about what the best recording engineers can do. A team of them, hours, weeks, months, cutting and splicing and shading and highlighting. True, they can't camouflage sloppy play, but sloppy play was not my problem: I was producing a heavy, spiritless sound, with no spark or passion, and despite the engineers' technical expertise, and the dozens of takes I did of each piece, measure by measure, that problem was not solved but concealed, even to the most critical ears. Finally, though I was playing every note, I began to feel like a charlatan, a supposedly great soloist with the equivalent of ghost writers in the recording booth. Of course I needed that fix of the live audience, and that was one reason I had pushed myself into this tour. But the bigger, the more urgent prod was the overflow of my self-disgust: either I could do it or I couldn't, but I wasn't going to prolong my career any further on the basis of these recording studio marvels peddled as virtuoso performances.

"I hope it's nothing really serious," she said, studying me closely.

"No." I felt uncomfortable. Here she was in limbo between life and death—though she had obviously resigned herself to the latter—and I was playing coy about my professional travails. The fact was that it really did seem insignificant at that moment—the tour, the recordings, everything—though for months I had thought of little else.

"The layoff has been good for me," I said lightly. "I just have to work off the rust now."

She let this pass. "When you want to talk about it, we will. Though I don't know that I have much to offer you." Her face brightened. "Listen, I remember the best bit of advice you ever got. It's one of my fondest memories. You remember, in Paris?"

I smiled. "From the Maestro. Of course I remember. He said to 'make music'—no more, no less."

A wonderful memory, indeed, which I did not mind calling forth at that moment, when my spirits were sinking. I had met Artur Rubinstein in Paris when I was twenty-two and he already an old man. Orana was on tour with me in those first golden months of our marriage, and we were permitted to visit the great man backstage at the Salle Pleyel, a very high honor. I called him Maestro of course, and I was immensely flattered that he knew who I was and what I had done. Taking my hand in both of his he wished me success in the many adventures that lay before me. That was the word he used, adventures—musical adventures—and that touched me deeply. How many other pianists would have expressed it that way? He smoked a large Havana, sipped champagne, and had a beautiful svelte lady companion at his side. He was brimming with good cheer. His eyes were a young man's; they still retained a sexual hunger and a sense of the comic, the absurd. And what most impressed me was the complete lack of the prima donna in him. Overfastidiousness infects so many older pianists who become pompous spokesmen for the integrity of the instrument—at the worst a Clementi, who got rich in the end manufacturing pianos and only deigned to play when demonstrating a new model. There was nothing rigid about Rubinstein. As he had said many times before, and as he repeated to me that night, "There are dozens of pianists who are my technical superiors, who put me to shame with their virtuosity and acrobatics—but how many of them make music?" Make music, and forget all the rest: that was his advice. And that was his great virtue and his passion—that and his obsession with women, which I shared.

If only I had taken that advice eleven years before and left the rest of my life clear and uncluttered—in service to my talent. But that had never been my way.

There was a knock at the door and two nurses wheeled in a cart loaded with alcohol, towels, and linen. One of them started fussing with the bed. I kissed Orana on the forehead and she smiled faintly.

"Next time," she said, "leave that hangdog stuff out in the hall. That's not what I need. This is the healthiest half-hour I've spent in months, talking to someone who cares about my soul as much as my body."

I felt a shiver run through me: was it true, did I really care about her soul?

"If we can talk about your troubles—if you have any—" she smirked, "and not mine, it will be a luxury for me."

"All right, we will. But is there anything else I can do?"

"Will you come tomorrow?"

"I wish I could, but I have to be in court. I'm being sued again."

"The other Mrs. Randal?"

"No. Ellen."

"Even better," she said drily.

"I'll be back on Saturday," I said, and she grabbed my hand with surprising strength.

"One other thing: are you close to anyone now, or still just giving chase?"

"I'm with someone," I said.

She nodded. "I'm glad for you. Good-bye, then."

During the drive home, I felt relieved, even uplifted. And I felt guilty for it, as if I had drawn strength from someone with woefully little to spare. Orana's fortitude had heartened me, and somehow, because of this, I no longer felt so sorry for her.

I took a detour and stopped by Patty's bookstore. I bought the only set of Gibbon she had, a real beauty, the three-volume English edition of 1882 bound in red morocco.

That night I practiced for seven hours at white heat. It was the only way I could keep my mind off Orana. The reality of her circumstances looked even grimmer at two a.m. Sitting by her bedside had taken more out of me than I cared to admit, and it caught up with me hours later. Characteristically, I threw myself into my work.

Maybe I shouldn't say that. In truth, while my powers of concentration were by necessity highly developed over the years, I would not describe myself as the sort of musician who "escaped" through his music—in the romantic sense. I did not go into dream-reveries that obscured the harsher aspects of my existence. I wish I could have. I'm afraid the nature of my escape was more bound up in professional diligence and craftsmanship. Of course I lost myself in my music in that there was nothing else in the world for me while I was playing it: otherwise, I wouldn't have been worth my salt. And then too there is the question of whether one who is not inspired can possibly inspire others (in my case, a live audience). I think the answer is obvious. But what I am getting at is that I used my playing to escape, to withdraw, more in the physical sense than the artistic. I tried to exhaust myself to the point where there would be nothing left in me, not a square inch of fertile ground in which my grief could take root. Whether this was because I was coldblooded or cowardly, I don't know. But, as often occurred at such times, I made real progress that night—maybe more than I had in the previous two weeks.

I spent three hours practicing the Schubert, using one of Liszt's old tricks for peeling the deeper layers off a piece by practicing it in different keys. I shifted from B-flat to F to E, experimenting with various tempi, testing out the second movement especially with its tricky dynamics and odd fingering, trying to work through the third with more pedal than Schubert recommended, and then going back to the long legato stretches, improvising around the opening theme, with good and bad results. My third teacher, Olga Chernov, encouraged me to improvise, and I found it an invaluable tool. The great early pianists, Beethoven and Hummel and Moscheles, were phenomenal improvisors and—at least in their roles as virtuosi—their public laid a far higher premium on their improvisational abilities than their competence with strict renditions. In fact, it was expected that the pianists of their day would improvise freely in concert, and only the dolts performed as the twentieth-century pianist does, treating the sheet music as scripture. Of course I would have been put out of business had I gone onstage and embroidered a piece to my heart's content, and I had little interest in turning back the clock two centuries for the benefit of the music public, but I did improvise constantly while preparing a piece, and I have no doubts it enhanced the subsequent performance. I must say, I prided myself on my technique, and early in my career I was most scrupulous in what I accepted and rejected out of the miasma of methods, the hundreds of schools of thought, most of which are an insult to the serious pianist. Once, I had boasted that "Beethoven taught Czerny who taught Liszt who taught Leskowicz who taught Chernov who taught me—so you see I'm in direct line to Beethoven." Obnoxious, but true, I'm afraid. If the scholarly theories of piano technique that nonpianists impose on us have any validity, I was certainly more inclined to the fiery Beethoven than the formalist Hummel, to the showman Liszt than the cautious Leschetitzky. When Orana set me my reading course in the history of the piano and the lives of my distinguished predecessors, I saw from a critical standpoint what I had always known instinctually about the course I had taken in the process of creating myself as a performer. For that is perhaps the true difference between the performer and the artist: the performer uses the medium to create a persona, and the artist creates the medium itself out of the persona he has shattered.

I should add here, since I have taken such pains to lay down my notions of a performer's role, that my career as such was never something I felt I had chosen in the conventional sense. Nor did I honestly feel it had been chosen for me, however much I used to rail about my mother's and my teachers' aggressive tendencies. That was nonsense. My talent was always just there for me, as long as I can remember, and my career flowed out of it quite naturally. Perhaps one in a thousand concert pianists do not start performing very young, but I was not one of these exceptions. My talent was there like my two hands, my eyes, my ears, my stomach which I had to feed and later my sexual urges which I had to quench. It was a part of the organism, with its own peculiar sort of appetite, difficult to appease and often with little relation to what I craved in my mind or heart or body. After a time it was the tyrant whom I always feared I would fail. But it took me many years to realize this and accept it, and before that happened I mistakenly put a number of people in my life into that tyrant's role and loaded onto them the fear and loathing I harbored for my own gift.

Be that as it may, such theorizing and self-examination were rarely in my head when I played, and certainly not on that hollow night after my visit to Orana. First with the Schubert and the Liszt, and then some Rachmaninoff that I dragged out of mothballs, I played like a demon and hit my stride as I hadn't in weeks. Especially the opening of the Schubert, which I had struggled with in the morning. And then the Scherzo. Suddenly there was some fire in it. All was not well by a long shot, but at least there were some glimmers in the darkness. There are few more wonderful feelings for the pianist than that surge of exultation when he hears the first signs of transcendence in a piece behind the mere playing of it. He can feel all the disparate elements coming under his command after an interminable anarchy and can imagine himself on the threshold of higher zones—at least for a moment.

After six hours, as I tried to circle the same ethereal possibilities in the Liszt, greedy after my first intoxication, my arms gave out and my left wrist began to throb again. My fingers were hot and sore, Band-Aids on four of them, and my head was pounding. I felt the huge emptiness of the room around me. I had always enjoyed my time alone with my instrument, my intimate adversary. These were the most honest hours of my life, ruled by their own strict code of ethics and morality, one which seemed sorely lacking in my dealings with people. In my solitude I felt like an honest man, for I never lied to myself when it came to my playing. But on occasion, less often as I got older, I found the sheer vacancy of space around me, the distinct lack of a listener, oppressive. When I was married, there was often someone in another room, and I took comfort in that. These feelings went back to the earliest days when I lived with my mother and sister and my efforts were *heard* before rocketing into oblivion. But those days held more pain than pleasure, and for years flung up stinging memories.

First and foremost there was my sister, Stella, now the wife of an English surgeon. Poor Stella, I remember the shrill voice of her adolescence hectoring me mercilessly. My practicing drove her crazy. She was a normal kid who liked to have friends over for the normal sorts of pursuits—records, clothes, gossip, sex—and here she had this kid brother who was a hothouse freak. Always playing the piano. People had to walk past the living room on tiptoe, and were never allowed to use the hall bathroom, or enter the kitchen via the dining room, and were never ever permitted to interrupt me unless the place was on fire. These were my mother's strict orders. My mother exacerbated things, of course, for she insisted the piano be in the living room, the center of the house. It was a Steinway concert grand, the kind I still play, the biggest they make, and it echoed through the whole damn apartment. It was a huge apartment, nine rooms on Park Avenue, part of my mother's divorce settlement, but even so, as Stella informed me bitterly, even if you were in the farthest room from the living room, with two pillows over your head and the windows open to traffic, you could hear every note I played. My teachers advised my mother that a more intimate and private practice space would be better for me, but she would have none of it. I had to be the boy Mozart of Sixty-second Street, on full display—especially to her friends, who would listen to me from the dining room over cake and coffee. My mother's argument, always in bellicose terms, was that my playing was more important than anything else going on in the house. Is it any wonder Stella was so resentful? I'm only surprised she liked me at all. Her frustration hit the breaking point one scalding afternoon when she planted herself in the hallway, covered her ears, and at the top of her lungs shouted "Shut up!" at me a dozen times until my mother ran down the hall and slapped her while I cringed, terrified, at the piano. Stella ran away from home that day and holed up with one of her girlfriends for a few days until my mother tracked her down. I was resentful too—maybe even more than Stella—for I knew that my mother was behaving badly and had made me the fall guy, a role I didn't relish. It's amazing to me that she didn't make basket cases of us—or maybe she did. Stella has been in analysis for twenty-two years, and I play the

...ay every day, the same pieces over and over again—
...n't care how good you are, how accomplished, there's
...mething crazy about that. But of course I loved to play,
a... I secretly relished having listeners around.

Castiglione, another of my finds through Patty, had something
to say in this area. He insisted that music should be performed in
the exclusive company of friends, especially ladies, "for the sight
of them softens the hearts of those who are listening, makes them
more susceptible to the sweetness of the music, and also
quickens the spirit of the musicians themselves." To this day, I
remember that pretty sentence verbatim. He goes on to add that
one should avoid playing music in the presence of a crowd, of
common people in particular. Well, what other kinds of people
are there nowadays? Castiglione antedated the first formal piano
recital by a few centuries (it occurred in his own country, by the
way, in Rome, at the hands of Signor Liszt himself, who discarded his accompanists and became the first true soloist), but
maybe he had a point, however effete it may sound to our modern sensibilities, our sense of "fair play," which of course should
never extend to the arts. Perhaps I wouldn't have been undergoing such lacerating tortures of self-doubt on that damp night if I
had discarded this notion of my comeback, of playing before
crowds, and had restricted myself to performing for the various
ladies in my life. But when I thought hard on this, the crowd
somehow seemed less forbidding than the ladies—and anyway,
performing was my business. It was a nasty, ruthless business if
one wanted the material rewards, and there were no glittering
insular royal courts anymore, such as the ones Castiglione knew,
to which people like me could attach themselves, could eat,
drink, and sleep well, and play some fugues and minuets on the
odd night for the prince's family, all of them accomplished
themselves on the pianoforte. No, I was a trained seal for the
American rabble, the self-made and the born-rich and the tat-
tered intelligentsia, all of whom required musical diversion at
high prices—a seal very highly trained and proficient, but in the
end, let's face it, the performer is a mirror of his audience, and
there were no Medicis or Hohenzollerns where I plied my trade.

My head spinning with distractions, I paced around the loft, circling the piano every so often, thinking I might squeeze in another hour of work if I took a long enough break. But this was not to be. I would have to find another refuge. And at that hour Boston was completely gone under, black in every direction. I had come to relish those early morning hours, by necessity, through my protracted bouts with insomnia over the years. After a while I had to accept it more and panic less, for sheer peace of mind. Or as Amos Demeter used to tell me, "Sleep is just another realm of the consciousness, with its own dynamics, and who are we to try to regulate it, like the idiots who try to constrain their thoughts or submerge their desires." A more adventurous soul than I, he had no trouble dealing with such problems on a purely metaphysical plane. For my part, I was content to have accepted my sleeplessness. I no longer tortured myself lying awake in bed for hours, and I didn't try to knock myself out with numbing doses of bourbon and Nembutal. I listened to my tapes, or I read, or on particularly restless nights I went out driving through the streets, deserted and blue like a stage set. That night, with my head outracing my body, I passed out at some point on the couch, the tape deck playing back my assault on the Schubert and a novel lying unopened on my chest.

While my visit to Orana filled and overflowed the darker recesses of my mind, my superficial thoughts revolved around more immediate tangles: my foray into the dangerous country of the law the next day, a disagreement I had had with Sarah the week before, and my failure to return Margaret Demeter's many phone calls. When the telephone, six inches from my ear, woke me with a start at six a.m., I was absolutely certain it was September 12, that I was in the Plaza in New York taking my customary prerecital nap, and that in two hours I would have to walk onstage and perform. I cannot tell you how much this waking fantasy terrified me. So much so that I didn't answer the phone. After a polite interval, it started ringing again, and this time, having assured myself that it was still June and I was still in Boston, I picked it up. And cursed myself. And cursed Amos. It was Margaret again, beside herself with this other crisis I had done my utmost to avoid and which she seemed determined to foist upon me. Having caught up with me again, her determination was going to pay off.

After hanging up, though, I was more disturbed than I expected to be. I left a note for Sarah, who would be coming by while I was in court, asking her to pack a bag and join me—if possible—on the improbable mission I had promised to undertake that evening to Amos's farm in the Berkshires. I searched for a way to convey the exact nature of our business, but finally settled on three words in boldface: AMOS IN TROUBLE. Little did I know that it was I who, in addition to my domestic and professional problems, was about to embrace a whole new brand of trouble that I never even knew existed. If Theocritus is correct, and misfortune multiplied becomes good fortune, this was to be my lucky day.

At exactly 1:55, Sweeney and I mounted the steps of the State Courthouse solemnly in the blinding sunlight. Government Center, that dizzying bureaucratic maze of steel and glass, loomed around us, so many depthless surfaces punctuated by the usual megasculptures and dull murals that adorn public places. But our business was in the old courthouse, a throwback to the thirties, solid, dank, and green, and after riding up in the antiquated elevator and wandering down some murky corridors, we were ushered into a waiting room outside the judge's chambers by a diffident law clerk.

First I tried to fall into a reverie, my usual device when I found myself trapped in such places. I stared out the dusty window attempting to fix on the sliver of a single perception, as Bashō advises us. But this time it didn't work. I didn't even come close. I was too edgy. So I used the five minutes we shared on the uncomfortable bench to study Sweeney. He of course was in his element; he had come to life. Sluggish after our lunch of steak and lobster tails and his ponderous explanation of the briefs, he led me to the courthouse with an almost reluctant air. I had begun to worry about his effectiveness, but suddenly there in the waiting room he was all snap and polish. His face glowed with a calm, but aggressive, light. Personally, I sniffed disaster in the air, but even so I studied Sweeney, trying to imagine his inner workings. This was a great weakness of mine, a drug which sent me on prodigious imaginative journeys, all futile in the end, for unlike the true artist, the composer or painter, I had no creative release for my findings. I even felt a little guilty about these inner journeys. I suspected they were wasteful distractions, another way of avoiding a real and painful breakthrough where I most needed it—in my music.

At any rate, you would think I would have been acclimated to waiting rooms by that time. True, in the green rooms I was accustomed to, in concert halls, I was waiting to be applauded rather than attacked, so the habits I had developed in them had ill-prepared me for the courthouse variety. I usually sat in limbo, priming myself, balancing the inner scales before going onstage. At the best of times, I daydreamed. I never did understand those pianists who practice or study sheet music to the very end backstage. If you're not ready to play cold by concert night, you might as well pack it in and go home. I used to eat lightly, nap, and then go to the hall an hour or two before I went on. I usually waited backstage alone. In New York, Willy would come by. Orana rarely waited with me. But my second wife, Greta, almost always did. Alone or not, I tried to think about anything but the evening's program. I think this is essential for a first-rate performance, for then the best of your energy, the surprise, the spontaneity (especially on tour, playing the same pieces night after night) properly emerge before the audience.

But daydreaming and mental limbo did not serve me well in this waiting room outside the judge's chambers. So, uncomfortable and apprehensive, I made my aerial reconnaissance of Sweeney's inner life. In his office before lunch I had studied the photographs of his wife and kids while he instructed me in how to answer the judge's questions. They were a handsome, open-faced family. Sweeney himself was tall, with a tennis player's build, and carefully parted straw hair. He wore six-hundred-dollar suits that hung badly on him. His tortoiseshell glasses seemed a trifle too small. I imagined that while not exactly sexy in private, in the sack with his tennis-firm wife, he was nevertheless a horny sort of guy. He had that sheepish look of a man who has been hot for the same woman for many years. You see, I believed that no matter whose inner workings you were talking about, from Sweeney, to Leonardo (with his sexless boys and caged birds bought to be uncaged), to Lord Byron (with his boys, girls, sisters, and menageries), the whole confabulation spins on an axis of sex. Of bliss unrealized and forever sought.

Byron especially, at that time, ever since Patty sold me his diaries and journals in eleven volumes, had intrigued me. I began studying him carefully, as I had once thrown myself into the works of Freud and Rank, in order to clear the shadows from my own complex relations with women over the years. I flattered myself that Byron shared some of my own bizarre outgrowths in this area. His monasticism, for example, set up as a parallel pursuit to his sexual life. In Venice it was a literal monasticism: visiting an Armenian monastery where the monks taught him their native tongue, long hours of grammatical exercises which he followed up with a lurching circuit of the bordellos where he ran through his sexual paces. Of course I considered my hours locked up with the pianoforte as the equivalent of Armenian lessons, I deemed the city of Boston my monastery, but I seemed to have less need of an equally fervid and complementary sexual setup as I got older. At least not to the troublesome extent that I did in my early twenties. But then, I doubt that even Byron enmeshed himself in domestic nets such as I had knotted over the years. As far as I know, he married once and then avoided long-term liaisons assiduously. I was not so smart. I was the sort that began many long-term liaisons, carried through on none of them, and was left with the multiplying consequences, including guilt.

Having probed no further into Sweeney's inner life than his possible relations with his wife, I was startled when the clerk reappeared with a dim smile and led us into the judge's sanctum. Its rich furnishings, tasteful oil paintings, walnut paneling, and discreet lighting contrasted sharply with the bleak waiting room. I was surprised Ellen and her lawyer were not there first. The judge, Judge Edward T. Ryan, was a florid Diamond Jim Brady sort. He would be a fixture at the choice tables at Anthony's Pier 4, where the great barristers and politicos who ran the city gathered for lunch. Men of the world—to put it mildly—and I was reassured to find that one of them, and not some mealymouthed parvenu, was to be the MC in our little drama. Judge Ryan, big across the shoulders, with gravelly voice, sharp blue eyes, and snowy hair, beckoned us to two of the four chairs set up on the Persian carpet before his desk. He seemed indifferent to my carefully chosen blue suit—my most subdued and respectable outfit outside of my performing duds—gray tie, and black shoes. Everything about me was subdued.

"My wife is a great fan of yours, Mr. Randal," he said amiably. "I've heard you play on two occasions and both times enjoyed it thoroughly."

Sweeney beamed and my spirits climbed. I thought: wonderful, for once the judge is a music lover, sympathetic to the difficult pressures of my profession, the unintended repercussions in my personal affairs, et cetera. I got carried away after his innocuous compliment, all sorts of nonsense flying through my head. If the judge's wife were a fan, surely he would be in my corner. This sort of compulsiveness was always getting me into trouble.

"What particular recitals—" I began, but at that moment the walnut doors were thrown open and the clerk stepped aside as Ellen swept in with her lawyer, Joe Pagano.

She smiled pleasantly in my direction. She looked sleek and terrific—but not too fancy—all in white. Sweeney greeted Pagano and the two of them began ruffling papers out of their briefcases with authority. The comedy was about to begin and my spirits swan-dived once and for all.

"How are you, Max?" Ellen asked indulgently, as if I had been laid up for months. "Everything okay?"

"Sure, I feel great," I said. "How's Daphne?"

"Never better," she said airily.

"We are here today," Judge Ryan intoned, shutting us up, "by mutual agreement, to settle several questions outside the court proper. Is that correct?"

Absolutely correct, I said to myself, and immediately tuned out of the proceedings. I had been caught up in messier legal hassles than this, with more at stake, but wrapped up in my comeback—which carried with it plenty of financial pressure—I felt particularly vulnerable this time around. Also, Ellen was never my most merciful antagonist: my legal outings with my wives were pleasurable by comparison. Uncle Louie, my father's brother, a tough successful New York lawyer whose clients were in the mob, the shipping business, and the unions, reassured me the last time I went to court with Ellen: "Look at it this way: at least you didn't marry that tomato. If you had, she would have gotten the pot you pee in by now, and your pecker into the bargain. Give her what you can and keep it out of court, no matter what. Resolve it in chambers and you'll come out ahead. That's what I told your father years ago, but he wouldn't listen to me and your mother took him to the cleaners—no offense. Go to court and you'll be playing an organ on the street with a monkey on your head." Uncle Louie never pulled his punches. However, though Ellen and I had never married and so had never had a chance to fail in that department, we had produced a child. My daughter Daphne, age nine.

My one bit of fathering I managed to squeeze into the narrow gap of years between my two marriages. I was on the rebound from my breakup with Orana. Ellen—sitting six feet to my left, with her streaming jet hair and perfect profile and the elegant, put-upon Hapsburg manner that she cultivated growing up rich in Phoenix, Arizona, where her daddy built jet engines—had shared eleven glorious and six miserable months with me in Rome and Paris, the European idyll of my youth. She had presented me, at the American Hospital at Neuilly, with a blond baby girl, spitting image of my mother's mother and surely the sweetest child ever to have sprung from such belligerent parents. Daphne was truly the person I loved most on this planet. She brought me more joy than I deserved.

The history of her conception, the odd circumstances that brought her mother and me together were very much in my head that afternoon in Judge Ryan's chambers as Sweeney and Pagano delivered their respective monologues.

When Orana's lawyer had called me from New York at Amos's farm to inform me of the divorce, I was sprawled out on the bearskin before the fireplace, reading *Bleak House*, that intricate miasma of lawyers, lawsuits, and courtroom horrors. I was supine and unsuspecting, and they got me. I hurried to New York like a madman, though when I hit the city at nightfall there was absolutely nothing I could do. I slept at Amos's apartment, for Orana had locked me out of our loft, and drank too much bourbon, and the next morning, exhausted, dropped by Willy's office for a much-needed royalty check. Before I had a chance to cry on his shoulder, he sprang the news on me that the European tour had been moved up a month and expanded. He pulled out a sheet of paper with a neat list of cities and dates and informed me at once how many additional francs, lire, and Deutschmarks I would bring home. He expected me to put up a stink, but I agreed at once, happy to get away after the blow I had received.

Two weeks later, after honing my repertoire and licking my wounds, and drinking myself into a light stupor listening to Mahler every night (I was not so strict about my training in those days, but it had little effect), I set out for the Continent. It was a successful tour. And my instincts had been sound: I was too busy to indulge my depression. There just isn't time for self-pity when you're performing five nights and one afternoon a week. And the European audiences are tough—they come to listen, and they listen hard. Even the philistines among them know more about music than the philistines in North America. So I saved a lot of what was going on inside me for the stage, and I played well. In fact, I got wonderful reviews. Each night after my performance, I ate supper alone and dutifully returned to my hotel room—to my mineral water, champagne, and Dickens. The people from Willy's office doing the advance work and publicity for once didn't have to oversee my extracurricular activities because I didn't have any.

It was in Vienna, the fourth city on the tour, that I met Ellen. I had played London, Amsterdam, and Berlin, and the next stops were Belgrade and Budapest, then Milan, Venice, Rome, and Paris. Ellen was twenty-three, taking her Continental tour in style after Vassar and a year at the Sorbonne. And here I was, limping into town, withdrawn, famous, and obviously available. In my wallowing I had compounded my mental anguish by remaining celibate, so I was ripe for the picking.

Sitting in the judge's chambers, I thought of Byron again (I should have stopped reading those damn journals), who claims it was he, not his lady friends, who was always the victim, the seduced, the patsy. Certainly, dosed heavily with self-righteousness, and not a little vanity, this was the role I felt I played with Ellen. It was I, the shell-shocked world traveler, abandoned husband, and international performer, not she, the blooming wealthy American college girl, who was victimized and out-maneuvered. Ellen was a complicated case, as will become clearer. But I should set one thing straight before I go on. Doubtless by now I have painted myself (not unwittingly) as a Casanova of no mean proportions, particularly at that time of my life. This was not quite the case. In fact, except for two periods of relative promiscuity, I was for most of my youthful years a monogamous person. And unlike the true womanizer (that cold mechanic), for me women were never a means to an end, but always an end in themselves. That's probably why I got into so many jams: I took it all so seriously. I never thought of the women in my life as road signs, briefly lit up along the black highway of my psyche, there strictly for my convenience, and leading finally to that complete, thalassic Woman at the end of the carnal rainbow. I preferred hunting out complete women along the way, and sharing with them the bright and dark earthly highway that we all must traverse to quite a different destination.

At that moment, while Judge Ryan and Sweeney and Pagano droned on in their measured bassos, while I waited for the ax to fall, the very clear and warm memory of my first meeting with Ellen was painful. I felt light-years away from that sweet misty night in Vienna, a truly civilized city in the best sense, when I played the Beethoven Opus 111, Schumann's *Carnaval* and Chopin Waltzes. A program I will never forget. My best recital of the tour, possibly the finest performance I had given in two years, a night on which everything—chemistry, passion, angst, illumination—had converged and evolved, enabling the music to transcend the piano and me and reach the audience as a live entity, an organic whole. Afterward, I was flushed with genuine triumph, full of myself in a pellucid, ego-less way—though that seems a contradiction. Many performers will say it is their sense of power that is gratified when they move an audience. Despite my reservations about glorifying recitalists, I would suggest it is our sense of personal magic, of spiritual mastery, that finds fulfillment. Bergson says that to hear is to speak to oneself. He insists that the power of music lies in repeating to ourselves the sounds we've heard until we are transported into the psychic state in which they were composed. The more powerfully the performer plays, the greater will be the listeners' intensity in repeating the sounds they are hearing. The audience that strays, that is bored, is one that has ceased to repeat in the chambers of their brains what they are hearing. And what could be more magical for the nonscientist than to enter those chambers—in my case, by playing a piano.

I was flying, and the idea of going back to my hotel room alone, to my mineral water and my books, seemed out of the question. I knew when I returned to the dressing room, the applause of three curtain calls reverberating in my prideful soul, that I was ready to rip. And I had the old feeling, from my early touring days, of hoping the night would never end. It's a wonderful feeling, like a very short lease on immortality. In this frame of mind, I couldn't bear to be alone, and hearing my admirers milling out in the hallway, I threw the door open and embraced the chaotic scene that tumbled in on me. A week before, the same crowd, in different cities, made me queasy: reporters, distinguished dilettantes, the producer and his entourage, music students, and assorted hangers-on. But I couldn't get enough of them that night. I was hungry for their praise. If my worst enemy had been in that hallway, I would have ushered him in with fine speeches. To the astonishment of Willy's people, I uncorked the complimentary magnum of iced champagne and ordered glasses for everyone. And three more magnums! And flowers for all the ladies! The producer's wife immediately cornered me with her two daughters and started speaking French. I signed programs. The music students asked intelligent questions. People shouted and clinked glasses. The producer asked me to stay on and play the next night: a special performance, a percentage of the gross—the works! I tossed off three glasses of champagne, the suburbs of my brain lit up, and I tried to take stock of things. I scanned the room for more interesting company on this night to end all nights. It was not a producer's wife and daughters, nor conservatory students, I was after. I spotted a pretty brunette just inside the door, smiling curiously in my direction. She was holding a clipboard and seemed vaguely attached to the producer's staff. Perfect, I thought. And how different certain aspects of my life might have been, how obvious that I would not be sitting in this judge's mortuary chambers had not this brunette with the clipboard and the winning smile chosen that moment to step aside and reveal, in the shadow of the doorway, a truly exquisite and bewitching young woman, tall, raven-haired, Circean, in a long white coat, wearing teardrop diamond earrings. And that was Ellen.

By the time the magnums, and the dressing room, were empty, she was on my arm, in a crowd, en route to the producer's opulent townhouse on the Richtenstrasse for an enormous reception. Had I still been suspended in my moribund state, I would have made a token appearance at this bash, sipped a soda, and slipped away to my hotel before the caterers had even wheeled out the first cart of hors d'oeuvres. But on this night I led a procession in a miraculous set of Mercedes limousines, and with this beauty (whose name I hadn't caught in the commotion) tucked in sweetly beside me, and the producer's wife still chattering in French on my right, I watched the blue lights of the city snake by like strung pearls in the thickening mist. Intoxicated by the crosscurrents of the ladies' perfumes, I gazed out at tall brass statues, and baroque churches that spired into the clouds, and white parks full of fashionable pedestrians until we reached our destination. It felt like half the city must be there, all the local bankers and burghers, the fellows with season boxes at the Opera House and overdressed wives who spoke French. And of course there was the obligatory delegation of local intelligentsia, a stern and scornful bunch.

Ellen was reserved, cool and beautiful, but she was eating it all up too. She had wanted adventure and romance of the sort she read about in nineteenth-century novels and now she had found it, on a scale even her Bircher father, with his desert millions, could understand. We were fêted and flourished and buffeted about the grand ballroom like a very special sort of hors d'oeuvre. Europeans love to discover and rediscover that Americans possess any capacity for sculpturing or writing poetry or playing Schumann on the pianoforte. Their vision of the American, I am sorry to say, often consists of a spoiled and self-righteous creature, with a hubris that is shameful. A population of blusterers with a fanatical love of money and gadgetry, and a childish world view. So the European elite was exceptionally indulgent of an American like me, whom they imagined to have risen from the muck and mire of vulgarity against all odds. I was accustomed to this phenomenon from previous tours, but for Ellen, who until then had only met various Frenchmen and Austrians under the auspices of her rich daddy (a blusterer if there ever was one) and her rich friends, this was all very new and heady. For a while I puffed out my chest under the delusion I had picked up a woman of incredible beauty—so crude was my pride in those days. Then I realized it was the other way around: a fellow-countrywoman had picked me up, and attached herself as if we had been inseparable for years. Some Viennese ladies actually asked how long we had been married!

Such is the enormous and rather graceful power of certain clever women and the phenomenal stupidity of a man like me, my head filled with absurd macho notions, my dull and inflated ego repeatedly setting me behind the psychological eight-ball in any amorous encounter. For Ellen and I lost no time in getting to that phase of things, and by sunrise, exhausted and red-eyed in my hotel suite, her languorous long-limbed form curled beside me under the satin comforter, I was sublimely trapped and netted, ready to dance in the streets for that girl. And I would dance, all right, I was still dancing that day in chambers. She had come to Vienna on a whim, to study the architecture, to see Freud's house and Klimt's studio, to hear concerts in the magnificent halls, and instead she had bagged a live pianist, met the mayor, drunk champagne with opera stars, and enjoyed breakfast in bed in the best hotel in town while listening (through a barely opened door) to the pianist give an interview to the music critic from *Der Spiegel* at nine a.m. The pianist not at his best, head pounding and hangover suddenly upon him.

Of course one thing led to another, and with no pressing reason to be in Vienna, Ellen, suddenly full of purpose, accompanied me to Belgrade, Budapest, and so on through Italy and on to Paris. She sat in the front row at every concert. She took it upon herself to speak for me (*ex officio* as it were) to anyone willing to listen. She carted me to all the museums and four-star restaurants we could squeeze into my hectic schedule. My sedentary hotel routine was blown to bits. In Milan we rented a car and drove around the lake district. She entertained me with long recitations about medieval history. At the Sorbonne she had written her thesis on Roger Guiscard and the Venetian doges. She was smart and she was funny. But she was terribly spoiled. The one and only princess, North American variety, I have ever fallen in with. Between discussions, gourmet meals, and sexual horseplay, she sent her daddy a cable informing him that she had "eloped" with a famous American musician. She posted an explanatory letter the same day with a bunch of my clippings. And because it was postmarked in Yugoslavia, the old man's initial reflex was that his little girl had run off with a Communist. If only that had been the case! Then who could she have sued nine years later? The cable and the letter proved fatal. Even before Ellen and I parted in Paris fourteen months later, even before her father learned that not only had she not married but that she was pregnant, he cut her off financially. From then until now, she had been supported by her mother, who sent cash on the sly, and by me, her consort for barely four hundred days. Actually, most of the money I contributed went to supporting my daughter. But it galled me that this guy in Phoenix, swimming in dough, fifteen, twenty million dollars liquid, had cut this girl off for a youthful indiscretion and that I, never ungenerous for all those years, was still relegated to the role of villain.

My daughter Daphne was conceived in Venice. Byron's favorite city, that metropolis of bad dreams and grand illusions. We were there for five days and I was sick as a dog, barely getting through my performances, bolstered by vitamin injections and smelling salts. I had a viral anemia, which I'm sure I picked up during our tour of the lakes. Despite this, we managed a single go-round in our enormous bed under the mock-Tiepolo mural, Ellen climbing on top of me in the middle of the night at my insistence, so sure was I that I would expire before dawn and anxious not to leave this world unsatisfied, sexually agitated, with juice to spare. It was short, hardly satisfying to either of us, and forgettable, except for the fact it marked Daphne's entrance into this life.

In my mind I was still in Venice, still on my back, virally in-capacitated, staring out the nine-foot windows at a pastel sky, a mauve and rose cloud bank, but there in Boston ten years later a voice, low and insistent, was addressing me across a vast ex-panse. The voice of Judge Ryan.

"Do you remember that occasion, Mr. Randal?" he was insist-ing, not unkindly, and I felt Sweeney's elbow in my side.

What I had failed to achieve in the waiting room, to prepare myself for this scene, I had accomplished at exactly the wrong moment. I had fallen into a deep reverie. Sweeney, Pagano, the judge, and Ellen were all staring at me, waiting for an answer.

"Do you remember?" the judge repeated, and I wondered how he could possibly have been privy to my thoughts, my memories. . . .

"Yes, of course I remember."

Sweeney went white. "I don't believe my client understood the question, Your Honor."

"Why not? It's a clear enough question." The judge was irri-tated. Things were going badly and I didn't even know why. "I'll repeat it once more," he intoned, leaning forward, his cheeks flushed.

"Mr. Randal, do you remember promising Miss Voigt in No-vember of last year that this June the first, your child support payments would triple to offset the inflationary rises not fully covered in your paternity agreement? Do you remember this conversation?"

"What? No! Absolutely not. I had no such conversation."

Sweeney shook his head sadly.

"I have two witnesses, Your Honor, who would be happy to appear," Ellen piped in wearily.

"What witnesses? Last November—where? You mean, at Thanksgiving—"

"Of course."

"But we were alone that day. We barely said a word to one another."

"Max, you know you tend to forget these things. I was *not* alone. And we spoke for nearly an hour."

"That's a god—"

"Mr. Randal, remember where you are. Both of you. This is not a counseling service. These are my chambers and I will have no bickering. If you cannot settle your differences here, civilly, then you will appear in my court, under far more rigid conditions."

I knew from Sweeney's face that losing my temper had been a mistake. Exactly what he had warned me not to do. Her lawyer, Pagano, spoke up now, oily and confident. He had a gilded, tortoise look, his bullet head pushing forward out of his pinstripes. He wore a pink tie with a gold pin.

"Your Honor, allow me to apologize on behalf of my client. She has been under great emotional stress, and is frequently goaded into these exchanges in private by Mr. Randal. That is why we are here today, I'm afraid."

Son of a bitch. But now it was Sweeney's turn to earn his fee. I leaned back and listened carefully. And it didn't take long for me to grasp what had transpired while I was roaming the past, to understand exactly what Ellen wanted from me. I realized in a flash that this courthouse/chambers business was an exercise in futility, a fantastic sham. Ellen had already won her battle and we were all wasting precious hours of sunlight going through the motions like puppets. Sweeney was merely trying to contain the magnitude of our losses—that is, the actual amount of cash I would part with. The judge, it seems, was predisposed to this inflation question a priori, and my notions of storming in there in my sober outfit wielding moral arguments and fine distinctions was so much nonsense. Everyone else knew that; only I had come stuffed with delusions. And was this really so sinister? It seemed like a bit of theater—provided by the State—in which I might be humored.

When Sweeney was done, Pagano put in his two cents, the judge did some muttering, and the figures, the new reality emerging from all this mumbo jumbo, were laid on the table. But none of it seemed worthy of further attention on my part. I was studying a set of jade figurines on the judge's mantelpiece. There were four of them, three women and a man, with the look of Matisse's dancers, swooning around some central point, into one another's arms. They reminded me of statues I had seen in

Stockholm and Oslo, but the jade didn't fit in with Scandinavia. Yet they certainly weren't Oriental. I turned to the judge with new interest. He seemed to broaden before my eyes. Perhaps I had underestimated him, pegging him for a gourmand and beer-swiller, a florid high-class crook of Pagano's ilk. And of course he was that to some degree—he must have been, to become a judge in Boston. But, still, I couldn't imagine Pagano or Sweeney displaying that piece in their offices. The judge was put off by my stare.

"Is there something you wish to say, Mr. Randal? Something you object to in these figures?"

They were throwing around so many figures, I had lost track of them.

"Just one thing, Your Honor, before we go on."

"Yes?"

"Those jade figurines on the mantel. Where were they sculptured?"

He was dumbfounded, and I felt foolish suddenly for having said this. Ellen now had the perfect excuse for rolling her eyes in her spoiled way and sighing, as if to reaffirm what she had to put up with in dealing with me. And maybe she had a point. Maybe I had played the clown in order to undercut my own already eroded position—at once a self-destructive stroke and a way of thumbing my nose at them.

"The jade," Judge Ryan said. "Yes, my wife bought them when we were in Pakistan. She's a collector."

Pakistan. I would never have guessed that.

"They're exquisite," I said.

"Thank you," he mumbled, slipping on his glasses. He was neither pleased nor displeased. I think he just wanted to get rid of us.

The lawyers argued some more, the judge listened, and after another fifteen minutes it was all over. In addition to her mortgage payments and taxes, which I took care of outside of our legal agreement, Ellen would now receive two thousand a month for Daphne's support. This was up from the thousand she had been getting, but not the three thousand she wanted. Sweeney considered this a victory. Even the judge seemed to realize that you don't need three thousand dollars a month after taxes to feed, clothe, and school a nine-year-old. But I was doing some quick calculations: coupled with my alimony to Greta, which was thirty-five hundred a month, my monthly output for one daughter and one ex-wife was now fifty-five hundred. That was sixty-six thousand dollars a year before all other expenses, including my own support!

But my real agitation was not financial. Ellen had only extracted another twelve thousand per annum, and that was no big deal. It was probably even fair. What most upset me was that she always insisted we do our business through the legal system. She knew I would do anything in my power for Daphne. And she knew I hated going to court. If she had told me she needed more money, that would have been the end of it. I had dreaded that day for weeks simply because of where we were meeting, and the attendant convolutions, not because of the money. And I resented it. Also, to be truthful, I suppose it *had* hit me finally, in those august surroundings, how much I had been dipping into my capital just to meet this payroll of my past follies. To think I had cursed Willy for prodding me into this tour, my comeback, the rest of it. I should have kissed his feet with the kind of income I now required to stay afloat. If need be, I could perform a hundred times a year. I had been idle too long. I would restore my lost reserves. Suddenly I felt buoyant. Maybe Sweeney was right, maybe this was a victory. These things could work in strange ways.

But they had a surprise for me. I was already standing up, relieved to be on my way, when Pagano started in again.

"About that other matter, Your Honor, involving the child's visits to her father."

Sweeney seemed surprised, and I didn't like that. They're trying to pull something, I thought. It's not the money, it's this.

"I thought all that was settled," Sweeney put in.

"Something has come up in the last week," Pagano continued.

The bastards are going to try to keep the kid away from me, I thought. For the first time in that room, I was all ears, ready for anything.

"Due to unforeseen circumstances, my client will require the child to make her annual two-month visit to her father, not for the month of December and in week-long stretches during the other seasons, but all at once this summer—that is, the months of July and August."

"July and August!" I blurted. "But that's in two weeks. And the whole summer—you can't do that. I'm preparing for a tour. I can't take care of her properly while I'm practicing ten hours a day. It's impossible!"

"Mr. Randal, please calm down," the judge interjected. He seemed sympathetic. "Is there valid reason for this, Mr. Pagano?"

"Yes, Your Honor. My client has to travel abroad on urgent business to further her career."

This was too much for me. "Career? What career?"

"If you took any interest, Max, you'd know that I've started my own business. Importing antiques. I'm beginning to do quite well at it, too," she said, but Pagano cut her off with a glance.

"Yeah, maybe that's where all the money has been going, setting you up in business."

"That's a terrible thing to say."

"Quiet, please. I've warned you both not to bicker in these chambers."

We were all standing in a circle, very excited. Only Pagano was calm.

"Getting back to the issue at hand," he said. "Miss Voigt's original agreement with Mr. Randal covers just such an eventuality. I direct you to page 12, clause 3b, Your Honor. And you, Mr. Sweeney."

I could tell from Sweeney's face that Pagano had gotten us.

"But don't I have any say in this—about what's best for my own child?"

"Not according to this clause, Mr. Randal. It is left entirely to Miss Voigt's discretion when the child is to see you for visits of longer than a weekend. Only the total number of days per year is immutable."

I thought back venomously to the lawyer who served me when Ellen had this thing drawn up. I had paid him five thousand bucks so I could keep getting screwed for years. Inflationary rises, visitation rights, the whole thing was a mess.

I tried to assume a reasonable tone. "Look, Ellen, you know what it's like when I'm preparing for a tour—"

"Do I?"

I took a deep breath. "In December, after the tour, I can give the kid my undivided attention. We can do things together. Go skiing, buy Christmas presents, the theater. The next two months are going to be crazy—as if she's visiting a monk, a hermit. It will be awful."

Ellen snickered. "You, a monk? That's a good one. No, July and August it is, my plans are already fixed."

"But what about *my* career considerations?"

She shrugged.

"And why the hell didn't you know about this beforehand?" I demanded of Sweeney, but his head was buried in his briefcase.

I turned in desperation to the judge. "Your Honor, is what I'm saying so unreasonable? About seeing my daughter under the proper circumstances?"

The judge seemed to feel sorry for me. "I can appreciate your feelings, Mr. Randal, yes. But you signed this agreement, and it is absolutely binding. It's not in my hands. You will be prepared to receive your daughter on the 1st of July, and to return her to her mother on the 31st of August. And beginning on the 1st of September, you will send Miss Voigt two thousand dollars per month, every month from that day forth. I believe that concludes our business here. Good day."

The money was one thing, but this could be disastrous, gumming up my work schedule and my relationship with Daphne in one stroke.

They had one last surprise for me. When I burst out of Ryan's chambers three steps ahead of Sweeney, I discovered, in that drab waiting room, on one of the hard benches, my lovely daughter Daphne leafing through a magazine. For a moment, I could not understand how or why she was there. Ellen hadn't mentioned her, so I assumed Daphne was home with a sitter. More spontaneous than I, she broke into a big smile and ran into my arms. I melted, for in this entire awful world there was this little creature with my mother's hair, and Ellen's eyes, and my hands, and a golden heart, who loved me unquestioningly, completely. The sight of her renewed my spirits.

"Daddy, I thought you'd never come out. I wanted to come in and see you."

"I'm glad you didn't, sweetheart. It was very boring."

"You mean, you and Mom were arguing," she said sadly. "I guess that is boring."

She was always too smart for me. She had my father's dry sense of humor. She was intrigued by him, her paternal grandfather, whom she had never known, so much more interesting than her Bircher grandfather who spoiled her, despite his hostility to her mother and me, but whom I don't think she fully trusted. I knew, though, that the old man had earmarked several million dollars for Daphne in his will, so she was set up for life. And this took some of the heat off me financially, in terms of the long haul. In fact, I thought, unless he outlived me (which was possible), Daphne would even be able to keep me out of nursing homes later on if my affairs went completely haywire and I ended up broke. I had the feeling too that the old buzzard would soften up toward Ellen in his last years and provide for her outright. But at least I knew that my daughter, in addition to being beautiful and talented and sweet-dispositioned, was also going to be rich. In temperament, she was her mother's opposite: no guile, no instinct for subterfuge. She didn't resemble me much either in the inner workings department. She showed no signs of the morbid self-consciousness and furtiveness that I displayed so early on—probably from being so isolated and from dealing with a truly crazy woman like my mother every day.

The previous year I had taken Daphne to London for Christmas, to visit Stella and her kids—her first cousins—and they had a ball. She loved Stella. She was the kind of kid who found something good in everyone. As for her interest in my father, I could never really understand it. In a little boy, it would have been obvious: a grandfather who was a boxing champion, a tough guy, all that stuff. But a little girl? I got hold of films of three of his title fights, paid plenty for them from a boxing archives, and Daphne had me show them to her over and over again. Certainly the old man, known as a dancing master with his fancy footwork and quick hands, was nice to watch, but I never could get her to tell me exactly what it was about him that so fascinated her. She would back off vaguely. She didn't want to talk about it. This was never the case when it came to my work. She loved to hear me play, she listened to all my recordings at home, and we had long discussions about them. Since she was only five when I last performed publicly, she had never seen me onstage, and I had promised her she would attend a recital on the upcoming tour, probably in New York.

I wanted to talk with her now for a few minutes, to discuss this two-month visit coming up. As soon as I saw her, I was happy about it, despite my real fears. We had never spent that much time together, ever. Pagano and Sweeney were behind us, chatting amiably, fraternity pals suddenly comparing golf notes—or maybe fees.

"I'd like a little time with her," I said to Ellen. "How about if we go for a soda and then meet you in front in a half-hour?"

"Can't do it," she said breezily. "Sorry, but you've got all summer, Max—thanks to me. It's just impossible now. We're taking the four o'clock shuttle to New York, and we've only got a half hour to get to Logan."

"New York? What for?"

"We're visiting my sister for the weekend. And I have some business there."

Out of the corner of my eye I saw Daphne's face darken. I knew she disliked her aunt, Ellen's rich sister Caroline, and her two bratty cousins in their giant pad on Fifth Avenue. She had told me stories about those kids which gave me a greater under-standing of Ellen's upbringing.

"Well, can't you take the shuttle at five?"

"No, I can't. Caroline's car is picking us up at the airport and I'm not about to change all my plans so you can have a soda."

"But it's all right for me to change my entire summer plans at the drop of a hat, is that it?"

"I'm sorry, Max."

She had taken Daphne's hand and I was walking alongside them to the elevator, the lawyers trailing me. I saw there was no point in arguing, so I tried to control myself for the kid's sake. I didn't like her to see us fight, yet that was all we seemed able to do.

And, truly, I deserved anything I got. With all my Byronic pretensions and messy dealings. Even chaotic violent men like my father seemed able to control the extent of their entanglements. But not me. I vividly remembered my own parents' divorce proceedings, probably much as Daphne would one day remember these afternoons she spent in judges' waiting rooms.

After getting into the elevator with her and Ellen, I hit the "Close" button, hurrying the door shut on the astonished faces of Pagano and Sweeney and terrifying Ellen, who thought I was about to assault her. At that moment my heart went out to my child. If all I was to have with her on that dismal day was the lousy elevator ride, then so be it, I wasn't about to waste time bitching with her mother. I leaned down and she buried her face in my neck and hugged me, her pretty hay-colored hair in my face, and we walked out across the lobby and through the revolving doors into the muggy Boston afternoon. She held my hand while I got them a cab. Then she gave me a big kiss, waved out the cab window, and they were gone.

This was how things stood as I returned to my loft to prepare for the drive to Amos's farm. My monastic summer, my attempts at a spiritual rebounding, would be attended by circumstances that just a few days before would have seemed outlandish: Orana had come to town to die, my daughter was going to live with me almost until my opening recital, and my friend Amos, according to his frantic wife, had disappeared in the company of his latest guru, a psychologist-shaman named Dr. Winters. I was at low ebb as I trudged in and tossed aside the mail. Disgusted at having had to waste my workday with the likes of Sweeney and Pagano, I would now proceed to blow my evening on a wild-goose chase. I had serious work to do and instead I was running in circles.

Sarah came down the hall from the kitchen in turquoise shorts and a big white shirt, barefoot, a pencil behind her ear. I noticed her overnight bag stowed neatly behind the door. Typical of her, for unlike me she never allowed herself to waste time. She looked me up and down.

"Get a job in a bank?" she said drily.

I had forgotten about my subdued outfit, now rumpled with heat and anxiety, shirt open, tie askew. For all the world resembling a junior bank stiff after another deadly day.

"No, this is how I look when I get fleeced."

She poked a finger into my ribs. "How much?"

"Another thousand a month."

"What's a thousand dollars to an executive like you?"

"It's not that. Ellen's finagled it so that Daphne is coming to stay here all summer. And you know my schedule and the pressure I'm under."

"Why now?"

"She claims she has urgent business abroad." She followed me into the bedroom as I pulled my clothes off. "You know, I'm happy Daphne's coming, but I'm afraid I can't work the way I have to and still take care of her the way I want to." I sat down on the bed. "I guess I'm really just afraid of letting her down. I've never had this much time before to botch things up."

"It'll be all right. And what's this crisis with Amos?"

"I'll tell you during the drive. It's too complicated. How did your readings go?"

"Okay. Sold a pile of books."

"Like a night on the town in New York? I planned to go next week anyway to see Willy, so instead I thought we'd sleep at the farm and drive down tomorrow."

"Fine, I have business there myself. I'll make some sandwiches for the road. Why don't you take a shower and cool off."

I closed my eyes and let the water run off my shoulders. I was partial to showers and baths. When I moved in, I had this shower fitted with three high-speed nozzles, one overhead and two at rib-level. A poor man's jacuzzi. I once owned a real jacuzzi, a Christmas gift to myself, back in my old loft in New York, but it had become the property of Greta. I loved that place, which Orana and I bought and fixed up and made into a home. I would never have sold it for any price, and in the course of a half hour of double-talk, another judge, this one in south Manhattan, had awarded it to Greta as part of her settlement. Everything except the last year of mortgage payments, which were my share of the deal.

Such was the negative spiral of my thoughts. I tried hard to think about my music. My umbilical cord to the piano was something I mocked to my intimates, but they knew and I knew that without it I would have been lost. I reassured myself that even if I was sacrificing a couple of days' work at the keyboard, the pieces were in my head and I could work over some theoretical problems. This was a delusion. Nevertheless, I succeeded in distracting myself, musing about Kierkegaard's theories of music, which I had been studying that week.

I had discovered much of interest in Kierkegaard. He is far more trustworthy and less abstruse on the subject of music than the stuffed shirts who usually write about it. He claims that music only exists in the moment of its performance. No matter how skillfully the notes are read, and how lively the imagination behind the reading, there is no music until someone is playing it. I agreed with that, while continuing to insist that the performer is an interpreter and not a creative artist. Kierkegaard also says that music is the art of the spirit. But that because of its lack of spatiality, it also lacks sensuousness in the ultimate degree, and must finally betray the spirit. He concludes that *Don Giovanni* is the greatest of musical works. The apex. And the exemplar of self-betrayal. Which brought me back to Don Juan, Byron, my Casanova researches. For Kierkegaard states outright that in Don Juan Mozart found the subject that is "absolutely musical," a high epic of the musical-erotic, as he calls it.

And why was I dwelling on all this, eyes clamped shut in my overheated shower in the midst of the city's worst heat wave, my paramour doing her daily sit-ups on the bedroom rug, my car double-parked below? I knew the reason even then, in my confused state. I had reached the point in preparing myself for my work where it was no longer enough for me to run through some yoga exercises and map out my technical explorations. No, either from maturity or boredom, I required more incentive than mere technical curiosity to lose myself at the hammerklavier. I craved spiritual and sensual connections, though I was not yet sensate enough to recognize them as such. Inner linkages which would propel me away from the self, the ego's hub, the lotus-land of everyday life with its opiates of pain and despair. I craved, in short, what the true, creative artist already possesses: an absolute link between the sexual and artistic impulses. The musical-erotic. It was for this reason I was now attempting—in last-ditch fashion—to convert the raw material of my sexual history, its lusts and follies and higher flights, into the fuel that would make my playing a vehicle of inner consciousness and not just a virtuosic distraction. Perhaps the supreme misadventures of my twenties would make me into a truly great performer in my thirties. What vanity! But if Mozart found in Don Juan the "absolutely musical" subject, perhaps I too could find in the portion of myself that embodied the seducer's life-and-death struggle with his darker shadow (for the true seducer attempts to seduce death so as to prolong life) the greater depths of my own musical soul. At any rate, such mental gymnastics had become a necessary prelude to any sustained work. I had rediscovered, after years of coasting, that the piano demanded as much rigorous intellectual training as sheer unflinching physical discipline.

It seemed to me that what had been instinctual for me, musical and otherwise, ten years before, was no longer so. Back then, I sought out women, both lovers and friends, to fulfill my inner longings; now I had to turn to Kierkegaard and Molière. Was this such a bad thing? And, musical questions aside, had it indirectly improved my relationships with women? I don't think so.

Certainly my relationship with Sarah could have marked a turning point. She lived a life of the mind, and I could discuss these points with her as if we were chatting about the weather. But I—who was often wrong about women, impulsive, going overboard, yet usually preferring women's company to men's— had suddenly grown cautious at the age of thirty-three. I was trying to be sensible and I hadn't the faintest idea how to go about it.

It was only a week before the first day of summer and the days were long. As we purred out of Boston, the sky was bright, without a single cloud. The humidity lifted and the air cooled. I put the top down, ate a ham sandwich, settled back with a cigar, and tried to repeat to Sarah what Margaret had told me on the phone at the crack of dawn. Our destination was Lenox, in the heart of the mountains, two and a half hours away, but we were comfortable in the Cadillac's giant leather seats. Sarah let her hair fly loose, her sunglasses reflecting the oncoming cars. I had called Orana just before we left, and she thanked me for the Gibbon. I told her I had to leave town for a couple of days and would be by on Monday. She sounded weak, drugged up, and this had depressed me further. I was almost grateful for this wild excuse to get out of deadbeat town before it fell in on me—hospitals, courthouses, and the rest.

But the open air was working wonders. I related Margaret's tale with relish. And what a tale it was. As always, when my affairs were in upheaval, Amos seemed to enter the scene from the wings.

Amos Demeter was my oldest, dearest, and really my only close friend. We had known each other since we were twenty. We were exactly the same age, born the same month and year. Unlike me, with my occupational blinders and single unswerving purpose, Amos had played many roles, enjoyed many adventures that, logically, should never have belonged to the same lifetime. He had broken his chains, the ones we are all swaddled in from birth, but rather than discarding them, or clanging them angrily in the night as the disaffected do, he built bridges with them, connections to higher realms and purer spheres of action. His one anchor, his relatively permanent incarnation, was as a photographer. This was how he made his living, outside of various business schemes. And as a photographer he had excellent credentials—a Pulitzer Prize, in fact, for a series of photographs he took in Vietnam at the height of the war. By sheer recklessness, he had insinuated himself in the wrong place at the right time and caught a shocking scene of refugees under fire. The experience did not sit well with him, however, and he soon gave up straight news work. He published three books of photographs—studies of Indonesia, Tibet, and African nomads—and he often worked on assignment for the glossier magazines to fund his latest project. He had also, in his early years, been a scuba diver, ballroom dancer, manager of a nightclub on Rhodes, and a tour guide in Barcelona, his favorite city.

Amos's spiritual quest was decidedly external. His worldly activities were complicated, and, a creature of impulse, he never thought twice about how or where to funnel his vast energies; in this respect, he and I were polar opposites. This was perhaps one reason we had remained close friends for so long. His marriage to Margaret, a model, was then entering its seventh year. She had continued to prosper in her career, and rarely interfered in his pursuits, however bizarre. And they were often quite bizarre: a trek to Angola to excavate a subaqueous city, a holistic clinic for avalanche victims, a scheme to make protein bars from algae. He did have his serious moments and was a constructive, and objective, critic when it came to my playing. He knew about music (his mother had been a concert violinist), and I trusted his judgment. I had confided in him completely about my problems with my work, and he had tried to help me in his indirect, illogical way.

At any rate, because of his history, and her usual tolerance, I had reluctantly taken notice when Margaret expressed alarm about his latest shenanigans.

She told me he had gotten it into his head to do the first extensive photographic study of Albania by a non-Albanian—a hopeless notion from the start. It was almost impossible for an American to enter Albania, much less to do so with a bag full of photographic equipment. The Albanians didn't have an embassy in the United States, so he went by their U.N. Mission on Eighty-seventh Street in Manhattan, had a fruitless interview with a dour attaché named Sinonescu, and promptly forgot the whole business. A few weeks later, however, he received a phone call from a Dr. Winters, who said he had been given Amos's name by Sinonescu, his sometime squash partner. Winters introduced himself as a psychologist and theosophist, the president and founder of the Eagle Institute of New York and London, and a specialist in neurovisual harmonic phenomena. Margaret didn't know what this meant. Winters said he had heard that Amos was a man of adventure. He said he was embarked on an undertaking of the utmost delicacy that demanded the skills and services of such a man. Of course this was just the bait for Amos, and he met Winters the next day. He came home that night extremely agitated, but he would tell Margaret nothing except that Winters was an extraordinary man. He began visiting this Eagle Institute daily, and suddenly one morning told Margaret he had to travel for a while, but refused to give her any details. They had a tremendous row, and he left. After a couple of days, she tried to locate him, in vain, and as a long shot called the farm in Lenox. A woman answered the phone very rudely. Then a man got on, identified himself as Dr. Winters, said Amos wasn't there, and hung up.

That was three days ago. Margaret had called me then, but I had put her off, hoping Amos would turn up. Now she claimed she was worried to distraction. She believed anything might have happened—after all, she said, what did she know about this fellow Winters? Amos had taken their car, and she was afraid to go there alone, anyway. So I was enlisted for the job.

"But is that all she said?" Sarah asked.

"Isn't that enough? It's hard to believe that much."

"And he told her nothing else about Winters and his institute?"

"Nothing. She said he sometimes came home and asked her cryptic questions."

"Such as?"

"About souls transmigrating, and whether she believed the soul operated outside of time—solar time."

"Has he always been like this?"

"Amos? Always. This is all nonsense, but I have to get Margaret off my back. I'm only bothered by this Winters being at the house without Amos, and hanging up on her. Doesn't sound right. Amos loves that place. He usually keeps to a somewhat normal life-style there. It was part of his mother's legacy. She worked on her music there. Even now, he usually goes to the farm to recover from his excursions, not to initiate them. And I have my own sentimental feelings about the place. I don't like the idea of a stranger having the run of it."

Sarah lit a cigarette and tugged at her lower lip with her thumbnail. This was the sort of stuff that appealed to her imagination. She would stew over it. I had other things to worry about—business with Willy, and I had to start thinking about taking care of Daphne day in day out, and of course there was Orana. So Amos's adventures did not hold their usual sway—even vicariously. I mollified myself with the reminder that a beautiful old Steinway awaited me at the farm, a prewar job with gold leaf and mother-of-pearl inlay, on which, if circumstances permitted, I would be able to put in a few hours that night.

I put a tape into the cassette machine and Mozart's last string quintet washed over us. It was Amos who introduced me to Sarah, by the way, at Tanglewood, back in April. She was up there to see her father conduct. He was the famous Franz Lengford, conductor of the Philadelphia Symphony, with whom fortunately I had never worked. I doubt we would have hit it off in that capacity, though I had the greatest respect for him, and he for me, as it turned out. Amos was photographing the season's opening at Tanglewood for a national magazine, a lark since he was spending the month at the farm anyway. I was visiting him for the weekend and tagged along that night. I enjoyed the concert (Brahms' Fourth Symphony), and at the reception afterward, one of those glittery indoor-outdoor affairs with Japanese lanterns by the lake, Amos brought me over to meet Lengford and his family. He knew Lengford well, for Lengford and his mother had been friends. They were engaging people, and after talking shop with the maestro and exchanging pleasantries with his wife, I was about to go on my way when their eldest daughter appeared with a bottle of champagne. She asked me to join them, and I did, to Amos's amusement.

She was terrific to look at, a honey brunette with wide-set dark eyes, fine cheekbones, and a straight nose that highlighted her facial symmetry Donatello-style. She was a writer, she had published a book of stories and a novel the year before. She lived in Boston. But all of this was irrelevant to me. I was used to meeting beautiful, accomplished, and talented people, and trusting very few of them. What I was taken with at once was her poise. She seemed to possess great reserves of inner calm, which, for me, translated into spiritual peace. I immediately envied her her detachment: it seemed integrated somehow.

That night after dinner Sarah and I drifted away, drinking more champagne and talking, and at two o'clock, when the great lawn was nearly empty and the stars blazing, she drove back to the city with me. It was a bittersweet drive, for enamored as I was, I was also a little sad and apprehensive, caught up for the first time in my life with my age. Later, this would seem absurd to me, but on that night I thought, Here I am with a young woman, barely twenty-five, which is nothing new for me, but have I already reached that juncture, that vaguely sad plateau, where I am dating the daughter of a colleague, a friend of my own best friend? Lengford himself was only forty-seven, and that seemed closer to me in age than, from the other direction, twenty-five. I believe now the true cause of my angst was the larger fear of leaving my youth and entering the suburbs of the great middle realm before the final descent. It must have been, because thirty-three and twenty-five is actually a fine pairing, and just two years before I was running around with a girl nineteen without a qualm. Was it my fault that Lengford had become a father early and that because of my professional precocity I had colleagues, professional equals, who were twenty years my senior? But I am playing too much on my melancholy, for it was also a night of rare beauty, one of those times when Nature drops her adversary role and seems present solely for our benefit. I never had such a night again with Sarah. Our relationship didn't come close to fulfilling the romantic expectations engendered at that first meeting. But I wonder now how long it had been since I thought I might possibly fall in love again, whatever that worn phrase meant to me, clotted as it was with years of contradictions and qualifications? Obviously, it was something I craved, for cutting down the open highway with the top down, the radio humming, and this girl beside me telling me her great plans for herself, her ambitions, I congratulated myself for still being lucky with women. I should have exhausted the capital of my luck long ago in that department, I thought, but perhaps that too was something I had inherited from my father, whose luck was legendary until the end. Instead of congratulating myself, I should have kept my ears open, and asked myself exactly what Sarah wanted, and indeed what I wanted. If I had forgotten what it was to fall in love, I had forgotten too the language that is spoken in that terrain. Sarah and I certainly weren't speaking it, though we spent the rest of that night and much of the next day in each other's arms. Perhaps despite my idealization of her (for I always idealized women), I already harbored qualms about her that I wouldn't admit to myself.

But as on that first night, now, driving into the sinking sun, it was Sarah's inner calm that I continued to envy and covet, that detachment which, apparently, she could summon at will. It seemed almost sinister. I was so desperate for it myself that I hoped some would rub off on me. Sarah needed no meditation room or cell. Cafeterias, gas stations, movie houses were perfectly adequate. It amazed me, for I could only find a vestige of such calm—on a hit-and-run basis—within the frenzy and torment of practicing. And even then what I called calm was more a negative quality, an obliteration of self, a subsuming state in which I became one with my music. And this deficiency, I fear, did me great harm, for rather than leaving me in a neutral state, it swept me under with great waves of anxiety and inferiority and panic.

Sarah was an intellectual, which by my definition meant that she lived more for her mind than her body. She had few friends, and those I met were a cold, sullen crew. They were political, in a literary sort of way. She wrote articles for highbrow journals and attended fund-raisers for worthy causes. She was horrified that I didn't read the newspapers, that I hadn't voted in years, that I got out of jury duty by fabricating a criminal conviction, that, as she put it: "Your social consciousness is nil." Of course her father was very active politically, a humanitarian, despite the pressures of his career. One night I told her grandly that my business was the human heart, where the true revolution would occur when all the manifestos turned to dust. She didn't appreciate that, either, but she dropped the whole subject.

On another, loftier plane, I did owe her a debt, for she was always reading aloud to me, around the house, in bed, in the car, and it was always good stuff. Between her own varied selections, and the many books Patty was throwing my way, I felt I was rounding off my formal self-education, but also crazing myself with wild theories, justifying one day's mood while canceling out another's. A few days before, she had read me a poem by Christopher Smart, and one line particularly delighted me: "The right names of flowers are yet in heaven." It set off bells in my head. I decided that the right names of almost everything were still in heaven, and we, in our world of multiple divisions, were fussing constantly with names, objects, and notions that had nothing to do with the real essence of life. I felt we took a certain jealous pride in this insularity, as if lack of true vision were a virtue. Indeed, that is what is drummed into us from the first, in school. I was always grateful that my career had disrupted my formal education. I hated school. They only let me through because of my musical precocity. As a kid, I had tutors because I had to practice so many hours a day. And when I went to Juilliard later on I was all right. But then my mother and Willy got it into their heads that a first-rate university was essential, to give me breadth, et cetera: sound enough in theory, but in practice a disaster. Off I went to Harvard, where outside the mainstream there is always room for people like me—dictators' sons, expert fencers from Ghana, and the odd prodigy. That is how I originally came to know Boston. I was given all the breaks, but I never even completed my junior year. After all, I had a full-time career. My classes were halfheartedly sandwiched between my playing engagements and other commitments, and though I was majoring in Renaissance literature, trying to acquire some real knowledge outside of music, I spent most of my time in the practice rooms of the music department, the swimming pool, the billiards club, and the Radcliffe dormitories. I lived off-campus in an apartment with two pianos, and when I look back, it wasn't a bad life for a student. But the stuffiness soured me, and years later when Daphne entered school, I had tedious arguments with Ellen about her plans for the kid, a rigid tour of the sort of private academies my sister Stella attended. Ghastly places with subtle methods. Certainly their wardens were not looking for the names of flowers or anything else in heaven—or hell. But I prayed I would always be looking, for what does that line of poetry, composed by a man in an asylum, mean except that once heaven is stumbled upon or fallen into, all sorts of metaphysical wonders will shower upon us. Roses, lilies, orchids, poppies— these will assume new names and therefore new meanings, new purpose, just as we shall, by discovering our truest selves. As it is with women: seek out their heavenly selves and they will take on new names, new significance, new connections in the inner self. I had spent half my life seeking in women what Smart sought in flowers, and perhaps that was why, like him, I had made so many unfortunate choices. Like Samuel Pepys, another Englishman, who explained that music and women were the two things on this earth he could never resist. Perhaps the Maestro Rubinstein when I met him in Paris, with his svelte companion and his contented sexual eyes, knew that this was a virtue, not a vice, the virtue of the Dane Kierkegaard's musical-erotic, the adventure of life resonant in the music of heaven.

The back roads in the Berkshires were splashed heavily with blue and gold wildflowers and zigzag patches of forsythia. Their colors were liquifying in the orange light, and red shafts from the horizon line were firing only the highest reaches of the oaks and pines. The air was alive with insects and birds, and the wind carried a dizzying mix of pollens from the fields and gardens—neat hedged-in patches that alternated wildly with tangled forests. Puffing my Macanudo, plotting a change of fingering at the end of the Schubert, my urban senses intoxicated, I nearly drove past the access road to Amos's farm. Sarah was fiddling with the radio and munching a pear. She seemed utterly serene, but since I never quite knew what she was thinking, I always felt a little off-guard. Having grown up as Lengford's daughter, in the pressure cooker, I had assumed she understood what I was going through in preparing for the tour. Sometimes I wasn't so sure.

The long driveway was lined with apple and cherry trees, and the new fruit was still green. There were forty acres of property around the house, providing a rare and blessèd privacy. I had my own key, and an open invitation, but my rhythms were so attuned to the city, whether Boston or New York, that I rarely took advantage of this. After driving up a hill and cutting through a field of lavender, we saw the house suddenly on another, flatter rise.

"There's a girl on the roof," Sarah said. "Oooh-la, and she's in the buff."

Indeed she was. A naked girl in crucifixion position at the juncture of the sloping main roof and the flat sunporch roof. The shock of her black hair was startling beside her pale skin.

"She's going to get a bad burn," Sarah added drily, for though it was still warm, there was only a trace of sunlight touching the roof, and that a good twenty feet from the sunbather.

I hoped this didn't mean Amos was cheating on Margaret and that I would now have to lie to her. But it was not to be so simple as that.

The house was a sprawling Gothic colonial, weathered shingles, white shutters, a wraparound porch, built beside a large pond. The pond could be reached by a long wooden stairway behind the rose garden. There was a barn about fifty yards from the house, and beyond that, a stable and a greenhouse. Amos's car was not in sight, but a shining blue Mercedes sedan was parked near the barn. The windows in the house were all curtained. Except for the sunbather, there was no sign of life. She glanced down at us coldly and then lay back again.

"This is going to be interesting," Sarah said.

"You think so?"

As soon as we got out of the car, the front door opened. A man I had never seen before stepped out calmly, smoking a pipe and cradling a cat. He wore slippers and a blue silk robe, and under the robe white ducks, white shirt, and a dotted bow tie. He looked very much at home. He was around fifty, bald, short but sturdy, with large hands and a moon-face indented with washed-out oval eyes and a wide mouth. He didn't seem surprised to see us.

"Good afternoon." He had a low pleasant voice, with a non-Englishman's English accent.

"Hello. I'm a friend of Amos Demeter's. Is he around?"

He studied me with a faint smile. "You are Max Randal, of course. I once heard you play in New York—seven years ago."

It seemed everyone I met that day had heard me play. First the judge, and now—

"Josef Winters," he said, extending his hand and walking down the steps. "How do you do?"

"This is Sarah Lengford," I said, and we shook hands with him.

"Franz Lengford's daughter? Very nice. To answer your question: Mr. Demeter is not here. May I offer you a cold drink, or some coffee?"

"Where is he?"

"He has gone away for a while."

"Can you tell me where?"

"Certainly. First Ireland, after that Yugoslavia, and then Hungary."

He said this as if he were telling me Amos had hopped into town for groceries. I was staggered.

"Well, you know, I'm here—"

"At the behest of Mrs. Demeter," he interrupted.

[70]

"Did you speak with her today?"

"No."

"You know, I think I could use some coffee. How about if we go inside?"

"By all means."

I was put off by all the parlor talk. This fellow laid it on a little thick for my taste. Ireland, Yugoslavia, and Hungary! Whatever it was I had expected to find, a nude sunbather and a moon-faced man in a robe did not quite fit. There were two black suitcases in the foyer alongside an attaché case, an umbrella, and a portable cassette recorder. The suitcases were monogrammed J.W. The house looked in order, neater than when Amos was around. I peered into the living room. The couch and coffee table were overflowing with books and tape cassettes. Some fresh irises were arranged in a vase by the window. On the armchair nearest the door was a book on fly-fishing, a biography of Liszt, Gray's *Anatomy*, and a world atlas filled with paper markers. But Winters steered us toward the kitchen. He dropped the cat, a big gray tom, in the hallway, and after leaping around and hissing at Sarah, it disappeared up the stairs.

"Your cat?" I asked.

He shook his head. "Emma's," and he nodded upward—toward the roof, I assumed, unless there was another girl on the second floor.

The coffee was brewed and there were three cups on the table. Also a bowl of fruit and a homemade white cake.

"Expecting someone?" Sarah said.

"Not exactly. Mr. Randal—black. And you, Miss Lengford?"

"Black."

"How did you know I took it black?" I asked.

He smiled. "Mr. Demeter told me you are something of a night owl, and the night owl customarily does not like to dilute his fuel."

"What else did he tell you?"

"That you might be alarmed at his precipitous departure. So I will not delay in passing on the message he left, for you and his wife, to receive today—no earlier."

"But you haven't told her?"

"No, she has not answered her telephone today. Mr. Demeter will return sometime this summer. He has gone to Ireland to get something for himself, to Yugoslavia to get something for me, and to Hungary," and here he paused with a broader smile, "to get something for you, Mr. Randal."

"For me?"

"That is correct."

"Well, what is he going to get?"

"What he is getting for himself is his private affair. What he is getting for you is a surprise and I am sworn not to reveal it. I can only tell you what he is getting for me, which is probably the simplest of all: he is meeting a man in Skopje who will give him some research material that I require."

"What kind of research?"

"Medical. But I cannot tell you any more about it."

I had been expecting farce, and though indeed this may have been farce, it was of a high order. One thing was certain: Winters was a serious man. He meant business and held his cards close to the vest. If they were from a shaved deck, it was his secret.

"Would you care for cake, Miss Lengford?"

"Thank you. You know, Doctor, Max and Amos have been close friends for over twelve years. You don't have to be so mysterious. Why not just tell us what's going on?" She put a chunk of cake into her mouth. "Delicious."

No mincing of words for Sarah, no jousting. But Winters was unruffled.

"I have no desire and no time to indulge in intrigue. Mr. Demeter asked me quite specifically to say nothing of his business—not even to you, Mr. Randal. Would you want me to betray that trust?"

"How about his wife?" I said. "Don't you think she has a right to know?"

"He is her husband, not I. Don't you think it was his business to inform her of what he was doing? Given the fact he left here only yesterday, and could easily have spoken with her—doesn't that tell you something? Who am I to tell her what he did not want her to know?"

I couldn't argue with that.

"Amos has not always been the most predictable person,"

Sarah said. "In your opinion, was he in a rational frame of mind when he started off on this trip? And is he undertaking something you yourself would?"

"Rational? What is rational?" he replied. "I do not like the word. Do you mean, was he out of his wits? Or are you insinuating that I have bamboozled him into some dangerous undertaking? That there is something illicit in his actions?"

"Bamboozled" sounded strange off Winters' lips.

"I'm not insinuating anything," she said. "But would you say he was out of his wits?" She dabbed some icing from her lip.

"Of course not. Absolutely not. He is more in touch with his inner feelings than ever before. He went off with a sense of purpose and a lively spirit, which is worthy of him. And, quite frankly, I had expected to see more of that same spirit among his close friends. I am disappointed, Mr. Randal, that an artist of your accomplishment would not have a more open mind."

"I apologize. But, you see, I'm very busy myself these days, and I'm not in the habit of keeping tabs on my friends. Margaret is usually cool about these things, and she seems worried—I came here to make sure Amos is all right. Nothing more."

"Well, then," he said, standing up abruptly, "your mercy mission is completed. He is absolutely all right, and you can pass that information on to Mrs. Demeter, though I assure you, I intend to call her myself."

He was dismissing us, and this made me a little hot.

"Now, wait a minute. She told me she called here the other day and you hung up on her."

"That is not true," he said, the moon-face flushing.

"She wouldn't lie to me about that."

"I am afraid she has lied, if you will excuse my saying so. I ask you again, Mr. Randal: why did her husband not tell her his business? Why are you making me the culprit? I believe his wife is behaving hysterically—and insincerely. It is because she is frustrated with Mr. Demeter's actions and cannot address him directly that she blames me for what he does not tell her. What am I to do?"

"Look, I find you in my friend's house, you tell me he's gone on some cockeyed trip, and then you can't or won't offer any explanations. How would you feel in my position?"

"I have no idea. Amos Demeter is a client of mine. Now we are also business associates. We were working here together until yesterday. I have stayed on at his express invitation. He told his wife he was going away, did he not? He has not been kidnapped. His reasons for secrecy are his business, not mine. I will be leaving for New York shortly. Now, that is all I can tell you, Mr. Randal."

The door opened and a young woman in a black jumpsuit, with black cap, boots, gloves, and the gray cat in her arms, stepped into the room. It was the sunbather reincarnated as chauffeur. She had a thin, tight-lipped face and hard eyes. She wore a single earring, a silver pyramid.

"Will you be ready to leave at eight-thirty, Doctor?"

He glanced at his watch. "Yes, fine. Emma, this is Max Randal and Sarah Lengford."

She nodded at us and retired. I had had my fill of this circus. But I had to admit that Winters was right: Amos was the one who had chosen to keep everyone in the dark, including (maybe especially) Margaret.

"Will you excuse me for a moment, please," Winters said, cool and collected again. "I have something for you."

When we were alone, Sarah said, "What do you think?"

"I think we're going to have a wonderful dinner in New York tonight."

"But—"

"I don't want to stay here. I'm too tired to work tonight, anyway."

"Do you think he's telling the truth?"

"Why should he lie? A guy with a car like that, a silk robe, a chauffeur from the Folies Bergère—what do you think? That he bumped off Amos and broke in here to swipe the rare books? Come on. He's right. Margaret is hysterical, or she has an ax to grind with Amos, and I got dragged in, god knows why."

Winters returned and handed me an envelope. "In addition to what I have told you, which is what Mr. Demeter asked me to say if you called, I was to mail you this today."

It was addressed in Amos's hand, and dated the previous day. It, too, was typical of him.

Dear Max,

Be back August, maybe sooner. Sorry about all the mystery, but it's vital. Have made astounding discoveries! Think I may have an answer for you. Trust Dr. Winters in all he says: he's a great man & a real friend. I'll be in Europe when you receive this. Onto something big. Absolutely no need to worry. Oh, & please call Mike, if you can, & tell him I can't make it Wednesday.

Ciao,
Amos

I passed the note to Sarah.

"I owe you an apology, Doctor."

Winters nodded graciously.

"Who's Mike?" Sarah asked.

"His cousin. Wednesday is their poker night. That's Amos, all right. Turns things upside down and then worries about a poker game."

Winters cleared his throat. "Will you be staying on tonight?"

"No, we're going to New York."

He walked us to the door. It was nearly dark and the air was cooling fast. Winters watched me put the top up on the Cadillac. He seemed quite small and harmless suddenly. Margaret's theatrics had gotten me into this, and I half hoped she would call me again so I could tell her off. What was the point, though? Amos was playing out some elaborate scheme, Margaret had her own problems, and all of it was over my head. I didn't care anymore.

Winters came around to my window as I started the car. "Mr. Randal, this has been an awkward first meeting. I would enjoy lunching with you in New York sometime. Will you be there long?"

"Just a few days. But I'm often in town."

"Here is my card." He smiled. "Allow me to meet you again under the auspices of a music lover and a fan."

"Anything but that. But I would be interested to know about what you do. I've heard only bits and pieces."

"From Mrs. Demeter, no less."

"Yes."

"It would be an honor. Come by the clinic and we'll dine in my office." He touched my arm. "Tell me, Mr. Randal, do you believe in miracles?" he whispered with a twinkle in his eye.

I was startled. "Sure, I believe in miracles," I said. "Have you got any for me?"

"Perhaps, if you need one. Our lives are so very short, and so little of what we feel can be explained. There are provinces of our minds we never touch, like virgin forest. This is true even of an artist like you. So I shall look forward to our lunch." And he walked away.

"What was he saying to you?" Sarah asked as I sped down the driveway.

I hesitated. "He asked me if I believed in miracles."

"And?"

"I said I did."

"But are you really going to have lunch with him?"

"Why not? It might be interesting."

"And what about this big secret of Amos's—this 'answer' he has for you. Answer to what?"

"I haven't a clue. But he hasn't lost his baker's touch."

"What do you mean?"

"That cake. That's what convinced me Winters was telling the truth. Amos baked it. He loves to cook. And he's been baking the same cake for ten years. I'd know it anywhere."

We rushed headlong for Manhattan in the gathering darkness. By the time we hit the suburbs and the factory lights and the first of the ghostly bridges, I had forgotten about Amos and Margaret and Dr. Winters. A fearful hook of anxiety dug deeper into my entrails as we approached the scene of my comeback, the capital of the world. Despair had overtaken me and left my mouth full of black dust, and I was certain that for the first time in my professional life I was going to choke on that dust, and fail utterly on the appointed night in September. And then, sixteen more cities and fifty performances in which to finish the job. What a fiasco it could be! Away from my piano, from the weeks of manic feverish preparation, I was terrified I would be shown up in a few months for what I had become: washed-up, a has-been.

Except for the fact it was my first visit to New York since signing the contracts for the tour, I could not account for this sudden surge of fear. I was muddled and scared, and I didn't know if I could live that way for the next three months. It's easy to ride high when you're on top, and I had been there for many years. Now it would all be uphill. I would find out what I was really made of, as the gentlemen in my father's racket liked to say.

"You know," Willy said, pushing aside his plate of chicken Kiev, "Mendelssohn also describes how much Jan Dussek liked the good life and how it was his undoing."

I groaned and continued to eat.

"Jan Dussek, my dear," he explained to Sarah, "was the first fellow to play with the keyboard at a right angle to the audience. Before that, they all played facing the house. But Dussek turned the piano, not for the better acoustics, but because he was so overweeningly proud of his profile! He couldn't resist showing it to the ladies while he played."

"We've heard about Dussek," I said.

"*You* have heard about him—and not enough."

Dussek was one of Willy's whipping boys, along with Gottschalk and Albéniz. A fine early master of the pianoforte, Dussek had squandered his talents and dissipated himself with wine and women. Willy constantly held him up to me as a warning, even when I was living like a hermit.

Willy liked Sarah. He "approved" as he almost never approved of the other women in my life, with the exception of Orana. He loved Orana, and he thought when I married her it was the best thing I had ever done. He figured my life (and career) would be in order from then on, and he was bitterly disappointed when we were divorced. He was so upset he wouldn't even discuss it with me for a long time. But in fact he was predisposed to Sarah even before he met her in Boston in April. Her father, it turned out, was an old friend of his, and any girl with such a distinguished musical lineage had to be all right.

Willy (Wilhelm Stroëker to the maitre d') invariably lunched at the Russian Tea Room, and this day was no exception. We were staying at the Plaza, a nice room overlooking the park, and so it had been a short walk up Fifty-seventh Street to the restaurant, where we found Willy, punctual and cheery, waiting at his favorite table. My spirits had improved with a good night's sleep, and even the fact that Carnegie Hall was next door didn't throw a damper on my meal. My terror seemed to have receded in the light of day, at least for a while.

Willy, as always, looked distinguished, ready to charm and be charmed. He wore a beige suit, tailored in London, and a beautiful checkered tie, Italian design, with a ruby pin to match his cuff links. For someone who was always lecturing me on the quicksand of the high life, he was inordinately fond of jewelry. He never wore less than three rings as well as his platinum watch with the diamond numerals. I am about six feet, and though Willy is only slightly shorter he always seemed much more so. He was portly in an odd way, his shoulders narrow, his waist thick, and his legs disproportionately thin. He had sharp blue eyes and wore a neat moustache, the same slate-gray as his hair. His German accent had softened over the years. Women found him attractive, and since his wife's death twenty years before he had remained a bachelor. She was his great love, and he once told me he had no desire ever to remarry. At sixty-two he always had a regular lady-friend, but never let things go beyond a certain point. I believe this prohibition limited his perspective in later years, making him not so much overcautious as overfastidious. He worried a great deal, and now that he was rich, with no children, no family, he worried almost exclusively about his health. He had a faint heart murmur. I knew that he was closer to me personally than to his other clients. He had taken me on when I was a boy, and there was always a hint of the surrogate father about him. Just what my mother had wanted.

One of his peculiarities was his bottled water. Willy never went to the tap, and he would not drink just any mineral water. His Choaspes was St-Jean, an Alpine spring he had visited in his youth. He swore it accounted for his robustness. He kept cases of it in his apartment and office, and like a Persian king, he always traveled with it. He had other quirks: a superstition about the number six, a fear of ships and open water, and an aversion to the color orange.

Of course we had two large bottles of St-Jean at our table and Willy was pleased to see me downing it liberally. He even tried to cajole me into ordering a single martini, but I refused.

"Is this for my benefit?" he asked Sarah, "or is he really taking care of himself?"

"He even goes rowing twice a week," she said, "for his wind."

Willy grew alarmed. "Rowing? Rowboats?"

"No, sculling," I said. "Very small boats."

"But is that good for the tendons, the fingers? It could be dangerous . . ."

"Don't be ridiculous. Now, let's talk turkey about this new contract. Why are they hedging on another three-record deal? And why the quibbling about my up-front cash? They've made plenty on every one of my recordings, even when I haven't been performing."

Willy's index finger went to his mustache, as it always did when he talked business. His voice dropped. His eyelids drooped. His irises froze. I expect his entire metabolism shifted gears. For obscure psychological reasons, I liked to think of him as a stock character, the bumbling generous uncle in a Spanish comedy, but this was absurd: he was a tough, shrewd businessman, and if he had to lecture me about high living, it was only because he himself had put me in a position to enjoy it.

"Now that is it, Max. You have hit the nail on the head. As I predicted last November, it is because you have *not* been performing that they are hedging. And mind you, it is just that—a ploy to bring down our money demands and dilute the preferential clauses. I will not let that happen, so don't worry. But as you know, they have been eager to see you perform again for some time. They know I still got top dollar for you in every hall you will play. This is good. It was to be expected. You are coming back fresh. The public is intrigued. There is some mystery here. But it is also why this tour . . ."

He didn't have to finish his thought.

". . . Of course there is more to it," he went on, lighting my cigar. "They are not handing out the kinds of contracts they once did. There used to be more courtesy in this business. Now, each time around you have to fight for every comma, every cent. You are an established name, the very best, a guaranteed money-maker, and you are young with a strong following that will last. But let's look at another side of it. . . ."

And we proceeded to look at six or seven sides of it. Sarah sipped her espresso and sat back demurely, curious as always. She probably listened more carefully than I to Willy's analysis of the tawdry Byzantium that is the record business. By the time he was through, I was exhausted and numb. I realized one thing clearly however, one bit of truth that shined through the fog: I had not exaggerated the importance of this tour. Both artistically and businesswise, it would be a turning point—either up or down. I had to play better than I had in years, I had to be at my very best, or I would simply lose my standing, the hard-earned capital of my reputation that I had spent seventeen years in building up.

"I think I will have a drink," I said to Willy. "How about Rémy, like in the old days?"

"Excellent. It will do you good. Excuse me a moment."

He went off to call his office, and Sarah leaned over to me.

"You haven't told him, have you."

I pretended not to understand. "What?"

"You haven't told him about your trouble at the piano. He just thinks you took a sabbatical. 'Temperamentally burned out,' he calls it. Nothing serious . . ."

"That's right. I've never really talked to him about it."

"But I thought you talked to him about everything."

"Not everything. Look, he would just start worrying even more, and that would make it harder on me. He'd be calling every other day, sending helpful letters, panicking slowly. I'd be able to *feel* him worrying two hundred miles away."

"But he might help you."

"Nobody can really help me with this, Sarah."

"Why not? You've got yourself into this all-or-nothing mentality that can eat you alive."

"That's not true," I lied. "But I don't want to talk to Willy about it. Not now. Anyway, he's not so far off: I was burned out, but not in the way he thinks."

"I still think he could help."

Willy came up behind us and smiled pleasantly. "Help with what, my dear?"

I shot a glance at her through my cigar smoke.

"Help us choose a surprise for Daphne," she said. "We want it to be something special."

"Such a beautiful little girl. How is she, Max?"

"She's great. You know, she's coming to live with me for the summer."

"That's wonderful, but won't it be difficult?"

"I'll work it out. I was in court yesterday." And I summarized the proceedings for him.

His face reddened. "That woman. There's always something with her. Foolishness is all she knows," he said, poking the air with his corona.

I shrugged. "These are fine cigars, by the way."

"Real Havanas. Remember the old cellist, Piguer? Well, he's retired to Venezuela and he sends them to me every month in a candy box." His face darkened. "Max, now that you mention Ellen, I remember that your other wife, Miss Greta, called the office yesterday. She wanted your number in Boston, said she has to speak with you, that it's very important."

"Oh? What does she want?"

"She wouldn't tell me anything. And we didn't give her the number."

"I'll call her today."

"Your Uncle Louie has been calling, too. You know, it's nice you have that unlisted number, but it doesn't deter people."

"What does he want?"

He grunted. "How should I know what that man wants?"

Willy had ill feelings toward Uncle Louie, my father's brother, ever since Louie questioned him once about my residuals. Willy was deeply offended and called me up the same night to complain about a man "who is almost a criminal" daring to question *his* ethics. "Can you imagine?" Willy asked me at least a dozen times. Of course I could imagine it very well. Louie was a nervy sort of guy. That was his nature, and the nature of his business. But I knew he cared for me and never meant any harm. In his own brash way, he had been as protective toward me early on as Willy.

"All right, I'll give him a call too."

Willy looked a little worried. "Have you met Uncle Louie?" he asked Sarah.

"No, I haven't."

He grunted again. "Max's mother was a great lady, and his father despite his profession a fine gentleman—may their souls rest in peace. But some of his relatives, let us just say they live in a different sphere."

"Oh, come off your high horse, Willy. How about a toast," I said, raising my brandy snifter. "To a beautiful day."

"And to the tour," Sarah said.

We clinked glasses.

"Yes, to beauty and art," Willy intoned. "What else is there?"

What else, indeed. We parted company on Fifty-seventh Street. Willy had left word at his apartment that I would be coming to work at the piano. My night at the farm had been blown, and I was getting jumpy at the prospect of another day without practicing. Sarah had set up a meeting at her publisher's for the rest of the afternoon, and I had planned to browse in the rare bookstores for a few hours. But after putting her in a cab, I walked a few blocks and got one for myself. I had a sudden urge to visit Greta. I tried to call her, but the line was busy, so I figured I'd just drop in.

She lived in SoHo, in a once peaceful and private neighborhood—a haven for Orana and me—that was now fashionable and noisy. My cab hurtled down Seventh Avenue, the driver cursing fluently, and I sat back and enjoyed the rest of my cigar. It was another clear, beautiful day, not nearly so hot, and I amused myself reading the latest porno titles on the marquees and watching the crowds swarm by. New York was my town for better or worse, and the chaos was familiar and comforting after months in Boston. Stopped for a light on Thirtieth Street, my eye caught on an attractive woman walking toward Eighth Avenue. She was wearing a plum-colored dress. I watched her until she turned into a doorway under a pale blue sign and I suddenly found myself carried back rapidly to another June day many years before, a day shared with my father.

He had an intriguing knack for turning up when and where he wasn't expected. Seeing him was always a surprise in some way, maybe by his own design, though my mother would attribute it to his fickleness. They were divorced when I was seven, but he stayed in New York at first, and I saw him every weekend. Two years later, after he moved out west, our times together became very irregular. On that particular June day, he showed up at the apartment unannounced while I was practicing. I was thirteen, and at that time used to practice without fail nine or ten hours a day. I was often alone all day, and indeed my mother and Stella were both out when the maid answered the doorbell. I assumed it was a delivery, but a few minutes later I glanced up from the piano, across the sacred ground where no foot trod during my practice hours, and there was my father in the doorway, watching me intently. I froze. He never inspired fear in me, just awe. I hadn't seen him since Christmas. Dapper as always and trim, he wore a cream-colored suit, plum-colored tie with matching handkerchief, white carnation, and two-tone glove-leather shoes. He was very particular about his shoes. They were custom-made in Milan, a dozen pairs a year. At that time he was forty-six, retired nearly twenty years and still in excellent shape. His black hair was just graying, cut full, his face still darkly handsome.

I hurried over to greet him, but after a quick embrace, he sat down abruptly and signaled me to return to the piano. I had been plowing through Liszt's *Dante* Variations, but thinking he would enjoy a more bravura performance, and certainly wanting to show off, I launched into the *Waldstein*—a piece I knew inside out—and played my heart out. I only dared to glance at him once, upright and attentive on the couch.

I knew he was impressed with my talent. I learned after his death, when some of his papers were turned over to me, what close tabs he had kept on my career. It was something special to him, and he was big on that—doing something special, out of the mainstream, the chosen few, that sort of thing. Coming from where he did, against suffocating odds, this was not difficult to understand. And his business—like mine—was blatantly elitist: you were on top or you were nothing. Like most fighters, he was born poor and clawed his way up.

"When I was a kid," he told me in a rare confessional moment, "my greatest fear was not being poor, you know. It was the fear of being unknown. You make your name, Max, and at least you'll know that you lived."

This was my father's perspective on fame. I believe he was more existentialist than Social Darwinist, though neither label would have meant much to him. He firmly believed that our lives are tiny sparks in a gulf of blackness, and that a few people in their match-flicker of eternity are born with extraordinary gifts, and a handful of those actually accomplish something. He liked to tell me—without malice—how his older brother Ray was stronger and quicker and regularly beat the hell out of him as a kid, but that Ray had no willpower, no discipline, no real ambition. He had notions of becoming a fighter but quit within a week because of the roadwork. My father believed willpower was ninety percent of any battle. He didn't put much stock in environment or education. That was for humdrum people, the ones who kept the machinery of society oiled and running. If you broke away from that enormous prison, you could make your own rules. So my precocity at the piano was an easy thing for him to accept. In fact, unlike my mother, he took it in stride, and I appreciated that, probably more than he knew. He figured I inherited it from him. Which tells you what he thought of my mother. For her, my playing was a source of eternal vexation, though she would never have seen it that way. She was proud of me—too much so—and devoted herself to my career early on. But, unlike my father, she had few accomplishments of her own, so her devotion was an unhealthy one. Her great delight in my abilities was leavened by this vexation of hers. She was always trying to get at my precocity, to dig up some explanation, some concrete link that would verify her authorship not just of my biological body but of my gift so she could in this way account for herself in the general scheme of things. Spiritually and emotionally, she was a pedestrian person beside my father. The man's raw energy and physical guile—far more delicate qualities than we usually suppose—endowed him with a kind of genius that she could never approach, much less understand.

When I said he grew up poor, I should have amplified. My grandfather was Welsh, my grandmother Greek, and they were the offspring of immigrants. My father was the second of four sons. My grandfather was a house painter. After my father died, the only members of his family I ever saw were his kid brother Louie, and (rarely) Uncle Ray's widow and daughters, my first cousins, who lived in New Jersey. Ray left them nothing but gambling debts, but Uncle Louie took care of them. Louie's law practice, the shippers and union big shots and the mob guys who gave him their legitimate operations to handle with white gloves, was lucrative and thriving. Louie, his wife, and four kids also lived in Jersey, but in a posh suburb with five acres and a pool. My father and Louie grew up on Ninth Street and Avenue B, a hard place even back then, without the junkies and zip-gun boys. Louie was the only one who went to college. My father paid his tuition out of his first ring earnings, and of course Louie never forgot this. Ray and Tommy, the youngest brother, became construction workers. Tommy was killed in an accident and Ray died of cirrhosis. And my father, the queerest of the lot and the most respected within the family, became a boxing champion. When I was a kid Uncle Ray told me—still astonished at the recollection—that my father, at age seventeen, every day did five hundred sit-ups, five hundred push-ups, ran eight miles rain or shine, and never drank, smoked, or stayed up past midnight.

Jackie Randal fought thirty-nine fights as an amateur and forty-one as a professional, and he only lost once, and that June afternoon as I concluded the *Waldstein* and glanced over at him—he wasn't a big man, five-ten, 150 pounds—I calculated, as I often had before, rather romantically, how many shots he must have taken through those fights and how they still paid for my rarefied existence, these insular rooms on Park Avenue and my custom-made Steinway, and the fine clothes my mother bought us, and all the rest of it. Other boys, I'm sure, appreciate the efforts of their lawyer, doctor, and hard-hat fathers, but I always thought of it in this soppy, fanciful way—the number of cruel blows this quiet man had absorbed so I could play the piano all day.

I finished the Beethoven with a flourish and he clapped softly, nodding his approval. De Quincey wrote that music is an intellectual or sensual pleasure, depending on the temperament of the listener. Well, for my father it was decidedly sensual and it showed in his face. I had been right to choose the *Waldstein*; something in those hard chords and long runs and fitful suspensions had gone straight to his heart.

He embraced me again. "Where's your mother?" he asked softly.

"Out shopping."

"And Stella?"

"They're together."

"Can you play hooky for a few hours?"

"Oh, sure," I said, delighted at the prospect.

"You haven't had lunch, have you?"

He had a hired limousine downstairs, for he disdained taxis, and we rode through the park and ate a huge meal at Gallagher's. Usually, on such outings, we would also go to a ballgame, or visit his tailor to buy me a new suit. He seldom talked boxing and had never taken me to a fight, despite my frequent requests. Generally, except for a rare testimonial, he had little to do with the boxing world. He was proud of his accomplishments, but he said he liked to keep the past in its place. So I was surprised when we pulled up in front of a ratty building on West Thirtieth Street. We entered the doorway, under the same pale blue sign through which the woman in plum disappeared as I watched from my taxi.

"I thought you might enjoy this," he said, and for the first and only time we entered a boxing gym together. It was Gleason's Gym, and it was a madhouse. My father waded through the crowd with me in tow, and men on either side called out to him, Champ this and Champ that, in friendly waves, and though I was accustomed to hearing people address him respectfully, there was a different timbre to it there in the gym. The place was jammed with pugs, as Eddie the bartender would have pointed out, but only two champions, my father and the lightweight king of the day, a handsome young black fighter who came over for introductions and a photograph. It was this lightweight champion who taught me how to thumb an unscrupulous opponent on the sly, a trick I have not forgotten to this day, metaphysically and otherwise.

That night, my head still buzzing, my father gone, I should have known better but I couldn't restrain myself and I recounted my adventure to my mother and Stella. Whether out of meanness or jealousy, they feigned astonishment at the fact that I, who had been introduced to Horowitz and Arrau and Stokowski at the age of twelve, should be impressed by such a place and such people. I hated them for that. Later on, when I learned how badly and frequently my father had betrayed her with other women, I could forgive my mother. But I don't think I ever forgave Stella, who was simply ignorant and snobby, and who had tipped her hand the year before when we were filling out our passport applications and she had leaned over to mine and blacked out "Boxer, Retired" which I had written in the space for Father's Occupation, and replaced it with "Sportsman." That was what Stella had picked up in those boarding schools in which Ellen was so hot to enroll Daphne.

Sifting through these memories and choking my cabbie with Willy's giant Havana, I pulled up in front of Greta's building on Spring Street, my old house. The brick corridors still smelled the same, the cast-iron elevator still knocked at the fourth floor, and at her door I could hear a tremendous racket: there was a party going on! Friday afternoon and she had some of her pals over for high tea. A young man with a crewcut and a red leather suit showed me in and promptly disappeared into a mass of bodies. The loft was jammed, the kitchen, the hallways, everything. There was a long buffet table and bar under the skylight, where my pianos used to stand. And people radiating from that yellow circle of light, eating, drinking, shouting, full of laughter.

I was dazed. I had expected to find Greta alone. Maybe to have a cup of coffee out on the terrace under the fruit trees. I tried in vain to find out what the party was all about. When I twice asked a girl in a straw hat standing alone, she winked at me and floated away. Finally I heard someone say something about an opening.

That made sense. After a few more inquiries, I learned that it was Greta's opening—a new show of her work. I got myself a brandy and soda, figuring another drink wasn't going to kill me, and went off in search of her.

My marriage to Greta can be summarized briefly. She was a jewelry designer now, but when I met her she worked as a fashion model. She was a friend of Margaret's. It was Margaret who introduced us one night, and we took to each other like tigers. We met on a Thursday and were married the following Monday at City Hall. Then we went off to St. Kitts and didn't leave our hotel room for a week. We never needed other people much when we were married. Greta was Danish. She was blond, a rare exception in my long line of dark-haired companions. She was ravishing. And she was an eccentric. A real oddball who got me involved in all sorts of distracting pursuits, from Sufism to astronomy to a diet of all-white foods—milk, bread, vanilla ice cream, cauliflower, et cetera, that lasted a full year! But she was also a wonderfully kind and considerate woman, bright and imaginative, bighearted, trustworthy, and a good companion to me as a performer. During our marriage, I gave more recitals than ever before, and cut some of my best recordings. And our lovemaking was in itself rare and unique: she was a sexual athlete, with a worldly finesse that, as an American, I could only marvel at. So why, you may ask, were we divorced four years previously, after only two years of marriage? I suppose it was because we were never in love, absurd as that sounds. We loved each other, and we had fine times, but there seemed to be no real spiritual foundation, as there was with Orana, nothing deeper than our compatibility and shared thirst for novelties. We gradually grew restless. She felt cloistered, I withdrawn, and quite amicably, without recrimination, without the usual backlash that hits a couple deeply, painfully, in love, we were divorced by mutual consent. I hate to make it sound so cut and dried, but that's the way it was. Perhaps after Orana and Ellen and countless misfires in my fervent search for a lifelong love, I had been relieved to find Greta and share two charming, active, reckless, and decidedly restless years. A strange hiatus in my quest for a heavenly passion. That was what I told myself at the time.

So Greta was doing well, though she apparently still needed her alimony to throw a bash like this. She told me after our divorce that she had outgrown modeling, that it was not fit work for a grown woman with a brain. During our marriage she had plenty of time to pick out a new career. And she had always been a jewelry buff, making her own stuff in gold and silver and constantly tinkering with new designs. She had come a long way in four years. She had been written up a few times, and her work was gradually appearing in the better stores.

I found her holding court in the bedroom, in a crowd, everyone in high spirits. I saw her before she saw me, and she looked more gorgeous than ever. Magnificent, in dark blue, with her blond mane tumbling over her shoulders and her tiny cornflake-colored freckles gilding her tanned skin, she was leaning against one of the brass bedposts. She was laughing. At the head of her bed, propped up as always, were her three white teddy bears, the three wise men she called them: Bobo, Hobo, and Max—after me. I wondered if Max's name had been changed. Someone passed me a joint and I drew on it absently, as if it were a cigarette. I hadn't been high in months, and it hit me like a rock.

A woman just in front of me turned around, and to my surprise and dismay, it was Margaret. Her eyes popped. I wished I could have disappeared. I had left a curt message on her answering service that Amos was fine. Now I wanted no part of her. She embraced me and kissed my cheek.

"Max, what on earth are you doing here?"

"I was in town, and I thought I'd surprise Greta."

"You haven't talked to her yet? She'll be thrilled. Come on—"

"I'd rather do it myself, thanks. Did you get my message?"

"Oh, yes, thank you again for going to the farm." Margaret was a redhead. One of her eyes always seemed slightly off. And though pretty, she was too skinny for my taste. Her gaiety was annoying.

"I thought you were worried to death about Amos," I said.

"I was," she said earnestly. "It was terrible. But I feel much better now that you've looked into it. I guess Winters is kosher. He called this morning to reassure me." She threw her hands up and smiled. "And you know how Amos is."

I wasn't prepared for this. "Sure, I know how he is. But Winters told me you lied, that he never hung up on you."

She winced. "Dr. Winters and I had a misunderstanding. I was worried. I know Amos has pulled some stunts before, but this was different, creepier. You can understand that, I'm sure."

I didn't understand any of it. Especially her about-face.

"Just count me out of all this, Margaret," I said sharply. "This is a bad time for me, and you and Amos are playing games."

She seemed genuinely surprised. "Well, I like that," she said. "Some friend you are. Let me tell you, Mr. Prima Donna, you're going to be sorry someday for the way you treat people. Winters didn't say much, but I got the impression Amos is doing *you* the favor of your life. I can't imagine why!" She turned on her heel and huffed off.

There was something screwy going on, and I wanted no part of it.

As I crossed the room, Greta turned and saw me. Her eyes widened and she ran up to me with open arms. I hadn't expected this either, and her warmth and big smile gladdened my heart. Her blue irises looked aquamarine in that light, brimming mischief. I hadn't seen her in nearly two years, and then just for a moment in her lawyer's office.

She kissed me on the mouth, and before I could say a word, took my hand and led me through the crowd.

"Max, I can't tell you how happy I am that you came like this. Such a surprise! You got my message then from Willy?" She pronounced it "Weely."

"Yes. I tried to call but—"

"No, no, this is much better. I should have thought of it myself, but I know you are funny about these things. You know, burying the ax and all that."

She had lived in New York for six years, spoke French and English fluently, but Danish was her native tongue, and she still had trouble with American idioms. I always enjoyed the way she improvised on them. "Let's knock them back a few" was one of my favorites. "Come, we must talk at once," she said, "in private." I began to feel uneasy, for I realized she was taking me to the master bathroom.

The door was ajar and a tall woman was combing her hair before the mirror.

Greta coughed politely and pushed the door open. "Hello, Marion. I don't believe you ever met my husband, Max Randal. Marion Kent."

"The pianist," she said. "Yes, of course, I'm a great fan of—"

But Greta was already hustling her out. "I'm sorry, Marion, but it's very important, and this is the only privacy there is."

"I understand, dear . . ."

"Goodbye," Greta said, and locked the door with a sigh.

And suddenly we were alone in the large bathroom. There was my prized jacuzzi, and forgetting everything for a moment, I lovingly stroked the pink-and-gray marble. I was flooded with memories. Lying there alone after a long day, letting my muscles expand in the jets of hot water, and reading the Sunday papers with Orana propped up on rubber pillows, and finally Greta, with whom I had enjoyed tremendous fucking bouts as the water poured over us and shot up from below, the room dense with steam and eau de cologne, which she loved to spray around at such times.

"Fondest memories, Max?" she said, coming up behind me.

"Yes, as a matter of fact. I was thinking of the jacuzzi just yesterday."

"And of me?"

"And you too, Greta," I said warily. "Now, what's this all about?" I sat down on the edge of the tub. She put down the toilet cover and nestled herself onto the white fleece. She hitched her dress up and crossed her legs, and I couldn't help glancing at them, exquisite, tanned with that same golden glow and with the tiniest softest filaments of blond down tapering to her ankles. I remembered those legs, too. . . . And suddenly, achingly, out of nowhere, I wanted Greta. Like I wanted no one else. I imagined getting into the tub with her or rolling around on the plush black rug.

"I'll tell you everything, Max, but first have a sniffle of this," and she held out a silver vial with a spoon attached to its cap. Before I knew it she had the spoon, brimming with its shiny cargo of cocaine, poised under my nose.

"I didn't know you fooled with such naughty toys, Greta. Something new?" and I snorted it.

"I don't fool with it. Someone gave it to me today. I would throw it out, but I know you like it."

She refilled the spoon and put it to my other nostril.

"Good stuff," I said, feeling it singe the back of my throat.

Eighteen hours in New York, I thought, and I had gone from complete, compulsive asceticism to this. I was feeling pretty loose, ready for anything, and the coke made me want Greta that much more. Sarah flew through my thoughts and my stomach went cold, but I assured myself this had nothing to do with her. This was something else.

"Greta, you look beautiful. I've never seen you look better."

"Thank you."

"And judging from the crowd, your show must be wonderful."

"Yes, I'm very proud. It's the best work I've done. It's a big step."

So is this, I thought, and pulled her to me gently. Sliding my fingers into her golden hair, I kissed her mouth, and when she returned the kiss, moved to her neck. Before I knew it her dress was unbuttoned to the waist and she was unhooking her bra. Her breasts were also tanned, large and golden, and I remembered that she always sunbathed in the nude, on the terrace— I'm sure to the delight of the neighbors. Her perfume invaded my head, carrying its own memories, and left me reeling. I was smothering her with kisses—face, throat, breasts.

"Slow down," she whispered. "I am glad you feel this way. It will make it so much easier for me. Very glad . . ."

My eyes were closed and my ears humming. "Easier?" I murmured.

"Yes, much easier," and she undid my pants, unzipped them, and slipped her hand in.

"Make what easier?"

"Oh, darling, to know you feel this way." She pushed me away with a kiss so she could stand up. She let her dress fall and stepped out of her panties. Then she kicked her shoes off and peeled off her stockings. When she started to unbutton my shirt, it took what willpower I possessed not to pounce on her and tumble to the floor. She had a wonderful body and she knew it. I never knew a more graceful woman, or one more attuned to her own subtleties.

"To know you still feel this way, Max. That you want it to be like this again. Why, that's half of it, isn't it? It makes so much logic."

"Half of what?" I asked dreamily, as she pressed her breasts into my chest and reached around to pull my shirt down off my arms. "What logic?"

"Perhaps this *is* the best time," she said, laying her arms on my shoulders and looking up into my eyes. She snuggled a little closer and locked her arms behind me. My pants had slipped to my ankles and, gingerly, I was trying to step out of them, but each time I moved, my cock jammed against her stomach and prodded her. She started laughing. Another few seconds, I thought, and it would be all over . . .

"Yes, let me tell you," she began archly, wiping away a few tears of laughter and running her tongue along my lower lip. Just then, someone knocked at the door.

"Shit—"

"Shhh," she whispered. "Please go away," she called out. "There is another bath near the kitchen, and we have a small emergency here."

An emergency is right, I thought, finally getting one leg free of my pants.

"Here is my idea," she said softly.

"Why don't you tell me later?"

"Oh, no, it will make you happy now." She winked.

"I am happy, Greta. What is it?"

She rose up on her toes so that we were nearly the same height, and I thought I would fall into her eyes. They looked like perfectly round baby-blue lakes seen from an airplane.

"I think we ought to get married again, Max," she said evenly. "I really do."

"What?" My voice went funny.

"Live together and then get married. Remarried—you know, the second merry-go-round. Is that how you say it?"

That was it, all right. If she had flung a pail of icewater into my lap, the physiological effect would have been the same. I was speechless.

"That's why your feeling like this makes it easier to tell you," she said, closing her eyes. "Passion brings out the best in us, no?" Then she realized something was wrong below. She tucked in her chin and gazed down between her lovely breasts. "What happened?" she said in bewilderment. "You needn't worry—we won't be interrupted again."

"It's not that. Tell me more about your idea. And please stop doing that now." For she had started running her fingertips along the inside of my thigh.

A shadow crossed her face. "You don't want to make love now?"

"I'd just like to hear what you have to say first, Greta." I brushed her cheek with a kiss.

"Well, it was the other night," she began, shifting her weight from one leg to the other. My temples were throbbing. I figured the gods—those few that still cared about this world—had been testing me all week. And now this! Standing there naked with one leg caught in my trousers, and Greta warm, silky, open-hearted, leaning against me and explaining why we should re-marry.

"The other night I was lying in bed and I was thinking: what if Max were here again? Could it be different for us? Did you make a mistake? Could we really and truly fall heels over heels for each other a second time around?"

"Head over heels."

"Yes. Like that."

"And so—"

"Not so fast. You're always too sure of yourself, Max."

I nearly laughed aloud, under the circumstances.

"So I thought about it," she went on. "I thought about those things, and though I couldn't answer all my questions, and there are no guarantees, I decided we should try again. Really try. Let me finish. This is not so sudden as you think. I've grown a good deal in the last four years, and I've learned a thing or two about myself. About you, too. I may be impulsive, but I am not careless. And I do think we made a mistake. We didn't give ourselves enough time. Not nearly enough."

"It's possible. But—"

"I also know," she said, looking me in the eye, "that within a few months of our divorce you stopped giving recitals. You haven't performed even once since then, have you?"

I was startled, for I had never thought of it that way, never related it even remotely to Greta. Greta, my fellow-acrobat. I knew I had done some of my best work during our marriage, but this other angle—that the layoff, my staleness, had begun when the marriage ended—was a new twist.

My mind went blank and then flashed brightly: could Greta's departure from my life have been more internally traumatic than I thought? Could it be the cause of what was missing in my playing?

It didn't seem possible, but I listened to her carefully.

"So, you see, how can you have been happy without playing your piano for the public—which you always loved to do. You have not played because you have been unhappy. And you have been unhappy because you have not been with me. Now, that is what makes so much logic, you see?"

"I see what you're getting at," I said, trying to gather my thoughts. "But it's more complicated than that. Here, let's sit down." We assumed our previous positions, but stark naked now. Somehow, I felt more comfortable that way. Perhaps this shouldn't have surprised me: the physical culturists insist it is a prerequisite for harmony. But it was a dubious scene, the two of us facing each other intently, ardor laid aside, the two most reasonable, congenial former spouses in all of Manhattan.

"But even if all that is true, Greta—and that's a big 'if'—what would this hold for you? You seem to think I would be happy, and perform happily, but what about you? Remember, it wasn't all rosy for you at the end of our marriage."

She waved this away. "Don't worry, I'm thinking of myself. I knew nothing back then. Neither did you."

"What makes you think I do now?"

Her eyes softened. "I am hoping you do. I am willing to take a chance. We were foolish four years ago. I want to be with you again, Max. I have missed you too often. That is what I thought when I was lying there alone. I want us to overcome our adversaries and make a second chance."

"Overcome adversity."

"Yes. And we can do it!"

I was truly touched, for I saw that she meant it, even if she could not explain it. I had no idea what emotional journey of her own over the previous few years had led her to such a conclusion, and she seemed unwilling, or unable, to share its particulars with me. Her impetuosity about such things—matters of the heart—clearly had not changed. And perhaps I was a fool to be wavering at such a moment. But it was an overwhelming proposition she was laying before me. I didn't know what to say, and I felt like a heel. I certainly wasn't prepared to say no—and this staggered me. Until the last hour, I thought I might possibly be falling in love with Sarah. How could I now, after four years, out of the blue, contemplate such a radical turnaround with Greta? It seemed insane. Things didn't work that way. But on the spur of the moment, in one of those decisions we only comprehend long after the fact, I decided not to tell Greta about Sarah. This did not seem dishonorable: Greta had planted a seed and I wanted to keep the ground clear, in case we allowed it to sprout. But what it told me about my feelings for Sarah was a revelation.

Someone else knocked at the door and got the same business about an "emergency." We had reached a lull in our conversation. I was staring at our clothes on the rug. Her panties draped over my shoes, my shirt coiled inside her dress, her bra looped around my tie—they mirrored my feelings. We were all mixed up, intertangled, Greta and I, and our bonds were stronger than I had ever dreamed. My heart was full suddenly. Maybe I had been wrong all the time.

"Listen, Greta, we have to talk about this some more. This is very serious."

"Of course it is." She stroked my cheek. "I knew you would be surprised and I didn't expect you to take it in all at once. But once you have thought about it as I have, you will see things as I do and feel as I feel." She kissed me full on the lips. "To me, it is as if we have never been apart. You know, I could never talk to other men the way I talked to you, Max. Sometimes talking to you I could have been talking to another woman. You are smiling."

"No, I understand." Dr. Selzer had said I had a powerful anima—for good and bad.

"We were meant to be together," she went on. "Maybe the break was the best thing for us. Maybe we needed it. But let's not make another mistake now." And she kissed me again.

"I will think about it, Greta, I promise you. I guess we'd better get dressed. People might miss you at the party."

"People!" She pulled a face. "Since when have you worried about what people think? We cannot come this far and then leave, like this, roused . . ." She murmured the word wonderfully, a soft growl.

"Really, it's all right."

She kissed me again. "Maybe for you, but not for me." She leaned over and turned on the jacuzzi jets, all seven of them. The tub started filling rapidly. She slid over beside me and tested the inrushing water with her foot, then got down on her knees. The hot mist rose and settled on her golden hair like a fine blue net. She was right: we were both overheated, to say the least, and it took her less than a minute, using her lips and her tongue, to return me to my former glory. My legs were shaking now and the sweat was running off my back as the water thundered behind us and Greta's soft mane brushed over my thighs and tickled my belly. I had my eyes closed and I was holding her head gently between my palms.

"For old time's sake," I murmured.

She stopped and looked up at me with wide, unblinking eyes. "Oh, no, Max, for the times to come. I think you are ready to set sail now, without a doubt. Come . . ."

And we climbed into the tub, kissing and cooing. The hot jets from the sides and below caressed our undersides, and by the time the tub was full, we had slipped into our once-favorite position, half-underwater, she straddling me on her knees, hands gripping the edge of the tub while I lay on my back, legs extended, spine arched, and her breasts pearled with moisture brushing my face as she rocked back and forth. Afterward we collapsed sideways in each other's arms, only our heads above the foaming water, and the steam so thick we could no longer see the door.

I was afraid to admit it, but I hadn't felt that good in months, in years, with Sarah or anyone else. I didn't care if I never moved again, and even the would-be intruders who knocked and were sent packing, and the din of the party, did not hamper the voluptuous afterglow we enjoyed, still loosely embraced, the water churning around us. But while my body glowed, stupefied with pleasure, my mind was working overtime. I was thinking hard about what Greta had said, thinking that indeed it was moments such as these, repeated daily, weekly, ad infinitum, that "made so much logic." In my haphazard quest, I hadn't found a fraction of the inner peace I was enjoying just then with that lovely woman, suspended in hot water with the world at bay. Perhaps this was the true crux of the spiritual life, with exactly the right person at exactly the right time and place, and my error in my previously disordered sexual life had not been a lack of selectivity but a general animal approach with a premium on sensual annihilation rather than sensual enlightenment. I felt I might be entering a higher realm, acquiring a new insight into the meaning of bliss, and that if there was such a thing as a sexuality of the intellect, then perhaps Greta was its finest practitioner ever to come my way. And why, if this were true, had it taken me so long to figure out?

All of this devolving from a chance rendezvous during a cocktail party. By then my ex-wife and I had spent over an hour in that bathroom and word must have gotten around, for people had stopped knocking at the door altogether. We finally forced ourselves out of the jacuzzi and dressed slowly together as in former times. In the same mirror, Greta combed out her hair and I knotted my tie, keeping our eyes to ourselves. Oddly, we experienced our first moment of real awkwardness—for how were we going to take leave of one another now? What kind of goodbye came to one's lips in such circumstances? Obviously thinking along the same lines, she introduced a new subject.

"And how is Daphne?" she asked, applying her lipstick.

I had forgotten how fond they were of each other, and I felt bad for it.

"She's fine."

"You know, we correspond every so often."

"No, I didn't know that."

"She writes darling letters. And for my birthday, she always makes up a card from scratch."

"She's going to be living with me all summer in Boston."

"That's wonderful. Do you do that every year now?"

"No, this is the first time. Ellen is going abroad."

"Perhaps I can come up and visit you both. Would you like that?"

The moment of decision had arrived. "I would like that, Greta. But maybe we ought to sleep on it for a while and make sure about things."

"Make sure?"

"So that neither of us gets hurt. It's no small thing."

"What do you mean?"

"Well, seeing each other again after all these years. Visiting . . . Do you feel that casual about it?"

"It's not a question of feeling casual, Max, but of making a second chance, of being happy together—can't you understand that?"

"Sure, I understand. I even like the idea." I saw that we could dance in circles like that for hours and get nowhere. And I thought of a cynic's response to all this, a hypothetical voice in the wings, asking, "If you didn't fall in love when you were married for two years, why should you now?" As yet, I had no hypothetical answer. I only knew that people change, that life changes us—for the better, if we're lucky.

I put my arm around her. "Let me call you in a few days from Boston, and either you'll come up there or I'll come back here and we'll figure it all out. Okay?"

"Yes, that's what I want is for you to think it over. I know it comes out of right field—"

"Left field."

"Left field. So, good, we'll talk soon, we'll see each other soon." She planted a kiss behind my ear. "And, Max," she murmured, patting my stomach, "wasn't it wonderful? Even better than the old days? Isn't that the way it should be?"

My answer was yes on all three counts, and after a few more hugs and kisses we emerged from the bathroom and she walked me to the front door. A new wave of guests was coming in, and not a few eyes followed Greta and me as we passed. The fellow in red leather accosted her and whispered something. She nodded and he disappeared.

"Who's that?" I said.

"Oh, the director of the gallery where I'm showing."

But this had triggered a line of thought in me. As we stepped out into the hall, I said, "Aren't you seeing anyone now, Greta?"

"A man?" She smiled and winked. "Not really. I have not been a priestess for these four years, but if I were deeply involved with someone I would never think to talk to you like this."

"A nun, not a priestess," I murmured.

It didn't seem to have occurred to her to ask me the same question. She was not thinking along those lines. She was on a higher plane. After one last languorous kiss at the elevator, and a solemn promise to telephone in two days, I was off.

Sarah retired early that night, tired and irritable after the meeting with her editor. She didn't even want to talk about it. She was in a dark mood. I, who had broken my abstinence and drunk brandy, smoked ganja, snorted coke, and then fornicated with my ex-wife, felt vitalized and not in the least bit tired. After a listless dinner in our room, I left her reading in bed and rode up to Willy's place to put in my time at the piano. His sprawling apartment, a real gem twenty-five stories above Fifth Avenue, was cool and dark and gloriously empty. I had it all to myself for four hours, planted at his fine Baldwin by the picture window above the twinkling expanse of the park. I spent the entire time working on the Brahms sonata, without once rising from the piano to dawdle, and I played it better than I had in weeks.

You might think I would have been besieged by waves of guilt when I saw Sarah again, but not a bit of it, and I can't say I wasn't further put off, even saddened, by this realization. Perversely, it disillusioned me in her, not myself. I harbored no regrets for my interlude with Greta. When I returned to the Plaza and saw that remorse was not about to set in—no delayed reaction, nothing—I began to think very seriously about Greta's overtures. Though not prone to infidelity, when I had slipped in the past the Furies had worked me over well. If I did not now feel unfaithful or remorseful, I reasoned, then my feelings for Sarah must not run very deep. My relative ease at the piano also seemed significant. Could Greta's magic work that quickly and subtly?

Caught up in these deliberations, I had of course forgotten to return Uncle Louie's phone calls. The next morning, on my way out of town, I stopped by Willy's office to say goodbye.

He ran over some last-minute business with me, and then said, "Well, what did that man want?"

"What are you talking about?"

"Your Uncle Louie—what did he want?"

"Jesus, I never called him. Can I borrow your office for a minute?"

"Certainly," he sniffed, "but I hope it is nothing illegal."

I had to go through an elaborate chain of lackeys before getting Louie on the line. He was gruff and to the point, as usual.

"You're harder to get hold of than the governor," he said. "Are you hiding?"

"In a way. I'm preparing for a tour, Louie."

"You're paying your taxes, aren't you?"

"I'm trying."

"And those shysters your ex-wives hire, are they still fleecing you?"

I didn't want to depress him with news of my latest courthouse adventure. "Really, things are fine, Louie."

"Your little girl?"

"Just fine. She'll be with me all summer."

"Yeah? That's great—then you can bring her with you."

The preliminaries were over, he was down to business, and I grew cautious. "Bring her where?"

"Jeannie is getting married next month, and Shirley and I want you to be there."

I scrambled for a moment. "Jeannie! That's great, Louie." Jeannie was his eldest daughter, my first cousin, and the last time I'd seen her she was about seventeen.

"Yeah, if you called us once in a while, you might have known about it. She's been engaged for six months."

"I've been pretty busy . . ."

"I know, I know. So you'll come, right?"

"What day is it?"

"The ninth. July 9, a Saturday."

My first, reflexive reaction was to fish for an excuse, but after a few seconds another idea entered my head. My mind racing, I played for time and thought it through.

"How old is Jeannie?"

"Jesus, you know, you're even worse than your old man. He kept to himself, but at least he remembered that *he had a family.* You, you're a loner, Max, a wolf." He paused, and I could hear him relighting his cigar. "Jeannie's twenty-one. She just graduated from Penn State last week, with high honors in business administration."

"So she plans a career?"

"Of course she plans a career. All the young women do nowadays. And she'll raise a family on top of it."

He sounded as if he was trying to sell me something. That was his style.

"Where will the wedding be?"

"In a church, where do you think?"

"In New Jersey?"

"That's where I live, isn't it? Listen, enough questions, you're going to be there, aren't you?"

I sat back in Willy's big chair and gazed out at the skyline. "I wouldn't miss it for the world, Louie."

"Good. And you'll bring Daphne?"

"Absolutely. And another guest, if that's all right."

"Huh? Oh, sure, of course it's all right. What's the matter

with you? Now, give me your address—if it's not classified—so we can send you an invitation with all the details. Listen, and you tell that manager of yours that the next time I ask him where I can reach my nephew—"

"I'll tell him. I'll give you my phone number too, in case you need it."

He grunted. "This is a big tour, huh? Shirley got tickets for the New York date—Carnegie Hall, right?"

"You're going to be there?"

"Don't sound so surprised. I know you think I'm a short step from the caveman, but I enjoy good music. Anyway, you're my nephew and I get a kick out of seeing you in the big time. I used to go to your father's fights, and I come to your concerts," he added matter-of-factly.

He equated the two, which flattered me, actually.

"I'm happy you'll be there," I said.

"Now tell me, how's your health, Max?" he said, and I knew we were entering the last stage of the conversation. "You taking care of yourself?"

"Never better."

"Health foods, huh?" he said with distaste.

"Not anymore. I just watch myself."

He grunted again. "And no drugs, I hope. Grass, pills . . ."

"I'm clean, Louie. Honest."

"I'll see you in a few weeks, then. Don't forget now, Max."

"I won't. Love to the family."

I said my goodbyes to Willy and left. Sarah was sitting in the car, double-parked on Fifty-seventh Street. I felt good walking out into the sunshine. My motive for accepting Louie's invitation, despite my tight practice schedule, was really quite simple: if I went to the wedding it would give me an excuse to come to New York and see Greta. She would be my "other guest." If I had any lingering doubts about the importance of my visit to her the day before, they were gone. Sarah was still out of sorts, taciturn, absorbed in her own affairs. She muttered that New York was a town of sharks, and I concurred halfheartedly. She couldn't wait to get home, she said. When she fell asleep near Hartford, I was glad for the time to myself. I had a lot of thinking to do, even more than when I had left Boston two days before, which was not what I had expected.

I asked myself, as Dr. Winters had asked me, if I believed in miracles. I told myself that if I didn't, I was going to be in big trouble. And I was right.

For the next week I threw myself into my work. It seemed the best defense against further complications. I went sculling with Tim, and I spent two nights fixing up the spare room for Daphne. It was a good-sized room down the hall from my bedroom, bright and airy, but it was too spartan for a little girl, with a bed, a table, and one lamp. So I bought a white rug and curtains and flowered sheets and I put some pretty lamps around and lots of cushions and pillows, and I was pleased with the effect. I practiced each day for eleven or twelve hours, until my fingers went numb. I would start off with two hours of exercises, scales and arpeggios over and over again, to build up my stamina. The acupuncturist paid five house calls and my left wrist improved. My back still hurt, and my shoulders, but I was too far along to whine about aches and pains.

As for Orana, I wasn't able to see her when I first returned: she was undergoing a week of intensive tests and was permitted no visitors. Telephoning was pointless because she was always drugged up after the tests. They told me her condition was worsening. The following Monday, four days before Daphne was to arrive, I arranged to visit her in the evening. And I had the florist send another dozen white roses.

That afternoon at five Sarah showed up unannounced with some Chinese food. I had just finished working and was sipping a beer by the window, gazing out at nothing, exhausted. Ever since the trip to New York, I had forsaken my rigid abstinence. After all, what good had it done me? I still wasn't going out at night or touching hard liquor, but some beer or wine and a couple of cigars in the evening seemed to be doing me more good than harm. Sarah had kept a low profile all that week, and I knew something was in the air. She had taken on a slew of book reviews, and was working on her new novel at night, and the way I was going I wasn't good for much anyway, so we hadn't seen each other. And my adventure with Greta lingered in my mind like a glowing coal, growing brighter in the evening and ebbing in the morning when I had my work before me. I had talked to her several times by phone. It was warm and relaxed, but we had never been good on the phone. I believe our affinity was too physical for such a disembodied medium. I had invited her to Jeannie's wedding with Daphne and me, and she was delighted. But I was in a quandary as to my relations with Sarah.

Sarah was shrewd in these matters, as I was to learn, and her antennae were up. She had not the faintest notion what had happened in New York, but she knew something was amiss. That afternoon she seemed more cautious than usual, and reserved. She fetched herself a beer, and some plates, and ladled out the chow mein and shrimp. I saw she had something on her mind.

As I mentioned, Sarah had been no exception to my tendency to idealize women. I was a knee-jerk rhapsodist, and I always played the same tune with my *inamorate*. With Orana and Ellen and Greta, and even with my more fleeting conquests, it had always been the same tedious roundelay of overblown expectations and sour repercussions. Or, as Dr. Selzer had incisively observed in one of our better sessions: "Despite your preening self-absorption, you are no Don Juan type, Max. The true Don Juan type keeps his detachment intact. He is fully possessed, all his mechanisms fine-tuned to the chase. His only concern is with numbers, lists. His passion lies in repetition, not in novelty or perfection. Does that sound like you? With you, it is not quantity—you are no Lothario, and most of your lasting friendships have been with women—it is quality to an obsessive degree. You do not want dozens of women, for their own sake, you want the perfect final woman. You have a Beatrice complex. Numbers only enter into it for you because of course you will never find such a woman, so you continue to chase enigmas, the ghosts and shadows of ghosts of your mother, your sister, and several other women in your early life. Your first teacher, for example, was a young woman, no? You idealize compulsively because it is the ideal you desire and can never have. You would tend to have a woman on a pedestal before the introductions were complete."

Beatrice, not Don Juan. Later on, I saw that her observation had been most accurate, but at the time I refused to accept it. I was a terrible patient, and our two years' efforts brought me little enlightenment. At any rate, I had gone through the same routine with Sarah from the moment we met that beautiful spring night at Tanglewood, and while I wasn't rejecting outright the bright picture I had painted back then, enough of it had faded in the intervening months so that my visit to Greta impelled me to examine the brushwork even more carefully. I was not so fickle as to let the jacuzzi romp alone turn my head, but that too gave me another slant on things. It was not primarily that I enjoyed lovemaking with Greta more than with Sarah (who I sensed was constantly battling her indifference), but that I felt a bigger heart and more generous spirit at work in Greta. Not just toward me, but in all ways. So what was it I had initially seen in Sarah to spark my idealizing? Youth, wit, keen intellect . . . I had it in my head in April that I needed a woman who lived a life of the mind, and to me the mind and the spirit were one—a gigantic error. And above all there was that inner calm that I have described. What I wouldn't see at first was the true nature of her enormous ambition, which was icy and cold-blooded. I didn't know whether this sprang from her famous father, or had other roots, but I sensed it had sent previous romances to the dogs. I knew she was casual about friendship, holding on only to those "safe" and accommodating friends who understood that her writing was the center of her universe. She told me outright—that week, in fact—that she needed a man like me, both ambitious and already successful, who would not feel threatened by her. People like her father and me, she explained through the telephone, who had climbed to the top in a world whose very air was hard ambition, were best suited to her. Kindred souls. And that may have been true, and we may have enjoyed smooth sailing, if indeed I had been a man like Franz Lengford. But I wasn't. I had other needs that existed outside of my career, needs that required a different kind of air. Because I was having difficulties with my work (which she dismissed as a temporary aberration, a kink), my other needs were more important to me than ever. So she and I had come together with mutual misconceptions. She saw me as an ambitious man who would tolerate her ruthlessness and offer succor, and I saw her as a keen-witted woman who lived and worked by the spirit and would connect with me on that level; she overlooked my over-passionate nature and I ignored her genuine coldness. And there we were . . .

Though I must admit that at that moment, munching a spare rib and uncapping my second beer, some of these thoughts were still inchoate. I felt unsettled but not yet disillusioned.

"Max, I've been thinking," she began, spreading mustard on an egg roll. "What would you say to our living together, seeing how it would work out?"

I froze, and sipped some beer.

"I guess there comes a time," she went on, "when you have to turn the corner, test the waters, whatever."

I nodded.

"What's the matter? I thought you would be pleased with the idea."

"Nothing's the matter." I poured some more beer.

She sat back. "Is it because Daphne's coming? Would she get upset?"

"I don't think so."

"But you did want her all to yourself. I know you've never had two months together."

"I had that in mind. Really, I'm just surprised. Why now?"

She shrugged. "It just hit me last night. I went home, I was alone, and I wanted to be with you. I know that sounds kind of corny, but that's what happened. So I thought, fuck all this coyness: let's do it. Let's take a chance."

Suddenly people were missing me at night, women in my life past and present were lying in bed mooning over my absence. First Greta, now Sarah. And after four idle years, four years in which for me one night was just like another, this was occurring at the one time I actually needed to be alone a great deal. Where were they during those years when *I* was lying awake lonely at night? Willy had been right, after all, I thought ruefully. When I moved to Boston, he had said: "Why bother? Nothing is going to change for you, it will just be the same commotion in a different city. If you are smart, and you really want to avoid distractions, you will go to one of the rural conservatories and rent yourself a studio for six months." He had been right but I couldn't live like that. I would have gone stir-crazy.

But what was I going to say to Sarah now? I couldn't account for this sudden gambit on her part. Unless her antennae were even better than I thought. I didn't want to live with her. And I didn't want to play games. Experience had taught me that when you get mixed up with two women at once, when you start lying and plotting, you end up feeling like a heel with both women, you cheat them, you diminish yourself, and you cripple your chances of happiness. So I tried to think clearly for a change.

"You did touch on something," I said, "when you mentioned Daphne. The way things are between her mother and me, I want this to be a very stable move. No fireworks, no clutter. Anyway, what you're talking about should be considered very carefully."

She was peeved. "You mean, put off indefinitely."

"Frankly, I don't think it's right for us."

"You don't think we have any future?"

"Let's just say it's hard for me even to think in these terms now. I've been practicing night and day. I barely have a free moment. It's a big step—not something to be half-assed about. I've made too many mistakes like that in the past."

"You don't have to bring up the past, Max," she said bitterly. "I'm well aware of your mistakes."

I didn't say anything. I felt bad.

"So you don't even want to discuss it?"

"Not now, no."

She shrugged. "I'm sorry, then. I guess I jumped the gun. I see your point about Daphne. But you've been so preoccupied—I've felt a bit neglected since we got back from New York."

"I can't help it. You know what a hard time I'm having. Look, I'm glad we talked."

She glanced away. "Sure."

"Jesus, it's late. I have to get dressed for the hospital." I stood up abruptly and she followed me into the bedroom.

[*110*]

"Is she finished with her tests?"

"For now, anyway."

I picked my clothes with care. I put on a sky-blue shirt, because Orana liked that color, and some beige trousers. Usually I wore a lot of dark colors, or white or black, and I was avoiding that. I went into the bathroom and Sarah sat down on the bed.

"You know," she said, "if we did do it at some point, I would still keep my apartment. That's where I would write every day. I couldn't do it here, with you practicing all the time."

"Of course," I said, combing my hair. I didn't feel so bad anymore.

"It would be like an office."

I came back in and put on my jacket. "I get the idea." I wanted to change the subject once and for all. "Did you tell your father that Willy sends regards?"

"Not yet. He's in Stockholm."

I put on my sunglasses. "Can I drop you anywhere?"

"No thanks."

As we walked out to the street, she turned to me casually. "By the way, your ex-wife—the one in New York—did you ever get back to her?"

"Greta? Yeah, we talked. The usual, some problems with her lawyer."

She waxed sympathetic. "Max, I wish you'd gotten yourself better lawyers back when."

"It's not so bad, really. Sometimes I think I've gotten away with murder."

"Why?"

I shrugged and drove off, relieved to get away.

Orana was asleep and I didn't want to wake her. I brought a chair to the bedside and took off my jacket. I was sweating. The room was again full of amber light and heavy barred shadows. The fresh roses were in a vase. The set of Gibbon was propped on the bedside table, but I gathered she hadn't done much reading. She had lost more weight. Her skin was blanched and taut. The sheet was pulled up to her chin, and her fists were clenched on her chest. They too were white. Only her hair offered a contrast. Otherwise her body might have been one with the sheets, embossed there, like one of those saints' sarcophagi in France on which the prone likeness of the martyr seems to have risen from the slab beneath it. I watched her, afraid she might open her eyes and catch me unawares, with fear in my eyes. I was convinced I ought to serve as a bearer of hope, a conduit to the "outside," without really knowing that she wanted such a conduit, without any notion of what hopes she cherished, or what "hope" meant to her now. I supposed that her inner vocabulary must have changed radically, but not knowing how, I could only keep alert for signs and patterns, as one does in a foreign country where the language is incomprehensible. I had had some experience of death, violent and so-called natural death, but none of terminal illness.

When I was twenty, my mother suffered through a severe kidney ailment. At first it appeared fatal, but they saved her by removing one kidney and bombarding the other with drugs. It was then I developed my dread of hospitals. She was in for four months, and she was a great sufferer, my mother, no stoic. The night she died, nine years later, it wasn't in a hospital. I was in Montreal that night, alone. I always seemed to be in cold places when death struck members of my family. I was asleep in my suite at the Ritz-Carlton Hotel, three hours before a recital, when Stella tracked me down from London. It was snowing hard, the sky black-and-blue, the clouds billowing, and I was sitting there naked trying to decipher Stella's voice through the transatlantic static. I used to like the cool anonymity and solitariness of hotel rooms when I toured, but that room felt cavernous and cold. The big windows were so clean I thought the snow was going to swirl in on me. My mother had angina for years and had moved to Zurich on the advice of a quack who convinced her the ionic mountain winds would expand her arteries. It was the day after Christmas, which at that time meant little to me: I had no real home in the States, I had just been divorced from Greta, and my life was in limbo. Willy had booked me to the gills on what turned out to be my last tour before the layoff. My mother was visiting Stella for the holidays, and though she was a hypochondriac I knew she felt safe in that house because her son-in-law was a doctor. My niece had run upstairs to wake Mother on Christmas morning and found her dead in an armchair. It was ghastly. Stella told me that on her last night on this planet my mother had insisted they play my recordings, the Chopin Ballades and Bach's French Suites, which I knew were her favorites of all my work. And there was Stella, bawling through the impulses of cables and satellites, across the icy wastes, and I had nothing to offer her. I was silent, shamed by the years of estrangement that had numbed me to my mother and sister. All those years we shared with that woman— Stella couldn't go to her husband with that. Only to me, alone in a hotel at Christmas, performing festive music for holiday audiences—and for Stella I might as well have been on Mars. I performed that night, without a word to anyone. A real professional, I told myself, but now I know better. Afterward I drank and tried in vain to call her back. What would I have said? I could think of nothing. And that night it was not the good things I remembered, but all the truly terrible things my mother had ever done or said to me. It was only at dawn, in the shower, that it hit me like a sledgehammer.

I blinked and saw Orana staring at me with enormous feverish eyes.

"Where were you just now?" she asked softly.

I took her hand.

"Have you been here long?" she said. "I waited and then I must have dozed off."

"No, it hasn't been long."

There was a small machine with red and green lights wheeled up beside the bed, humming softly.

"What is that?" I said.

"A monitor. Blood pressure, temperature, vital—the usual." Her voice had grown weaker. "They told me you tried to come all week. The tests . . ."

"I know. Is it difficult for you to talk?"

"Oh, no. Just sleepy. The Gibbon," she smiled faintly, "you shouldn't have."

"Would you like me to read to you?"

"Maybe later, okay? I haven't had anyone to talk to."

"Sure."

"How's the music? Working hard?"

"It's getting better. It's . . ."

"What?"

"Nothing. Just mechanics. Rust. The layoff, you know."

"You're lying. You lied the last time you were here. You're having trouble, aren't you? Real trouble."

I looked at her. "Yes."

"What is it?"

"My playing is flat, listless. No magic at all. I can play the pieces but—"

" 'Play the pieces'? You're a great performer. What are you saying? People like you don't go flat for no reason."

"True. But I don't know the reason."

She peered at me closely. "You will be touring—that's not changed?"

"No. You see, I booked the tour as a last resort, to break out of this thing. I have to tour."

"You'll be all right."

"I think I'm getting on the right track."

"I wish you hadn't been so secretive last time. I was thinking more clearly then, I might have helped." She paused. "Do you still have trouble sleeping?"

"Sometimes."

"What does Willy say about your trouble?"

"He doesn't know."

"It's that bad. And your girlfriend, what does she say?"

"She has nothing to do with it."

"You've confided in no one?"

"Amos. But he's out of the country." I hesitated. "And Greta, my—"

"I know who she is. I met her in San Francisco, when you were first married. You know, I liked her very much."

"You did?"

"I thought she had a real sweetness to her. She was very kind to me when we were alone."

She breathed deeply and one of the red lights started flashing.

"What's the matter?"

"I don't know. It does that every hour or so."

"We've been talking too much."

"It's not that."

The light stopped flashing suddenly.

"What did Greta think of your dilemma?"

I was still staring at the machine. "I didn't even have to mention it to her. She said right off that she could tell I'd been unhappy. She thinks my troubles started four years ago when she and I were divorced. That without her, I went stale. I don't know . . ."

"Why so skeptical? It's possible. What else happened four years ago?"

"I don't know. I'm sick of the whole business."

"What else, besides your divorce?"

"I was in a car crash in Rome. No one hurt, but the car was totaled. That shook me up."

"Your father died in an automobile accident."

"What has that to do with it?"

"Anything else?"

"Well, I've avoided the *obvious*. You know, my mother died four years ago."

"Ah."

"I know it sounds ripe, but I went into all that with my analyst right afterward. Without much success."

"I didn't know you were in analysis."

"For two years."

"And this led nowhere? Her death, I mean."

"You knew my mother. We had a mutually tormenting relationship. Her unhealthy ties to my career, and the rest. I'm sure her death had a profound effect. I can lay things at her door, but not this."

"If you say so. It's the only thing you seem definite about. But you'll figure it out. Immerse yourself at the piano, let the music take you over. When the trouble is physical, it's one thing. But when it's here," and she tapped her forehead, "you have to be careful. It could be anything at all, it could lead anywhere."

I nodded. I wanted to drop it.

"Daphne's coming this week to stay with me. I thought I might bring her to see you."

"Oh, no, you mustn't bring her here. Please don't. How old is she now?"

"Nine."

"Already? Imagine, Max a father. What will they think of next?"

I laughed. But I felt uneasy, for Orana had wanted a child when we were married and I had insisted it was impossible. I was afraid it would interfere with my career. It was a sore point, and I often wondered what part it had played in her decision to leave me.

"You must be excited," she said.

"A little scared, too. It's for the summer."

"Just don't try too hard."

I didn't want to go into that. "Orana, I haven't had an opportunity yet to talk to your doctor. He canceled on me last time. And he's out of town today."

"There's not much he can tell you. Unless he's keeping things from me," she said drily.

A nurse came in and said I had five minutes left. I looked out the window at the cars on the Drive.

I said, "Here we've spent the whole time talking about me again."

"You're a bit thick—I told you it's a welcome change for me. Don't you have any juicy escapades to report?"

"Afraid not." And I thought of Greta and our Roman bath.

I leaned closer to the bed. By now the room was dark and her green eyes were glittering in the shadows.

"Do you remember that time in Chicago? The green room, the night I played the *Emperor*?"

She blinked. "You would remember that. So embarrassing . . . that man from the *Tribune* walking in on us—on the floor, no less. You told him I was your page-turner."

"That's right."

"How did you get me to do those things? You're a wicked man, Max."

"He gave me a great review."

She started laughing softly, but after a few moments I saw tears shining on her eyelids and sliding down her cheeks. Then she closed her eyes.

"Better go now," she whispered. "Sorry . . . I guess I'm more tired than I thought. . . ."

I was angry with myself. I squeezed her hand. "Don't you want me to read to you? We have a few minutes."

"Next time. Please, just go."

I drove away from the hospital quickly. I went about five blocks and pulled over and switched off the headlights. And I cried my eyes out like a baby for the first time in years, since that night in Montreal four years before.

The night before Daphne arrived, my relations with Sarah took another turn for the worse.

I was dining alone at Billy Diamond's. Eddie had the night off, so there was no boxing talk, which was just as well. I was nervous about Daphne's arrival, and I had been pushing hard at the piano, still with lukewarm results. And I had to attend a benefit reception, which I dreaded. I usually avoided those things, but it was for a good cause—music scholarships—and Mrs. Patterson, who had procured Orana her nice room, had personally invited me. I couldn't refuse. Decked out in another of my fine, sober suits, I devoured a swordfish steak and put away an icy white burgundy, and things began to look up. I had a table in the back under a palm tree, and secure in my solitude I studied the women around the room and enjoyed the music. It was very pleasant. I ought to do this more often, I told myself. Dr. Selzer had been correct, as my further readings in Kierkegaard had confirmed: I was no Don Juan type at heart, for among other things, the Don Juan type invariably dines out alone, and I almost never did. I had to dine with a woman or the meal felt incomplete. This intrigued me, especially with a bottle of my wine in me, but I had no time to develop the idea for I was called away to the phone.

Only one person knew where I was going that night, so I wasn't holding my breath. "Cooled" isn't the right word: my relations with Sarah had rather frozen since our talk about moving in. I hadn't seen her since then, and on the phone she had seemed surly, at loose ends—which was out of character. Even her writing was blocked up, she had told me glumly, and this gave me a shiver. Could my own malady be catching?

Her voice was giddy and urgent, and a little too sweet. "I hope I'm not disturbing you, but something important's come up. Very important, or I wouldn't be calling at the last minute."

"What is it?"

"I know you have that reception tonight, but I'm going to ask a big favor."

"I can't back out of it now, if that's what you mean."

"Of course not. I just need an hour of your time afterward. I have a party of my own, and if you could stop in and meet some people it would mean a lot to me. It would also be nice to see you," she added drily.

"What, a book party?"

"No, nothing like that. It's a cocktail party . . . at Harvard."

I groaned.

"I've never asked you to do this kind of thing before—can't you put aside your prejudices just once?"

"Prejudices?"

"Forget it, then," she said coldly.

I was ready to concur and hang up, but I didn't. "Why is it so crucial, Sarah, that I make an appearance?"

She knew she had me hooked. "Remember that teaching post? They make their decision next month. It would be a perfect job, give me tons of time to write—"

"I remember. So?"

"So tonight the dean has asked me over. Just to get acquainted. I think I have the job in hand if I play my cards right."

This was depressing. "Don't tell me—his wife's a music lover?"

"You needn't be unpleasant, Max. Forget it."

I'll say this for Sarah, she had plenty of nerve. On some level, she obviously knew the score on us, romantically speaking, and it didn't temper her.

"So you just want me to show up like a dancing bear and do my act. You know how I hate that sort of thing."

"I'm really surprised to hear you talk this way," she said sharply. "It's nothing like that, but you've just told me a lot about how you think of me."

"Think of *you?*"

"Listen, I'm inviting you there as my friend, my lover. I

thought it might be a welcome diversion for you, something different, locked up as you are day and night. It happens they *are* fans of yours—also of my father's. They're interesting people. I've done you plenty of favors—"

"All right, just give me the address. I'm sorry."

"You don't sound it."

"I've had a long day. The idea of a second soirée gives me a headache, but I'll be there. I'll even try to have a good time."

"Don't bother."

"Sarah, give me the address."

It didn't take much more coaxing to get it, and I returned to my table in a dismal frame of mind. She had done me some favors, but whatever my faults, I didn't keep an account book in that department and I was more embarrassed than surprised to hear, from her own lips, that she did.

The benefit reception held no surprises. A bigwig's townhouse near Beacon Hill, a string quartet, a large crowd, and plenty of champagne. Mrs. Patterson and I had a friendly chat, and she was most solicitous about Orana. Members of the Symphony were there, and a handful of soloists from the area. I met the three scholarship winners who were pianists. They asked me for autographs and wanted to know what I had been doing of late. I talked about the tour. None of them was about to be rude or impolitic with an established soloist, in a position to help them, but I wish they had been more frank and less admiring. In my ivory tower, I had no contact with other musicians and I wondered what the word was on my comeback. Suddenly it was time to meet Sarah. In fact, I was late. I tossed down one last glass of champagne and slipped away.

I never made it to the dean's party, or even to Cambridge. I was deflected from my distasteful mission in a way I would never have chosen myself. To save time, I took a shortcut across town and found myself in the "combat zone," Boston's version of Times Square. But much sleazier. Red-light hotels, leather bars, and blocks of crumbling, bombed-out brownstones with pimps and hookers lounging on the sidewalks. There were the usual sailors and lowbrow types around by day, but at night it could be rough, more than satisfying the newspapers' weekly crime quota. It was a warm, drizzly night, and usually, in my vintage car, prudence would have kept me off those streets. Was I, I asked myself later, under the guise of haste pursuing other demons in that wasteland (for surely none of us ever ends up in a place totally against our will), in order to be distracted from my very tangible problems at that time?

There was nothing complicated about what happened. I witnessed one crime, a confidence game of a crude and ugly variety, and was the victim of another. I had stopped for a light at a dark intersection. The surrounding buildings were all gutted. The street was full of trash. There were two men on one corner, a hooker on the other. A truck sped through the intersection, and a pair of cars. Then I saw the men exchange glances and one of them backed up into the shadows while the other remained on the curb. A station wagon came around the corner and, with expert timing, the man on the curb, feigning drunkenness, staggered out and was apparently struck by the front fender. He spun around facedown onto the pavement while the car screeched to a halt. The driver and his companion, who looked like students, jumped out to help. At that moment the man in the shadows, and another hiding in a doorway, crept up brandishing clubs, beat the students from behind and pinned them to the ground. The "victim" meanwhile had leaped up to rifle their pockets. By the time I got out of my car, terrified but moving on instinct, the hooker had disappeared, and the three men had leaped into the station wagon and roared off into the night. I stood there in the rain staring after them and my stomach flip-flopped. This was not my usual brand of crisis. Aside from a mugging on Fifth Avenue, and several noisy but antiseptic bar-room brawls I had seen in my halcyon days, I had little exposure to criminal violence. I ran over to the students and turned one of them over. They were no more than twenty, and well-dressed. The one fellow had a gash up over his ear and another on his chin. His friend was out cold. Several other cars cruised by and slowed long enough to see they wanted no part of what was going on. I tried to flag down a van and nearly got run over. I tied my handkerchief around the young man's head, locked up my car, and set off in search of a phone. There weren't any. The phone company had obviously written off that part of town. And except for hookers, the streets were empty. I had to walk two blocks to find a bar.

Now, it hadn't struck me until I entered this place that it wasn't very smart to be running around there in my pinstripe suit and silk shirt, a target if there ever was one, and I cursed myself for forgetting the old raincoat I kept in the trunk of the car. There were some pimps in the bar and a few bikers. Otherwise, it was so dark that I couldn't see much. The black walls seemed to flow on forever. I could have been at the bottom of the Atlantic. The stench was terrible. The bartender, openly hostile, directed me to a phone booth in the rear that reeked of urine. I called the police and they told me to wait at the scene until they arrived. As I left the booth, two men stepped out of the darkness and took my arms firmly.

"Slummin', Mac?"

I couldn't see their faces, but they were both about my height. They smelled of gin and they were wearing leather jackets.

"Whaddya' want here?"

"Just to use the phone."

"Jus' t' use the phone," he mimicked.

"Well, there's a fee for outsiders, dude," the other one said thickly.

"How much?"

"Now, don't be stupid. How much ya got?"

I was a little slow. All they wanted was to roll me. And, despite the sacred memory of my father and his iron fists, what I had in my pockets was not worth a knife in the kidney or a broken arm—though if I had truly been a darker, more self-destructive sort, the latter would have taken care of all the metaphysical angst about my comeback in one stroke. I could throw a punch and that would be the end of it. Instead, I flipped out my wallet and removed all the bills.

"I've got seventy-three dollars." I didn't tell them I had five twenties in my sidepocket. I had my pride, after all.

"That'll do. Now you stand right here, lover, and count to ten, then go on yer way."

After what I had seen on the street, I felt grateful, as if I were getting off easy. By the time I got back to my car, the cops had arrived and an ambulance was on the way. The cops were skeptical about me, and my fancy car, in that neighborhood, and when I told them I had been robbed, they shrugged. Then they took a statement from me, though my description of the assailants was woefully sketchy.

Finally on my way again, I realized it was almost midnight and I had probably blown it as far as Sarah's party was concerned. I pulled into a gas station and got the dean's phone number with some difficulty. Sarah had just left. I stopped again ten minutes later and reached her at her apartment.

"Sarah, I'm sorry. I ran into some real trouble—"

"I don't want to hear about it. You succeeded in humiliating me and there's nothing more to say. You didn't even have the decency to call."

"Listen, I witnessed a bad assault and got mugged myself trying to get help."

"Don't make me laugh. What was her name?"

"That's the truth. I'm sorry I couldn't call, but the cops took forever."

"You're sorry? You never had any intention of coming. I don't know why you feel you have to lie about it," she added bitterly.

"I don't give a damn if you don't believe me. Good night," and I slammed the phone down.

I knew she would be mad, even incredulous, but I hadn't expected such nastiness. She must have really wanted that job.

I was more shaken than I thought by what had happened. I had pumped out a lot of adrenaline that my body was trying to burn off all at once. I had to keep myself from driving too fast and jumping lights. When I got home, I showered and poured myself a double Scotch. I put on my bathrobe and sat at the piano. I couldn't imagine going to bed but I don't know what I thought I was going to do at the piano. My hands weren't steady. I poured another drink, a weak one, and sat there in the dark for a long time thinking about Greta.

"All right, Dad, now you stir the vegetables and herbs in with the tomato sauce, let it sit for five minutes, and then add the meat."

"You keep the heat low?"

"Uh huh."

"And what do you call this?"

"You call it Mongolian goulash. You'll like it."

"Don't you sauté the meat first?"

"Uh uh. It cooks in the sauce. How many minutes left on the rice?"

"Six."

"And you don't have white pepper?"

"Is that crucial?"

"No, this'll do—but you *should* use white."

"I'll remember that."

"Now, don't stir too much, just let it simmer."

"Where are you going?"

"Be right back. It's seven o'clock and I promised my friend Ginnie I'd call her. Is that okay?"

"Of course."

"Don't forget, cover the rice when it's done."

We were having a fine day. We'd gone for a drive by the river, visited the aquarium, and taken in a movie, a Western, for they were her favorites. In addition to redecorating her room (which she liked), I had stocked the kitchen with her usual staples. The refrigerator was overflowing with soda and cold cuts, candy bars and desserts. It turned out she had a newfound taste for health foods, so we bought a lot of fruit and nuts and granola. I had planned to take her to Billy Diamond's, but she insisted we dine at home her first night—and she would cook.

Daphne was a beautiful kid, and I would say that even if she weren't mine. Blond, with Ellen's dark blue eyes, petite but not delicate, she had small hands and feet and powder-puff skin. Her mother had braided her hair, and she wore purple jeans and a pink T-shirt that I bought her on her last visit. Though it was seven a.m., and she was in a taxi packed with luggage, late for her flight to London, Ellen was very pleasant when she dropped Daphne off. She looked lovelier than ever with her black hair shining in the sun and she seemed truly relaxed for a change, even with me. It was one of our better moments, and I was grateful for that, for getting off on the right foot, because this visit had taken on great importance for me. Maybe Ellen sensed that. Neither of us brought up our session at the courthouse. While still apprehensive, I was very glad Daphne would be with me for the summer and ashamed I hadn't arranged such a long visit before—without the help of a judge. True, Ellen had seemed resistant to Daphne's visiting me beyond what our agreement stipulated, but I had never really pushed the point. Maybe I had fueled her resistance, not wanting to rock the boat, for as holiday companions Daphne and I had always been just fine. But if I couldn't now prepare myself for the tour while also fulfilling my paternal obligations, I was a sorrier soul than I would ever want to admit. At any rate, my day had been made from the first when I realized how happy Daphne was to be with me. It was a warm breeze through my heart.

As I stood daydreaming at the stove, she sashayed back in, whistling, and sat down at the butcher-block table to dice carrots. She had a fluid, confident walk for a little girl; she was aware of her body, not in a lewd way certainly, but you felt she had good and delicate inner connections between her senses and her limbs. That, or she kept an imitative eye on her mother, who—there was no denying it—was a very sexy woman.

"I covered the rice and I didn't stir the meat too much," I said. She nodded. "Smells good."

"How's your friend?"

"Fine. Her brother caught a gecko today."

"Yeah? I didn't know there were geckos in Massachusetts."

"There *aren't*, Dad. Ginnie lives in the desert. The Baja."

"The Baja?" I was surprised. "Do you call each other often?"

"No, really we're pen pals. I met her when I was in Arizona last year at Grandpa's. But she called me last week 'cause she didn't feel like writing. So I told her I'd call her back."

She and Ellen lived in a big house on a duck pond near Lexington with a garden and lots of trees. Ellen, who grew up in the Southwest, had always liked New England. She bought that house after a couple of unhappy years in New York when Daphne was a baby. I often wondered that spring if I had not chosen Boston for my exile because they—or at least Daphne—would be nearby.

She was studying me now: aproned, the cooking glove on my left hand and the spatula in my right.

"Where'd you learn to cook, Dad? Not from Mom," and she pulled a face, "she's terrible."

"No, not much from her." How could I, I thought, when we were eating out twice a day at four-star restaurants.

"From Greta?"

"Mostly." I wasn't a bad cook, and my cuisine, such as it was, was an amalgam of Polynesian and Scandinavian, from my wives. Lots of fish dishes and strange salads. "You're fond of Greta, aren't you," I said.

"I sure am. I liked it when you were married. 'Course, I might not say that to Mom," she added.

"You're going to see Greta next week in New York."

"At her house?"

"Sure. We're all invited to a wedding. My cousin Jeannie is getting married."

"She must be my cousin too, but I don't remember her."

"You were a baby when you last saw her."

"Who is she marrying?"

"That's a good question. I don't know."

"How come?"

"Well, I rarely see her, to tell you the truth."

She pondered this. "You know, Dad, I think you work too much."

"And so I'm out of touch with the relatives, huh?"

She nodded. "I guess it's worth it, though. I mean, working too much."

"You think so?"

"Well, Mom said you're the greatest pianist in America."

I stopped stirring the goulash. "She did?"

"Uh huh."

"She's just playing favorites."

"No, she meant it. I know you are. I sent Ginnie two of your records and she really liked them."

"I'm happy to hear that. Are we going to play together after dinner?"

"I've got three pieces all prepared."

"Mother told me you've been practicing hard lately."

"Uh huh. Mozart sonatas for violin and piano. And one by Haydn. I wanted to be ready for you."

"You're sure I'll be able to handle them?"

She rolled her eyes, just the way Ellen did—but in Daphne it wasn't spoiled, it was lovely.

"Come on, Dad, you're always teasing me. Will you play me what you're going to perform at your recitals?"

"You're going to hear that stuff so many times in the next two months that you won't want to come to a recital anymore."

"I bet I will."

"We'll see. You don't mind that I practice tonight, do you? You understand what I explained to you before?"

"Sure, I know you've got to do it every day." She pretended to shiver. "Boy, if I was going to get up in front of thousands of people, I would practice plenty."

"And you don't mind having to be quiet all that time?"

She clucked her tongue. "I'm not a little kid, Dad."

"I keep forgetting that, somehow."

"You see, you're always teasing." She folded her arms on the table and rested her chin on them. "Dad?"

"Yeah?"

"Do you ever get scared when you give a recital?"

"Sure. But as soon as you start playing, you forget all about the audience."

"How?"

"You have too many other things to think about. If you're thinking about the audience, or the lights, or what you had for dinner, it's a sign you're not playing well."

"What you had for dinner?" she repeated. She thought this was very funny. "Have you ever made a mistake?"

"Lots of times."

"What did you do?"

"I fainted."

"Come on."

"I just kept playing. People rarely notice mistakes or wrong notes, except the other musicians in the house."

"My teacher, Mrs. Matthews, says when you make a mistake you should go back and start the piece all over. Even if it's just one note. Isn't that dumb?"

"Did you ask her why?"

"She says that's the way you learn."

It certainly was dumb, but I tried to think of something constructive to say. "I think there are other ways. You can just practice that section of the piece until you get it right. Do you like Mrs. Matthews, otherwise?"

"Not really. But Mom checked into it and said she was a good teacher."

"What happened to your old teacher?"

"Mrs. Notti? She moved to Ohio in January."

"I'll tell you what. I'll look around for someone new and then talk to your mother about it. There are plenty of good teachers around Boston."

"Dad, how much did you practice when you were my age?"

"About nine hours a day."

"Jeez, did you ever have time to play outside or anything?"

"Not very much in those days. You see, my mother and my teachers already knew I was going to play professionally, so it was all very serious."

"Do you think I could play professionally?"

"If you wanted to, if you set your mind to it, I'm sure you could. You have a lot of talent."

She shook her head glumly. "Yeah, but I asked Mrs. Notti if I was a prodigy like you were, and she said she couldn't tell yet. But I think she was just being nice."

I put my arm around her. "You don't really worry about that, do you, sweetheart?"

"Sometimes."

"You just put that stuff out of your head. A prodigy is simply someone who begins playing seriously very early on. And you're still quite young. But all that counts if you want to be a violinist is how you play when you grow up, and how hard you practice now, and how much you love music. You understand?"

"Uh huh."

I kissed her forehead. "You know, sometimes we all think we'd like to do what our parents did, but then we find out we're really better at something else. I bet you know what I wanted to be when I was a kid."

Her face brightened. "A boxer, like your dad."

"But it just wasn't for me."

"You weren't tough enough, huh?"

"Well, I wouldn't go that far."

"You know, Dad, sometimes I think I'd like to be a figure skater. Or maybe a doctor," she added seriously. "That's what Mom says I ought to be."

"You've got plenty of time to work it out." And I remembered Dr. Selzer explaining Jung's theory about prodigies to me, that they are a specialized form of the Divine Child, guided unerringly by nature and instinct, and incarnating in their particular gift "the inability to do otherwise." I had had no choice but to play the piano, according to her. It was an ability that, by its very power, negated all other options. I did not see Daphne in that position. Clearly, she had other choices. She was lucky.

Our dinner was excellent. Daphne had laid out a formal setting, put on my recording of Chopin Waltzes, lit candles, and sat us at opposite ends of the table. It was the most romantic dinner I'd had in a long time.

"By the way," I asked, "where did you learn this Mongolian goulash recipe?"

"You liked it, didn't you. Uncle Amos taught me."

"Amos?"

"A few months ago, when he visited us."

"At your house?"

"Where do you think? He visited a few times. He's nice. He reminds me of you, except goofier."

"Thanks."

"He showed me pictures he took in the Amazon. Spiders and things."

"And he and Mother are friends?"

"Oh, sure, he didn't just come to see me, even though he is my godfather."

This was mind-boggling. Amos visiting Ellen! I couldn't imagine their having much in common—even less, having an affair. But, then, maybe my imagination was growing stultified in that department. After all, I found myself dwelling on women who had gone out of my life. Amos had never evinced any particular warmth toward Ellen before, but of course people change in tortuous internal ways and you never know how the respective changes will affect their mutual chemistry when they cross paths again. But I was thinking of myself and Greta and grafting the possibilities onto Amos and Ellen. And obviously jumping to conclusions. He was an unpredictable man—perhaps he had been taken with a sudden urge to see his goddaughter. Somehow, though, I didn't think it was as innocent as all that. I was intrigued, but I didn't want to badger Daphne with questions and put ideas into her head.

Still, I couldn't resist a couple. "I'm surprised," I said breezily, "that Uncle Amos didn't call me while he was up here. Was he very busy?"

"I guess," she replied, tuning her violin. "He and Mom were working on a project in her office—she calls the den her office now, you know."

"What kind of project?"

"I don't know. They worked on it a lot, though."

Worked on the couch was more like it, I thought, succumbing to a wave of jealousy. There I was, crestfallen, furious, jealous of my best friend and the mother of my child—a woman whom I hadn't thought of in years with the slightest romantic inclination. And in my mind's eye I could see her copulating wildly with Amos while Daphne was dispatched on discreet errands. Ellen could be sneaky—but Amos! I expected more from him. A little loyalty. Yet when I stepped back from this vulgar fantasy, all I could do was laugh. What was it to me what they did? I knew one thing, though: Ellen would not play Amos's games with him the way Margaret did. Ellen played by major-league rules.

So I had something new to think about.

"Okay, Dad," Daphne said, "I'm ready to play. Here, I brought two sets of the sheet music."

I sat down at the piano and glanced over them. "Who accompanied you while you were learning these?"

"Mrs. Matthews. Sometimes her assistant, Miss Ford. I told Mrs. Matthews I was going to play them with you. She's a fan of yours, but she said Mozart isn't your strong point."

"Is that so? I'm sorry to hear it." That clinched it: Mrs. Matthews would go.

"Let's start with the Sonata in G Major. Ready?" She poised her bow, tapped her foot, and nodded for me to start.

She played with a sweet touch, a shade tentatively at first, stealing glances at me until she fell into the music. She was indeed very good, better each time I heard her, with real style and expressiveness, and I wondered what I would say if she ever really decided to make a career of the violin. She was a perfectionist but she took great pleasure in her music, sensual pleasure, which I believe is essential. There have always been too many mechanics out there and not enough sensualists. She looked so pretty standing beside the piano, the city lights twinkling behind her through the big windows, her face glowing a soft honey color and her lips pursed.

Playing a duet can be a jousting match onstage, or sometimes a case of two drivers trying to negotiate the same vehicle, but when you do it privately with someone you love, it is a very intimate experience, all the interweaving of harmonies and the dynamic give and take. I found it soothing and I let my mind wander.

It wandered inevitably to the events of the night before, as it had all day, even during my sunny excursions with Daphne.

The police had called to inform me that the two students had recovered, the car had been found abandoned, and the punks had escaped. It was obvious they wouldn't be caught. There had been a small item in the *Globe*'s police blotter column detailing the incident and mentioning my name along with the victims'. Sarah, who read the paper religiously, and also, I imagine, had second thoughts about her harsh words, called to apologize, and even to praise my good citizenship. She seemed astonished that such a hermetic personality might be capable of any beneficent action. When she went on to call it "heroic," I nearly gagged, and suggested we forget the whole incident.

Even had it remotely applied to this situation, the role of hero was not one I yearned for in any capacity. No, that's not true: when I was very young, I wanted to be a heroic pianist, in the tradition of Liszt or Godowsky or Anton Rubinstein. A bravura demon who, like Liszt, would arrive at the concert hall in a coach drawn by twelve white horses, and depart supine on the shoulders of beautiful women. This was before I had beaten my own style into shape on the cold anvil of the live stage and in brutal competitions, where such fancies were rapidly dispelled. But good samaritanship was not my idea of a heroic pursuit.

Yet, perhaps it had been a useful lesson for me—with my rarefied, musical notions of the infernal—to stumble through an infernal realm in the concrete world. To watch those three wolves descend on their fellows so viciously for some loose change and a joyride, to see their predatory cunning firsthand, was instructive. Though Augustine tells us evil is no more than the diminution of good, and Aquinas that evil (in itself nonexistent) simply signifies the absence of good, and Chrysostum that evil is but a turning away from the good, I was convinced that if those gentlemen had found themselves at that dirty intersection, witnessing even such a relatively minor outrage, they would have recognized what we in this century of mass horror and fiendishness take for granted: that evil is an active thriving force in itself and not a pale counterpoint to theological goodness. That hell is here and now on terra firma, subdivided according to social, economic, and spiritual gradations, and when Dante arranged his vision he was not toying with allegory but drawing up a blueprint of everyday reality. For my father, as a boy in the tenements, the circle of violent crime was just a notch or two down the scale, easy to fall into. For me, considerably more insulated, it would have taken a longer and more self-willed fall. And Daphne was that much farther away. Evil, to me, was not some exotic brew on life's byways: it was the power behind the inevitable dividend one was issued for failure, poverty, and weakness. It was the trapdoor in the dark that awaited us all after we exhausted our quota of folly. One thing, at least, those early theologians had right: Lucifer was not a fellow easily bribed, and thus he derived his leverage. But history told me he was no longer a dandy in tails that fellows like me could conjure up for an evening's amusement by playing Liszt's *Faust*. He was everywhere and in everything.

Such were my mental diversions even while playing Mozart duets with my angelic daughter, her bright eyes intent and dreamy as she drew from her violin those long winding runs that always remind me of snowscapes and delicate ornate architecture (in whose very ornaments the wind makes its music) and black trees and rivers overlaid with ice, thin as lace. Mozart always struck me as a winter composer. And Daphne played him beautifully, rich and full-textured, with none of the careless impatience that is the pitfall of the student. She told me her best composers were Mozart and Vivaldi, and I wondered if this was because her mother and I met in Vienna and conceived her in Venice. Of course in my phenomenological wanderings I had long since come to believe that such things were not only probable, but generally more valid in terms of real life—the life of the heart and the spirit—than mere facts. Mere facts would have insisted that she was proficient at Vivaldi because her previous teacher Mrs. Notti had an abiding passion for him. But I knew better: I knew that the city that had inspired his music had on the day of Daphne's conception fully permeated the bloodlines and glands of her parents, that in fact Vivaldian electrical life-impulses—perhaps emanating from the silver fog that enveloped the city that day, especially the nearby church of San Salvatore, where his *Four Seasons* was performed that very night—were everywhere, and who is to say what generative effect they had on the momentary genetic network of a concert pianist (despite his viral anemia) and a beautiful and receptive woman who at that time (so she said) was intoxicated with music. I should have been surprised had Daphne *not* become enamored of Vivaldi! I watched her, small fingers and small serious face, ears and lips which were Ellen's and hands which were duplicates of my own, the fact of my fatherhood living and breathing before me, flesh of my flesh, sprung of my loins, playing music with me, which in some crazy symbiotic way was like playing both instruments myself. That I was this child's father still amazed me. Dr. Selzer, again, would have insisted this was not merely a case of biological wonder, but that my unresolved, still-childish portion, left fatherless early, had difficulty connecting with the emotional reality of its own fatherhood. Be that as it may, the fact that I, a male who had known many women, had produced from my body this girl who would become a woman, was truly a miraculous thing to me.

Daphne shared my musical pleasure, for reasons of her own. She grew more radiant as we played on. She told me she wished we could do this all the time.

A few hours later, Sarah phoned to apologize again. I think she was more sorry about making such a fool of herself than about her obvious bad faith. In truth, I hadn't given her much thought one way or the other. I wasn't even particularly sore at her, despite the fact her attempt to parade me before her academic bosses had been the catalyst of my misadventures. I was tired of the whole business. And not a little dumbfounded at how carelessly she had let her customary shrewdness slip.

"Well, I have a million other things to tell you about," she said blithely, and her voice softened. "But when am I going to see you? Everything's been so upside down."

I didn't know what to say. I was counting the days until I saw Greta, who was in Chicago just then. I winked at Daphne, on the couch in her pajamas, sipping a Coke and waiting patiently to listen to me practice.

"I'll give you a call. Daphne and I have been pretty busy, just settling in and all."

"Would you put her on? I'd like to say hello."

"She's in the tub just now," I said.

"Oh. All right. Max, I'm really sorry, let's just forget last night, okay? I wasn't myself, you know."

I almost smiled at that. "It's forgotten," I said, and wished her a hurried good night.

I sat down at the piano and opened up with the Brahms. It was faultless and flat. It never took off. It seemed the more I played, the flatter I got. My doubts loomed larger than ever.

Three days later, on the Fourth of July, Daphne and Sarah and I drove out to Revere Beach to watch the fireworks. It was the first time I had seen Sarah in nearly two weeks and she was upset about the way things were going. For good reason. She hadn't been back to the loft since the day she talked about moving in. Of course we had not gone to bed together in that time, and even she, not so sensitive as I in that department, was distressed. The more I had thought about her callousness the night of that Harvard party, the more it soured me. It confirmed all my earlier qualms. And her sweet talk and cleverness weren't going to change anything. I wanted to clear the air with her once and for all. To finish things. I couldn't just keep avoiding her. It was cruel. After the fireworks, she came home with us for supper. A cold supper, because the heat was ghastly, even with the air conditioners running full-tilt.

I had continued my marathon practice sessions without interruption. Aside from increasing technical strength, the results were the same. Daphne, as I had foreseen, was a stabilizing influence as well as a joy to have around. Cheerful and busy, she practiced the violin, wrote long letters, and painted watercolors on the roof. She made us sandwiches at midday, brewed tea at four o'clock, and was waiting to get dinner going with me (still by candlelight) when I knocked off in the evening. My wives and paramours had never treated me so royally. She had other recipes from Amos: chicken stuffed with pineapple, chili Madrid, lobster stew Trinidad. As a consequence, I heard some more about his "visits." Just bits and pieces: the llama rug he brought Ellen on her birthday; the time he arrived at midnight with a pilot from Iceland; the mohair sweater her housekeeper had knitted for him. That particularly galled me.

No one had ever knitted anything for me. At night Daphne and I went to the movies or took long drives. She loved riding in the Cadillac with the top down and the radio blaring. One night we heard chamber music at Symphony Hall and I took her backstage to meet the musicians. We had plenty of other activities planned.

But on that hot night, after the late meal, she was exhausted. I tucked her in and mixed myself a manhattan. Firecrackers were still sputtering in the street. An occasional Roman candle sailed over the rooftops and exploded in a cloud of rubies. The city was alive with patriots, all of them honking their horns. I found Sarah gazing out the window in my studio.

"Would you like a drink?" I said.

She shook her head. "I feel like a stranger here."

I wanted to be as gentle as possible, but I didn't know where to begin. "We should talk."

She shrugged and crossed the room. "I'd like to hear those tapes you were telling me about. How old did you say they were?"

"Busoni recorded the original discs in 1919. These tapes were made about ten years ago. I got them from a collector."

"Will you play them?"

I had an elaborate stereo system with speakers run into all the rooms. If you put on, say, a Mahler symphony and ran it through the whole system, it felt like the roof might take off. The first tape was the *Don Juan* Fantasy, one of Busoni's mainstays. Ornate and exquisite. It was strange to listen to a pianist who had been twenty when Liszt died, who had known Anton Rubinstein and Pachmann and played duets with Godowsky. I considered Busoni the first truly modern pianist, the thundering link between Liszt and Horowitz, a man who presented titanic programs night after night. At his farewell concerts, he performed twelve Mozart concertos. A wild man. The *Don Juan* was only a fragment, succeeded by the *Goldberg* Variations. His version was very different from Tureck's or Gould's—controlled, but with the oversustained tremolo and too-liquid arpeggios with which they flowered Bach in those days. Busoni's training, his instrument, his instincts were all a world removed from my own.

I could lose myself with those tapes, and I thought I had better have my talk with Sarah before it became too awkward. It was already too awkward. But she started the conversation for me.

"You know, Max, these fears you have about your playing . . ."

"What about them?"

"I listened from the kitchen before, when you played the Schubert. It sounded wonderful."

"It's not right," I snapped. "If you knew what I *expect* to hear, you wouldn't think it was so wonderful."

"Jesus, don't bite my head off."

"I'm sorry."

"You never used to talk to me like that. Nothing's been right since we went to New York."

"I'm sorry. I'm not a good democrat when it comes to my music. I know it sounds adequate, but it's not even close yet."

"Oh, stop being so melodramatic. You'd think this was your debut. You've been performing for—what?—seventeen years."

"Seventeen minus four."

"Bullshit. I was talking to Daddy about it when he called from Stockholm, and he—" She stopped short.

"You what?"

She was flustered and angry. But she had blown it this time.

"Damn it, you know you shouldn't be talking to anybody about this."

Predictably, she took the offensive. "Not even with my father?"

"Especially with your father or anyone else in the business. You think I want to broadcast this? All I need is for people to get wind of it . . ."

"Like who?" she said contemptuously.

"Like the record company executives negotiating with Willy. And some critics who would love to have my ass."

"Don't sound so persecuted."

"Don't you understand, this is business—business! You think these people care about art and gentility? If they knew I had *any* doubts, if they knew why I had stopped performing— Shit, what's the use. I don't care who you talk to."

"But my father is fond of you. He has great respect for you. Don't you think he might be able to help?"

"Your father barely knows me. This is something personal, not a problem in music scholarship. Just what did you tell him?"

"What you've been saying . . . about losing your edge, all of that. He said it's just a mental block. Happens all the time. He said perhaps the answer is to stabilize your life."

"What the hell does that mean? That maybe you should move in? And what else did you tell him about my personal life?"

"I was trying to help. How dare you—"

"Why don't you help yourself and cut down on the transatlantic calls to papa?"

This was too much for her. "You can go fuck yourself," she shouted. "I hope you get everything you deserve—in spades." She stormed into the kitchen to get her bag.

I waited for her in the foyer, holding the door open. She was furious. She looked right through me as she turned the corner and stalked out.

"Good-bye," I said, and locked the door after her.

I was glad she was gone. I switched the Busoni onto the bedroom speakers, stripped down, and sprawled out on the bed. It was a blessing to be alone. My heart was thumping. I turned off the lights and stared up into the darkness, letting the music wash over me, when I heard Daphne call out. First I thought I must have imagined it, for she wasn't the kind of kid who got scared of the dark or demanded a glass of water. Then she called me again. I put on my robe and rushed down the hall. Maybe the fireworks were disturbing her. I hoped she hadn't overheard my argument with Sarah.

I found her sitting up in bed in the dark. She wasn't crying, but her eyes were bright and troubled.

"What's the matter, baby? Was it a bad dream?"

"No. I couldn't sleep. I had to talk to you." She switched on the lamp.

I sat down. "What is it?"

She shook her head pensively.

I stroked her cheek. "Come on, Daphne, you and I have no secrets. What's wrong?"

"I wanted to know if you were in love with Sarah."

I sensed this was only the tip of the iceberg. "No, I'm not. She was—she's only a friend."

"So you wouldn't marry her?"

"No. What gave you that idea?"

She shrugged and rubbed her eyes.

"Not in a million years," I said. "Okay?"

She shrugged again. "You told me once why you and Mom didn't get married."

"Uh huh. Did you have other questions about that?"

"No. She explained it to me, too. But she said you and she still love each other. You know, in a different way, like friends."

"That's right."

"Well, I was thinking about Greta," she said slowly. "How come, since you're divorced and all, she's coming to the wedding with us?"

"It's kind of complicated."

"Is that why you told me not to mention it to Sarah?"

"I shouldn't have done that. It was wrong. But I didn't want to hurt her feelings."

"I still won't tell her."

"That's all right. Sarah won't be coming here anymore."

"How come?"

"I'm too busy, and she's busy, and we're just not getting along. We haven't been seeing each other much."

"Oh."

"As for Greta, I saw her recently after a long time. And it was very nice. We thought just maybe we had made some mistakes when we were divorced and we ought to talk things over and spend some time together now."

"Oh, I think you did make a mistake, Daddy," she said solemnly.

"It wouldn't be the first. But really things are up in the air now. I felt it would be good for the three of us to be together— Greta's dying to see you. The wedding seemed a nice way to do it."

"I can't wait to see her. I just didn't understand how you could love her and Sarah at the same time."

We were getting closer to the iceberg. "I couldn't. I wasn't in love with Sarah. In fact, you know there's only one girl I really love . . ."

"Me."

"More than anybody, ever." This, at least, I was sure of.

She was silent. Then her eyes clouded again. In a rush, she said, "You know, I said you weren't, and he said not to talk back, but Grandpa said you were a playboy."

"What?"

"He said it to Mom and I said it wasn't true and he got mad."

That Bircher SOB, poisoning me to my own kid. Playboy! He had his nerve, the hypocrite. Ellen once told me about the two Mexican enchiladas he kept stashed away in his beach house. "It's not true, Daphne."

"Mom told him he was wrong to say it."

"I'm glad." So Ellen had proclaimed me the greatest pianist in America, and had even defended me to her old man. I was shocked. But I was fishing at that moment in deeper waters, for the right thing to say. Daphne's own love-life, down the road, could be affected by this. I had to weigh my words and think of the future for once in terms of someone else.

"I suppose I've had a different kind of life than most people," I said, trying not to sound feeble. "I've taken some wrong turns. I imagine your friends have parents who have always been together."

"And who got married," she chimed in.

"Yes, that too. I know it's hard for you. My own parents split up. It's small consolation, but you must never forget that your mother and I loved each other very much when you were born. Lots of married people don't love each other and they just stay married and unhappy."

"And they have kids?"

"Some of them. But that doesn't make it any easier for you. Mom and I were very young when we met. We fell in love and we didn't stop to think things through. My marriages didn't work out for other reasons. Sometimes, Daphne, people who are lucky in one way are unlucky in another. I've always been lucky in my work, and I'm very lucky to have a daughter like you, but I haven't been lucky enough yet to find the right woman."

"I wish it had been Mom," she said softly.

"I wish it had been too, baby. But I wasn't right for her, either."

"And after her, I wish it had been Greta."

"I know." I took her hand. "But you must understand, a playboy is someone who just runs around, and thinks about himself, and never falls in love."

"You mean, he's just in it for the sex."

"Something like that." I cleared my throat. "That's not the way it should be. Without love, there isn't anything in life that's worth very much. Do you understand? Now, this is all between you and me, you let your grandfather think what he wants." And he'll get his one day, I thought. His ticker will give out in some cathouse.

"All right, Dad." She yawned. I gathered that had been the iceberg. She didn't like the notion of my being a playboy, whatever that conjured up in her head.

"Feel better?"

"Uh huh, I do."

I kissed her. "Now, don't you worry about this stuff anymore. Okay?"

"But will you tell me when you find the right woman?"

I kissed her again and tweaked her nose.

"Come on, Dad . . ." and she rolled her eyes in that funny way, like Ellen.

"Sure, you'll be the first to know."

"Okay." She switched off the lamp and pulled the sheet up to her chin. "Just don't be too picky."

Dr. Winters poured me another glass of red wine and ambled over to the enormous window behind his desk. He had a fine view of the river, the Statue of Liberty shining like a brilliant toy, the decrepit ferries chugging through the milky sunlight, and the gulls circling like stray confetti. I was impressed by the quiet dignity of his offices, the Eagle Institute comprising the whole of a well-kept brownstone on a sleepy street in that indeterminate neighborhood between the Battery and Tribeca. A glass tower in the next block cast a gigantic cool shadow over it at that hour, as if it were at the foot of a pyramid or a monolith. Two of Winters' "attendants" (nurses, for my money), serious young women in pale blue uniforms, were clearing the remains of our lunch from the conference table. The best curried lamb I had ever tasted, topped off by an almond mousse. The wine, too, was delicious, and I had already imbibed more than I should have. I was still surprised to find myself in that room at all. Winters was an utterly congenial and old-fashioned host. I was anticipating the pleasures of the brandy, coffee, and cigars that were apparently on the way.

I had not been able to hold out until the day of the wedding to see Greta. I had been thinking about her night and day. And with Sarah gone, there were no further obstacles to my pursuing her wholeheartedly. So, a day early, and with a clear conscience, I packed our bags and Daphne and I set out for New York at the crack of dawn. On a whim, I had called Winters and told him I would be in town and would like to take him up on his luncheon invitation. He was delighted. Daphne and Greta were at the zoo for the afternoon, and I was sipping my wine trying to guess what would happen next. We had engaged in nothing but small talk over the meal.

Winters seemed to know what he was about, though. My first impression, from our absurd encounter at Amos's farm, had been reinforced: he looked small and harmless. And kindly, as well. His moon-face beamed, pale and untroubled, around his washed-out eyes. Even in this imposing setting—for his office, oak-paneled and richly appointed, with its big soundproof windows and Indian carpets, encompassed the entire fifth floor—he struck me as a bookish, elusive sort. He was wearing his silk robe and a dotted bow tie again. And when, midway through lunch, he fed the fish in his aquarium—a tremendous tank built into the bookshelves—he put on white gloves first so as not to contaminate their pellets. That idiot Margaret, with her gangster fantasies, had misled me completely. It wasn't the only thing she had misled me about, as I was to learn the next day. And yet, I still didn't know exactly what the nature of Winters' profession was—his neurovisual harmonic phenomena—and I knew nothing about his "business" with Amos. I had assumed I would be enlightened on these points, but except for some very sketchy scraps he offered me, I was wrong.

From what I had seen riding the elevator to his office, peering out when it stopped on other floors, I guessed he had a staff of about twenty. A trim, busy, serious bunch. Each floor was marked with signs: Examination Rooms, Library, Laboratory, Audiovisual Room, Floatation Pool, Meditation Tanks. And there had been a good dozen people, all well-heeled, in the waiting room. A pretty slick operation, I concluded.

Hands clasped behind his back, Winters seemed to have resolved something while gazing out the window. He sat down and looked me straight in the eye.

"Mr. Randal, the poet William Blake wrote that 'every man's wisdom is peculiar to his own individuality.' "

Laying my wineglass aside, I tried to concentrate. Winters shifted gears quickly; the small talk was over.

"You don't mind my speaking frankly, I hope?"

"On the contrary."

"Good. Clearly, what Blake was repudiating was the notion of generalized wisdom—especially of the empirical sort. The kind of fly-by-night nirvana that our society peddles to its—shall we be kind?—to its less inquisitive members. The point is that there is no 'wisdom' per se. One puts together his life well or badly, uses his experience and talents fruitfully or squanders them— yes? And what is wise is simply what constitutes the most fertile avenue along which one pursues his dreams and desires, and even his fears. I see you agree. Good. Now, when we are truest to ourselves, when we are not lying to ourselves, we are most apt to find enlightenment, to fulfill our individuality. Most people can never even contemplate this because they never stop lying to themselves. But what is the nature of this enlightenment for those who are true to themselves: placidity, hallucination, fear-lessness? No. I would posit that it is a state of submergence to the furthest depths, of a deathless calm, of a realm of total communication with the living and the dead. The Zen masters claimed to aspire to the state of water: more powerful than any solid, and at the same time shapeless, soft, unconfinable, open."

He paused and I squirmed slightly. He took a small cassette machine out of his desk. He pressed a button and a wave of piano music rushed over me. I listened carefully, and then looked up with surprise.

"Of course you recognize it," Winters said with a smile, switching off the machine.

"That's me playing the Chopin Fantasy in F minor. But I never recorded that."

"Quite right. Beautiful, isn't it? I taped it myself seven years ago—surreptitiously—at Avery Fisher Hall. I hope you don't mind. Mr. Randal, I will get to the point. Amos Demeter told me about the problem you have been having at the piano. Have you solved it yet?"

I was beginning to wonder who *didn't* know about my problem, and didn't have a solution to offer. But it didn't bother me with Winters as it had with Lengford, because I trusted Amos. In fact, I was eager to hear what Winters was getting at, though I suspected I wasn't the first person to have received that speech about submergence. And deep down, I wasn't at all sure I wouldn't have been better off uptown at Willy's apartment, practicing, instead of playing the man of leisure, lunching and philosophizing.

"No, I haven't solved the problem yet," I said. "I'm not sure I'll even understand the nature of the solution when I do find it."

"I understand. That is exactly my point. You will need to pass through a dark night of the soul before you find your answer in the light. To touch your lowest low in the darkness before you can approach the heights again. That is true for all of us, and there is no way around it."

I looked at him.

"The last time I saw you, I asked if you believed in miracles. I had a reason for that. Now, forget your usual associations with the word 'miracle,' cheapened as it has been over the years. Forget, too, the primitive religious appropriation of the word. Miracles were with us long before Jehovah took the stage. The true meaning of a miracle is an act, usually of healing, that is *wondered at*, that floods the heart with wonder. The miracle has nothing to do with one's god, and everything to do with one's heart. Your heart, I would venture to say, is closed to the one source that will truly heal it. You may try a thousand makeshift cures, but so long as you do not open yourself to this source, none of them will be effective."

I waited, growing warier, but hopeful. "Yes?"

"The voices of the dead in your life. And those dead unknown to you with whom you have a spiritual affinity. For what are we in our essences but a composite of those voices?"

I let out my breath, disappointed. For an instant, sitting there comfortably warmed by food and drink, I had foolishly hoped this man would pass me a sage and ready answer, like a nugget of candy for my hungry soul.

"I know you have undergone analysis," he said. "Well, I assure you, you can leapfrog psychiatry, psychology, and all their permutations with my method."

He was finally getting down to the sales pitch, I thought glumly. "And what is your method, Dr. Winters? Are you talking about clairvoyance, or sciomancy?"

He pulled a sour face. "Mr. Randal, please, spare me such insults."

I shrugged. "Are you speaking metaphorically, then?" I was all for phenomenology—but in the world of the living, not the dead.

"I am speaking literally, I assure you. Through the proper external stimuli of light and sound, and after careful mental and emotional preparation, the subject begins to submerge, deeper and deeper, until he can commune with those voices—residing in the rarest layers of his own consciousness—and learn things that are normally inaccessible in this chaotic world. Blake also wrote that 'man has closed himself up, till he sees all things through narrow chinks of his cavern.' "

"So it *is* like a séance, but with an electronic medium."

Winters looked truly hurt. "No, I am sorry, but I can see you are not taking my words seriously, as your friend Mr. Demeter did. *He* has used my method."

I had grown impatient suddenly. "Yes, and now he's off dashing around Europe. I don't have time for that sort of solution, Doctor."

He shook his head sadly and pushed his chair back. For the first time, he took his eyes off mine.

"Where is he now, anyway?" I asked, relieved at the digression. "Have you heard from him?"

"Since you were polite enough not to inquire until I mentioned his name, I will tell you that he is at this moment in Skopje, Yugoslavia. He has completed his business in Ireland—with great success," he added thickly.

"Oh? Can you tell me now what his business was?"

"I am afraid not. Not because I take pleasure in withholding this information from you, but as I told you in Lenox, it is his wish."

"Sorry, I forgot. And he's in Skopje on your behalf—medical research, you said."

"Yes."

"That's in the south, near Albania, isn't it?"

"That's correct. How did you know?"

"I once visited Dubrovnik when I was on tour."

"Getting back to you, Mr. Randal. I had hoped to be able to help you, but I do not think it is possible."

"Well, why don't you tell me more about it—what exactly do you mean by these 'voices'?"

"What would be the use? Mr. Demeter warned me that you would not be receptive, and he was correct. He knows you well. He came up with his own idea to help you. He discovered it while taking my treatment, I might add. Possibly, it will work. I hope so, for your sake and his. But, enough—I have already said too much."

He stood up. It appeared that our interview was concluded.

"I had hoped to show you around," he said with dismay. "But perhaps some other time our work here will be of more interest to you."

I nearly asked him to show me around anyway, for I was curious to see his modus operandi. But it didn't seem right. Amos would have been disappointed in me, I thought guiltily. And I was sorry about that. We rode down in the elevator and Winters saw me out very graciously. I glimpsed Emma, his chauffeur and major domo, down a corridor in a laboratory smock. When Winters appeared, the clients in the waiting room stood up briskly, smiling, and offered their greetings. He was their deity, apparently. Perhaps, I thought, I had been too hasty—what the hell did I know about his "method"? And one treatment might have been interesting, in the way of a visit to a mind reader or a palmist. But what of it? I had other things to worry about, and I was itching to see Greta.

We crossed the George Washington Bridge with the sun pouring down on us, hair flying, merrily on our way to cousin Jeannie's wedding. It was a fine day to get married, not too hot, the sky brilliant, and even the poor abused Hudson River, which I well knew was pea-green up close, was sparkling and opalescent. I'd had the car washed and waxed, so it shone like a mirror, and Daphne (in white) and Greta (in pink pastel) both looked beautiful. Outfitted gaily in a white suit and splashy yellow tie, a yellow rose stuck in my lapel, I was very proud of my little ensemble. Greta was especially irresistible that day, her blond mane shot through with gold, her lovely legs crossed beside me, eyes mirthful and spirits bubbly, and if Daphne had not been leaning on the back of my seat, her head between us, I don't know how I would have refrained from attacking Greta right there. Thanks to my overcautiousness, we still hadn't had a moment to ourselves to talk, much less go to bed.

I had checked into the Plaza the moment I reached New York, despite the fact that Greta had invited us to stay at her place. I was sorely tempted, but then decided we had to talk things over carefully before taking such a momentous step. Staying there, in my old digs, with Daphne in town, seemed like the point of no return. I knew Greta didn't intend it as such. She was merely being congenial and openhearted and following her instincts. But I didn't trust my instincts, so I hemmed and hawed about having to be in midtown to practice at Willy's, to do business, et cetera. Hoping we could talk at her place later on (and, with a little luck, make love), I hadn't counted on the fact Daphne would be exhausted after the car trip, the zoo, and a night on the town. So after dinner, Greta went home and I returned to the hotel, cursing myself, having spent more time that day with Dr. Winters than with her.

But this was a new day. Greta was excited about the wedding, and she and Daphne were happier than larks to be together again. They really did get on wonderfully, and they'd had a ball the day before. It was because of Greta's generosity and good taste that Daphne had her lovely white dress. Stopping by the Plaza after leaving the zoo, while I was still downtown, Greta had asked Daphne to show her the dress she was wearing to the wedding. I had picked it out of her closet in Boston, without much care, I confess, so absorbed was I in rushing out of town as early as possible. One look at it and she took Daphne by the hand, marched down Fifth Avenue to Bergdorf's, and bought her this new dress, with little shoes and gloves to match. I was warmed to the bones by this sort of kindness, and not accustomed to it anymore.

At dinner, after expressing my admiration for the outfit, I had reached for my wallet and asked Greta how much it cost.

She was deeply offended. "Don't be absurd, Max. It was *my* present to Daphne. Anyway, it's all in the family."

This first mention of "family" by Greta was to set the tone for many such remarks at the wedding. In addition to its being a family affair, celebrating to the hilt the virtues of an institution that Uncle Louie so venerated, there I was, usually fast and footloose, arriving in my Cadillac with my blond daughter and my blond ex-wife (whom everyone assumed—and why shouldn't they?—was my current wife), looking affluent, comfortable, and gay, astonishing Louie himself most of all with my sudden emergence as an exemplar of the nuclear family. The very first lady I was introduced to outside the church, the groom's mother, glanced admiringly at Greta and Daphne off to one side, and said, "Your little girl looks exactly like her mother. You're a lucky man." Of course I concurred and threw a paternal smile in their direction. This was new terrain for me.

Uncle Louie, though not a religious man as far as I knew, nominally belonged to the Greek Orthodox Church. He had sent his kids there to Sunday school, and regularly donated large sums of money. My grandfather the Welshman was a genial agnostic and allowed my grandmother to raise her sons, including my father, as she saw fit. But Louie was the only one who kept up his church affiliation after age fifteen. So despite the fact the groom was a Christian Scientist, the wedding was held at an Orthodox church, to Daphne's amazement and pleasure, for she was intrigued by the ikons and gold leaf and stained glass, and the intoxicating smoke of the censers. Louis spotted us at once and greeted us warmly as we crossed the neat suburban street to join the crowd in front of the church.

It was going to be a huge wedding, over two hundred people, and Louie was in fine fettle, bursting with pride, greeting people effusively, bussing women, everywhere at once in his smart tails with an enormous white cravat. Louie was a bigger man than my father, bigger than me, about six-two, stout now, never athletic, always the studious one in a household of bruisers, but imposing in his own way. He had a crazy foxy twinkle in his gray eyes, thick black hair combed straight back, bristling mustache, big cow ears and a wide mouth that could, and usually did, accommodate a large cigar and a telephone receiver without effort. After a double-handshake, he bear-hugged me, kissed Greta, whom I know he didn't recognize at first, and then mauled Daphne with kisses, all before we had a chance to catch our breath.

"You made my day, Max, coming like this. And look at you—spiffy as always, like your old man. Here, stick this in your lapel—it's for members of the family," and he plucked out my yellow rose and replaced it with a white carnation. "And you brought your family, you son-of-a-gun lone wolf. Look at this little cupcake—I could eat her alive."

"Congratulations, Uncle Louie, on Jeannie's wedding," Daphne piped up sweetly, and made him a little curtsy. I nearly died, and Louie was overwhelmed.

"Congratulations, Uncle Louie!" he echoed, and mauled her cheeks again. "You little doll, you watch it or your Uncle Louie's going to kidnap you and never let you go. Where did you get a kid like this, Max? A guy like you, you don't deserve it."

"And, Louie, you know my ex-wife, Greta. You met before."

"Of course we did. Thank you so much for coming, Greta. You look lovely. Come on, Shirley's right over here. She's been dying to see you."

And as he led us through the crowd, he pulled me close by the nape of the neck. "What is this 'ex-wife' stuff? Are you a sap? Is *that* the girl you divorced a few years back?"

"That's the one. We're seeing each other again, Louie. You know, on and off—"

"On and off? I'd grab her back if I were you. What a jewel! Stop wasting your time with floozies. Ah, what's the use, you don't listen to me. But, Jesus, it's good to see your goddamn face. You look fine, Max, just fine."

Shirley was a quiet, plump woman, a suburban matron who had watched over Louie and kept him in line since the early days when they had to struggle. The rest of his family, two teenage daughters and his fourteen-year-old son, and assorted in-laws, were milling around her, so we met everyone at once. The bride was still at home with her maid of honor, and the guests were killing time in the sunshine, talking business and pleasure. Louie went off to greet a group of men who arrived as one in a fleet of Lincolns, like a funeral cortege—clients, he said—obviously mob guys, and Greta and I were left with my young cousins, the girls fussing over Daphne and introducing me to family friends. Nice people, curious about me, it seemed, because of Louie's boasting, including three ladies from Shirley's reading group who asked for autographs.

And I realized that to Louie's family—like my father before me—I had assumed the position of family celebrity, an oddball who had made it big in a glamour profession. For to these people who worked hard in business and family, who piled up annuities and acquired luxuries one at a time, who took an enormous pride in their sheer steadiness of course along the expensive highway of life, what I did and what my father had done must have seemed unreal and exotic. Sports and entertainment, after all, were their great diversions, even if my sort of entertainment was a bit rarefied. And though most of them, including Louie, would have been horrified to hear their progeny express interest in a career as a boxer or pianist, they nonetheless, as outsiders, admired success in these pursuits. Actually, I was the outsider, and it was brought home to me palpably that day that if my father hadn't stepped off the well-trodden path many years before, tried for the brass ring in one of the all-or-nothing fields and beaten the odds to grab it, it would not have been so easy for me to keep off that path. Not just socially and financially, but emotionally. Perhaps I felt as guilty about this as I was grateful.

Jeannie looked pretty, and slightly bemused, in her elaborate lace gown, so long that three little girls carried the train. Louie, beaming ear to ear, walked her down the aisle, and she winked at me as they passed. As the vows were exchanged and the priest juggled the nuptial crowns, Greta squeezed my hand. We were seated in front, and Uncle Ray's widow Francine and her two kids were beside me, not nearly so well-dressed as Louie's family, and my heart went out to them. They wore that look that said "poorer relatives." They didn't recognize me at first, and they had never met Daphne, to my embarrassment.

Afterward, I followed the procession of limos, everyone blasting their horns, back to Louie's house for the giant reception. Daphne was propped up on the backseat. I ran my hand up Greta's dress, up along her thigh and back several times until I slid it up a little too far and she frowned and pinched my wrist. She felt as luscious as she looked, and I was dying for her, hoping we could slip away to one of the bedrooms and grab a few golden minutes together. Greta had filled out slightly since her modeling days, and I thought she looked better for it. When we first married, she was quite thin, and always offered the same explanation when I complained: that all models photograph ten to twelve pounds heavier, so she had to stay down to compensate. "The camera fattens you like grain fattens the goose," she liked to say. I didn't buy this, for even when she stopped modeling she was loath to put on weight. Now, working at home, her time her own, and turning thirty on her last birthday, nature had done the work for her and she looked terrific. Not zaftig by any means, still slender, but with her curves rounded and plentiful.

Louie had spared no expense for the reception. His imposing white ranch house lay nestled in the rolling hills west of the Palisades. The large lawn and the flower gardens were especially manicured for the occasion. The oval swimming pool glistened like a gem. There was an eight-piece band in blue tuxedoes on the terrace, tables adorned with orchids spread around the lawn, a gargantuan buffet, two bars, waiters patroling with trays of champagne, the works. Greta and I were seated at the head table, and Daphne at a table with all the kids. The first thing I did was get a double-bourbon to fortify myself. Greta, with her usual talent for such things, had discovered the one eccentric in this suburban crowd, a young woman, a zoologist, who had just returned from four months in Tierra del Fuego, and was deep in conversation beside the swimming pool. Daphne was on the swings. I was about to make a leisurely reconnaissance of Louie's property when I was accosted by a large man in a charcoal suit, about sixty, with an unlined stone face, black eyes, and a gold cigarette holder. It was one of the mob guys. He walked straight up to me and extended his hand.

"I knew your father well," he said by way of greeting. "In the old days. My name is Frank Lancio."

"I'm happy to meet you."

"Chivas with a splash," he said over my shoulder to the barman. "You probably don't remember," he continued, his eyes locking on mine, "but you and he and I went to a ballgame together years ago. At Yankee Stadium. You must have been five, six years old."

I remembered many such ballgame outings in those years, but I didn't remember this man. "Sure," I said, "I remember."

"He and I used to go to the track a lot. He was quite a guy. Always did everything his own way." He tinkled his ice around and inhaled the aroma of the scotch. "Louie tells me you've done real well. He says that—"

But I was never to know what it was he had said for at that moment Louie himself interrupted the band's rendition of "I'm Crazy About You," took over the mike, and bellowed for everyone's attention.

"My good friends, please give me your ears for a moment. Before we start the festivities—and let's hope they go well into the night!—would you all come around to the front of the house. Thank you very much."

Daphne ran over to me and, along with Frank Lancio, we

joined the exodus filing around to the carport at the head of Louie's driveway. Louie was standing in front of the garage with Shirley. He was grinning, hands in pockets, waiting for the assemblage to settle down.

"Jeannie and Mark, come up here," he boomed, and I swore he was even louder without the microphone. The bride and groom joined him, and Louie kissed them both. They were twenty-two and they looked like kids to me; yet when I had married Orana at twenty-one I felt I had a good deal of life behind me.

"I'm not one for speeches," Louie thundered, and there was laughter. Even Frank Lancio grunted his amusement. "Let me just say that there is no holier state than matrimony, except maybe motherhood—and we can expect a little of that in the next few years, eh, Jeannie?"

More laughs.

"But just to get you rolling in your first few years, Shirley and I thought this little surprise might help. So good luck and lots of love to both of you—two great kids."

With that, he pulled a gadget from his pocket, pushed a button, the garage door rumbled up, and a gleaming white Eldorado, a young man in a white jumpsuit behind the wheel, glided out to a collective gasp. There was a bouquet of roses on the roof and a "Just Married" banner across the trunk. Jeannie started crying and kissed Louie, and his son-in-law caressed the hood and looked bewildered.

"It's nice," Daphne chirped admiringly, "but when I get married, Dad, I want you to give me your car."

"It's a deal."

"Sweet kid," Frank Lancio said, pinching her cheek. And before we trekked back around the house, he gripped my shoulder firmly and leaned close. "Your father was a man who never asked for anything, but he was always generous. He did me a great favor at one time. If there's anything—anything—I can ever do for you, you let me know. You understand?"

He meant it, too. "I'll remember that," I said.

"What did he mean, Dad?" Daphne inquired, wide-eyed, after he had left us.

"Just what he said, I guess."

"Why didn't you ask him for a million dollars?"

"What do I need with a million dollars?"

"Mom said you love to spend money. She told me I should always get only what I need—but that some people need more than others."

"That's for sure. Daphne, do you like the other kids here?"

"Oh sure, they're nice kids."

"And you don't mind sitting apart from me?"

"Dad," she said, rolling her eyes, "you've got to cut out this baby stuff."

"I'll try. Go on now."

I got another bourbon and spotted Greta on a stone bench in the garden, still holding forth with the zoologist from Tierra del Fuego.

"Max, I'd like you to meet Miss Strom."

Miss Strom looked like a tough cookie. Very butch. "A pleasure," she said coolly.

"Nice to meet you." I took Greta's hand and hurried across the lawn. I saw Louie in our path, so I veered off to the left and up the back steps. We went through the kitchen, where four cooks were at work, and then on to the second floor.

"What is it?" Greta asked. "Is Daphne ill—"

"I'll explain in a minute."

I opened the various bedroom doors: Henry's wouldn't do, he was liable to barge in; then there was the master bedroom—no good; the younger girls'; and last was Jeannie's room. There was a large picture of Mark, the groom, on the bureau. Perfect, I thought, and hustling Greta in first, I locked the door and pulled her onto the bed on top of me.

"Max, you're a devil. *This* is why you dragged me here? It's not right—this is Jeannie's room."

"Don't worry—she's married now."

It was heavenly, even better than our escapade in the jacuzzi. I couldn't imagine what worlds we would conquer when we actually had a bed to ourselves for an entire night, no party surrounding us, and no time limit. I had to take my pants down halfway and lift her dress carefully, and it had been many moons since I had employed that technique, not a garment removed and barely a ripple on the bedcovers. Greta, the daughter of a country baker in Denmark, one of nine happy and closely knit children, descendant of potato farmers and fjord fishermen, sprung of the Arctic winter, had enough fire in her veins for a dozen such as me and more expertise than the Attic priestesses who devoted their lives to the cause. I was lying on my back, expired, ruminating, as she toyed with my ear, the band playing a tacky rendition of "This Is the Night," and I decided it wasn't just a matter of fire and technique, it was the passion Greta kept kindled in her heart—something Sarah had sorely lacked. I loved Greta for that, and feared that in my heart of hearts I might resemble Sarah—a devastating notion. Greta overflowed with love and vigor. That I had missed the boat with her once was suddenly an indictment against me in my own eyes. I wanted to tell her how much I loved her. But at that moment she stood up. There was someone in the hall.

"Max," she whispered, zipping up my fly, "we had better go down now. We have lots of time later. Tonight . . ."

Tonight, indeed, I thought, and we sneaked downstairs like a pair of felons.

"Poor Miss Strom," she murmured as we took our seats. "The way we just left her there."

"I think she had the hots for you."

"Your mind is in the gutter, Max. People who live in greenhouses should not throw stones."

"Glass houses."

"Same thing."

The meal arrived in waves, platter after platter, and the champagne flowed heavily. After the cake and ice cream and the endless toasts, each blearier than the last, people started to dance and some of the gayer blades threw one another into the pool. The musicians drank their fill too and their tempo grew sassier. Louie danced a few numbers with Greta; I danced with Jeannie, her mother, and sisters. And after a while, as the afternoon shadows deepened across the blue lawn, and the laughter grew more raucous, I found myself marching into the house with my arm around Louie, each of us clutching a bottle of Taittinger's. He led me into his study and closed the door with no small measure of relief.

"Jesus, I need a breather. Sit down, Max, get comfortable. You want a glass?"

"The bottle's fine."

There were two enormous leather couches and we each had one to ourselves. He loosened his cravat and rested his feet on the coffee table. I took a swig of champagne and lit a cigar. His eyes brightened.

"You got another of those stinkers? The doctor told me to lay off 'em, and Shirley watches me like a hawk, but what the hell, it's a special occasion."

I lit it for him and he drew in the smoke lovingly. Then he sipped some champagne and looked hard at me.

"Don't worry," he said suddenly, "I'm not going to get maudlin on you. You know me better than that."

I was sure he would, as soon as he said that.

"Quite a day, huh?"

"It was a fine wedding, Louie. Jeannie's a terrific kid."

"Sure, they're all terrific kids. And as long as I've got it to give to them, I'm going to give it. That car—shit, Shirley and I saved up two years to buy our first car—in installments. What the hell."

I knew he was tighter than usual because he was never one for Horatio Alger routines.

"Ah, you know, here my firstborn got married and not one of my brothers lived to see it. All gone. Your father . . . I'm glad you came, Max. You're the only real link I have to all of that. Francine, her daughters—what a fuckin' mess. Ray was a jerk, may he rest in peace. But I've taken care for them. If I kick off tomorrow, they'll be all right." He grinned. "You know, that Greta of yours, what a doll. I got to tell you—you're my nephew, after all—but when I was dancing with her, the old heart was pumping, the hormones were flying. Christ," he howled, "I didn't know I even had hormones anymore."

I took another sip and we laughed.

"And look at you. You know we're all proud as hell of you. When I was growing up, that lousy three rooms we had—who the hell could have imagined a concert pianist, an international talent, would come out of that. Not your old man certainly. Jesus, he had a voice like a goat, he couldn't carry a tune." He grunted. "I wouldn't have any of this if it weren't for your father."

"You would have done fine under any circumstances, Louie."

"You think so? I don't. I didn't have to wash dishes or wait tables at night. My bills were paid. With your father, people remember the good days, the cars and the trips and the broads and those handmade shoes he was so fond of. Hell, did you know that for a while, before he turned pro, Ray and I were his cornermen? What a joke. Ray thought he was tough, but he didn't know anything about the fight game. And me—the whole business terrified me. I took my mother to Jackie's first fight and the two of us got sick. After that, she'd only listen on the radio. I remember seeing him piss blood a few times—I mean, bright red—and puking half the night. And the cuts, the bruises bigger than grapefruits, the swollen joints." His eyes were glassy. "Here I said I wouldn't get maudlin on you, and I'm talking crazy. What the hell's the matter with me?" He looked down. "You know, Ray and Tommy always had disaster written all over them. No surprises there. But your father, he was something else. I thought he would live forever. I'll never forget when that lawyer of his called me up. That son of a bitch. He said, 'Mr. Randal, I regret to tell you your brother was killed yesterday. I'll need your permission to bring his body back from France.' Just like that. No condolences, nothing. Lawyers are pricks, Max. I know—believe me, I know. Something went dead in me that night. All those years, all the knocks, the breaks. And then a couple of drunks run him off some shitty road. Why were those bastards there? Why does anything like that ever happen? You know, the drunks lived. And the broad who was with him lived. That's the kind of shit life hands us when we least expect it." He flicked his cigar ash. "Just listen to me—and on my daughter's wedding day. Why the hell am I dumping all this on you? Let's have a drink to forget."

We clinked bottles.

"I'm sorry, Max. I'm turning into an old woman."

"Don't be ridiculous."

"For years, all I could think about was making dough, building my practice, making, making—for what? The priest, who chases me for donations? It's expensive to be respectable. And what the hell does it get you? They laugh at you behind your back." He sat back heavily. "I envy you. Your best years, you've been able to enjoy them. I know you work your ass off, but you didn't forget how to squeeze the wine from the fucking grape. How to live! This life doesn't have to be a goddamn jungle. The bastards I deal with every day—that's how they live. It can be a paradise. But suddenly you're too old to enjoy it. Ah, fuck 'em all. You got a light?"

I relit his cigar. He was high, and he was maudlin, but I was touched that he could unload himself to me. He was a man who kept a tight lid on his feelings. Opening up was a sin, not a virtue. I didn't really know how to reply. There was something, though, I had always wanted to ask him.

"Louie, maybe you can fill me in on something."

"Shoot."

"It's about my mother. I don't know much about her early days with my father, when they first met, all of that. I was around later for all the rough stuff. What was she like back then?"

"Your mother?" He let out a long breath. This was one out of right field, as Greta would say. "We never got along well, Lynn and I, but you know, I liked her. I was wary at first—your father was on top, and always a little crazy where women were concerned. And one day he calls up out of nowhere and says, 'I'm in Key West and I just got married. Say hello to my wife.' Just like that. She was no simple case herself. From a good family in Frisco, with dough. Educated. Sort of a kook. And she marries a prizefighter from New York. Now, if *I* was surprised when they called me, imagine her folks out on the coast. Must have been a scream for them." He grunted. "So I wasn't sure what she was after. His dough, the limelight, whatever. But, after I met her a few times, I came to like her. I realized she wasn't after anything. And they were crazy in love, the two of them. They used to do wild things. Parties, trips, they'd show up at your door in a limo at five a.m. with a box of lobsters from the Stork Club, or a magnum of this stuff. Shirley and I had two rooms in Queens, and for us they were living a dream. This was before you and Stella came along, of course. Your mother and I, I guess we always had our guards up—we were such different types. I was rough as granite, and she was doing her best to polish up your father like marble. But it was the women screwed things up. He was my brother, and I loved him more than I love anybody outside my wife and kids, but I have to tell you, he brought it on. He was a bastard to her with the women. It was his Achilles' heel. He was the sweetest guy in the world, but he wasn't made for marriage. He needed other women—I don't know what he got from them. It wasn't just the sex; it never is with guys like that. The attention, the novelty, the sense of conquest—how the hell should I know? I've been with the same woman for thirty-seven years and I never cheated on her. Don't tell anybody, though. I'm a workhorse, a family stiff, not a stud. Anyway, I think your mother could have put up with other things. Money problems, or drink, or the emptiness that can kill an athlete when he's through. She could have helped him through any of that, but he didn't have those problems, and when she got wise to his two-timing, she turned sour. That's when she got mean and a little nuts. You know, he would have let you think he was leaving her because of that meanness, but it was his two-timing came first. That was the root of it all. She became another person. I did like her and I'm sorry I never told her so. She turned on me, too, 'cause I was close to him, so I never really had the chance. But you can always make the chance. You gotta tell people certain things before they're gone. Poof, they're gone just like that, Max."

His cigar was out again and he leaned over for another light. "That's the truth, anyway," he said, his eyes big and still glassy, peering at me through a cloud of smoke. "Is that what you wanted to know?"

I nodded and toyed with the lip of the champagne bottle.

"Now, I know you and Lynn had your run-ins when she was bringing you up alone. Your career meant everything to her, and that must have been tough on you. But I know she loved you kids. Of course you can't remember her the way she was in the early days. All the blame shouldn't be laid at her door—and you know I'm the last guy to put the knife in your father."

"I know that. No, you filled in a few blanks. I've seen pictures and heard stories, but I was curious about how they were at the very beginning."

"You know they met on a train? Your father was in a high-stakes poker game, and this girl stumbled into the car by mistake and asked if she could watch. Daffy sort of girl. Within an hour, with her sitting behind him, he wins nine hands out of twelve. And he turns to her, cool as ice, and says, 'You must be the girl I'm going to marry.' " Louie chortled. "I always thought it was too good a story—maybe the two of them just made it up. Maybe they met in the waiting room in Philadelphia, who the hell knows."

Daphne was asleep on the backseat when we crossed the bridge back into the city. Greta had danced her fill and Daphne had run herself out with the other kids. I had drunk four cups of black coffee before we said our goodbyes, and my head was pounding. And now we were expected at Willy's at nine for a dinner party, the last thing we needed. I was tempted to cancel, but Greta insisted we go. Daphne could rest in one of the bedrooms, and we would all have a fine time.

"I forgot to ask you last night," Greta said, applying some lipstick, "but how was your visit to that fellow Winters?"

"Disappointing. I think he's a quack."

"Too bad. I'm surprised Amos didn't know better."

"Why? Amos is crazy."

"But he's smart too. He does crazy things, but there's always a reason for it." This was true, but it nagged at me that Amos had fallen for that stuff about voices of the dead. I had always associated him with Pan, the god of mad music, not Anubis, the tour guide of death. I could accept some of Winters' ideas, the business about wisdom and submergence, and the dark night of the soul, of suffering as a necessary prerequisite for joy and renewal. But, all things considered, and despite my faith in Amos, I thought Winters was a charlatan, albeit a highly refined one. His sales pitch had made me wary.

"Look," I said, "I don't even know what Amos is doing. He's

running around Yugoslavia, and then he's going to Hungary. He wouldn't even tell Margaret where he was going, or why."

"Why should he?" Greta huffed. "Don't you know what's going on with them?"

"What do you mean?" I had told Greta only that Amos was involved in a scheme with Winters. Nothing about my excursion to the farm, Margaret's hysteria, or even that I had met Winters there. That day in the jacuzzi I had had better things on my mind.

"They are both fooling around, having affairs with other people. It's no secret."

I was shocked. It was no secret, but of course I didn't know about it. "With whom?" I said, as if I hadn't already guessed in Amos's case.

"With him, some woman from out of town. I don't know who she is. With Margaret, it's a furrier. He's fat and rich. Stupid, too."

"So if they're estranged, why the hell was she so excited when Amos ran off?"

"Was she?"

"She sure acted like it." I glanced back to make sure Daphne was still asleep, then lowered my voice. "Look, I think the woman he's having an affair with is Ellen, her mother."

Greta's blue eyes widened into saucers. I told her about my dismal visit to the farm at Margaret's urging.

She listened carefully, then clapped her hands. "What a serpent," she whispered. "Don't you see, Max? She knows about him and Ellen. She probably thought Ellen was the woman who hung up on her. And that Winters was one of Amos's buddies, covering for him. So she lied to you. She pretended to be worried and she sent you up there to find Amos with Ellen—to poison things between you and the two of them."

This was dizzying. "Just for kicks?"

"No, no, there must be an ulterior motive. Wait! I've got it. Maybe she thought you would be so angry upon finding them together that if she called you as a witness against Amos you would gladly testify."

"Margaret wants a divorce?"

[*162*]

"Yes, of course. And you see, if she nabs him for adultery, she'll get everything. The farm, what money he has."

This was all too devious for me, but Greta had it figured out in a minute. "But I don't care what Ellen does," I said, forcing myself to whisper. "Why should I screw my best friend?"

She eyed me slyly. "Now, weren't you angry when you heard about him and Ellen? Just the slightest bit miffed? Come on, the truth."

"I still wouldn't screw him."

"Yes, but if you did stumble on them and she subpoenaed you, you would have to testify, like it or not."

"But that's insane, to go to all that trouble. It's so complicated."

She shrugged. "What trouble? What did Margaret have to do, after all? She got wind of his going to the farm, she suspected his mistress would be there, and with a good cow-and-bull story she sent you up as her errand boy. What did she have to lose?"

She had a point there, though I winced at being described as an errand boy. And I was too deflated to tell her it was "cock-and-bull."

"Don't you understand, Max," she concluded, "that is why Margaret behaved so oddly when you ran into her at my party. She was never really worried about Amos in the first place, she was just setting a trap. And that was why Winters was so indignant at the farm. He was as confused as you were."

"Sure, he was the other fall guy," I said listlessly. "She's sick, they're all sick."

"Yes, she certainly turned out to be a real snake," Greta said energetically, sweeping some imaginary dust off her lap. "So what are you going to do?"

"Do? Nothing. I'm too busy to waste another minute on all this nonsense. Let them destroy each other like scorpions, what do I care?"

We were the last of Willy's guests to arrive. He greeted us at the door, and though he wasn't the mauling type like Louie, he gave Daphne her second red-carpet welcome of the day. He was cordial to Greta, but when she and Daphne went into the living room he took me aside.

"I didn't want to ask you on the telephone," he said, "and it is none of my business, but what has happened to Sarah?"

"She's in Boston."

"I can see that."

"We're through, Willy. Didn't work out."

"I'm sorry."

"Don't be. I haven't felt so happy in years as I have lately, with Greta. She's got a real heart, and I never appreciated it before."

"I hope you're right, Max," he said doubtfully, pulling at his mustache. "I never know what you're thinking."

"Stop worrying." I clapped his shoulder.

Greta came back out. "Excuse me, Max, I must talk to you. I'm sorry, Willy."

"Use my study, dear," he said, "but don't be too long."

She took my hand and led me down the hall.

"I didn't want to ask you in front of Daphne, but you will be coming to the loft tonight, won't you? It would be foolish for you to stay at the hotel again."

This time I didn't hesitate. "Of course I will. I'll check out of the hotel on the way downtown."

"Good."

"I was hoping you'd ask again."

She shrugged. "I never know what you're thinking."

It seemed nobody did. Including me, for I had intended to stay at the Plaza until we had our big talk. Talk seemed superfluous now.

"You go on ahead," I said, kissing her. "I just need to clear my head for a minute."

I sat down heavily. I had a dull headache. I combed my hair and savored Willy's marvelous view of the park, the trees thick and neat as puffs of black velvet, the lights topaz-colored, the sky violet, and the buildings across the park, the great stage set of Central Park West glittering like one of Marco Polo's mysterious fortresses on the road to Cathay. I glanced around his study, and nothing had changed. There was my photograph, hung in its customary spot with my medals framed below it. My face at twenty, serious and concentrated, looked a shade younger than it had the last time I had been in that room. I smiled at the lack of humor in my expression: I took myself without any grains of salt in those days. And though that photograph had been my standard publicity shot until I was twenty-five, and I had seen it a thousand times, I could never remember when or where it had been taken. I tried, by reading the eyes and the turn of the lips, to imagine what I might have been thinking at the moment the shutter caught me. Did I know that one day I would have a daughter named Daphne? Did I have an inkling of how I would feel the night my mother died? Could I have known that on this July night thirteen years later I would be staring dumbly at the image the camera was capturing? What was percolating behind all that seriousness? Probably I was thinking of whatever girl I was going to see that night. Orana once told me that all our actions and words, our mistakes and misdeeds and our luck, everything that happens to us is pregnant within us from the first and merely unfolds a second or two ahead of our awareness—as if all of our lives are, so to speak, after the fact. Certainly it is a proposition that cannot be disproved. But was there the acknowledgment in my eyes at that moment that they would one day be gazing back at me, back at themselves—for, however remotely, there is always that fractional self-awareness. To me, it is the essence of the photographic portrait, built in on a dizzying scale, something like a two-dimensional mirror trick.

I adjusted my tie, smoothed out my jacket, and walked out to the party.

It was quite a switch after the wedding bash. Willy's apartment, with its paintings, wood sculptures, and exotic plants, was like a little gallery. There was a fine Matisse hung at the end of the hallway, which I always paused to admire: a woman in blue hovering behind a bowl of floating irises. And his guests couldn't have been more different than Louie's—though there were a few fellows who were simply Frank Lancio with French tailoring and season boxes at the Met. It was the usual cross of literati and glitterati that I suppose Willy found amusing. He got me a bourbon (inquiring, of course, about my forsaken asceticism) and introduced me around. There were about two dozen guests. I met a fashionable lady who owned a gallery, a Broadway producer, an art critic, an ambassador, an Iraqi poet, and other notables. I was growing despondent when to my delight I spotted an old friend, who greeted me warmly.

Kim Long was another of Willy's clients, a violin soloist. He was a reedy fellow who looked as if he had just stepped out of a woodprint. As a small boy, Kim had emigrated to the States from Korea. His mother had put him through school on a shoestring, and we had been classmates at Juilliard for three years. We went back a long way. As always, his life and career were completely in order compared to my own, and I found it vicariously soothing to hear about his affairs.

He had just returned from a tour of Eastern Europe—thirty recitals in three weeks—and he was exhausted.

"So you had good houses?" I said.

"Excellent. The people love their music and they let you know it. Warsaw and Sofia were dull, but Budapest is still an exciting city."

"I haven't been there in years. I remember it had a real night life." Maybe Amos was there at that very moment, I thought, crossing the Szécheny Bridge with his collar turned up, embroiled in his mercy mission.

"That's your department," Kim chuckled. "I was so beat I did nothing but sleep. You know, I thought of you over there. In Prague I played a duet—a special program—with one of their pianists, a chap named Koslacz who won some big prize. And we did the Haydn duets—you remember that?"

"Sure, that was a great night. Only Willy could have conned us into it on a week's notice."

Kim and I had performed together just that once. It was a charity program at Fisher Hall, and Willy, serving as chairman, had enlisted half his stable to perform free. Kim had been a joy to work with.

"We should do that again sometime," he said. "Here in the city. Maybe two performances one weekend."

"I'd like that."

"I hear you've descended from your ivory tower to rejoin the rest of us galley slaves. When does your tour start?"

"September 12." And still, when I said that date aloud, it sent a cold bolt through my heart.

"What happened—tired of being a recluse?"

"It was just time."

"The way I feel now," he sighed, "I could use some of that recluse stuff myself."

"So what are you going to do?"

"Nothing."

"But where? How?" This was what I wanted to hear.

He looked at me a little strangely. "What can I tell you? I still have my house on Nantucket. I'm just going to lie around all summer with my wife and my dogs and watch the ocean roll by. Do some gardening, catch up on my reading, swim—the usual stuff. How do you do nothing?"

"Frenetically. I'm not good at it."

"Ah, you've always been a little edgy. You shouldn't fight it."

"Why the hell not? I want some serenity. I want placid waters."

"You wouldn't know what to do with them. That's not what you're after, Max."

I couldn't bear to trundle out my problems to another soul, especially someone like Kim whom I respected—and more to the point, frankly, who respected me. So I held back.

"Maybe you're right," I said.

"You're the one who should be doing thirty recitals in three weeks. You always thrived on that. And I should be lying in a hammock under the apple tree—that's my style."

"Maybe we got our wires crossed. Tell me more about Nantucket."

It sounded lovely, and I envied him. A peaceful airy house, his one and only wife (of ten years), his record collection, swimming pool, and apiary, his ten months of touring and two months of sunning himself, year in, year out—his entirely well-ordered private life which nurtured, rather than sabotaged, his professional life. Kim was content as I would never be: my forte seemed to be intellectualizing about contentment while doing my utmost to avoid it. I was still seeking momentary pleasures, whimsies, chimeras, without any real inkling of the bigger picture. Only the dimensions, and to some degree, the quality of my quest, had been enlarged. But when it came to the bigger picture I was still a blind man. A nihilist.

Before we sat down to dinner, Kim took my arm. "Listen, how long will you be living in Boston?"

"Just until the tour."

"You're so close by, Valerie and I would love to have you down to the island some weekend. Any time before September."

"I'd love to, Kim. But time is short for me right now . . . you know how it is."

"One weekend won't hurt. Call me and we'll set it up." He handed me a card. "And here's the name of that acupuncturist I mentioned. She's aces. Now, don't forget to call. I'll give you a crash course in forgetting everything."

Exactly what I needed.

We left early, just after dessert. I checked out of the Plaza and we drove down Fifth Avenue to Greta's house. Daphne, after two parties, was in overdrive, alert and talkative. Life with Daddy was apparently a great adventure, and it agreed with her. The late hours, the rich food, the friendly faces at every stop, Daddy's confused but lively personal tangles—how different from my own childhood, I thought, all cloistered and cozy with my mother as jailer.

It was strange for me to be in my old loft as a guest. Much stranger than the day of Greta's party, with the hordes of people and the din. It was nighttime now, cool and silent. The long darkness of the front hall, the varnished floorboards, the whiff of fuchsia from the terrace, the spiderwork shadows in the kitchen, and the wedge of blue neon angling into the studio from the street were all achingly familiar, ingrained in my memory from the eight years I had lived there. Each time I entered a room, or turned on a light, or touched a doorknob or faucet, another flood of sensations carried me back, not so much to memories of Orana and Greta with whom I had shared my time there, but to physical memories of the place itself, of its objects and my tangible intimate relations with them. When I passed the old building on Sixty-second Street where I had lived with my mother and Stella, it left me cold. But this place had housed the best part of my youth.

We helped Daphne settle into the guest room, brought her milk and cookies, and no sooner had we switched off the lamp than her excitement left her, literally in a wink, and she fell asleep. Greta and I retired to her bedroom—our old bedroom—and it was awkward at first, as it had been three weeks before when we stepped from the jacuzzi and got dressed. There was something very formal about readying ourselves for bed again side by side. But this passed. We had been man and wife, after all, and it was funny how, despite everything, the habits of those days, the little bedtime choreography, fell back into place. She showered first, and I undressed and waited on the usual chair, one I had purchased in Orana's time at an antique fair. She fetched a bottle of mineral water "to ambush our hangovers"—just as she always had—and gave me one of my old black towels (preserved out of sentiment?) and a kimono. It had hit me as I packed my bag at the Plaza that for all intents and purposes the die was cast with Greta. I didn't even refer to her as my "ex-wife" anymore. There I was sitting on her bed in a red kimono, Daphne asleep in the next room, gone to a wedding decked out as the last word in nuclear families, gone to my manager's operating under the same illusion, and now returned home with nuclear family intact and snuggling in for the night. I wasn't unhappy about this—just shocked. Out of my several families, had I put together this perfect combination to buttress me in my time of crisis?

Greta reemerged from the bathroom, bathed, perfumed, and powdered, in a lacy negligee. She was reinvigorated after the long day.

"No jacuzzi?" she teased.

"Not tonight."

She cuddled up next to me. "But, Max, you didn't think that on your first night home" (that word again) "after four long years we were just going to go to sleep? What kind of a woman do you think I am? Passion declares its own holidays. We must celebrate . . ."

Passion declares its own holidays—and I thought I came up with good lines! As I kissed her, her big eyes loomed like blue planets, planets of turquoise seas spinning toward me through a benign space, and again I fell into them like a man falling effortlessly, pleasurably, safely, from a tremendous height into deep soft water.

I ran my hands up and down her wonderful strong legs. Greta

was always partial to her legs, and she kept them shapely through her constant regimen of yoga and, in the winter, skiing. She was a great skier. In the old days when she used to get me up to Vermont, and once even to Aspen, I would content myself with hot toddies and billiards in the lodge while she went down the master slopes in her skintight outfits, helmet, goggles, her blond hair streaming behind her. Like a boxer, she knew that the essence of strength and leverage, sexual and otherwise, resides in the legs.

"They are not used to such naughty sights," she murmured, exiling her three teddy bears to a chair across the room.

"Is that really true?" I said, pinching her.

"Let's just say I always move them." She lifted off her negligee.

"Are they still named Hobo, Bobo—"

"And Max. Of course. Max is the naughty one," she laughed.

"I bet he is." I switched off the lamp. "You know, I'm just mad about you," I said. "I'm in love with you. I don't know how we could ever have gotten divorced. We must have been out of our minds."

"No, Max, we needed to meet all over again, at the right time. I have a theory about it . . . I'll tell you later. . . ."

Time passes like lightning between lovers, says Pindar. And moments of ecstasy, according to the Persians, blind us to everything but heaven. So, all things considered, I shouldn't have been surprised when I flipped open my eyelids after what I had thought was the briefest of blissful post-coital levitations and, focusing on the clock, saw that it was 2:40. Greta's head was on my chest and her lovely fragrant hair across my shoulders. Gingerly, I lifted her head, slid a pillow under it, and slipped out of bed. I peeked in on Daphne. Then I walked around my old house one last time, still knowing my way in the semidarkness, drawing both pain and delight from my memories. I drank a glass of milk and crawled back into bed. Greta emanated warmth and security. I laid my arm across her and buried my face in her hair and lay awake for a long time, despite my fatigue. I was afraid to dream, for my dreams never worked out this well.

I was sitting at the piano gazing out the window while Daphne grilled us hot dogs. The inferno had hit deadbeat town. For a week, even at night, we had barely ventured out. Down on the adjacent rooftop, my old friends the sunbathers were still pursuing Helius with a passion. By now mahogany-colored, I didn't see how they could take much more. I had exactly six weeks and three days before my opening recital, and since our return from New York I had been putting in my time heavily. Daphne was a patient kid—I wondered that she didn't go out of her mind hearing those pieces over and over again. But she never said a word. One morning she persuaded me to buy her a black kitten—named Mango—so at least she had company.

Despite our high-powered air conditioners, my whole body felt on fire from within. Kim's acupuncturist had done wonders for my wrist, but playing as I was, twelve, sometimes fourteen, hours a day, the heat was leaving me drained, punchy. I had lost ten pounds since the wedding. Every morning I squeezed four quarts of orange juice on the machine. That, dozens of vitamins, and poached eggs, were my staple. And hot dogs.

Greta couldn't come to Boston for another week because of business commitments. She was traveling around to a dozen cities, meeting with buyers and finding outlets for her designs. Often she called me for my opinion on some deal, or simply to let off steam. I hadn't seen her for eleven days and counting. She was going to move in for the rest of the summer, and I couldn't wait. Only when I was practicing did I get my mind off of her.

Castiglione, who thought (like me) that he knew as much

about women as he did about music, informs us that for the ardent lover, the absence of the beloved "widows" his soul and plunges him into torment. Good Platonist that he was, Castiglione seconds Socrates by advising us to begin our lifelong quest for Absolute Beauty with the contemplation of physical beauty. I had always been a Platonist as far as that went. But then he ambushes us and adds that it is this very concentration on the physical—on a *single* object, in fact—that will lead the lover into a terrible trap, into this soul-widowing when the beloved is gone. The trap can only be avoided if, at the right moment, the lover casts aside all thought of the beloved and proceeds to the next rung on Socrates' ladder: the appreciation of moral beauty. Rather a raw deal for the beloved. And impossible for me. I had never succeeded in taking that step while crazy about someone. To me the physical was an end in itself, not a precondition for ethical improvement. So I seemed to be knocked out of the picture where Absolute Beauty was concerned.

All of which is neither here nor there except that it helped me examine my longing for Greta in light of my past history. I have already mentioned my tendency to idealization, which sent me up the wrong path from the first with Sarah. But perhaps my deeper, truer affliction was cathexis. The investing of one's libidinal energies in a person, object, or idea, says the lexicon. With me, it was always a person, a woman. When Cupid got to me (in Greta's case, the second time around, with a vengeance), I put on blinders of the most opaque variety. As I also said earlier, I tended to monogamy when I was in love. I ran on a single rail. When I was merely promiscuous, my libido radiated 360 degrees without a qualm, but tie my heart strings to a single woman and I was a different man. Dr. Selzer shooed away all my talk of cathexis and Plato and reduced it to a simple Jungian formula: when I found a woman with a strong animus, I connected completely through my anima; when I bedded someone (or she bedded me) who was a mere refraction of my Shadow, my lesser and darker portion, I only connected biologically.

I couldn't disagree with this, but how I longed at times for those days when I was free and footloose. What did I care if I was chasing my Shadow—with or without a capital S? Things had been so much simpler, I told myself in moments of frustration, forgetting what those days were really like. Though separated by years and marriages and commitments, the footloose periods could all have been rolled into one. There was little variation among them. I traveled alone fitfully (without the restraints of performing), and drifted in and out of haphazard relationships, and constantly created diversions to ward off ennui—even those that ran against my own grain.

It was that part of me, perverse and essentially dishonest, and the accrued folly of those times, that propped up my Byronic pretensions after the fact. That so enlivened for me, now that I was back in tamer pastures, those letters of Byron's and encouraged me to seek out parallels in my own experience. I thought these would testify to my breadth of amorous knowledge, and the resultant expansion of my emotional range as a performer. Byron, divorced and cut loose in carnival Venice (for a time, he too with a "natural" daughter—named Allegra!—in tow), making assignations, attending orgies, and tumbling into the Grand Canal in flagrante—it sounded terrific. But, let's face it, it's no way to live. It's a hollow shell. And the twentieth century is not so conducive to such clowning. *My* life when I let out the stops grew so complicated that my ardor and would-be libertinism were effectively smothered by anxiety. It took me years of self-conscious exploits to realize I was not cut out for the Carnival. It took Byron only a few months to abandon that life and take up the role of *Cavalier Servente* to a stable young princess, quietly domesticated Italian-style, but I fought my good senses on and off many times, beyond all reason—looking for what? My youth which had been lost to the damn piano, that convenient villain? Or worse—my boyhood? Or did I cater to my frivolous side out of sheer self-destructiveness, to keep myself from higher pursuits?

Daphne and I ate our hot dogs in the kitchen. We were waiting for the piano tuner to come by. Two keys were off and the pedals needed adjustments.

"Is that why you have two pianos, Dad—in case one breaks?"

"I guess so. I've always had two. Superstition, maybe."

[*173*]

She thought about this.

"You know, in the old days," I continued, "many of the concert pianists performed with two pianos onstage. They would go back and forth between them."

"How come?"

"Well, in those days they actually did break strings very often. Liszt, von Bülow, Beethoven—they were all great piano wreckers."

She laughed. "Were they that strong?"

"No, silly. The pianos were much more fragile. They were all wood, no steel. Now it would be very difficult to break strings."

"I bet you could do it."

"Let's hope not. The string tension is about thirty tons per square inch. Do you know what that means?"

I was still explaining it to her when the piano tuner arrived, and leaving him to his work, we went out for a drive. We took some peanut butter sandwiches along for dessert. Daphne seemed to be adopting my oddball eating habits, and I scolded myself for neglecting her nutrition. Her yen for health foods was gone. I tried pushing meat and vegetables on her, but she had taken to canned ravioli and turkey pies and cornflakes for supper. At least twice a week we still had our romantic dinners, but otherwise it was bachelor cuisine. I resolved to change this as of the next day. That night we read together and played with Mango, and when they turned in, I went back to work. If only I were playing well, I thought, I could have gone on with this life-style forever. Willy once told me about seeing Landowska at Town Hall in the late forties. She was performing the first book of *The Well-Tempered Clavier* in a series of recitals, and she had the stage set up like her living room: lamps, tables, carpet, harpsichord, and she even wore her robe and slippers. The audience loved it. Maybe that's what I needed: a smoking jacket and slippers, a cigar, and Daphne and Mango curled up on a large divan center stage. Maybe then the audience would love me, too. But Landowska played flawlessly, and that helped.

It was to be a day of reckoning, but I didn't know that yet. I had put in my ten hours at the piano and gone for a long walk. Orana called, somewhat agitated, to make sure I was coming by the next day, as I had promised. I assured her I was. Then, with grave reservations, I called Sarah. She had left four messages in the previous two days, which I had ignored. I wanted to keep the books closed with her. But I also didn't want her bothering me. She was curt and unfriendly: she had to pick up the clothes and books she had kept at the loft. I suggested meeting her in the lobby with the stuff, but she insisted I wouldn't find everything—and she wanted *all* of it so she wouldn't have to come back. That was fine with me. I told her to drop by at seven.

This conversation depressed me. I had made a bad mistake about Sarah. All my crazy delusions in the spring seemed laughable. I blamed my comeback, opening up my insides like a Pandora's box. And my isolation. But maybe I just wasn't very smart anymore. That quietude of hers that I had so envied had turned out to be a pocket of gall. With all my misgivings, I don't know what I expected. Her kind of ambition was never centered with calm. The fulfillment I desired resided in the generous country of the heart, Greta's terrain—not in the spleen.

Suddenly I couldn't understand what I had been waiting for with Greta. The sooner I saw her, the better. I cursed her damn business trip. Rather than fretting, waiting for happiness to come to me, I should have joined her for a few nights on the road. I had talked to her that morning, but on an impulse I tried to reach her again at her hotel in Montreal. I was ready to fly up there that night. To propose! Of course, she had just checked out and left for the airport. It was 5:05. I knew her next stop was Detroit. Maybe I would fly there in the morning with Daphne. Just thinking about it gave me a lift, and I went back to work.

The circumstances, the physical details, attending a crisis are often easy to recollect—even when we'd rather forget. I remember exactly what was going on two hours later when Sarah rang the doorbell. At that moment, 7:10, the loft glowed with rosy late afternoon sunlight, and the air conditioners were whirring at top speed. I was wearing white trousers and a tank shirt. I hadn't shaved in two days. I was sucking on a mint candy. Daphne was in her room reading Jules Verne. The cat Mango was watching me practice from his customary perch, atop one of the stereo speakers. His tail, as always, snapped back and forth like a metronome, though not (I must confess) in tempo to the twenty-second of the *Diabelli* Variations, which I was playing just then with great intensity. That particular variation is a deviation from the other thirty-two. It is in C major, but instead of basing it on Diabelli's original waltz tune, Beethoven strangely enough derived it from a theme of Mozart's *Don Giovanni*—my old friend Kierkegaard's apex of all musical works, the ultimate expression of his theory of the "musical-erotic." That I should be playing this particular theme at that moment (minutes before my own love life was to be tossed into upheaval) is somewhat ironic. Why Beethoven inserted into his work, out of nowhere, this strain of Mozart, is itself bewildering. The *Diabelli* was his last major piano piece. For years, until von Bülow stuck it in his repertoire, no first-rank pianist had ever performed it. Diabelli himself was a music publisher and hustler. He commissioned an odd bunch of composers (including Moscheles, Hummel, and the Archduke Rudolph) to write variations on his waltz tune. The others' variations are forgotten, but Beethoven, for unknown reasons, was intrigued by the original, primitive musical line, and took off on it, modeling his set on Bach's *Goldberg* Variations. Orana told me it was his farewell to the pianoforte, dense with musical ideas, past and future. Always difficult to perform, I had recorded it, but never played it onstage. I thought it would start off my comeback with a bang. And I was working hard to make each variation ring distinctly and vitally. Of all the pieces on my program, it was the one I felt most confident about.

Running through the twenty-second variation, thinking of Leporello and Elvira, Mango gazing at me sleepily, I was interrupted by the doorbell. I braced myself as Sarah breezed in with a suitcase, and without a word, headed directly for the bedroom. I had her clothes piled on the bed and her books on the floor. She started packing. She never even looked at me.

I stood by the door and watched her uneasily. I realized that if I said nothing, she wouldn't either. At first, I was smart enough to keep my mouth shut. Her movements were jerky. Her lips tight. She looked pale, dark around the eyes. She rummaged in the closet and found a few dresses I had overlooked. She took some books off the shelf and fetched a bottle of cologne from the bathroom. I was surprised how many of her things had accumulated since April. When the suitcase was nearly full, I made my mistake.

"Look, I'm sorry things have turned out this way," I said.

She glared at me so venomously that I winced. "I'm not," she said through her teeth.

"Fine."

She snapped the suitcase shut and slammed it to the floor. "I'll be happy if I never see you again."

"I'll carry your bag out."

"Don't you come near me." Her eyes narrowed. "You'll get yours, Max Randal. I hope you fall flat on your face. With your reckless egotism, you're going to be a loser, and you're not going to like the way it tastes."

"I think you'd better just go now."

"And it won't be long," she went on. "This tour should finish you off. I grew up around real musicians. Around my father. They didn't sit around feeling sorry for themselves, waiting for someone to pat them on the back, hoping for *miracles*."

"Come on, Sarah, you've got your stuff." I took her arm.

"Take your hands off me." She turned as if to get her suitcase, and from my blind side, swung up rapidly and caught my cheek.

Then she came at me with both fists raised. I gripped her wrists and pulled her up short.

"Let go of me!" she screamed. As soon as I released her, she spat at me and landed a punch on my ear.

All my anger flew out of me and I slapped her twice, harder than I wanted to. She staggered back and caught herself on the bed. Her lip was cut. Crying hysterically that I was going to kill her, she ran into the bathroom and locked the door. I was shaking. I had never hit a woman before. I was worried about what Daphne might have heard. I didn't know how to get Sarah out of the house without doing further damage. But all of that became academic, for I realized dimly that what had been a minor background distraction was again the insistent call of the doorbell. I couldn't imagine who it might be, and torn between keeping watch on the bathroom and answering the door, I finally ran down the hall and opened it.

It was Greta.

Smiling, happy, two suitcases beside her. I felt the blood rush from my head. It wasn't possible . . .

"Surprise!" She threw her arms around my neck and kissed me. "I just couldn't wait another week," she said breathlessly. "You kept saying, come, come—so here I am." And she picked up her bags and marched in.

"I flew straight down from Montreal," she said.

"Not to Detroit," I said dumbly.

"No, my meeting there was postponed, so I figured, why go back to New York—for what?—when I can go straight to Max in Boston?"

I can't begin to describe the panic that seized me. It required all my willpower to speak and move calmly. I remember thinking that the gods had it in for me, and there was nothing, nothing, I could do about it. I had apparently entered the realm of tragedy, where timing—the engine of comedy—deepens into inevitability, and all the clowns turn into Furies.

"So this is your house," Greta beamed, taking it all in. She looked cool and lovely in a dark green dress and kerchief. Why, I thought, why couldn't she have come five—even three—minutes later? One cab later in the airport taxi line. But I was already forgetting: inevitability, not timing. People missed cabs in comedies, not tragedies.

"What is it, Max? You look white."

"Just work. Listen, I have to explain something."

"Well, show me to the bedroom so I can stow these bags. I have a million things to tell you."

"I'll take the bags. First let me show you around. In here," I said, guiding her to the studio. "This is where—"

"What was that?" she asked.

I honestly was not pretending I could not hear Sarah's shrieks in the bathroom. Agitated as I was, I had succeeded in blocking them out.

"Max, what was that?" she repeated, starting down the hall for the bedroom.

I couldn't stop her, I was helpless. Daphne must have fallen asleep, I thought, glancing toward her room, for neither the doorbell nor the shrieks had brought her out.

"I'll tell you what it is," I said, taking her arm, as she peered into the bedroom. "I've just had an argument with a former friend of mine."

"It's a woman," she said, and at that moment she spotted Sarah's suitcase. She shook her head in bewilderment. "An argument?"

Sarah had fallen silent. Greta and I stood there transfixed, waiting for a fresh eruption.

"What is going on here?" she demanded, alarmed now. "And where is Daphne?"

"Daphne's asleep in her room."

"Asleep? She is probably hiding—scared. Please tell me what is going on, and who is in there."

I didn't have to, for the door flew open and Sarah stepped out. She was holding a washcloth to her lip. It was spotted red. Greta and I shrank back. Sarah was as startled as we were.

"Who the hell are you?" she said.

"Who am I?" Greta echoed, raising her head up. "My name is Greta Randal. Who are you and what is your business here?"

I closed my eyes.

"Did you say 'Randal'?" Sarah sneered. "You must be one of

[*179*]

the ex-wives. The Danish delight. The one who isn't dying—or are you dying too?" She stared at Greta's suitcases. Greta's eyes were wide. "And you're moving in, no less! Oh, this *is* good. Well, you can have the bastard. I sure don't want him anymore. He must have been two-timing us. But that's par for the course. Mr. Sensitive here is spoiled rotten, thanks to women like you. Well, he didn't get his way with me." She picked up her suitcase and took a step toward Greta. "Don't you have any fucking self-esteem? Look what he did to me." She pulled her lip down and Greta recoiled. "But don't worry, he only beats you up *after* he screws you." She pushed past us, stormed down the hall, and slammed the door behind her.

Greta was trembling, flat against the wall, staring at me. I couldn't imagine where to begin my explanation—it seemed pointless. I had blown everything. I still couldn't grasp what had happened.

Even if I had found my tongue, Greta wouldn't have listened. She picked up her bags without a word and walked down the hall. I begged her to stop, but she would have none of it. She opened the front door and looked at me blankly.

"Greta, you have to let me explain. You don't understand."

"No, I don't want to understand. Don't tell Daphne I was here. And don't cry alligator tears to me, either. Good-bye, Max."

"You mean, crocodile," I said meekly, but she was gone.

At eight-thirty I dropped Daphne off at Patty's bookstore and drove on to the hospital. I was dazed. But though one part of my little world had just collapsed, I still had immediate responsibilities to Daphne and Orana—a new phenomenon for me—so I couldn't wallow. I was only grateful that Daphne had somehow slept through the tumult. I was still too shellshocked to think about it clearly. And what was there to think about? I was determined to convince Greta that I was not an ogre and a liar. That, to some extent, I had been a victim of circumstances—vicious ones. That I truly loved her. I had my work cut out for me. I planned to take the shuttle to New York the next day to plead with her. I had already arranged for Daphne to stay with Patty again. I had to try, anyway.

I stopped to gird myself outside Orana's door. This was truly the realm of tragedy, I thought. My messy squabbles were reduced to trivia when I arrived at this door. I had finally met with Dr. Swenson, and he told me straight that she had one month to live. Two on the outside. Exactly what they had told her in California. Nothing had changed. I was devastated, for I had not abandoned all hope. I asked how she had taken it, and he said her attitude hadn't changed since the day she checked in. They had run every test he could conceive of, and there was still no firm diagnosis. The one remaining possibility—Swenson did not refer to it as a "hope"—was the tropical disease center at New York Hospital. This would be expensive. Her insurance would cover some of it, and unknown to her, I was putting up the rest. This disease center was a tough place to get into, evidently, and they couldn't move her down there for another ten days or so. Orana told me on the phone that she thought it pointless but had given her consent.

I found her waiting for me eagerly, sitting upright, her hair combed more carefully than usual. A white rose was stuck in the buttonhole of her dressing gown. The second volume of the Gibbon was open in her lap. Because of dizzy spells, she wasn't able to read for long stretches anymore, but she had gotten through Volume One in fits and starts. I wondered if she could possibly finish the whole set. This question sank down to the pit of my stomach like a stone. I was trying desperately to pull myself clear of the day behind me, its residue clinging like mud to my spirit. But seeing her for the first time since my talk with the doctor was excruciating. She squeezed my hand, her own so small and dry, and as I sat down, her eyes, glittering deep in her face, roused me.

"You look exhausted," she said.

"And you look fine. Maybe you should be visiting me."

"I'm sure you would amuse the nurses."

"How's the Gibbon?" I asked. "Any more allegorical discoveries to report?"

"Not today. I've been reading about Tiberius—a ghastly fellow. Tell me, how is Daphne?"

As usual, we began talking about me, not her. I had finally gotten the hang of this after a few visits. In the previous weeks,

Orana seemed to have acquired a greater sense of serenity than I could ever hope for, with my blundering spiritual exercises and half-baked self-analysis. She was walking a tightrope that had no philosophical nets beneath it, no religious padding, and there was a certain freedom implicit in that, perhaps the one compensation granted people in her position. Once she had entered the suburbs of death, the jackass conceptions of life, the mumbo jumbo we all feed ourselves daily, had fallen away like so much dust from the wings of a plane. Someone like me—with all my elaborate metaphors for death, my vague notions of Thanatos from the music I played and the books and paintings I studied— was ignorant of this sort of freedom, which Orana had achieved through suffering. I was ignorant, and perhaps Orana, who throughout her healthy life was predisposed to serenity and kindliness and a fierce appreciation of life, was saintly. For saints, to my thinking, were not passive people: they were the handful who achieved a pacific state, not despite, but because of, their knowledge of the horrific. They digested cataclysm and nourished their spirits with its essence, something akin to beauty outside of time and space. It wasn't just in Gibbon's Rome, I realized, that Orana recognized an allegory of the soul, but in the pigeons on her windowsill, the patterns of light on her ceiling, the fanciful tune a nurse hummed while bathing her—things she had described to me with an innocent fascination, even rapture. Life and death were part of the same allegory. Only those of us trapped in the world of frenzy, on the gigantic threshing floor of everyday life, were blind to this allegorical reality.

"How are the pieces coming, Max? Are you happier with your playing?"

"Things are coming along," I said vaguely.

"It looks like I'll be in New York the day of your recital," she said softly. "Six weeks . . ."

I thought of Swenson's words—a month, two on the outside—and my heart skipped.

"You think of me when you play the *Diabelli*. Remember it was I who introduced you to its finer points."

"I'll remember."

"Move a little closer—I won't break."

I slid my chair in.

"You know," she said, "I have no family. Some distant cousins in the Pacific, but no one, really. It's strange how we both ended up here in Boston now."

"I've thought about that myself. Providence . . ."

"Perhaps. You've been very kind—"

"I don't want to hear that."

"I guess you're all the family I've got—by default. I'm sorry to be such a burden."

"Don't talk nonsense."

Her eyes wandered to the window and back. "All right, I want to ask two favors of you. I need some legal assistance. I can't afford a lawyer, I'm afraid."

"I have plenty of lawyers."

"I need a waiver of execution. Sounds charming, no? As if they're going to put me up against a wall. Actually, it's a permissions release. Something about crossing state lines . . . they need it to move me to New York. . . . It's a lot of red tape and I don't have that much time."

"I'll get the lowdown from Swenson and give it to my lawyer. He specializes in red tape."

She smiled. "Just like that, huh? Max brooks no obstacles."

I was trying not to look as bad as I felt. "What else do you need?"

"This is more personal," she said slowly. "Can I count on you to take care of things afterward?"

"Afterward?" At first, I thought she meant after being moved to New York.

"Yes, after I'm dead. When you have no one, that's when the real trouble starts. Someone has to tie up all the loose ends."

"I'll be there," I said softly.

"Will you see to the funeral and the rest?"

"Of course."

"I want to be cremated. No burial. Promise me that?"

I nodded.

"I want the ashes scattered in the sea. I'm afraid it might be expensive—"

"Don't worry about that." My head was beginning to throb.

"And there are a few people who should be informed."

"Just give me their names."

She passed her hand over her eyes. "You see, you're stuck with me. You never really get rid of people . . ."

I took her hand. "I'll see to everything, don't worry."

The nurses wheeled in one of those monitoring machines. My time was up. I promised Orana I would call as soon as I had arranged the waiver. She called me back from the door and gave me a white rose. I didn't want it. I left it in a flowerpot in the lobby.

Crossing the parking lot, the big floodlights reflecting off the cars, I felt dark and numb. A damp foul wind was blowing in off the river. I didn't feel like the good samaritan I pretended to be. I thought that I, of all people, was not worthy to be Orana's connection to this planet as she departed it. Family by default, indeed. I was just someone who had failed her grievously at one time. Someone still around by process of elimination.

But even while I was donning my hair shirt, and suffering anew with the recollection of Greta's departure, I told myself that Orana's trust should have given me cause to feel humbled and useful and even to rise a fraction in my own bleak estimation.

But it didn't.

I was sitting on Kim's dock on Nantucket, staring out over the inlet where he and Daphne were fishing from a rowboat. It was a bright cloudless Sunday. The wind was blowing the wavelets silver. Sunlight flooded the horizon. Mango was in my jacket pocket, peeking out at the water. At that moment I wished I could have changed places with him. I'm sure in an earlier incarnation I was a cat, and as such a more intelligent and useful member of the animal kingdom. Maybe not. Maybe, like Margaret, I was a snake. Or a worm.

A week had passed. A terrible, eventful week, but the one event I had hoped for—my reconciliation with Greta—hadn't occurred. I hadn't even talked with her. She called the night of our blowout with Sarah and immediately asked to speak with Daphne. They spoke for some time. I gathered Greta was explaining why she wouldn't be visiting us—more "business." Before Daphne could say good-bye, I grabbed the phone back and Greta hung up on me. My shuttle trip to New York the next day was fruitless. I waited outside her building like a criminal for nine hours. Even when I ducked into the deli across the street for a sandwich, I kept watch by the door until the counterman started asking questions. Finally I gave up. I had to pick up Daphne at Patty's before six o'clock, or I might have loitered there all night.

The following day, I arranged Orana's waiver of execution. I called my old defender Sweeney, who despite our bitter parting in June, was friendly and helpful. He fixed it so I could get the document from the judge in a week's time—the bare minimum; it usually took a month.

"You may not like this, Max," he said, "but I explained the situation to him and he was very sympathetic. Really a good guy about it."

"What's wrong with that?" I asked impatiently.

"Well, it's Judge Ryan."

"The guy we saw with Ellen?"

"The same. He liked you a lot," Sweeney added halfheartedly.

"I'm glad to hear it."

"Orana has to sign it in his presence, with two witnesses. He's agreed to come to her hospital room the day it's ready."

And that was the next day, Monday. Patty and I would be the witnesses.

I also set up an audition for Daphne at the Brook Conservatory on Thursday, so she had been immersed in her practicing all week. She was delighted at the prospect of leaving Mrs. Matthews. But she was also brooding about something, and I couldn't get her to talk about it. I didn't know if it was the audition, or missing her mother, or something I'd said or done inadvertently in my gloomy state, but she was carrying a small weight on her shoulders. Even Mango seemed despondent that week. Then, on Friday morning, Kim had called and invited us down for the weekend. I jumped at the chance to get away, hoping it would lift us all out of the dumps. His wife was away visiting relatives, and I guess he was lonely too. He and Daphne were having a great time. He was helping her with the pieces for her audition, and she was just tickled. First I had set up the audition on short notice, and now I had gotten one of the best violinists in the world to tutor her. I could do no wrong in her eyes.

All week I had practiced manically and felt sorry for myself. It was incredible to me how I had bungled things. I played like a madman day and night, barely catching any sleep. I was back on my old insomniac diet of Jack Daniel's and Nembutal. I woke up with daily hangovers and belted back black coffee until noon. Fortunately, in five days I couldn't do too much damage to myself, and maybe this reprieve of sunlight and salt air would clear my head again. But clear it for what? After starting off the year full of good intentions, resolute and disciplined, I had come full circle in just a few months: I was drinking, awake and anxious all night, my personal affairs a shambles, my playing unimproved and uninspired, and my spiritual life (if it even deserved that title) floating in a vacuum of bad faith.

As for bungling things, Dr. Selzer, like any good analyst, would have told me that one never does this without a reason. Events don't conspire against you; your many selves conspire against one another. Nothing is accidental. Therefore I must somehow have engineered the ugly confrontation with Greta and Sarah through a chain of murky actions of which I wasn't even aware. Perhaps secretly I had been terrified at the prospect of remarrying Greta, and so—presto!—I had sabotaged it. If I had simply told her about Sarah in New York, how we were in the post mortem stage, sweeping away the rubble, all misunderstandings would have been avoided. But I had been secretive. Why? What suicidal impulse took me over at such times? Or had I simply taken Greta's love for granted, as I once did with Orana, who said I never shared deep down. Dr. Selzer had given me the answer, but I wouldn't listen. She told me I distrusted my mother because she tried to suffocate me. Married to an elusive, unfaithful, insensitive man, she would make sure her son was none of those things. I would be sensitive (an artist), open, and faithful—to her, anyway. She never anticipated that in rebelling against her I would in many ways emulate my father. And I had, with modifications. As a rebel in my eyes, and one who had escaped the prison I inhabited with my mother and Stella, my father was a tremendously attractive figure. He came and went as he liked. He answered to no one. His style and his way with women were qualities I admired as an adolescent. My mother's smothering also inclined me to remain detached from women internally even while I craved their companionship. Dr. Selzer proceeded to the observation that when I played the piano I was having sex with my mother. Quite a jump. At that point, I broke off my analysis. Had she hit a nerve?

Possibly. But knowing these things intellectually, and applying them to my experience, were two distinctly separate propositions. And my judgment seemed so poor. Maybe Louie was right and I was by nature a hermit, a lone wolf, not fit for human partnership—amatory or otherwise—at ease only in solitude with my music and my ideas and my insubstantial transitory intrigues, that essential rootlessness to which I had been able to cling because of the unusual nature of my profession. Again, like my father, as Louie well knew: a loner, a perfectionist, insatiable yet wary when it came to fame and money. Maybe Greta was lucky—maybe it was she who had gotten the reprieve.

In that week of frenzy and insomnia I had finally entered the outskirts of that dark night of the soul Dr. Winters had mentioned to me. I dislike hyperbole when speaking of soulful matters, and I wince at the notion of conjuring up poor St. John, but I can think of no better way to describe my ordeal at the keyboard at that time. I was afraid I would never play again. Not just that my playing would be uninspired, but that even the technical facility would be wiped out. That, in my happy-go-lucky way, beginning in June and continuing with a vengeance into August, I had succeeded in checkmating my own best demons and negating whatever magic remained in my fingers. Things seemed drastic. I had regressed even further, and had even begun to consider canceling the tour.

And why was I playing so hard and so purposelessly, dawn to dusk and then half the night before I got out the bourbon? Perhaps I thought if I overran myself I would kill my fears of never playing again. And of never seeing Greta again. The two were intertwined. My loss of her had triggered a deeper panic. But was it deep enough to render me impotent at the piano? Did it matter anymore? The booze was contributing its own demolition work on my teetering ego. I sat in the darkness every night raking through my remorse and self-pity like so much muck, trying to penetrate the insensible by dulling my senses.

Chuang Tzu advises us that the white dove need not bathe in snow each day to whiten itself, nor the black crow in ink to reaffirm its blackness. Neat advice, for doves and crows, but maybe not so cut-and-dried for devils like me. Can it also apply, after all, in black and white, when we look to our inner shades, to the multichromatic range of our souls? I would hazard that we must indeed renew our inner colors daily, deepen or even dilute them, but on no account allow them to fade out of neglect. Our spiritual life has its own landscape to be illuminated according to the repercussions of our external actions.

I decided that afternoon on the dock that my inner colors were fading fast, that my daily acid bath, two parts fever and one part liquor, was taking its toll.

Suddenly Mango jumped out of my pocket, and as I snatched him up from the edge of the dock Daphne stood up in the rowboat, the sun flashing off her golden hair and red bathing suit, and my heart leapt. She waved and Kim, laughing, held up a large, wriggling bluefish. I had little taste for fishing myself, but according to Kim, the Korean people were the greatest anglers in the world. I waved them in to shore, afraid that Daphne, with her fair skin, would burn badly on her second day out. I trudged up to the house, had two quick shots of whiskey, then opened a can of Coke and lit a cigar to kill the scent on my breath. Mango watched me with great curiosity—and with a tinge of sadness too, I thought.

Kim gave a small dinner party that night, and Daphne—who had a bit of the old man's ham in her—was asked if she would treat the company to a violin rendition. Before we knew it, she had Kim join her in a Vivaldi duet. Despite the baby grand in the room, no one suggested a trio. Not even Daphne, which surprised me. Was my moroseness so transparent?

I was to learn just how transparent I was in other areas when I went to Daphne's room to tuck her in. She was on her knees in her pink pajamas, hands clasped on the bed, saying her prayers. This was something she had picked up from Ellen's mother, who, like the wives of many corrupt men, was extremely religious. She peeked up at me through her blond bangs as I watched her small lips fervently mouthing the words. Mango, curled up on the pillow, gazed at me intently. I seemed to be an endless source of entertainment for him. He was always following me around. Some animals are more susceptible than others to music, and I believe Mango was utterly won over by the sounds I had produced for him on the piano. Now that I was really going bad, I thought, even he would lose interest in me.

Daphne scrambled up under the blankets. I saw she had something on her mind. Her eyes kept roving to the ceiling as they had the night of our "playboy" discussion. We talked about fishing for a while, and about Kim's apiary.

"I wonder where Mom is now," she said suddenly.

Good question. Daphne had only received two postcards, both from London weeks before. That wasn't like Ellen.

"Do you miss her a lot?"

"Sometimes. But I like being with you, Dad."

"I know, but you've never been away from your mother this long, have you?"

"Uh uh."

"Well, she'll be back in a few weeks now. September 2nd's not so far away."

"I hope she sends some more postcards first." She sat up. "Oops, I forgot to brush my hair. You know: a hundred strokes every night/keeps it shiny, soft and bright."

"But it's late. How about just fifty tonight?"

"I guess that'll be all right. Even Mom doesn't do it every night."

Ellen had beautiful hair, lush and wavy. Daphne reminded me of her mother when she brushed her hair, with that same ninety-degree snap of the wrist punctuating her humming.

"Mom bought me my own brush set, with two combs and a tweezer," she said, holding out the brush. "See, the back is silver and here are my initials, D.L.R. How come you gave me the middle name Laurel?"

"Your mother came up with it. We both liked 'Daphne.' And then she remembered the Greek myth about Daphne, how one day she changed into a laurel tree. So she said to me, 'Daphne Laurel.' "

"It was because someone was chasing her, who wanted to kiss her, right?"

"Uh huh. Apollo, the god of music and light."

"Do you pray to him?"

"I haven't recently. Maybe I should."

She got back under the covers. "Dad, tell me what it was like when I was born. What was it like in Paris?"

"Well, it was a wonderful, cool, rainy day. Rained buckets. When we got to the hospital, Mother and I were drenched. She lost one of her shoes crossing the street. We were very happy. And you arrived right on time. The doctor came out and made a little speech to me. You know, the French are very formal about those things. Then I gave out cigars to everyone in the waiting room."

"How corny."

"I couldn't help myself."

She assumed a serious look. "You know, I noticed you've been smoking more than you used to."

I wondered what else she had noticed.

"Too many cigars. I can help you quit, if you want to. I helped Mom quit cigarettes. She hasn't had one in two years."

"How did you do it?"

"First, I talked to her a lot about it. And then—do you know Dr. Drexel next door? He gave me a mask—you know, the kind they wear in operations. And I wore it every morning when I went in to wake her before school."

"And she got the message."

"Well, she had trouble for a while. She was always eating and doing exercises. She said she was going to gain twenty pounds if she kept eating so much candy. So I told her to chew gum, and it worked."

Her little brush set and this story opened my heart suddenly. I felt I had glimpsed a real living picture of her home life. I seldom gave it much thought. Usually, she and Ellen were in their world and I in mine. And my image of Ellen seemed locked in a time warp in Europe ten years earlier. I couldn't imagine her as a day-to-day mother, driving Daphne to school, putting dinner on the table, running the house. Even when I visited them, it was all unreal to me. Now, after living with Daphne for over a month, getting to know how her heart and mind worked, it had dawned on me that her sweet disposition and keen curiosity and warmth hadn't evolved out of a vacuum. She had been raised almost exclusively by her mother, so it would have been difficult to attribute those qualities in her to anyone but Ellen. Like so much else in my life, I had been aware of this intellectually, distantly. But that night it touched me deeply. This kid was the way she was because Ellen had a lot of good in her, a genuine spirit and real independence. I always knew Ellen had spunk. Whatever her private disappointment before we broke up, when I suggested we get married for Daphne's sake, she rebuffed me unequivocally. Said she would not be party to a sham, that things could never work out with us. And she stuck to her guns, even raising her daughter as a single parent—with a different surname. She had insisted Daphne use the name Randal. Through the years, through our legal skirmishes and disagreements, she kept herself distanced from my antics without alienating me from our child, and I respected her for that. But it had taken me nine years to realize just how much she had put into her mothering, something she never complained or boasted about. I promised myself I would sit down with her in September, thank her for all that, and try to make amends for some of my insensitivity over the years. Maybe she had pulled a fast one on me in June because she felt it was the only way she could deal with someone like me. Ellen was another person, I concluded glumly, that I had failed. And this realization, coupled with my despair and heartache, and the inordinate amount of booze besotting my nervous system, nearly brought me to tears as I gazed into Daphne's bright eyes.

But those eyes were clouding, and her brow furrowing, and I knew she was just getting around to what troubled her.

"Dad, I have to ask you something."

"Yes?"

"You told me Greta was coming to see us, and she promised me she would. Did you change your mind—is that why she hasn't come?"

I should have known what it was, but I was too preoccupied chasing after oblivion. "I'm sorry, Daphne, I should have told you what was going on. No, I would never change my mind about something that important. She just can't come right now. I know she talked to you about it a little, and I'm sure she's thinking about you."

"How do you know?"

"Because she loves you. But she's working hard and it's difficult for her to get away."

I wished I could have disappeared into my shoes at that moment. I was afraid to tell her the truth because I knew she would be angry at me. Her instincts, I noted painfully, were good. She had asked if *I* had changed my mind, not Greta. Had she already pigeonholed me as fickle and undependable?

I decided to bite the bullet. "Listen, Greta and I had an argument last week and she's mad at me. It's not just her business that's kept her away."

"Oh."

"And you should know," I continued, "that the argument was my fault. Ever since, I've been trying to reach her to make up. But she won't talk to me."

She looked hard at me. "So you think we won't ever see her again?"

"I wouldn't say that."

"When will we see her, then?"

"I wish I knew. Very soon, I hope."

She pursed her lips and stared past me. "How come you're always having arguments, Dad? You have them with Mom—and with Sarah and now with Greta, too." She was struggling to hold back her tears. "Once after Mom talked to you on the telephone, and she thought I was upstairs, I came in and she was crying. And she never cries. And now Greta won't like me anymore either, because I'm living with you."

I swallowed hard. "I don't know why Mom cried that time. You know, people have disagreements, but they still love each other."

"You don't love her. You're only nice to her because of me."

"That's not true, sweetheart. Remember, I knew her before you were around, and I fell in love with her. We still understand each other pretty well."

Tears were running down her cheeks. "You understand her but you don't like her. I know it."

"I do like her, Daphne. It's hard for you to see because we've never been together with you. And I've always been away so much. That's going to change. I'll tell you what. When she gets back, the three of us are going to sit down and talk about it together, like a family."

"But we're not a family."

"Well, we have to try to talk like one. Okay?"

She shrugged and dried her eyes.

"And as for Greta, you must never, ever, think that because I have a disagreement with her or anyone else, they won't like you. Especially Greta, who loves you so much."

"I know."

I bit my lip. "You'll see her soon. I'm going to make sure of it."

"Promise?"

"I promise. Even though she's mad at me, I know she wants to see you."

"I don't want her to be mad at you."

"I'm sorry I've spoiled it for you, Daphne."

"You didn't spoil it, Dad. I didn't mean to cry."

I took her in my arms.

"And I didn't want to be mean to you," she said.

"You weren't mean. You should always tell me how you feel. Always. Now, don't worry about it another minute. It's been a long day, just go to sleep."

She turned onto her side. "But don't go yet, Daddy. Stay a little longer, okay?"

I rubbed her back gently for a long time. Even after she was asleep, I kept rubbing it. I didn't want to leave her alone, and I didn't want to drink myself to sleep again. I was trying to sort things out, I was drifting, and when I opened my eyes again it was twilight, birds were singing, and I was stretched out across the foot of Daphne's bed. I didn't feel bad until I remembered why I was there.

It was dark and drizzling all afternoon. I was standing in the hospital parking lot beside Judge Ryan's gray Lincoln. The judge and Patty were huddled under her umbrella, and she was trying to light a cigarette. He lit it for her. The waiver of execution was completed.

Orana was dizzy and weak when we arrived. She had suffered through a night of nausea, coughing and vomiting, and she seemed only dimly conscious when we stood by her bedside. For an instant she looked terrified, as if she imagined we were there for the last rites. Judge Ryan, in his black suit, could easily have passed for a priest. She signed the waiver, Patty and I witnessed it, and that was it. Orana fell asleep at once. I couldn't wait to get out of there. This little gathering had shattered any vain lingering hopes I cherished for her recovery: the waiver was tantamount to a death warrant. A symbolic last gasp. It meant she was already leaving this world, already beyond my reach. At least she was exiting with dignity, I thought, and that is more than many of us can say in the end. It was more than my father could say, and he had been more obsessed than most with that particular sort of dignity. For my part, I merely wanted to ward off impending disgrace in this life. Dying, with or without my boots on, was the least of my problems.

Judge Ryan asked me to have a word with him before we left. "If there's anything else I can do, Mr. Randal . . ."

"No, but thanks for everything, Judge."

"You're an unusual man," he said. "After our first meeting I had quite a different impression."

I shrugged.

"I felt rather bad for you. But it seemed to me you brought your problems on yourself. That your music was everything to you—as indeed it must be, in a way. But I've seen another side today, and Sweeney told me some things. The people in your life are more important to you than you let on." He seemed ill at ease. "I'm sorry, we're not in my chambers now, and I don't mean to be presumptuous."

We could have left it at that, but I felt an urge to talk to him, and I thought he had something on his mind.

"Your first impression was closer to the mark," I said. "It's because I have been so selfish that I'm trying my best to make amends now. With my daughter. My second wife. Even Ellen, whom you saw me with at our worst. But my best isn't good enough, I'm afraid. And now, with Orana, it all seems futile. Too little too late."

He arched his white eyebrows. He had those cold, porcelain-blue eyes that should be a prerequisite for anyone aspiring to the bench. Even in that parking lot, I felt as if I were in the dock.

"I'll tell you, Mr. Randal, a judge is like a doctor. Nothing shocks him after a while. I've learned it's what we all do in the end that counts, how we use our mistakes, not the fact we made them in the first place." He hesitated. "The Greeks said it centuries ago: a man's character can't be changed, only his ideas change. I've met you twice, under very different circumstances, and I would vouchsafe your character in any court. Character is not your problem. Therefore, whatever is, is soluble. That much I know, for what it's worth."

I was bewildered at this effusion of kindness. Maybe I looked even worse, soppier, than I thought, and he felt sorry for me. Maybe he just liked to spout off. Actually, I think the scene in Orana's room, from which I had felt detached and fearful, had touched a soft spot in him.

As he slid into his car, I roused myself. "Well, thanks again, Judge. For the kind words, too."

He nodded. "How has it worked out with your little girl? Everything all right?"

"Better than that. Her mother did me a great favor letting me have her all summer."

He held up a finger. "You did yourself a favor when you signed the original agreement she invoked."

"It's hard for me to look at it that way, but if you say so."

"Give yourself the benefit of the doubt. If you hadn't left yourself open with such a loophole, it would say a lot, wouldn't it? About your character." He smiled, and purred off in his big sedan.

Pascal says there is no truth or goodness behind men's actions, but only a seeking after wealth and status. I had had my share of that—with disastrous results. And now was it truth and goodness I was primed for, or simply a restoking of my wealth and a refurbishing of my status? Such was my self-righteousness that I was asking myself these questions that week. It is always the self-righteous who are most full of self-pity when the chips are down. And self-pity was my new poison. I was sick of it, sick of myself. I wished I had the guts to shoot the works and see where I ended up. Maybe like Gottschalk, the first great American pianist (and frequent target of Willy's jibes), I should disappear into the tropics for a while. Gottschalk lived in Cuba for five years when his career was in a lull. He was a famous ladies' man. An oenophile and gourmand. A beachcomber. Maybe I needed a real exile—not Boston—but Lima, or Senegal, or the Seychelles. See what kind of truth and goodness I would dig up in those places. Or maybe like Barere (foremost interpreter of Liszt's *Don Juan* Fantasy), I could pull off something really dramatic on my big night—he died at the piano in Carnegie Hall, performing the Grieg Piano Concerto.

The drizzle turned to rain as Patty and I drove to the bookstore. Daphne was there, in care of the clerk.

"When do they move her to New York?" Patty said.

"Friday."

"Are you going along?"

"Just for a couple of days. She made me promise I wouldn't stay. She doesn't want to disrupt my work. That's a joke." I also planned, in my free time, to try to catch up with Greta.

That evening, after a cold supper, I packed Daphne off to bed and picked up where I had left off before our jaunt to Nantucket. I took some speed and practiced until one a.m. My playing was as flat as ever. The Schubert sounded like a dirge and the Liszt was muddy. The delicate, filigreed opening that I had labored over so relentlessly never got off the ground. Even in my patchwork recording sessions I had produced a better sound. Now I had slipped from staleness to futility. My insides were sluggish, my fingers sore, and when I started drinking late that night I had stepped somewhat beyond desperation, no longer dreaming of solutions, but escapes. I wanted out—badly.

Ever since my talk with Louie at the wedding, I had been circling memories of my father and his death. Perhaps because that afternoon I had smelled death in Orana's room, and because I was dying a slow death myself, I was drawn to those memories again. I dropped two Seconal, two black beauties, poured out a triple-bourbon and settled into the easy chair by the piano. I stared out the big windows at the blue-and-white lights that flowed to the river. An hour passed. The lights blurred and streaked, and gradually the window backdropped lights of a different sort, on some inner boulevard. Drifting, I kept fixing hazily on a question Dr. Selzer had several times asked me. A simple question: "When was the last time you saw your father?" I didn't know. It conjured a blank. As with my mother's death, I remember where I was when I got the news of his. I was twenty-two, on tour, married to Orana, who was at home in New York. I was in Copenhagen when Louie caught up with me, at the hotel desk paying my bill. I took his call in the lobby and then went on to the airport and flew to London, as planned. I don't remember feeling much of anything. And not such a trouper as I would be seven years later when my mother died, I canceled my two recitals and jetted home for the funeral with Stella and her husband. My father was buried in upstate New York, near an old farm he owned, where he used to train before his fights. I thought of him in his grave, how cold his perfect teeth must be, and how there must be nothing left of his heart, his eyes, his genitals, his powerful arms. But all this had nothing to do with Dr. Selzer's question: When was the last time I had seen him, talked to him, been in his presence?

I never could answer the question, until that August night in Boston, a thunderstorm raging, when I truly touched bottom.

No more sub-basements, but the bedrock, where Satan does his hammering. Rimbaud made hay from the "systematic" deranging of his senses, and other notables in my pantheon worked at psychic untangling while in the throes of narcosis (Byron with laudanum, Mahler morphine, Freud cocaine), but I had never found much revelation by way of booze or dope. I was a frivolous dissipator, in the company of good-time charlies, or a solitary, seeking escape hatches in my insomniac chamber. (For I can say now, with authority, that insomnia is a kind of sleep—a negative sleep—with its own highs and lows, textures and depths, and subtle rhythms, like REM degrees.) I had not slept well for over ten days, getting at most two consecutive hours a night. For four nights I had barely slept at all. And while worrying in a perfunctory way about my whiskey and pill intake, I had not thought seriously about the inevitable consequences of so much sleeplessness. Not only on my work, but on my mental stability. I was a frayed wire that night, insulation gone, outlet sputtering, sparks flying. In the ensuing hours, I yanked the wires from the kitchen telephone (because it was ringing, or not ringing, I'll never know). I finished off nearly a fifth of bourbon. I wrote a three-page letter of gibberish to Greta and tore it up. I threw out all the meat in the freezer. I burned the sheet music to *La campanella* in the bathroom sink. I drew a picture of Mango—lipstick on cardboard—but fortunately did no harm to the poor animal. There was more, of a trivial nature, but I see no point in listing it all. In fact, I only go this far, not to lend weight to these nihilistic fumblings, but simply to set the external scene, the result of my physical actions, for I had no memory the next morning of any of it. I remembered only one thing, very clearly, when Daphne found me passed out on the floor under the piano, a pair of gloves under my head and Mango draped across my ankles—and it was the same (and only) thing I had been aware of during my delirium. It was my only reality through those hours, and it was a dream, a nightmare.

It began when I stepped off the cast-iron elevator in my old building—Greta's building. Except that it was many years earlier and I was living there with Orana. We had been married exactly six months. I was bringing home a dozen white roses in honor of the occasion. It was November 14. It was cold and windy and the air smelled metallic. It had rained all day. My shoes were wet. I let myself in and two of her Siamese cats ran to greet me. I heard someone tinkling on one of the pianos. I called out to Orana and the piano fell silent. A moment later she answered me from the kitchen. I went into the studio and my father was sitting at the piano. He was wearing a dark gray suit, vest, and blue tie. He looked drawn and tired. There was no carnation in his lapel. He stood up and we embraced. Orana came in carrying a tray with a glass, an ice bucket, and a bottle of bourbon. She poured out a stiff drink and handed it to him. I was amazed, for never in my life had I seen my father take a drink. Not once. The two of them were speaking to me but I couldn't hear them. It was as if we were outdoors and the wind was carrying their voices. He sat down again at the piano and Orana and I sat on the couch. She was wearing a gray dress. She and my father talked somberly for a long time. Suddenly she took the bouquet of roses, which I had left by the door, and placed them in a vase. My father finished his drink and she poured him another. They spoke some more. I still couldn't hear them, but somehow this was not awkward. In fact, it seemed perfectly natural. I hadn't seen him in months. He was living in France. Orana had never met him before. The telephone rang and she hurried down the hall to the kitchen. She was gone for a long time. My father took my notepad and started sketching one of the cats. He was always a doodler—on napkins, train schedules, envelopes. Finally, faintly, down a tunnel, I could hear his voice. He told me he was having trouble with his health. Two ulcers, migraines, kidney stones. With his constitution (and having always thought him indestructible), I found this hard to believe. I said so, and he looked at me quizzically. Orana returned and he embraced her warmly. This too surprised me, for though she was his daughter-in-law, he had never been one to show much emotion, especially the first time he met someone. Then, abruptly, she left the room again. I called her name, in vain. My father joined me on the couch. Close up, he did look sick. He asked me to feel his hand. He had fractured it years before, in a fight. He said it was badly arthritic, that his knee was even worse, and they kept him up at night. I didn't say anything. He put his arm around me and pulled me close. His eyes were moist. He got up and poured himself more bourbon. Suddenly he urged me to play him something the way I used to. I said I had to talk to him, we hadn't talked in a long time, but he insisted I play first, then we would talk. I went to the piano reluctantly and he sat down on the couch again, just as he had years before when he paid me that surprise visit. I started to play. At first, the music was very distant, as his voice had been. It was an odd sensation not to know what I was playing. Then gradually I made out the piece. The *Waldstein* Sonata, the piece I had played him that other time. I played it with all the bravura touches he enjoyed. I fell into it and never even glanced over to see his reaction. The music caught fire, and when I was finished—and I had never played it better in my life, never played any piece better, onstage or anywhere else—I sat back and closed my eyes. When I looked up, he was gone. The couch was empty and the room was growing dark. I called out to him. And then I called to Orana, but she never came, never answered. The silence was suffocating. I shouted again, but it felt as if my voice could not carry in that air. I didn't look for them: I felt strangely paralyzed. When I did try to stand, my legs gave out. I was floating through space. The loft was pitch-dark. Something brushed my arm and I glimpsed one of the cats on my ankle. I caught a whiff of Orana's roses. I heard the blood rushing through my ears . . . roaring . . .

Then I opened my eyes and Daphne was staring down into my face. She was shaking my shoulders and shouting at me to wake up. She looked frightened, and the morning light was streaming down on me over her small shoulders.

I was going over my notebook at the piano when Daphne stuck her head in the door. "It's time, Dad," she called softly.

It was Thursday and it was time for her audition. She was wearing what I had suggested: a simple white dress, white shoes, and a tiny pearl necklace. I put on a jacket, ran a comb through my hair, and a few minutes later we were speeding down the Drive. After three days of wind and rain, a blue summer storm that had leeched itself to the coast, it was again hot and sunny. If Daphne was nervous, she hid it well. We had enjoyed a quiet lunch and then she had napped (another of my suggestions) while I worked. In fact, all had been milk-and-honey around the house since Tuesday, when she found me passed out. After my long flailing descent, I had crashed in a heap, and now a great calm had overwhelmed me. I stopped drinking, I cut out the speed and the downers, and I went to bed by midnight every night. That lethal anxiety which had been crippling me had receded. It was the way I had wanted things all along: I slept well, practiced, and in the evening cooked and read. There were no more all-night vigils, no more ugly scenes with lovers I had wronged or who had wronged me, and no more wallowing.

All of this was on the surface; underneath, a dense network of currents was swirling. But the water no longer seemed dark and dangerous. At times it even glowed with possibilities. Something had broken in me on Monday. In some limbo off death's highway, I had seen Orana locked in that *danse macabre* with my dead father, and whatever broke reconnected anew, for the better—or at least stopped dangling. I couldn't say what it was. For twelve years I had stifled that memory of my father's visit and of his disappearing while I played for him. It was the last time I ever saw him. Orana, departing this world, had taken me along a few steps of the way, and somehow shaken me up enough to jar that memory loose. I was only beginning to feel the consequences. I thought of Dr. Winters. Maybe I would have been better off undergoing his treatment. The electronic stimuli he had mentioned seemed preferable to the mess of destructive chemicals I had abused to hear my own "voices of the dead." I wondered if my rocky reawakening was a stroke of dumb luck, or if I had actually undergone a purge. Perhaps Dr. Selzer could tell me. I had made an appointment to see her on Friday when I accompanied Orana to New York. She had told me I was always welcome to come by, and I needed to talk.

With Daphne, I had been able to cover my tracks from that insane night. The damaged telephone, the discarded meat—I had gotten to all of that before she could. I told her I had been stricken with a virus, unable to sleep, and she said nothing one way or the other. I'm sure she had the score on me during that hellish period, but by tacit agreement, we were trying to put it behind us.

At the Conservatory, I took her straight in to meet the director, with whom I chatted until the chairman of the stringed instruments department, a tough genial Brazilian woman, Mrs. Rojas, joined us for tea. Then they left me in the director's study and whisked Daphne off to an audition room.

In this free moment, I put aside the nebulous machinery of my spiritual rehabilitation and concentrated on the concrete and radical steps I had taken in other areas. For one thing, I stopped making a jackass of myself trying to reach Greta on the telephone. I wrote her a brief, apologetic note inviting her to lunch on Friday. I said I would come by at one o'clock sharp to pick her up; if she didn't want to go, she could leave a note on her mailbox, and I wouldn't bother her again. I had also finally, unequivocally, broken real ground in my preparations for the tour. The inspiration came to me on Tuesday afternoon, with no hesitation, phony intellectualizing, or nail-biting.

I simply drew up a new program for the opening recital! Just like that. I threw out every piece except the *Diabelli*, and put together an all-Beethoven program. Liszt had always been one of my anchors, Bach too, and Brahms—but it was to be Beethoven. I had a feeling about it.

After months of maddening, excruciating work, it might seem the height of lunacy, in line with my previous erratic behavior, to make such a compulsive change. Gone was the Schubert in which I had invested hundreds of hours. Gone were *La campanella*, and the Brahms sonata, and the Scriabin I had worked up for an encore. Willy, whom I telephoned on Wednesday so he could inform the people at Carnegie Hall, was sure I had gone off the deep end.

"What kind of a program is that? Are you insane? That will be like a deluge, a musical avalanche, not an entertainment."

"That's what I want—a deluge. An avalanche. A stunner."

"Why not just set fire to the piano? Listen to reason for once. I am Bavarian, for Christ's sake, I *love* Beethoven, and even for me it would be too much."

"It won't be too much. It will be perfect. Look, I'm not throwing out the other pieces. I'll be using them all through the tour. It's only in New York I'm going to do this."

"Only in New York? Where else is there? This is where the real notices will appear. Why can't you experiment in Denver or Houston or one of those places where no one knows any better?"

"I'm surprised to hear you talk like that about your comrades in the hinterlands."

"Max, don't joke now."

"Willy, I've made up my mind. I'm doing this program in New York on September 12. Anton Rubinstein used to do Beethoven programs all the time. And Busoni—"

"Don't tell me about Busoni and Rubinstein! This is here and now."

"I'll bet even Dussek—even Gottschalk—did Beethoven programs."

"Gottschalk did his plantation pieces, and that's what you'll be doing if you continue your suicidal methods."

"I'm even playing a Liszt encore. A kind of maraschino cherry on the whole concoction."

He groaned. "What are we talking about here? Of course there have been all-Beethoven programs. But not like this. Why not a part of the sonata cycle?"

"I've done that. I have to break new ground."

"New ground? But the *Hammerklavier* and the *Diabelli* in one night? Have you been drinking?"

"No, I'm back to tea and soda water."

"Better whiskey, then." I heard him relight his cigar. "All right, Max. Just run through the program again. Let me write it down. Then promise me you'll at least sleep on it. Please. I'll call you in the morning, no more arguments, and you can tell me if you have recovered your senses or if you are going to persist in your folly."

"I open with the *Diabelli*. Then Opus 10, Sonatas 5, 6, and 7. Then the intermission."

"Why not play right through—why bother with an intermission?"

"Then the *Hammerklavier*. The *Waldstein*. And then my encore—one or two Liszt Etudes."

He groaned again. "A marathon. And aside from the *Diabelli*, you are giving yourself four weeks now to work up the Opus 10 and the *Hammerklavier*."

"That's about it."

He was chewing the cigar, restraining himself. "All right. I'll call you tomorrow at ten o'clock. Please consider what I've said."

I had considered it and I confirmed the new program to him that morning. I knew exactly what I was doing. All I had to do was play as I had for my father that day. I had heard it all in a dream. Of course I didn't mention this to Willy. But he had reconciled himself to the idea. Knowing him, I was sure he had consulted his music library and pored over the precise Beethoven programs that Busoni and Rubinstein had played. He muttered something about its being dangerous and unmodern, and then ultramodern, but he stopped arguing. By the end of the conversation he even conceded that if I pulled it off it would be a comeback all in itself.

I had brought along the *Hammerklavier* score and I busied myself with it during the rest of my sojourn in the director's study. I went through it with a fine comb, with complete confidence as in the old days, making dynamic annotations and fingering adjustments, my overall approach to the piece fully formed from the start. I felt as comfortable as if I were at the keyboard, and that was a new, a reawakened, sensation after a spring and summer in which I had felt utterly detached even while glued to the piano. It was not all sunshine, by any means: I still had plenty to do. But at least I was on the right track. It was a fresh start, and that in itself was a relief. My confidence was trickling back. And though I had hoped for months that whatever was missing from my work would reappear with a thunderclap, I was grateful for a trickle. I kept reminding myself not to press, but to let the dove come to me, as the Japanese say. So long as it was a dove, and not a vulture.

After forty-five minutes exactly—these people didn't fool around—the director's secretary escorted me to Mrs. Rojas's office. Daphne was beaming, so I knew it had gone well, and my heart jumped for her. Mrs. Rojas couldn't praise her enough. Her intelligence, her touch, her perfect form. Suddenly I was beaming too. There was a photograph on the desk of Mrs. Rojas, in her youth, with Casals. She told us about it. She inquired about my tour. Then she popped on her reading glasses, shoved some papers under my nose, and said they were absolutely delighted to have Daphne enroll as a full-time student.

I was dumbfounded. I had wanted her only to come for biweekly lessons. I didn't have the authority, I was about to say, to yank her out of day school—then I pulled up short. I was her father, for Christ's sake. Authority was another word for responsibility, and I couldn't assume it suddenly because, having been lax so long, I had no right to.

Mrs. Rojas peered at me as I sat there in anguish. Daphne, squirming beside me in a leather armchair, patted my arm.

"Isn't that okay, Dad?"

I roused myself. "Is that what you want, sweetheart? To leave your other school, and do all your schoolwork here, and play the violin every day?"

She nodded enthusiastically.

"You see, Mrs. Rojas, there's been a small misunderstanding. I brought Daphne in to audition for part-time lessons."

"Oh, I see. I'm very sorry. She is so accomplished and advanced for her age. And with her background, I assumed—"

"It's not your fault. It may be a blessing, actually. But, you see, she usually lives with her mother, in Lexington. She's just with me for the summer. Her mother's abroad, and I would have to clear this with her first."

"I understand, Mr. Randal. That's fine. The only problem is that we have very limited enrollment. This year, on Daphne's level, there are just two openings. So I could not hold her place very long."

"Her mother's coming back on September 2."

She shook her head sadly. "Oh no, as much as she is qualified, and even with her family name," and she smiled, "I could wait no more than a few days. Next Monday or Tuesday . . ."

Daphne's face fell. All this chitchat was accomplishing nothing. For once, *I* would have to make the decision. I was in a corner, though, for I didn't want to barge in and just take over with a heavy hand. I had to weigh this against what I truly thought was best for Daphne, and take the heat later.

"You're sure about this, Daphne?"

She nodded again. "What do you think, Daddy?"

"I think you should do it. I'll talk to Mother when she gets back. Where do I sign, Mrs. Rojas?"

As I leafed through the admissions contract, I tried to be practical, to ask the right questions, to think of what Ellen would ask. Was there a bus service to bring her in from Lexington? How many kids per class? How much emphasis was put on nonmusical studies? And so on. I wrote out a check for the first semester, and Mrs. Rojas walked us to the lobby.

She took me aside for a moment. "I must tell you again, Mr. Randal, though of course you know: Daphne has a wonderful touch and a real understanding for the music. You must be so proud of her."

"I am."

"Of course, she's had such a fine model in you."

"I hope so," I said, abashed.

"I believe she could embark on a career in her teens. I really do."

"That's wonderful," I said, petrified at the notion. "Thank you for your encouragement, Mrs. Rojas."

She took my hand. "I'm honored to have met you."

As we drove home, Daphne was floating on a golden cloud. "You know, Dad, I think Mrs. Rojas thought I was a prodigy, like you. I heard her say so to the other lady."

"She thinks you play beautifully. That you have real promise. But you must remember what I told you last month: just work hard, enjoy yourself, and forget all that stuff. I want you to have fun doing this, too. That's what is most important."

"I remember," she said, rolling her eyes.

And god help you, I thought.

"And why were you surprised when I agreed to see you, Max?"

"I don't know. I remembered your saying I was always welcome to call, but I figured that was pro forma. A gesture."

"You know I was not one for gestures in the two years you came here. It was a matter of trust, wouldn't you say? And a lack of it on your part."

"Yes."

"When you broke off here, you had reached the stage at which you were beginning to transfer onto me the persona of your mother. You had begun to relate to me as your mother, and your trust for me had diminished accordingly. In fact, it is probably the true reason you broke off your analysis so precipitously."

I studied her face. It seemed unchanged. About fifty, she was a slender, diminutive, gray-haired woman, wide-set dark eyes, high cheekbones. She spoke softly. She had a new Persian carpet in the office; otherwise little had changed.

"Well, your silence is a positive sign. When you left, you would have denied emphatically what I just suggested."

"I understand what you're saying. But I still have trouble accepting it. And it's spilled over. If anything, my relations with women are worse than ever. I thought I came here to discuss some things that have happened. But now I see that I really wanted to ask if you would take me on again as a patient. I'll be on tour, but after that. I didn't know I was going to ask you this until I walked in here."

She sat back heavily and screwed the cap onto her fountain pen. "Of course you can always come back. But there is one small complication."

"You have no slots?"

"No, I can make room. It's more a conflict of interest. You see, your former wife Greta is a patient of mine."

"Greta?" I was stunned. "I had no idea she was even in analysis. She never mentioned it to me."

"Why should she?"

"Well, I don't know. I've been—I had been seeing her this summer—but of course you know that, if she's your patient."

She shook her head. "I am sure you understand that, for reasons of confidentiality, I have nothing further to say about her relationship with me. I would not have brought it up at all had it not become necessary."

"Can you tell me how long she's been coming to you?"

"About a year and a half. She began five months after you left here. She had been seeing another doctor, right after your divorce. She wanted a change, and I took her on."

"I see."

"I would never turn away a former patient, Max, but perhaps under the circumstances you might prefer another doctor. That is up to you."

I felt despondent. Two weeks before, Dr. Selzer had not figured in my plans at all. I never intended to see her again. But now, this seemed a setback.

"Sure. I guess I feel sort of preempted."

"That is natural, and unfortunate. If you had remained my patient, I would not have taken Greta on. But I did not want to turn her away on the slim chance you might someday come back."

"That's fair enough. I'm glad she's with you. In fact, one of the things I wanted to talk about with you is my relationship with her. The way I've screwed it up."

She interrupted me. "Let me speak to Greta before we have our first formal session. She ought to know about this as well, don't you think?"

"Yes. But maybe you're right. Maybe I ought to consult someone else. This could be too messy all around."

"It needn't be. But I leave that up to you." She uncapped her pen again. "Let me give you the names of some colleagues. After a two-year hiatus, a switch would not be so traumatic for you. It is often beneficial, in fact, at such times."

"Sure."

"You did say you would be back in New York after your tour?"

I was surprised how much difficulty I had in replying to this. The prospect of remaining in Boston did not seem so dreadful anymore, especially with Daphne nearby.

"I'm not certain. Can you give me a few names in Boston too, just in case."

"Of course. I assume you would want to continue with Jungian analysis?"

"Yes. I don't think I would get along with a Freudian," I said drily. "I am not inclined to the notion that sex is at the root of everything."

She looked at me. "I'm glad to hear that. And would you still prefer your doctor to be a woman?"

"It doesn't—yes, I would. I would prefer that."

"That's what I thought. Here, I've put down five names. If you should choose not to return here, I think the first two would be best for you."

I left a bit dazed, but at 1:05, heart thumping and mouth dry, I pulled up in front of the old building on Spring Street. There was no note on the mailbox. I rang the buzzer, waited, rang again, and the door popped open. At least she was going to see me. As I stepped off the elevator, I was briefly transported back to my nightmare—except that I had no flowers now. I had forgotten to get flowers.

Barefoot, in jeans and a T-shirt, her eyes distant, Greta ushered me in without a word. My heart sank, for she obviously had no intention of having lunch with me. We went into the studio and sat at opposite ends of the couch, the same one where my father sat when I played for him. Greta sat erect, like a statue.

"Would you like something to drink?" she said finally. Her eyes were flat, distant. I had seldom seen her like that.

"No thanks." I was about to launch into my explanation, which had been going round in my head all day, but suddenly I had a lump in my throat. A whiff of nausea. I tried to collect myself. I loathe theatrics, and I didn't want her to think I might be self-indulgent and messy, reluctant as ever to take responsibility for my actions.

Greta had a big heart, but she was wary of me. When I glanced up, I found she had not budged an inch. She was waiting impassively.

I coughed. "I'm sorry."

"Let me get you a glass of water."

"Thanks. I guess you don't want to go to lunch."

"I go out to lunch to do business, or to have a good time. I don't think you are here for either of those reasons, are you?"

"No."

"Well?"

She wasn't about to let me off the hook—why should she?

"You did get my note?"

"Yes, of course." Her big blue eyes remained unblinking.

The sunlight was flowing in the tall windows, where my pianos used to stand, casting beautiful shadows around the palm trees that lined the far wall. There was a long walnut table beneath them covered with her jewelry designs. The stones were flashing in the light.

"Look, Greta, I didn't come here to give you a song and dance. I feel lousy about what happened in Boston. I want to explain—"

"No need to," she said flatly.

"There is if I want to have any sort of future with you."

She raised an eyebrow. "Is that what you want?"

"Yes. Listen, that girl—"

"Which one?"

"There was only one. She put on that little show for you two weeks ago."

"I didn't know it was for my benefit."

"We can play this game all afternoon."

"No, we can't," she said, glancing at her watch. "I have an appointment in an hour. I have to get dressed in ten minutes."

"You just want to bust my balls, is that it?"

"I have not the slightest desire to do anything with your balls."

"You're in good form today."

"Now you listen to me, Max. You didn't change, you haven't changed, you probably never will change."

"How do you know I haven't changed? And that you aren't misjudging me grossly?"

"I am not judging you. You think people have nothing better to do than sit around and pass judgment on you?"

"I'm going to explain to you what was going on that day whether you want to hear it or not."

"If I have no choice, go ahead. It should be good—you've had two weeks to prepare yourself."

"Two weeks of hell. You don't know what I've been through."

"Too bad. That girl! The mouth on her! The little vixen. And you stood there like an idiot."

"What did you want me to do—belt her?"

"You had already done that, hadn't you?" she said acidly.

I threw my hands up. "What's the use? You're still so pissed at me, you're not going to believe a word I say."

"You're right. Why should I believe you? You think you can come here and make a big speech and then everything will be all right?"

"No," I shouted. "Damn it, I'm in love with you, and I want to get married again. Sarah meant nothing to me. I dated her for a couple of months—before I saw you in June. My relationship with her fell apart after I came here that day. I never lied to you, never cheated. She and I were finished. We had a fight. I had seen her just once in two weeks."

"Please, spare me—"

"She never lived with me. She came by that day and I was stupid enough to let her pick a fight. I lost my temper. Then you showed up. I can see you don't believe that, but it's true. That's why she was so jealous—why she lashed out at you. Don't you see? And we're the losers, not her. I'm not denying it was my fault. I should never have let her come up. I dragged you into an ugly scene and you're right to hate me for it. I don't know what else to say, except that I'm sorry. I'm so terribly sorry, Greta."

Her eyes narrowed. "I don't hate you. You're just a mess. A man with your brains, your talent, your capacity for life—and you screw things up so badly. Why? Why are you like that? When will it change?"

I shook my head. "I don't know. I think I have changed."

"Oh, Max. I know you: you're in the dumps, you can't sleep, you pace around at night, you take pills, and after a few days—bingo!—you've changed. A new man. Reborn. It's not like that. That's what you wanted with your music too, and it will never work. You always thought you could figure everything out, calculate your feelings, your ups and downs. To clean yourself out, you have to go through the wringer—don't you know that yet?"

"I have been through the wringer."

"Maybe. But only after so much resistance, after putting everyone else through first. I feel so bad for you . . . for both of us. I wanted things to be so different."

"They will be different." This was my moment and I seized it. I slid over beside her. She didn't move. "I'd like you to give me another chance. Two months ago you said it would be good for us to get back together. I know you've changed since our divorce. Give me another chance to show you that I have, too. That's all."

"That's a lot," she said.

She studied me, yet I had the uncanny sensation she wasn't thinking about our immediate conversation but about something else, of bigger dimensions. Weighing other choices, deeper feelings, that I wasn't even aware of.

I cleared my throat. "How about lunch?"

She hesitated. "Maybe a sandwich," she said, "but I have to make a call first."

"You mean, you really did have an appointment?"

"Of course," she said crossly. "We'll go somewhere around here."

"Wait. Later, I'm going by the hospital to see Orana. Would you like to come with me?"

"She's here now?"

"They brought her down this morning, to a special clinic. Kind of a last-ditch move. She's failing, they can't do anything."

"Poor Orana, that's terrible."

"Will you come?"

"Would she want me there?"

"I know she would. She's fond of you. She remembers meeting you in California."

"All right, I'll come."

I wouldn't say I recovered much lost ground with Greta at lunch, but afterwards she was less wary, not so cool. We were talking again. At least on the surface, the ice was thawing. I was grateful to her for hearing me out. Grateful to have her by my side again, not, as in July, because I lusted after her, but because of her radiance. She was generous by nature and I had counted on that. But I was afraid I could not make things up to her.

We were both pensive during the drive to the hospital on that humid afternoon, crawling up First Avenue enveloped in bus fumes. If I had smelled death in Orana's room in Boston, here I expected to find him perched on her bed, beckoning. Love and death can strip away our masks—at least temporarily, until we fashion new ones. My recent tribulations had forced me to strip away some of my own. But, with or without them, I felt naked that day, and raw. The closer we got to the hospital, the worse I felt. I remembered that Rosa Lenz, my first teacher, a lovely young Austrian woman, had died at New York Hospital. It was she who taught me Thalberg's "three-handed trick" one rainy afternoon. Thalberg used to wow his audiences with this stunt, and it earned him the nickname "Old Arpeggio." He laid down a theme with his thumbs and then played arpeggios around it with his other fingers. That was it. Even then, when my reach wasn't a twelfth, it wasn't very difficult, but it really gave the effect of three hands on the keyboard. Rosa often entertained me with such diversions after an arduous lesson. She died of cancer a year later. Her family asked me and another of her pupils to play at the funeral service, but my mother refused because she said it would disturb me. It was my mother who disturbed me. I suppose it was easier for me at that moment to distract myself with such memories than to ponder Orana's terrifying physical decline. Rosa Lenz had died slowly. Orana was now on the last leg of an express ride that had picked up speed in the previous days. I was sure she would not live out the week.

In the labyrinth of the hospital complex, the tropical disease center was a long rectangle beside the school of surgery. We went down several long shiny corridors, and as we approached the reception desk, I glanced up and felt my knees go soft.

"What's the matter?" Greta said, taking my arm. She followed my eyes and read aloud the chrome lettering over the glass doors: THE JOHN M. RANDAL WING FOR TROPICAL DISEASES.

I shook my head. "Jesus Christ."

"Isn't that—"

"My father."

"But how?"

"I don't know. It's incredible."

"You mean, you didn't know about this?"

"I knew he set up a foundation to dispense his money. There was a scholarship fund, but the bulk went for research into tropical diseases. None of us could understand it. It was some personal concern of his, something in his own life. So the executors must have sent a big chunk of the dough here."

Greta got Orana's room number and I started speculating. What intricate, convoluted karma had over the long years brought Orana to this place, paid for with my father's ring earnings, to die? And what was his connection to tropical diseases, of all things? The Arthritis Foundation, the Police Athletic League, the Heart Association—with his background, they would have made some sense. Why the interest in such a remote philanthropic byway? Why, and for whom? I would never know the answers to these questions. I had asked his lawyers when the will was probated, and they knew nothing—or wouldn't say, if they did. This shadowy link between him and Orana, even more than their joint appearance in my drunken memory, was not something I would be able to explain through my esoteric reading. There was nothing like this in Kierkegaard. This was the domain of Tiresias, where the blind men draw the maps and the rest of us stumble in darkness.

When we entered Orana's room, I thought Greta was going to pass out. I had neglected to prepare her. For in that last week Orana's appearance had deteriorated considerably. They were giving her transfusions every other day, and those monitors were hooked up to her round the clock. She looked as if the blood had been sucked out of her very fiber. Her skin was taut and transparent. Her eyes gigantic, her lips parched, her hands tinier than ever. She was asleep—she slept most of the time now—and the nurse told us we could stay only five minutes. What difference did it make, I thought. She had a private room with a window and the usual bouquet of roses was set on a table. Maybe because of the new surroundings and their finality, the sight of those flowers this time filled my eyes with tears. I felt utterly powerless.

Greta had to sit down. I squeezed her shoulder. Suddenly I felt close to her again. Her golden hair stood out in sharp contrast to the gray and white hues enveloping Orana. The nurse woke her up. After the briefest hesitation, she recognized Greta and smiled. We were surprised at the strength of her voice.

"Thank you for coming, Greta. I am sorry we could not meet again sooner."

"Yes, I'm sorry too."

"Maybe this is a dream, but I had a feeling when you were divorced that you two would eventually get together again."

"You did?" I was surprised.

She closed her eyes. I thought she had drifted off again.

But she blinked them open suddenly. "And I knew from the way you talked in Boston, Max. . . . You know, they say a man always goes back to his ex-wives for one thing or another."

"So it seems," I murmured.

The sunlight slanting through the blinds was very bright. Greta went over to adjust them.

"No, please, leave the light."

There were no books on her bedside table anymore, no journals. Just the nurse's fashion magazines.

Orana followed my gaze. "I didn't finish the Gibbon," she said, closing her eyes again. She was drifting. "Read as far as the Emperor Domitian. He was better than the others. He reopened the theaters."

Greta didn't understand. She glanced at me, and I shook my head.

"Thank you for the roses again. But don't send any more."

The nurse leaned in and told us we should be leaving soon.

Orana looked at us curiously, then sucked in her breath. "Greta, may I ask you a favor?"

"Of course."

"Would you step over here? No, closer."

Orana whispered to her. Greta's expression didn't change, just a flicker passed across her eyes. She nodded.

The nurse came back. Orana was already asleep when we kissed her goodbye.

Out in the reception area of the John M. Randal Wing for Tropical Diseases, I took Greta's arm.

"What did she tell you?"

"I can't say. She made me promise."

And we walked out into the courtyard, full of blinding light and hot as a furnace.

Epicurus suggests we banish from our lives all gods and notions of death if we want to be free of pain. For ten days, back in Boston, I tried to follow his advice, without much success. I visited Orana once (she slept through it), shuttling to New York and back one morning, but that night she lapsed into a coma and they told me it would be pointless to visit again. The following morning she died. She never regained consciousness. They told me she didn't suffer in the end. How could they know that?

It happened so quickly, and we had so many arrangements to make from afar, that there was little time for grief that day. Without Greta, I would have been lost. Not only did she keep Daphne's affairs running smoothly, but she helped both of us stay afloat and kept me, especially, at arm's length from my worst inclinations. I stuck to my work, my sobriety, and my decent schedule, and didn't stumble into a swamp of melancholia. In truth, I felt relieved that it was all over.

There is not much to tell about our whirlwind trip to New York. I felt like a sleepwalker. Orana's body was cremated, and that evening Greta, Patty, Willy, and I attended a small service for her at a private chapel. Then we flew back to Boston, following for a few minutes the route the small hired plane would take at dawn when it scattered her ashes over the Atlantic.

Two days after our joint visit to Orana, and two weeks after the disastrous episode with Sarah, Greta had finally come up to Boston. She was going to stay until I opened in New York, and then we would see, as she put it. She wouldn't discuss the future in any more specific terms. She said there was a lot of dust that had to settle. I thought of it as our trial period. But she became touchy if I brought up our living accommodations after my tour, and would change the subject immediately. Then, when I mentioned marriage again one evening, she flushed and made me promise not to bring up any of these questions until after that first recital.

From then on, we got on well enough. Fortunately, this was the off-season in her jewelry work, so she didn't have to be in New York. She set up a draftsman's table in the bedroom and worked there every morning. The rest of the time she and Daphne were inseparable. Daphne was elated to have her back, and this cheered me up a great deal.

The house was calm, and I had my work cut out for me with the new program. The pieces excited me. I worked hard, finally with some sense of purpose. I didn't have much choice. Orana died on August 30, exactly two weeks to the day before I played Carnegie Hall. This was it. And though my playing was more vibrant, with some of the old resonance reemerging—at its core, its very essence, there was still something missing. I could find no technical weak link. I needed something that I couldn't summon with my will. My numinous self was at the mercy of my psyche, which was still a tangle. I thought myself a new man, infused with calm, yet I needed something more, and as the time flew by I no longer had the luxury of searching for it through contemplation. I couldn't allow myself to fret anymore. Within two weeks I was going to walk onstage. I knew that I would perform competently. I would play as well as I had to. But with all I had gone through, I required much more than competence to justify myself. And to satisfy the rabble. Something else had to click.

The night after Orana died, Greta took Daphne out for dinner and a movie and I put in four hours of extra work. Later, try as I might, I was too wound up to fall asleep. I kept thinking about Orana. For the first time, I broke my new curfew, and my promises to Greta, and slipped out of bed at one a.m. I brewed a pot of one of Greta's herbal teas. We were stocked up with herbs and protein powders of every variety. The refrigerator was full of health foods—no more canned ravioli and garlic knockwurst,— and when the three of us sat down to a candlelight dinner, it was still romantic but the cuisine was eggplant shashlik, or turnip and pilaf, or tofu with lichee nuts. Gone were the Mongolian goulash and the chili Madrid. I sat down in the living room and tried to distract myself with the newspaper.

I dozed off after the first cup of tea, and it was 2:10 when I opened my eyes again. I was having a bad dream, but couldn't remember it. Then I realized it wasn't the dream that had awakened me. Someone was knocking gently at the front door. Barefoot, in my black silk robe, an unlit cigar between my teeth, I went and peeped out into the hall. There was a man in evening dress, white tie, and a black fedora pulled down low, so I couldn't see his face.

"Who is it?" I whispered.

Silence.

Maybe I was still dreaming. "Who's there?" I demanded.

"Max? It's me—Amos. Open up."

Amos! The prodigal. Who else would be at my door at two a.m. in a tuxedo?

We embraced. Except for the tux, he looked the same as always. His sandy hair parted neatly under the hat, his blue eyes wide awake, twinkling. He was trim and alert as usual, lithe as a nocturnal animal, about my size but with smaller hands and an almost feline precision to his movements. He needed a shave, and he was shadowy under the eyes, but his handsome face was unlined and relaxed. The more frenzied his pursuit of the moment, the calmer he looked. He was a boy wonder, a prince of youth, at thirty-three still the eternal romantic. What amazed me was that such a man could exist in our times, a man who lived for the moment as if his life depended on it. Amos was a true hero—not like me. One of those mad pioneer souls who woke at six a.m. and collapsed nineteen hours later, and still complained that he had no time. Leaping time zones, subsisting on bad food, sleeping on trains and planes—this was his bread-and-butter. And that night was no exception. He was in transit, as he informed me immediately.

"Good to see you, good to see you," he said, throwing his arm around me. "I have to catch a plane at seven-thirty, so we only have about four hours. Put on some coffee. We have lots to talk about." He tossed his jacket on a chair en route to the kitchen.

"Where are you coming from?"

"Athens. Before that, Budapest. In the morning, Santo Domingo."

"Of course. Are you with a tour group?"

"I'll explain everything."

"Shhh."

He stopped short. "Sorry, I forgot about Daphne."

"How did you know she was here? You were away when she came."

"That's true, but I knew," he said vaguely.

"Did you also know Greta was here?"

"You mean, *your* Greta—the ex? How did that happen?"

"That in itself would take us four hours. I even want to marry her again, but I'm afraid she won't consider it now—though it was originally her idea."

"I don't follow you."

"Things have been kind of complicated."

"What happened to Sarah?"

"We came to a nasty end."

"I see."

"Why the tux? Did you come in by yacht?"

"I had to wear it in Athens, to a party. I rented it. I'll mail it back tomorrow."

"From the Caribbean?"

"Why not?"

I grabbed his neck and started laughing. "I tell people about you and they don't believe it, you crazy bastard. All that madcap business you got me involved in with that guy Winters, and Margaret."

He became grave. "That's serious stuff, Max. I don't mean Margaret—but Winters, he's something special."

"All right. I can't wait to hear about your hush-hush mission to Ireland and the Balkans."

"That's why I'm here," he beamed. "But first some victuals." He was already into the refrigerator. "Hey, what is all this?"

"Greta's put us on a strict regimen. The stuff in the bowls is sesame casserole and soybean whip."

"Jesus, I've got to get some real food in me. Don't you have anything decent stashed away?"

I climbed up onto a chair and reached into the highest cabinet. "How about corned beef hash and kidney beans?"

"Perfect. And you've got some eggs down here."

"Yeah, but they're fertilized."

"I don't give a damn."

He cooked and ate his meal in a matter of minutes, then sat back loosening his collar. "Maybe you can give me a clean shirt," he said. "My bag's checked at the airport. Max, you look tired."

"It's been a rough summer. A lot of strange things have happened." I hesitated. "Orana died yesterday."

"My god, I'm sorry. What happened?"

I explained it to him as best I could. It wasn't an easy story to compress. He was genuinely upset, for they had been fond of each other. The three of us had shared many good times together.

"Got any rum?" he said. He poured himself a shot. "Why is it always people like her who get it like that?" He shook his head. "And all the rats thrive. Margaret."

"Yeah, I didn't know you two were so on the outs. Why didn't you tell me?"

He averted his eyes. "I couldn't."

"Because of you and Ellen?"

"You know, then."

"Of course I know. The first day she was here Daphne cooked me your Mongolian goulash."

"You're not pissed at me, are you?"

"Why should I be?"

"I guess I felt like I was sneaking around. You know."

"That's absurd. What right would I have to be pissed? I'm happy for her—you are serious about it?"

"That's putting it mildly."

"I just never would have put the two of you together."

"Opposites attract," he smiled. "But let's get down to business. That's why I'm here. And I have to tell you everything in order or it won't make sense. First, a couple of questions. How is your music coming—still having trouble?"

"It's been a roller coaster, but things are better. Still not where I want them, but I think I've averted disaster."

"Don't worry—there won't be any disaster. No matter what else has happened, I've got some musical dynamite for you. Second question: what pieces are you performing? Any changes since the spring?"

"Plenty. I'll show you." I got him the printer's proof of the program Willy's office had sent up.

For once, even Amos was surprised.

"This is wild. I've heard of all-Beethoven programs, but the *Diabelli* . . . the *Hammerklavier*. It's perfect. That's all I had to know. Now I'm going to tell you why you're really going to knock them dead."

He poured himself another shot.

"About five months ago, I got an idea. Actually, I got it years ago in Vietnam, looking through a Chinese magazine. I decided to do a photographic study of Albania, the least-known country in Europe, maybe in the world. Do you know anything about Albania, Max?"

I asked myself why I was playing along with this lunacy. "Not much. It's Moslem, right? From Ottoman days. On the eastern Adriatic."

He raised an eyebrow. "Very good. You already score better than ninety-nine percent of your fellow Americans. It's a tight dictatorship. The last guy was in charge for forty years. They have diplomatic relations with nobody, least of all the U.S.A. Only Moslem country in Europe. Reactionary Stalinist police state. But what interested me was the topography, the amazing terrain, just a fraction of which I glimpsed in that Chinese magazine. At that time China and Albania were close allies. After Mao's death, the Albanians gave the Chinese the boot. Afraid they would regress to feudalism, or something. This Chinese photographer—who was no ball of fire—took shots that knocked my shoes off. Hundred-year-old peasants. Icefalls. Fantastic ravines. Steppe villages without electricity. White rivers untouched by man. And nobody, outside of the Albanians' government photographers—a sorry lot—have been allowed access. *National Geographic* can't get near the place."

"Enter Amos Demeter."

"Exactly. I have to do it. I'll go in there the way I did in Bali and Niger—and this book is going to make that stuff look like near-beer. But I'm ahead of myself. Now, the Albanians have no embassy over here, just a U.N. Mission."

"Where you went to see Mr. Sinonesco."

"It's Sinones*cu*. How did you know about him?"

"Margaret told me."

He shook his head in disgust. "Forget about her. Forget what she told you in June. Just listen and you'll understand everything. I went to the Albanian Mission and proposed my idea to Sinonescu. Told him I wanted only nature shots, and villagers and farms—nothing political. I promised to clear all my film with the government." He snickered. "He practically laughed me out the door. Told me not to come back. So I put my plan on hold. I had no choice. You can't even cross the border with an American passport, so there was no question of being cute and trying to photograph surreptitiously. Two weeks later I got a call from Dr. Winters. Said he was referred by Sinonescu, his squash partner, who in his capacity as cultural attaché, spoke with his Foreign Ministry and had second thoughts about my proposal. They had checked me out. The minister thought it would be good for Albania's maverick image, humanizing, and seeing as I had been acclaimed for my role in exposing the brutality of the imperialist war in Southeast Asia, and had attracted international attention to Third World affairs in Africa, a real man of conscience, they were willing to let me take my pictures under certain conditions. In short, I had to make a deal."

"I hope you haven't done anything stupid."

"Why do you say that?" he said peevishly. "It did get kind of tricky, though, because my relationship with Winters forked two ways. He served as my intermediary to Sinonescu—for his own reasons, which I'll get to—and he took me on as a patient at the institute, which is where you and I—that is, Ireland and Hungary—come in."

"You're losing me . . . What was the deal—photos of missile bases?"

"You know me better than that." He smiled mischievously. "I can't say there wasn't a smidgeon of cloak-and-dagger, but nothing involving our government. I told Winters I would consider a deal, within reason, and he said Sinonescu wanted to meet with me again—at Winters's office. Now, this is Winters's tie-in with the Albanians: he and they wanted a report in the possession of a doctor in Skopje, Yugoslavia, near Albania. The report was compiled in the fifties in southwest Yugoslavia by a team of psychologists, half of whom were Albanians working jointly with Yugoslav doctors. It was a parapsychology project on clairvoyance, ESP, brain waves, and hallucinogenics—well ahead of similar research here in the States, or in the Soviet Union. It was a pioneer work and, sparing you a lot of interesting details, in the end the Yugoslavs, for political reasons, reneged on the joint-venture agreement and kept all the research material for themselves. They deported the Albanian doctors posthaste, without explanation. The Albanians protested, of course. It was a blow to their national pride. Because of the Kosovo dispute, their relations with Yugoslavia have worsened. Meanwhile, the report is still of medical interest—especially to someone like Winters—but politically it's a dead football. Nobody in Belgrade gives a damn about it anymore, but they refuse to discuss it with the Albanians. The Albanians still want it. They're very much into parapsychology, you know. Their agents got to a doctor in the clinic where the report is filed. After a hefty bribe, he agreed to turn it over to them. But he refused to meet with any more Albanians. He said if his government got wind of it, they would destroy him and the report. The Albanians needed an intermediary above suspicion, from outside the Balkans. That's where I came in. I agreed to meet this doctor, pretending I was on a routine assignment, to get the report."

"You're lucky they didn't blow your brains out."

"The Albanians assured me I was in no danger. As an American, I could play stupid. The Yugoslavs would never suspect I might know all the background on the stuff. At worst, they would have deported me as a dupe and confiscated the report. Anyway, they didn't."

"And Winters was a party to this?"

"Why not? Sinonescu agreed to give him a copy of the report, for his private research, so long as he never disclosed that he had it. It was his finder's fee," Amos chuckled, "for finding me. In

Skopje it was gathering dust. Winters figures he can glean some helpful information. The moment I deliver the stuff to Sinonescu, I receive a two-month visa to Albania, a permit to photograph in nonrestricted areas, and even a free pass at the state hotels. That's my payoff. They get their report and I get my book."

"Incredible. And you actually did this?"

"I pulled it off to the letter. That's why I was in Athens."

"I'm losing you again."

"Well, I wasn't dumb enough to cross the border with this thing under my coat. Skopje is about four hours from Greece. I had a good friend of mine, a newspaper editor who frequently travels to the socialist countries, meet me in Skopje. He's never bothered at customs. We stashed the stuff inside his spare tire and he took it into Greece for me. I flew there from Budapest two days ago and picked it up. That's why I'm wearing this monkey suit. I had to go to a testimonial last night for my friend. I couldn't refuse after what he did for me."

"But where is the report now?"

"In a locker out at Logan. That's where you come in. You simply get it to Winters in New York. He'll make his copy and then pass the original on to Sinonescu, who in turn will give you—and only you—my visa and the rest."

"All right. But I've had enough adventure this summer. I don't feel like getting rolled in the name of Albanian national pride."

"You're not going to get rolled. Okay, that's Part One. Now we get on to the bonanza I'm about to bestow on you." He smiled broadly. "There is something far more interesting, and truly exquisite, in that locker. Just for you."

"Want some more coffee?"

"I'm already speeding my brains out. Okay, you met Winters, so you must have heard about neurovisual harmonic phenomena."

I hesitated. "Yes, I've heard about it."

"I thought so. I told him you'd be skeptical. Did you even let him get to first base?"

I felt guilty suddenly. "You don't know how chaotic things

have been. I had no time for his treatment. Six weeks with the voices of the dead, and all that."

He shook his head sadly. "A big mistake. Look, I'm as cynical as the next guy when it comes to hype. Have you ever known me to be a patsy for con artists?"

"No," I said grudgingly. "But you're always open to experiment. Much more so than I am."

"That's not the point. This guy is on the level. Anyway, I'm not here to sell you on Winters. It just would have helped if you understood more of the background."

"Try me."

"All right. The Albanian business was set up in May, but I had to wait a month because the doctor in Skopje was away at a conference. I had lunch with Winters again, we chatted about the report, and his work, I asked some questions, one thing led to another, and I started taking his treatment. Hell, Max, you out-think yourself sometimes. I figured I'd try it. If it was a washout, I'd lose nothing; if not, who knows what I'd pick up. Your problem is that you're always caught up in romantic hassles, and you neglect your imaginative development."

"Let's not go into that again."

He held up his hand. "Fine. No cheap shots. By the way, I saw a box of cigars in the fridge . . ."

I got out a couple.

"Macanudos, eh?" He blew smoke rings while collecting his thoughts. "So. Essentially, through a kind of advanced, state-of-the-art hypnosis—lights, music, suggestive sound, hyper-immersion, and self-analysis sessions before the hypnosis itself—Winters gets you in touch with remote parts of yourself. Things that have been out of reach for years. It's very comprehensive, utterly compressed. Daily marathon sessions until he really gets under your skin. The second week you start summoning up things you can't quite articulate. Shapes, shadows, snatches of voices. They're fleeting, but achingly familiar, and you sense the approach of more concrete perceptions. That's where Winters does his real work, the crucial stuff, around the third week. He hypnotizes you one-on-one and serves as guide. He helps isolate some of the phantoms. External stimulation is cut in half. Consciously, I don't remember much of it. If I did, my treatment would have been a failure. It's not what you might imagine: no strobe lights or spooky music or anything. The audio is attuned to your body rhythms, to chemical connections in your brain. And the visual is patterned to mirror inner reflections that accompany trains of thought or memory. Winters said my treatment was amazingly successful. That I'm basically an extrovert, inclined to a positive response. But I'm getting carried away."

"No, it's intriguing."

"We don't have time, though. The point is that I had a fantastic spiritual experience."

"You mean, you talked to the dead?"

"No, I received impulses, voices, spiritual stimuli, to which I was already predisposed. Through time and space, through a set of laws that has nothing to do with our so-called natural laws. You know what Blake said about the doors of perception . . . the particularity of wisdom? I received two very strong revelations out of the entire miasma. There were other things I learned, but quieter, private stuff." He lowered his voice. "I've told you about my father's more colorful pursuits, but I never mentioned that he was a good friend of Rank and Adler, and of Sergius Müller, the Austrian metaphysician. He locked himself away for a year reading Paracelsus, Böhme, Swedenborg, Madame Blavatsky—all that stuff. My mother thought it was insane. But it is an odd coincidence that my father was tuned in to some of these ideas. And it's significant that I had a direct spiritual confrontation with my father in the fourth week. It was nothing like the stuff in films—wispy silhouettes and murky voices. It was more telepathic. As if his thoughts overlapped mine, and I had suddenly come up with an idea that I could not have arrived at solely through my own thoughts and memories. An idea that required another agent. It was as if my mind was taken over, as if in a dream I had become someone else, with an alien set of notions—and insights. But it would take days to explain. It came to this: my father was Irish, born over there, and I had the idea when I emerged from my trance that there was a lost set of diaries I ought to get hold of that belonged to my grandfather. That I would discover its whereabouts by visiting a certain address in Dublin on a certain date. That they were bound in blue leather and tied together with a sailor's sash. My grandfather was an explorer, a geologist. My mother used to say I must have taken after him. But I didn't know much about him. I got to Dublin on the 'suggested' date and went to that address. I talked to a woman who was staying there for just two nights, who in turn introduced me to her sister, in town—for the first time in nine years!—on an unexpected visit, who directed me to another address, et cetera, et cetera." His face lit up. "The upshot is, after a chain of the most opportune connections, I found the diaries! Under very obscure circumstances. Bound in blue leather and tied with a red sash imprinted H.M.S. *Seacrest*!"

I looked at Amos carefully. "But couldn't this 'idea' simply have been a buried memory, something your father or mother once mentioned, and then with a few coincidences tagged on— there are a hundred possible explanations."

"A hundred possibilities, but the fact—the *fact*—remains that I 'remembered' or realized this bit of information while taking Winters's treatment. And in fact the diaries exist. The sash, the other details, were accurate. Not to mention that first address. You can't refute that."

"I don't want to refute it. I'm just saying—"

"I know what you're saying. Just try, for once, to discard your ultrarationalist shackles. Now, that was business of a personal nature. It reached into my ancestral past. But you tell me how I could have known beforehand what you're about to hear. We leave Yugoslavia and Ireland. Hungary was your baby, Max. It happened two days later in my treatment. I knew little about Franz Liszt's personal life until two months ago. Only the obvious stuff: friendship with Chopin and George Sand, ladies' man, Wagner's father-in-law—trivia."

"Liszt?"

"Yes, Liszt. Initially, I didn't understand what it was I had discovered in my trance. This time the 'idea' was meaningless until I did some research. It had come to me that outside Budapest, at the old country house of an aristocratic family named Festetics, there could be found the original manuscripts of three of Liszt's Hungarian Rhapsodies. And here's the kicker: they were Rhapsodies Nos. 5, 7, and 21!"

His eyes were glowing like a madman's. Though I had been

able to accept some of the things he had told me, at that moment I thought he was crazy.

"Don't you understand what that means?" he demanded.

"It means your trance was a little short on history. There is no Rhapsody No. 21."

"But there *is*, Max. That's the point!"

"Listen, Amos—"

"You listen, you jackass. You don't understand what I'm telling you." I thought he was going to explode in his excitement. "I discussed this 'idea' with Winters immediately afterward. He didn't know what it meant or where it would lead, but he felt sure there was something to it. That it was linked to my desire to help you solve your problem, which I had talked over with him. He made an obvious suggestion—what you would be doing now if your mind weren't encased in steel. He told me to get a biography of Liszt and check out the few facts with which I had been provided in the trance. And do you know what I discovered on the night of June 8 in a coffee shop on Lower Broadway? Franz Liszt, at age twenty-eight, already an international celebrity, made a triumphal homecoming visit to Hungary in December 1839. He arrived in Pest on Christmas Eve to a tumultuous welcome. He hadn't been on Hungarian soil in sixteen years. In addition to his sold-out recitals, and the ceremonies honoring him, he did some important composing while he was there. He was intrigued by the music of the gypsies. He visited their camps. They treated him royally and performed their music for him, sometimes through the night. It affected him deeply. Later he wrote a two-volume work on gypsy music. But at that time, in January 1840, he composed a set of pieces called 'Hungarian National Melodies,' based on gypsy themes. Ten years later he revised and published them as the Hungarian Rhapsodies. He published fifteen of them, mind you. The next two were composed years later, and the eighteenth, nineteenth, and twentieth were composed a year before his death. Now, we go back a little. When Liszt came to Pest by coach from Pressburg, he was accompanied by representatives of the Hungarian nobility. The most prominent of these were Count Esterhazy, Count Zichy, and one *Count Leo Festetics*, in whose house Liszt took up residence on Christmas Eve!" He sat back triumphantly.

I could barely repress a smile. This was the Amos I loved. The man who had ridden in caravans and searched for underwater cities. "Go on," I said.

"The same Leo Festetics who presented Liszt with the 'Sword of Honor' in the National Theater and served as his host, providing him with sleighs to visit the gypsy camps. The same Leo Festetics who, with his family, entertained Liszt for a week during the holiday season at his country house outside Pest! It was there that Liszt composed those seminal Hungarian Rhapsodies. He even performed a half-dozen of them for Festetics and Zichy and their families one night on the Broadwood piano in the drawing room. The music reduced them to tears, according to a letter from Festetics's daughter to her cousin in the capital. Liszt transcribed several of the rhapsodies as a gift to the Festetics family—in fact, he gave them his original scores and took the transcriptions back to Paris. All but one, that is. All but one, Max! Due to an oversight, or because it was misplaced later in Paris, the transcription of the twenty-first—actually, it would have been the sixteenth, if you follow me—was lost by Liszt. Only the original, given to Festetics, survived. A piece played only once in recital, for two dozen guests in that drawing room on that winter night. Do you understand now? Has it penetrated? I went back there and got hold of that manuscript for you—the Hungarian Rhapsody No. 21!"

"You got it for me," I said dumbly.

"*And you're going to play it as the encore at your recital!* A lost piece by Liszt—never before performed except by the composer himself! Do you know the sensation that will cause?"

"But this is fantastic. How did you find the manuscript?"

"The same way I found those diaries. I followed to the letter the 'idea' that came to me in my treatment. The Festetics' country house still stands. It's a nursing home now, run by the State, for war veterans. In my researches, I learned that Liszt did his composing in the chapel on the estate. It's used now as a storehouse for junk from the old house. Very rundown. All sorts of worthless heirlooms gathering dust. So it isn't exactly under guard. I had a hunch about it. I drove there from Budapest late at night in a rented car, broke in the back window, and rummaged around with a flashlight for nearly five hours. Only for you, buddy. Nobody had touched that stuff in years. For a while it seemed hopeless. Just piles of junk. Then—bingo!—I found the remains of an organ in the sacristy. And behind it, buried under a lot of books and religious artifacts chewed up by rats, there was a metal box with a coat of arms filled with yellowed sheet music—devotional stuff—and exercise books, and at the very bottom the three scores in Liszt's hand. I confirmed that the next morning at the National Museum. The box evidently belonged to Festetics's daughter. Over the years it was forgotten. The manuscripts of the other two rhapsodies will be of interest to scholars. I'll turn them over to some university. But No. 21," he concluded majestically, "is for you, Max."

"You mean, you stole them?"

"From the rats, I guess, because no one else was going to use them. And they might just as well be in a museum here as anywhere else."

I was speechless for a moment. "Amos, it's astounding. An incredible discovery, if that score is authentic—"

"It is authentic, I tell you. I fumbled through some of it myself in Athens, at Yanni's house. I'm no maestro, but I know Liszt when I hear it. And I hope you're not going to suggest," he said thickly, "that my mother told me about Festetics as a bedtime story thirty years ago and Winters simply dredged it out of my memory."

"But how do you explain it?"

His face fell. "For a guy who can produce divine sounds with a bunch of wires and hammers, spiritually speaking you have feet of clay. Don't you believe in miracles, Max? In acts of wonder outside the sweatboxes of science and art? I covered thousands of miles on faith alone, and you aren't even willing to suspend your disbelief for a few hours, on my word?"

I felt ashamed, but the fact is I thought he was raving. I was unwilling to accept any of it until I studied the manuscript and played and heard this Rhapsody No. 21 for myself. But he was

right: if it was genuine, this "lost piece" would cause a sensation—and not just at my recital.

Amos shook his head. "You've got doubt written all over your
face," he said. "You think I'm off my rocker."

I heard Greta calling for me down the hall.

"I'm in the kitchen," I answered. "Make sure you're decent,
we have a visitor."

She peeked around the corner. "Who—Amos! Is that Amos?"

"Hello, darling," he smiled. "Just dropped in for coffee."

"But what are you doing here?"

"Good question," he muttered. "I've been trying to talk sense
to a mule." He gave her a big hug.

"So the bad boy has come home again," she said, tousling his
hair.

"Just passing through, I'm afraid. Greta, you look lovelier than
ever."

"But what is this?" she said, examining the remains of his
meal. "What did you give him, Max—cat food?"

"No, some real food. Hash and beans."

Amos, ever the diplomat, interceded. "Your casserole looked
scrumptious, but in my travels I missed my American basics.
Max objected, but I insisted on the hash."

"Two liars," she laughed, "but at least one is a gentleman. Let
me fix you something good. Some eggplant with ginger?"

"No thanks, I'm full. But I could use a shower before I go."

"Go? You can't stay on a day or two? Where are you rushing
to—New York?"

"Nothing so obvious," I put in. "He's flying to Santo Domingo in two hours."

"What for?"

"It's a long story," he said uneasily.

"Come on, while you shower, we can talk to you from the bedroom. I wish you'd gotten me out of bed earlier."

While Amos, through waves of steam, regaled Greta with tales
of his travels, I brooded over all he had told me. For her, he was
like a breath of fresh air through the place, with his tuxedo, and
his pockets full of mystery.

"On the plane," he was telling her, "there were four Arabs,

young guys with English accents, playing Monopoly with real money. A pile of five-hundred-dollar bills on Free Parking, and instead of the doggie and the top hat they were using their diamond rings as pieces. Arguing like crazy. They invited me to join them—all I needed was fifteen hundred in cash. I was tempted, but that's about all the cash I have left on me, and I sensed those guys were not good losers—or winners."

"But why did you go abroad in the first place?" she insisted, for he had been sidestepping all her questions.

"Max will fill you in when he gets back from the airport. And I'll take you up on that shirt now, partner."

"White?"

"With French cuffs, if possible."

At six-thirty, shaved, brushed, and crisp, he was ready for the world again. We didn't have a minute to spare if he was going to make his plane.

Greta walked us to the elevator with Mango perched on her shoulder. "Just one thing, Amos," she said. "Will the divorce be effective at once?"

He was startled. "How—"

"Come, come, why else does one go to Santo Domingo—especially in September?"

"You've got me there. Yes, it takes effect as soon as I sign the papers."

"Well, good luck to you," she murmured, kissing him on both cheeks. "You're doing the right thing, but still it makes me sad. Margaret and I used to be friends."

"It's for the best, Greta, I promise you that. I'll see you in New York. Bon voyage," and he blew her a kiss.

We rode down to the lobby in silence. Here I am, I thought, groping in the dark all summer, trying to work up the nerve—when all was said and done—to go on tour, which is no more than my profession, and here is Amos, tracking down heirlooms in Dublin and breaking into nursing homes in Hungary, making a major musicological find, and running secret missions in Yugoslavia for the government of Albania—all in a day's work. Amos was a gentleman, as Greta said, but in the existential, Confucian sense, for as the *Analects* advise, he constantly asked himself,

"What am I to do?" Not "how" or "why," but "what." I must admit I felt a pang of envy for my dear friend. And a bit sorry for myself.

And he still had one more surprise for me.

As we walked to the garage for the car, he was deep in thought. We were an incongruous pair in the early morning haze, he groomed and spiffy in his tux and I unshaven and bedraggled in my white trousers and denim jacket. We passed commuters trudging off to work, people who had eaten well and slept eight hours, and yet beside Amos, who had eaten canned hash and not slept a wink, they looked like phantoms, wrecks. He had never had a nine-to-five job. He worked hard as a photographer, in the field, and he got by professionally and otherwise on his sharp wits. That life-style, the lack of a deadening routine, had kept him healthy and young, to a degree he should have been neither.

He insisted we stop at a grocery for a quart of grapefruit juice, despite the press for time.

"We have gallons of fresh orange juice at the house," I said irritably. "Why didn't you take some?"

"I saw the orange juice," he replied calmly. "But I always make a rule of grapefruit juice—no less than a quart—every morning. It will be the secret of my longevity."

"Funny, I was just thinking about your good health."

"You would do well to follow the tips I've given you over the years. And don't be so cranky—I'm the one who hasn't slept in days."

"You're not human."

He passed me the juice at a red light.

"Changing the subject a bit," he said pensively. "You know, Greta only had half the answer just now."

"Answer to what?"

"You are disagreeable, aren't you? I'd forgotten you're not a morning person. The answer to why I am jetting to the Caribbean with such speed. You see, I am not just getting divorced down there."

"What do you mean?"

"I mean that I am getting married, too. Jesus, can't you put two and two together?"

I looked at him. His eyes were bemused and slightly worried, and at that moment I did put two and two together. I *was* thick. It had not clicked in my head, even after I had learned of his visits to her house, that Amos and Ellen might be traveling together. That they had been in Europe together! My discrete and unrelated fields of thought about the two of them, with so many respective unknowns, had never merged until that suspended moment at the traffic light.

"Light's green, Max."

"My god. You're marrying Ellen. Why the hell didn't you tell me before?"

"I had to wait for the right moment. Even for us, it happened rather suddenly—en route from London to Belgrade, to be precise."

"But why didn't you tell me you were seeing each other before you went abroad?"

"Ellen thought you would be hostile," he said, glancing away. "She wanted to wait."

"How long has it been going on? Daphne mentioned your visiting them in April."

"Oh, long before that. Ellen used to see me on the sly in New York."

"Those trips to her sister! Even after we were in court in June, she flew to New York."

"That was me. She had to see me off to Ireland that night. We met up later in London. I can't tell you how happy we are, Max. She's a great girl."

"I know she is. Frankly, I always wondered why she never married."

"She was waiting for the right guy," he chuckled. "She's very particular."

"Sure." They were made for each other. Perhaps Ellen had always needed someone like Amos to bring out her passionate and offbeat side. And she, with her own sort of lopsided practicality, would open up new vistas for him. But wait until her Bircher father meets Amos, I thought with amusement. If he considered me a high-risk, pinko sort, Amos would really set him off. But I truly was happy for them. I was only upset that I had been so dense, and he so elusive, and now we had no time to talk about this. We had spent hours on Albania and the Liszt manuscript, and here was a development of far more importance, that would affect Daphne's whole future.

"You two are sure about this," I said.

"Absolutely. We discussed it endlessly. You know I'm careful when it comes to these things, Max."

This was true. From anyone else, I might have suspected a dig, but not from Amos. In all other ways mercurial, he took marriage and his relations with women very seriously.

"I'll be beating Margaret to the punch," he said, "though that has nothing to do with our decision. But this way she won't be able to drag Ellen and me through the divorce courts in New York. Even though her furrier pal is loaded, she wanted to get the farm from me, and the money my mother left me."

"But I'm surprised Ellen didn't come here with you. To break the news to Daphne and everything. Where is Ellen, by the way?"

"She was upset it had to be this way, but we had no choice."

"What are you talking about?"

"Look, she didn't write to Daphne after England because you would have known by the postmarks that she was with me."

"So?"

"She was afraid you would get angry. She saw in June that you were on a short fuse. And she knew you were in rough waters preparing for this tour. She didn't want to compound your worries."

"Oh." Once again, and I hoped for the last time, I had misjudged her.

"Of course she wanted to talk to Daphne herself, but she's counting on you to do it for her. And if you're worried about Daphne and me," he said gravely, "well, we get on famously and—"

"I know that, Amos. She's crazy about you. She's taught me all your damn recipes. And she uses your tricks at Chinese checkers."

He laughed. "At any rate, Ellen is in Santo Domingo. She had to fly on ahead yesterday. The law there is that you can't get married unless at least one of the parties has been in town for seventy-two hours. Don't ask me why. She was dying to see Daphne, but we had to do it this way."

I threw my arm around him. "Well, congratulations."

"You know, if we didn't have to tie the knot under a banana tree, you'd be our best man."

"I would have been honored."

"You really are happy for us, aren't you."

He was all business again as he opened the locker at the airport. His old battered briefcase, with its myriad belts, buckles, snaps, and zippers, was stuffed in with his camera case and a green duffel bag.

He handed me the briefcase with great solemnity, and whipped out one of his cameras.

"What are you doing?"

"This is a historic occasion. Now, stand right there by the open locker . . . that's it." He backpedaled into the stream of passengers on the rampway. "Try to smile, for Chrissakes, you're holding a piece of immortality . . . that's it . . . good." He slipped on his sunglasses. "Here, take this too," he said, handing me the duffel bag, "until I get back." It was very heavy.

"What the hell do you have here?"

"Shoes."

"You're joking."

"No. Seventeen pairs. They have the best shoemakers in the world in Budapest. I stocked up for the next two years. There's a pair of blue ones for you, with buckles—just your style."

"You carried these around Hungary?"

"Of course not. I bought them on my last day."

I started to open the elaborate briefcase, but he laid a hand on my shoulder.

"Do me a favor, Max. Not now. Not in this place. Open it at home, sitting at your piano—all right?"

"If that's the way you want it."

He lowered his voice to a whisper, though there was no one near us. "The Liszt manuscript is in the back compartment, with the double zipper. Everything else is for Winters and Sinonescu. Remember, give it to Winters, stay with him until his copy is made, and then hand it over personally to Sinonescu when he gives you my visa. Winters will arrange the meeting with Sino-nescu—don't you call him at the Mission. Just call Winters this morning. Okay?"

"What keeps them from revoking the visa after they get this stuff?"

He shook his head. "You don't understand these things. A deal is a deal, especially when you make it with an entire government."

"I just don't share your faith in that department."

"Come on, I've got three minutes to board."

The briefcase under my arm and the shoes over my shoulder, I watched him check in, and then we embraced.

"I'll be back for the recital in New York," he said. "I hope my little present works out. You just knock 'em dead, all right?"

I nodded.

"Ellen will call tomorrow."

"Give her a big kiss for me. And don't get her into any crazy trouble, damn you."

"Oh, she's used to it. You should have seen her in Skopje and Budapest."

"You took her along when you broke into that place?"

"Are you kidding? She was my getaway driver."

I shook my head. "I guess I never saw that side of her."

"She's all aces."

I grabbed his arm. "Amos, tell me one thing: do you really believe you talked to this Count Festetics, a guy who's been dead for over a hundred years?"

He sighed. "No, of course I didn't 'talk' to him. It's not like that. I'll explain it to you again in more detail when I get back. Just go play that piece and stop fretting. *Arrivederla*."

As I drove home with the precious briefcase beside me, I felt rotten about having given him such a hard time. I don't know what had compelled me to play devil's advocate—an ultrarationalist, as he put it—when in my private ramblings Locke and Bacon and the other materialists were anathema to me. I had always been convinced of the existence of telepathic forces, and Amos and Winters, behind all the talk of miracles, were simply expounding a very specialized, advanced, and wide-open form of telepathy. From my researches into cathexis, I remembered Freud's dictum that at its deepest strata the unconscious is built not on fantasies but telepathy. That the true building blocks of the unconscious are hidden connectives that provide *uncanny feelings of reference*. If so, Freud's telepathic theory deepens the unconscious beyond our everyday notions, making it a furnace for occult psychosomatic influences and powers—and this was the key, I believe, to Amos's treatment with Winters.

I deduced that Winters found in Amos a subject with an especially refined unconscious relationship to the world, given to heart-pounding impulses, a man of instinct with little innate guilt, who could translate his unconscious urges into immediate action and was thus open to the occult influences of telepathy. For what else could this be but a telepathy which, if compared to mere clairvoyance (my original misjudgment on Winters), is as, say, calculus to arithmetic. Primed by his musician friend's need for a radical cure, versed in musicology, a born adventurer, Amos Demeter had been just the man to stir the particular mulligan's stew that would render the unconscious "idea" (translate: telepathic manifestation) of finding a certain Hungarian Rhapsody in a certain locale. Who knows what spirits, living and dead, and what cathetic vibrations from other objects, had conspired to assist him. Even the ultrarationalist could not dispute the fact that Amos had gone where he sensed he ought to go, from another continent, and found what he "thought" he would find. Freud says, "Reality is not things, it is energy and instinct." By this definition, Amos, that most energetic and instinctual of men, was a master of reality. And in this battered briefcase, I had an example of his mastery, albeit a miraculous one.

His Albanian escapade, the Irish expedition, his impending marriage to Ellen, mother of my only child—I had pushed all these amazing developments aside temporarily. I had to take things one at a time. For what had actually happened in the previous six hours? Amos had come and gone hurricane-fashion, like a master chef—even dressed for the part—and set before me the dinner of his adventures, his concoctions of the summer, so different from my own, one quick platter after another slipped under my nose without time for more than a furtive nibble. Only when he was gone could I begin to digest his fantastic feast. And what better place to begin than, as he himself had suggested, at the piano?

Greta and Daphne were out. They had left a note informing me that there was barley porridge on the stove and fresh carrot juice in the refrigerator. I tossed the bag of shoes into a closet and went straight to the piano. It took me a while to open the elaborate briefcase. I rifled through the papers that Sinonescu and Winters awaited so eagerly. They were in a strange language, which I realized must be Serbo-Croatian. Later, I would take a peek at the photographs and illustrations. I came on the double-zippered compartment. However skeptical I had been, I had a moment's pause. I sat there staring at it, the sun filling the room, and I sucked in my breath. Was I really about to handle some sheet music penned by Liszt himself?

I peered in between the smooth leather flaps and gently extracted five yellowed sheets of music paper—a variety I had only seen before in collections. Willy had something like it, the score of a Strauss concerto, under glass. I looked to the last page first. It was signed all right, and the signature looked authentic! Then I went back and scanned the piece through. I knew at once I had never heard it before. It was in F major. It had the typical balancing of the two gypsy elements in the Rhapsodies, the *lassan (adagio)* and *friska (allegro)* in alternating bursts. I also noted the "gypsy scale"—augmented fourths of the sort found in Rhapsody No. 13. And there was the annotation *"a la zingarese"*—in the gypsy style—which I remembered from the other rhapsodies. This was a fast piece, much of it *allegretto*, some *presto*, some *prestissimo*. The fingering, even in the first few difficult measures, told a story in itself: it had to be either Liszt or a phenomenally competent parodist. No one but he would dream of asking a pianist to make some of the crossovers and interlockings and leaps (worthy of *La campanella* and the Caprices) that jumped off the page at me. There was also some very intricate pedaling of the sort he used—radical *crescendo* and *diminuendo* notations near the climax. And perhaps most telling, the unique rectangular marking he placed over a cluster of notes to indicate an *accelerando* appeared twice, and I knew that he often employed it in the period Amos mentioned—1840 or so—especially in *Ricordanza*, which I had once performed.

This was what my eye caught on the page even before I touched the keyboard. And while all that told me plenty, there was something else, about the feel of the pages and the watermarks and the ink. The manuscript seemed to glow. Was this my lack of sleep, or the effect of Amos's romantic tale of jeweled swords and gypsy music in the snow—or was it intrinsic? I suppose every man has some sacred ground in this life, outside of the people he loves. Perhaps this was as close as I came to sacred ground, to reverence for any sort of relic, this set of yellowed pages crumbling at the corners. I had seen Chopin's journal in some museum, and Beethoven's desk, and even a pair of Mendelssohn's gloves, but maybe because this manuscript was in my hands, mine alone for a short time, and because it was music itself and not a mere object, it was the only relic for which I ever harbored sentiment rather than curiosity. I was convinced already that it was genuine.

I put it in the page rack and, fingers poised, stared at the opening measures for a long minute. I began to play. I wasn't happy with my tempo. I started again. It moved very fast. Now I was sure it was one of the rhapsodies. It was in a direct line with the others, pieces I knew inside out. It especially reminded me of Rhapsody No. 9. It was a beautiful, sweeping, wintry piece, and after a few self-conscious moments, I lost myself in it. Deeply. But for once, as I played, I listened not only as a performer but as a passive listener. I heard it with a second ear. I let it soak into me. I could have been playing it for days, or for a second, and when I finished, I sat back slowly. I felt dazzled, overcome. I had played many pieces, before many audiences, to much applause; I had performed before older, famous pianists; I had heard the best pianists of my time and I had met them all. But those ten minutes in which I played that rhapsody alone in my studio, unrecorded, no one to hear it, were among my most satisfying moments as a pianist. And as if someone else were there speaking, I heard a voice—my own—ask me why I was crying. I put my hand to my cheek and it was wet, to my astonishment. After the bitter, terrible battles I had waged with myself, I had sat down and played this piece I had never seen before, that wasn't even supposed to exist, and it had brought me to tears. I sat for a long time, and then I played it again, but it was different the second time.

That damn Amos, I thought. I would have given anything at that moment to have had him there beside me. I would have to wait until they called to tell him how I felt. I stretched out on the couch and slept fitfully for an hour or so, and when I sat up again I panicked, wondering if Amos had come at all, if we had really talked into the dawn and driven out to the airport, or if all those stories had been elaborate dreams sprung of my insomnia. Then I walked over to the piano, and the manuscript was still there, and I played the piece again. I was still playing it a few hours later when Greta and Daphne came home.

The fitter turned me around before the four-way mirror and expressed his satisfaction. I caught Daphne's eye and she nodded approval. My old set of tails had been in mothballs for so long that I had ordered a new one for the tour back in July. They had done their work well. I savored the touch of grandeur in my bearing as I paraded before the mirror one last time, ordered some final alterations, and returned to reality, walking back out into the Fifth Avenue sunshine.

Daphne carried her violin case while I clutched the battered briefcase with its contraband. Greta, seeing us off that morning, asked why it wasn't handcuffed to my wrist. She had listened with the proper combination of amusement and awe while I related Amos's adventures. That first evening I had played Rhapsody No. 21 over and over again for her and Daphne. And so, just eight days before my recital, I had again commuted into New York for the day (for the last time, I hoped) on the oddest of my many oddball excursions into the big city that summer. I wasn't seeking distractions, for I had actually begun to enjoy my work again—our business was legitimate and we were solidly booked. But my portion of it was certainly odd.

I had talked to Ellen (at poolside in Santo Domingo) the day after Amos's visit, and in the course of a most pleasant conversation, she told me that they would be living in New York come October. She was upset about withdrawing Daphne from the Brook Conservatory. She couldn't say enough how happy she was about what I had done—it meant a great deal to her. That was fine, I replied, but the kid had real talent and potential. I had merely opened the door. If she agreed that Daphne should pursue her violin studies wholeheartedly, we could take other steps. Within five minutes, the obvious solution materialized: Juilliard.

I had set up another audition, and that would be our second stop that morning. Then, after lunch, the real fun would begin, when I visited Dr. Winters. Willy's secretary was going to look after Daphne. But to my dismay I learned that Willy was in Washington. I had wanted to tell him about the Liszt face-to-face; now I would have to settle for the telephone. As yet, I had discussed it with no one but Greta. We had to decide how to announce the piece—in the program, from the stage, whatever. I wanted it to be dramatic, but I was wary of putting it forth as a gimmick, a bit of cheap showmanship that would distract from the other pieces or lay a glittery icing on a recital that might otherwise be flat as a pancake. I had paid too many dues for that.

We were in a cab on Eighth Avenue when Daphne brought up her mother's marriage. Ellen had talked to her at length on the phone four days earlier, and we had a long talk at bedtime that night, but she hadn't breathed a word since. Not even to Greta. When I was her age, this meant something was eating at me. But Daphne wasn't like me. She was a healthier kid. She was capable of brooding, as I had seen when I was on the outs with Greta, but she didn't hide it, and in the previous days she had been chipper and outgoing. I realized it was our being in New York that triggered her questions.

"Daddy, will I still be able to call Uncle Amos that? I mean, now that he's my stepfather."

Her stepfather—the word jumped at me. "Of course. I'm sure that will make him happy."

"Can you take me by his house later?"

"You'd like to see where you're going to live?"

"Uh huh."

"They're going to look for a bigger place, Daphne. You won't be living in his old house."

"Oh. Well, I guess I'll go along when they look."

"I'm sure your mother will want you to have a say in it."

"And if I'm living here, I guess I'll see you a lot more than I used to. I mean, when you lived here and I lived in Lexington."

For an instant I froze. Ever since Dr. Selzer asked me where I

[*246*]

would be living after the tour, I had been vacillating. Somehow I had taken a liking to Boston, though its principal attraction, I knew, was Daphne's presence. Without her, it offered little more than anonymity. Another complication was Greta's continued caginess. The future was still a taboo subject. She was pleased, even wistful, about Ellen's marriage, but seemed most anxious to know when Daphne would have her mother around again. As if she herself were a surrogate. This got under my skin. Maybe she figured she was a wet nurse for me too, I said in annoyance, but she wouldn't be baited. I kept reminding myself that our trial period lasted until September 12. She would move back to New York and on the 14th I would start touring. After that—limbo. My Boston lease was up in December, and my Manhattan apartment, six rooms on the West Side, was sublet until February. I had been avoiding these dates and deadlines, but now, as Daphne looked up at me, I made a decision.

"You certainly will be seeing more of me. I'm moving back to New York after the tour."

"To your old house—I mean, Greta's house?"

My face must have darkened, for she glanced away. "I don't know about that just now. But I'll be in Manhattan, so we'll see each other all the time. It will never be the way it was before, once every month or so. Never."

I would like to say my ninety-minute visit to Juilliard was a sweet jaunt down Memory Lane, but except for Rosa Lenz, I had poor memories of that place. For me it had been a highly competitive, unfriendly mill. There was the pack, and there were the few who had already broken from the pack. For better or worse, Nature had tossed me into the latter group, and though I preferred to be envied than to envy, I did not find the atmosphere healthy or particularly conducive to music scholarship, despite the impressive faculty. The bickering and backbiting were salutary in one way: I realized that the harder I worked, the better my chances of sticking as a big-time soloist, and thus never being subjected to the deadly internal strife of orchestras and chamber groups and—at the bottom of the ladder—teaching faculties. Not to mention the fact that only a soloist could aspire to true self-expression. For soloists, the competition was fiercest of all, but at least, if you had guts, you were competing on your own terms. You were on top of the world, or you were your own worst enemy. But you didn't have to expend half your energy on politics. So through negative reinforcement, the school helped me to appreciate my talent in concrete, worldly terms, and it provided me the isolation in which I could refine it.

So why, with such mixed feelings, was I now sending my daughter into this wolf's den? For one thing, it was still the best music school in Manhattan. But, more important, I knew I had gone there from a rarefied, even crippling, background, having never attended school with other children, tutored at home under my mother's bizarre supervision, and already fixed on a solo career. Daphne had none of those handicaps. She got on well with other kids. She didn't have a stage mother. And Mrs. Rojas had been the first person even to suggest that she might become a soloist—in my case, nothing less would have been acceptable. Nobody was pushing Daphne. She could pursue her studies calmly and her path would quite naturally open up before her.

The red carpet was rolled out for us once again, so they must have had fonder feelings for me than I for them. I was treated deferentially and again planted in someone's comfortable office when they carted Daphne off for her audition. I put aside the brochures and catalogs they had given me and glanced one last time at the parapsychology report—that is, I flipped through the dozens of pages of photographs in the back.

There were monkeys and dogs, a bear, and two tired horses, wearing all variety of electronic apparatus: earphones, pulsars, helmets, microphone-studded collars, the works. What the animals were supposed to be seeing and hearing, I couldn't imagine. The human beings who succeeded them looked equally baffled, and frightened. They appeared to be volunteers in name only. Most of them rough-hewn, burly sorts, probably recruited from villages in Montenegro. All of them inside various cages, boxes, cells, along the lines of orgone and Skinner boxes. Some faced primitive television screens while bathed in infrared light. Some were suspended in underwater tanks. A few, in loincloths, had been blindfolded and harnessed in miniature steamrooms with flashing lights all around them. Finally, there were hundreds of mug shots of the subjects, apparently in various stages of hypnosis.

I was still pondering these hapless faces when they called me downstairs to meet Daphne's inquisitors. A parched, somber bunch. Daphne looked pensive and my heart sank. I thought they had turned her down. But no—Juilliard, not so informal as the Brook Conservatory, had a strict audition policy: the auditors reported to the admissions committee who reported to the board and then the chancellor. We would be notified of their decision within the week. Even for distinguished alumni and famous performers, no exceptions could be made.

I spent the next cab ride reassuring Daphne about her chances. She had expected the same warm, instantaneous response she had received from Mrs. Rojas in Boston. And I believe she was jolted to discover that my influence in the music world had its limits. So perhaps this democratic treatment wasn't such a bad thing.

I dropped her off at Willy's office and prepared myself for my amateur espionage work. I told myself it would be all fun and games—and why not? I was serving as middleman for a bunch of fringe-operators, professional eccentrics. Perhaps it was the perfect role for me. Winters was waiting eagerly in his office when I walked in at one o'clock. He had been talking to the gray cat I had seen at the farm—named Iago—who remained atop the highest bookshelf like a sphinx.

We sat down at the conference table. A nurse brought us tea, I lit a cigar, and without a word slid the briefcase across several feet of gleaming mahogany into Winters's grasp. I wondered if he could read Serbo-Croatian. He flipped through the report with great delight. The redoubtable Emma was summoned, decked out in her chauffeur's outfit. She shook my hand coldly, then disappeared with the briefcase.

"It should take her about twenty minutes to run off a copy," Winters said. "Do you have your car?"

"No, I flew in."

"Then you will use my car—unless you have any objections."

"Not at all. But where are we going?"

He coughed. "Mr. Sinonescu had second thoughts about meeting you here. Logistical reasons. He would prefer you meet in Central Park, if that is all right."

"Sure. Do I leave the briefcase in a tree or a rabbit hole?"

He smiled uneasily. "I always welcome your levity, Mr. Randal, but this is far more delicate for Mr. Sinonescu than you might think."

"So what do I do?"

"Emma will drive you up to Seventy-second Street. Mr. Sinonescu will meet you near the statue of Alice in Wonderland, by the pond."

"That's appropriate."

"You will give him the briefcase, he will give you an envelope for Mr. Demeter, and that will be the end of it."

"Of course he knows what I look like."

"He has several of your recordings, so he has seen your photograph. I will telephone him the moment you leave here. Any questions?"

"A few that you probably can't answer. I know why you want this report, but what are the Albanians going to do with it?"

He shrugged. "Mr. Demeter explained the political situation to you. That is as much as I know."

"So you don't think there is anything sinister in their getting it?"

"Come, come, Mr. Randal."

"Well, I've read a bit about Albania in the last week. Hairy stuff. When you leave the Cabinet, you go directly to the gallows. People disappear."

"People disappear everywhere. I am an apolitical man, but my guess is that this is really a question of pride with them. And that the medical interest is genuine. Surely you have no pangs of conscience at this point?"

He was right: it was late in the game to be fussing about the moral ramifications. The Albanians were a nefarious lot, but I was a middleman, I was Amos's agent, and I had to rely on his moral judgment.

"I assume you're going to have the report translated," I said. "Can you trust your translator?"

"Of course." He relit his pipe and smiled. "You know, Mr. Randal, you have not said a word about the *other* results of Mr. Demeter's trip. Ireland . . . Hungary . . . what do you think now about the treatments which catalyzed all that?"

"It's hard to say. I've thought a lot about it. About telepathy."

He nodded.

"About Amos's personality and his receptivity to such things. But the results speak for themselves. That the manuscript was in that chapel—it's amazing."

"So you no longer think we are merely conducting séances here?"

"I don't know what you're doing, but that piece of music didn't materialize out of nothing."

"It's beautiful, is it?"

"Magnificent. But can you explain to me exactly how Amos connected with this Count Festetics?"

He shook his head. "You still want it in black and white? I am afraid I cannot reduce it to a tidy explanation. At least you seem more curious now."

"Oh, I'm more curious, though I doubt I would be as ideal a patient as Amos. And right now I have too many affairs to straighten out in this world."

That was true. Maybe the shock treatment of my tour would have the same effect. Performing sixteen cities in fifty days, lights, audiences, applause, critics, hotels, airports—these comprised a branch of neurovisual harmonic phenomena unto themselves. If the tour didn't jolt me into a new state of consciousness, nothing would.

Emma reappeared, whispered something to Winters, and handed me the briefcase. I think he was amused (and she annoyed) when I opened it to check the contents. If I was going to be a middleman, at least I would be a good one. He took me down in his elevator. The crowd in the waiting room again rose to greet him. He raised his hand and smiled, then led me outside. Emma opened the door of the blue Mercedes.

"Thank you again for your help," Winters said. "And do not be put off by Sinonescu. He is a strange bird, a little remote, but not a bad sort."

"You know, Dr. Winters, I think I can answer a question now that you asked me back in June."

His face lit up.

"I agree that there are still miracles, works of wonder, even on a troubled planet like ours. Whatever you and Amos did, I know that I hear magic when I play that rhapsody. With all due respect to Liszt, I'm not one to deny credit where it's due. In this case, to you."

"If you're thanking me, Mr. Randal, it is not necessary."

"All right. But I'd like to give you four tickets to my recital at Carnegie Hall." I dug into my pocket. "I hope you can make it."

"I thank you heartily. I wouldn't miss it. And good luck."

Emma raced me up Sixth Avenue at breakneck speed, running the red lights skillfully. I asked her to adjust the air conditioner, for she had the car colder than a meat freezer. I examined the back of her head, the coarse short-cropped hair beneath the driver's cap, the strange vulpine ears. I watched her face, shielded by black wraparounds, in the rearview mirror. It never even twitched. I felt as if I were being transported by a mannequin.

I walked into the park near the sailing pond. I hadn't been there in years. There were schoolboys, and men twice my age, sailing model schooners and ketches on the green water. There was even a bearded man in an admiral's uniform. When I reached the bronze statue of Alice and her friends, I scanned the benches but saw no one who might have been Sinonescu. The statue was swarming with kids. It was really more a miniature playground. The bronze was rubbed shiny by the millions of small hands and feet that had climbed, scrambled, and slid to various perching points. There was the large mushroom, the Cheshire cat, the rabbit, and of course Alice herself, whose tempting nose had been rubbed shiniest of all.

I put on my sunglasses and relit my cigar. A swarthy, ramshackle man appeared, blinking in the light. He had a dachshund in his arms. Was this my man? No, he went away with a boy in a baseball uniform. Twenty minutes passed. It was pleasant sitting there in the heat with the pollen filling my nose, birds singing, leaves fluttering, children shouting. I grabbed a moment for some meditation. I had a lot on my mind. Orana's death had been weighing on me. It had finally sunk in, and there seemed to be nothing to it after the fact, nothing I could latch onto. They say allegory's final destination is always eternity, where despite corporeal ruin, our souls find their proper lights. Perhaps she knew what she was doing when she allegorized her Gibbon. I had understood it in Boston. But now it meant nothing to me. All I could see was that she had suffered, died, and been reduced to ashes. Spiritually, I had trouble getting past this point. It all seemed like a colossal waste, not an allegorical climax. Even the surface of her tragedy was still too painful to explore.

Less painful but more baffling was the counterpoint of tragedy and comedy in my personal history. I had been toying with this notion ever since the evening when Greta and Sarah had collided. Tertullian says eternal recurrence is universal law. Everything that happens has happened before. Marx takes it a step further, insisting all events and characters repeat themselves, but the first time they occur as tragedy, the second as farce. Had that happened in my own life? Had I fallen in with a cast of characters drawn out of my past tragedies, all of whom (with the exception of Orana, who had lived out her own tragedy) had now crossed paths with me on various levels of farce? Where would this pattern end? Did recurrence have only two sides, flipping back and forth, and would my affairs naturally return from the comic to the tragic? Was Orana's death, and now Greta's diffidence, the first sign of such a shift? Or was I simply a gloomy sort who possessed only a tragic dimension and whose detours were no more than comic relief amid desperation?

Whatever happened—or recurred—all my energies and tensions now seemed to be flowing into that first recital. Until it was over, I could not answer these questions. Perhaps the rest of my life would fall into place, perhaps it would be derailed once and for all.

A small, dark man, with a mandarin look, walked up to me at that moment. He wore a brown suit and tie, straw hat, and two-toned tropical shoes. He was pale, with a neat mustache, and clear-rimmed eyeglasses, 1950s variety, with flip-down shades. He carried a briefcase. Daydreaming, drawing on my sketchy knowledge of Marx, I was about to meet a Marxist of a different ilk than I had ever known. For Sinonescu would fit none of my preconceptions.

Soft-spoken and urbane, he seemed to have all the time in the world. His American-inflected English was impeccable, though every so often he lapsed into a British accent in the middle of a sentence. He looked like a genial philatelist.

"Mr. Max Randal," he said, extending his hand. "Telfet Sinonescu."

He looked up at the sky suddenly. "Unusual, is it not, to have pink cumuli at this time of day?"

Was this what Winters had meant by "a little remote"?

"At that height," he continued, "it is not dust but the density of the water particles and the angle of light."

I patted the briefcase. "I have—"

"Of course you do," he interrupted. "Your friend Demeter is quite a chap, isn't he. Wants to do a book of photographs of my country. Appears now that he will do it. My government is— well, it can be difficult to do such things in Albania, you understand? We are a free country, but we have our own way about us."

"So I gather."

"But your friend has good politics, doesn't he," he said approvingly.

"He's a good man, and you can trust him to keep his word."

"Of course. Winters said the same thing. And you, your interest in all this?"

"I have no interest in your business with Amos."

"You are returning a favor, then?"

"We've been friends for many years. I've lost track of the favors."

"I see. Good." He smiled. "I have heard of you, of course. I have your recordings of Brahms's Ballades. Also, the Hungarian Rhapsodies. Excuse me, but I have only heard one other pianist play them as well—and he was Hungarian."

"Cziffra?"

"Of course. György Cziffra. Marvelous."

"Mr. Sinonescu, I'd like you to have two tickets to my recital next week."

He was taken aback. "Really? No, I couldn't take them."

"Of course you can." I hadn't intended to make this gesture. But I thought it wouldn't hurt Amos if I were generous with these people. I was carrying around two dozen choice tickets that Willy's secretary had given me. "You can come, can't you?"

"Yes, no problem." He smiled wanly. "As cultural attaché, I often make such outings. Thank you very much." He studied the tickets with pleasure.

"Now I suppose I ought to get down to business," I said.

He nodded absently. "Do you place any credence, Mr. Randal, in the theory that Anton Rubinstein was the natural son of Beethoven?"

"I beg your pardon?"

He repeated his question.

"No, I think it's nonsense. There was a physical resemblance, but Rubinstein was Russian, raised in Moscow."

"You never know with the Russians," he said slyly.

"Winters didn't tell me you were a piano aficionado."

He smiled. "I am not, really. One picks up many odds and ends in my position."

I think he had dropped these tidbits—the Rubinstein and the Cziffra—in order to impress me. He didn't want me to think he might be ignorant of musical matters. It was a question of Albanian national pride again.

"Well, perhaps we had better see to our business now," he said airily.

"If you don't mind my saying so, Mr. Sinonescu, I was under the impression you were very eager to get hold of this report. Yet you seem so nonchalant."

"I am eager. That is, people in my government are eager—which is the same thing. Personally, between you and me, it is not a subject that holds much attraction for me. However, I am sure my comrades at the Institute for Advanced Medicine in Tirana will be thrilled. So." He held out his hands for the briefcase.

I fished out the first ten pages of the report, which I had separated from the rest at Juilliard.

He pored over them intently. "Yes," he muttered, " 'The People's Report on Parapsychology and Psychic Phenomena in the Kosovo District.' Fascinating. The rest, please?"

"I hate to be formal, but I'd like to see Amos's visa and papers first," I said coolly. "You understand."

He flashed me a wicked smile. "Of course."

He handed me a manila envelope crammed with documents in Albanian. All I could make out was Amos's name in English and "U.S.A."

"These could say anything," I said, pocketing the envelope and handing him the briefcase.

Transferring the contents to his own briefcase, he smiled again. "True. It could even be an irrevocable warrant to the effect that he will be sentenced to ten years hard labor in our bauxite mines the moment he enters Albania." He laughed gaily. "But it isn't. I too am a man of my word. And, frankly, I look forward to the book he intends to publish." He locked his briefcase and chuckled. "The Yugoslavs will be furious when they hear about this."

"How will they hear?"

"My government will make sure there is a leak at some future date."

"But why?"

"Mr. Randal, surely you can read between the lines. We simply want to let our friends in Belgrade know that it is we who have had the last laugh."

"But what about the doctor in Skopje, the man Amos saw?"

He shrugged. "That is not my department. I would say the fellow would do well to defect to my country. Or to look up any of the two million Albanians living in Yugoslavia. They are very unhappy over there and would be glad to help a bewildered traitor."

This was his gentler side, the sort of sensibility required in the Albanian diplomatic corps.

We stood up and he made a small bow. "It has been a great pleasure meeting you," he smiled. "If you would ever like to tour Albania, just give me a call."

"I'll do that."

I was hungry and tired of running around and decided I could put off our flight home for a few hours. I chose to indulge a whim. I stopped at Willy's to pick up Daphne, and soon afterward we were seated at a corner table in La Diva in Little Italy, one of my old haunts. It was the limbo hour between lunch and dinner. The place was half empty, cool and dark. I ordered an enormous meal with an extravagant Bardolino. The manager professed great joy at seeing me again and took Daphne off to tour the kitchen. She came back with a double shrimp cocktail, compliments of the chef, and a red carnation in her hair.

I was halfway through my scampi diaboli when a heavy hand came down on my shoulder. Across the table, Daphne stared up in astonishment, her mouth open.

"Hello, Max," a voice growled. "Didn't think I'd run into you so soon."

It was Frank Lancio, the mob chief from my cousin's wedding, the old friend of my father's.

"Mr. Lancio," I exclaimed, pumping his hand.

"Frank. Sit down, sit down, don't let me disturb your meal."

"Can you join us?"

"Thanks, but I'm here with some associates." He inclined his head toward the private rooms in the rear.

That accounted for the small fleet of limos in front. Lancio looked sharp as ever, blue pinstripes, burgundy tie, gold cigarette holder between his teeth.

"At least join me for some wine," I said.

"Why not. Excuse me, I'll be right back."

"Are you going to ask him?" Daphne whispered excitedly.

"Ask him what?"

"For the million dollars. That's the man who said—"

"I know, silly. No, I'm not going to ask him."

Lancio returned, and the manager was now even more deferential. He looked at me with new respect. I ordered a second bottle of the Bardolino.

"So, have you come back from Boston for good, or what?" Lancio said.

"Just in for the day."

"This is my favorite place. When you're back to stay, we'll come here for dinner, when there's music." He sipped some wine.

"By the way, I have a little something for you." For the third time that day, I pulled out a handful of tickets. It was good I had them on me. "For my recital on the 12th at Carnegie Hall. I was going to have them sent to you."

I had touched the right chord. "That's very generous of you," he said warmly.

We talked small talk for a while. He was gracious, and seemed more relaxed than he had been at the wedding. Daphne told him about her audition. Then the manager took her to the kitchen to pick some dessert. Something had been gnawing at me, but I couldn't discuss it with her around.

"Frank, I'd like to ask you a question. If you don't think you can answer it—"

"I won't." He smiled.

"At my cousin's wedding, you told me my father had once done you a favor. After all these years, you haven't forgotten it. Can you tell me what it was?"

He studied me for a moment. "It's ancient history. It was in 1947. My kid brother was a fighter too, a lightweight. A good kid. He won the Golden Gloves. He kept his nose clean and was working his way up through the pro ranks. He had nothing to do with any of my associates, if you read me. I kept him clear of all that. But one day some jokers at the Boxing Commission decided to strip his license just because of his last name. Guilt by association. That tied my hands. If I interfered, they could holler and justify what they'd done. If I did nothing, the kid was washed up. They held a hearing, and your father offered to testify as a character witness. He was the only one who would. He knew the kid and believed it was a raw deal. He was retired then, very respected, a private sort of guy. Never stayed in one place very long. His name was good as gold, he'd always been clean, but he knew they'd try to spread dirt on him in the papers if he testified. They did. And he testified anyway. I could never forget that."

"What happened?"

"The hearing upheld the Commission. My brother never fought again. He was killed in Korea three years later."

"I'm sorry."

Lancio shrugged. "That's the way it is. If he was still fighting, he never would have enlisted. But your father was a gentleman, a real champion," he added, as Daphne returned with cannoli and strawberry tarts.

After another glass of wine, he stood up. "Business is business," he muttered, gesturing toward the rear. He put his arm around me. "Listen, good luck on the 12th. And forget the tab here—it's taken care of."

Before I could protest, he was gone.

On the flight home, while Daphne slept off the rich food, I thought about Lancio's story. My father's courage and generosity didn't surprise me. It was the passing aside about his being an elusive sort that had hit a nerve. It had reawakened that memory again, particularly one detail I had done my utmost to avoid. Before my father slipped away that day while I played for him, he got drunk. All his life he was a teetotaler, but in the end, ailing, he drank heavily. In the end he was a mess. All those years I had blocked that out. I could not accept that he, a man physically invulnerable, like a Greek hero, a rock in my eyes, had ended up a cripple. When he had come to me in pain, all I could do was play for him. He was already a ghost to me. And so I had failed him as he had once failed me. And now Orana had finally gone off with him, disappearing, just as she had in my dream.

We celebrated at Billy Diamond's the day Daphne was accepted at Juilliard. Some Dom Pérignon, lobster for Greta and Daphne, and mashed potatoes and carrots for me. That was the sort of fare I stuck to the week before a recital. I was walking around with a propeller in my gut. I had three days left. Once I broke the ice in New York, and hit the road, I hoped to eat heartily again.

It had been a rough week, but at least things around the house were cheerful. Greta was vital and upbeat, in a detached way. I needed to be alone a lot, to collect myself, as if my powers of concentration were an intricate jigsaw puzzle that required daily reassembling, but I also needed her and Daphne. I craved warmth and affection, and at the same time felt I had to cut loose from everything. This didn't make me the ideal companion. I was constantly losing myself in inner space. We were an odd trio: Daphne practicing long hours in her room, preparing for school; Greta forever on the telephone doing business; and I— least productive of all in terms of hours—pacing, fretting, annotating, playing, my piano now less an antagonist than a fitful ally who demanded subtle coaxing. We had reached the point of symbiosis, the piano and I, and while I felt comfortable with it, and had regained much of my faith in my own powers, our mutual chemistry onstage—with the added unknown of the audience—was still a question mark. I could play, and the instrument would respond, but how would we sound to all those foreign ears? Maybe what I was hearing, and what Greta and Daphne, full of plaudits, were hearing, was nothing like what my full house in New York would hear. Where I imagined silvery flows, they might hear rattling tin, and nobody would be able to reassure me otherwise until I had actually performed.

As for the Liszt piece, I was amazed that I continued to feel ecstatic, even transcendental, about it after that first day. Even on such short notice, it was ready to go. I felt there was nothing more I could do with it. I had finally discussed it with Willy on the telephone. First I had to overcome his deep skepticism—and this took some doing, ultrarationalist that he was. Once convinced that I wasn't pulling his leg and hadn't been hoodwinked myself, he settled into a state of sublime astonishment and curiosity. That was his music lover half. The impresario in him immediately started weighing the pros and cons of how we might best announce the piece to the public, and to the "barracudas"— his pet name for critics.

"They will dice and skewer you for this, out of pure envy, if we don't handle it right. You understand? Even if they are convinced the piece is authentic, if you just spring it on them they will be offended. Let me think. Such a good problem, but still a problem."

His solution, I thought, was both tactically and aesthetically correct. He proposed that instead of a surprise announcement from the stage, bound to distract from the other pieces, we attach a tasteful addendum to the program, giving the piece's historical background *in breve*, some details on its discovery by Mr. Amos Demeter, and a further note announcing that the manuscript would be auctioned off and the proceeds donated to charity. Photocopies of the manuscript would be sent to the critics and other worthies the day before the recital, along with a press release. Larger photocopies would be displayed in the lobby at Carnegie Hall for the audience's benefit. That seemed to cover all the bases. Above all, Willy agreed, we had to defuse any talk of gimmicks, injected by destructive souls to tarnish my comeback.

"You have some enemies out there, Max," he assured me, "and I know exactly how to handle them."

It was not for nothing that Willy had been on top in his profession for so many years.

After our celebration, I gave Daphne a gold violin-pin, and we drove down to the Charles, out past the cemetery near Alton, where there were never many people around. Daphne went off with some bread to feed the ducks, while Greta and I found a bench under the willow trees. We watched the water, the sunlight coiling orange and yellow spirals off the far bank, and the shadows of the trees rippling out into the gold band that divided the river, like a river unto itself. It was fragrant and hot, an Indian summer heat, thick, ashen, the leaves just a few weeks from yellowing. I smoked a cigar and Greta toyed with some dandelions.

I had kept my promise about not bringing up the future. This time it was she who introduced a delicate topic.

"What did Willy say about the suite at the Plaza?"

"It's fine. Someone went over yesterday and checked it out. It's high up and there's a nice room for Daphne."

"It will be better this way, Max," she said, fidgeting.

When I had mentioned a few days earlier that Willy was reserving a suite for me, I wanted her to invite me to stay at her place—even if she knew I would refuse. Instead she announced that she would be staying at home: she had work to do, and the hotel would afford me the intense privacy I required. This was true. In fact, for this particular recital, it was essential. But when I used to play New York, I always stayed at home, and I wanted to hear Greta say, as she had in July, that the loft was my home. I told myself I was being peevish, that she was thinking intelligently, protectively, keeping our private affairs on a low burner until I had made my comeback. But I was disappointed.

Our unspirited sex life had also been weighing on me that week. Normally, I would have been devastated by any trouble in that department, but again I rationalized that the external tension had to effect its toll. We were making love—and frequently. But the exuberance, the lighthearted bawdiness we had shared in the jacuzzi, was sorely lacking. For two people whose marriage had been so predicated on their carnal gusto, this was disturbing. Our general reticence and caution had crept between the sheets with us. This was to be expected. At times it seemed Greta simply did not want to rock our little boat—perhaps because she was more honest than I about the condition of the ocean.

She was still blowing dandelion seeds into the wind. "What time are those people coming?" she asked.

"Four-thirty. I wish you could say I'm indisposed—flu or something."

"Don't be childish. You promised Willy you wouldn't cancel this time. One hour and they will be gone," she said, scattering another dandelion.

For a month Willy had been on my back to give interviews. Aside from building interest in the tour, they were the perfect forum, he said, in which I might discuss why I hadn't performed in four years, why I was coming back, and so on. "If you do the talking, Max, you preempt the barracudas, you take control and prevent others from weaving innuendoes." So at four-thirty an editor from *High Fidelity* was coming by, and at five a music reporter from the *Times*. Actually, I had gotten off easy. For a tour of this magnitude, I should have expected two interviews a day for two weeks. But I placated Willy by promising to do that after New York, on the road. My whole life had become one gigantic *mañana;* everything would be taken care of after the recital.

"I'm thinking of going back into analysis after the tour," I said casually.

"Yes?"

"It might be useful. There are questions, connections, that I've left hanging for too long."

"But you were so dissatisfied in analysis."

"My attitude was all wrong."

"And now?" she said, arching her brow.

"I'm prepared to clear out some of the muck that's bogged me down. What do you think?"

"You mean, do I think it would be useful?" She hesitated. "I suppose it might help you with your music."

"Jesus, it's not the music I'm concerned about."

"Yes, but you know, all roads run to Rome. With you, all roads run through your music."

"Then maybe I had better take a different road and live like a human being."

She brushed this aside. "And do what—sell insurance? How do you think human beings live? Since you were sixteen—no, before that—you have not lived like a normal person. Why should you now? You are not a normal person—you're a freak. You do something much beyond the capacities, the scope, of any normal person. So there must be a different logic to your life, different rules."

"You sound like me ten years ago. But that's kid's stuff. I have to live with other people, their rules, their logic, their troubles."

She flicked away the last dandelion. "Do you? Do you have to live with them, Max?"

We watched the river in silence. Daphne, surrounded by mallards, called up to us gaily. We waved to her. I relit my cigar.

"Dr. Selzer thought I should try again," I said abruptly. "She's going to help me."

"You're going back to her?"

"I don't know. But when I saw her, she told me that you were her patient now."

"When did you see her?"

"The day I came to your house, when we visited Orana. I had no idea you were in analysis."

"Yes, I have been."

"Has it—have you found what you wanted?"

"I don't know that I wanted anything. And I certainly don't know yet what I have found. We're still breaking the foundation."

I tried to suppress a smile.

Then she smiled. "Breaking ground, I mean. It has been interesting. I have learned a lot."

"Did you go because of our breakup?"

"Of course, that was part of it. We were both so nonchalant, so businesslike, about our divorce. I knew you thought that was healthy, but afterwards it troubled me. It didn't seem right." She paused. "I had an affair a few months later that went badly. Very badly."

"A bad guy? Abusive?"

"Nothing like that. Not even such a bad guy. Just a mess, you know. And I realized that was a reaction to our divorce too. Anyway, it's never any one person who makes you unhappy. Perhaps something you did, or something done to you, long before that person came along, left you vulnerable to some weakness of theirs. You asked me what I have found, and I wasn't quite fair. I have learned the obvious: that nearly everything that happens to us we bring on ourselves. The trick is to stop blaming others." She shrugged. "That is not an original notion, but when you discover it for yourself, it takes on new meaning."

I looked away. Implicit in her qualifier was the suggestion that I had never reached that point in my own analysis, or my life. Or if I had, I had never acted upon it.

When I looked back on this conversation, it struck me that I had tried to use this idea of reentering analysis to convince Greta of my inner transformation, my new leaf. I was not trying to deceive her, or myself, I think, for only as we rose from the bench and strolled along the riverbank with Daphne, hand in hand, *en famille*, did I realize I had no intention of returning to Selzer or finding a new doctor. And this came as a shock to me. I had been utterly sincere about the whole business. But once I was reconciled with Greta that day in New York, there was no need to bring it up. And now that I had told her, and seen it make no real impression, I dropped the idea entirely. If anything, I agreed with her: if I put my music back in order (and I wasn't sure analysis was the way to do it), which was in effect putting my house in order, then other things might fall into place.

The two interviews blessedly merged into one. The woman from *High Fidelity* was late and the young man from the *Times* early. I was amused to learn that they were both named Brown—no relation, they assured me. Greta put on coffee, I fixed Miss Brown a spritzer, poured myself carrot juice, and we were off. Daphne drifted in, was introduced, and sat demurely at the piano. Greta, of course, introduced herself as Greta Randal.

Miss Brown turned to me with a smile. "You know, your daughter is a dead ringer for her mother."

"So they tell me," I said, smiling back.

Miss Brown was a good editor, a pro, and she had been through all this many times. She was laid back. For Mr. Brown, interviews were not so old hat. He had arrived early, eagerly, with dozens of prepared questions. He wanted to discuss my strategy for the Opus 10: the dynamics, the coloring, *the attack*.

What did I think of Gould's and Horowitz's recordings of the so-natas? Did I plan to record them myself?

This went on for a half hour, and I must concede he had formed some intelligent questions about the *Diabelli*, which I enjoyed answering. Then he got a bit picayune. How, he inquired, would I treat the pauses between the thirty-three variations—equally or variably? I kept a straight face.

"Oh, I think you have to treat them equally," I said, clipping a cigar and stroking Mango. "Otherwise it becomes a distraction."

"Will you have your piano shipped down?" Miss Brown asked. "Didn't you always use your own piano in New York?"

"That's right. In fact, it's already there. This one is my spare."

"But won't you take it on tour?"

"Oh no, I'm not that finicky. I want it for the first recital, then it will go into storage until I come home."

"You will be moving back to Manhattan, then?"

"Yes."

"Were your reasons for living here in Boston strictly personal?"

"No, professional. I wanted a change of climate, a different pace, while I prepared for this tour."

"Some people said you had retreated from live performances permanently," Mr. Brown said with a twinkle.

"People say a lot of things. Retreated? No. Just catching my breath after seventeen years."

"But four years . . ."

"Wasn't long enough," I laughed, and Miss Brown laughed with me.

"No other reasons for your sabbatical?" he persisted.

He was a bit of a bloodhound, I thought, but I was relaxed. Back in June I would have been up on my hind legs.

"Not really. I feel very strong now. I sensed the fires needed restoking. The juices had to build up again. You choose the metaphor. I needed to be away, aside from recording, which is a different kind of discipline. I'm not the first pianist to step back for a while."

"Yes, but on your level—"

"Especially on my level," I said evenly.

Miss Brown was tired of Mr. Brown. "The two you yourself mentioned are good examples, Ted. Gould and Horowitz." And before he could get in the last word, she turned back to me. "What can you tell us about the all-Beethoven program? I know you changed repertoire in midstream—why?"

Things went smoothly, and after a full hour, as we had planned, Greta returned and stood beside me, indicating that the interview was concluded. We had discussed the Beethoven angle in detail, and my plans for future recordings, and a possible European tour in the spring. They both seemed satisfied, and thanked me and we started for the door. But it had gone so well that I was feeling particularly expansive. I had an idea. Willy wouldn't like it—but, then again, he might. It was the kind of gesture he always recommended. Or, as Uncle Louie would say: it isn't how you play the game, or even how you win it—it's how you rig it beforehand that really counts. Usually, I was too busy trying to figure out why I was playing in the first place.

"If you have another minute," I said, "I'll show you something else that may interest you. You and your colleagues will receive a press release in two days, but right now nobody knows about it outside of my family and my manager." I smiled. "Are you good with secrets, Mr. Brown?"

I gave them each the press release, the addendum to the program, and then I pulled out the Liszt manuscript itself, now laid between sheets of plastic.

"This is fantastic," said Mr. Brown.

"Amazing," added Miss Brown.

This gladdened me, for I had been apprehensive about their reactions. After all, here were two New York critics in the flesh—ideal guinea pigs—and they passed my litmus test with flying colors. They were so appreciative it made me squirm. Willy would have been pleased. He was pleased, in fact, when I called to tell him. There was no whisper of gimmicks, even from the buttoned-down Mr. Brown. They were simply excited; it was a real story, Miss Brown exclaimed. A whopper. Trying to remain low-key, and swearing them to secrecy, I gave them more background than the press release contained. The program addendum was a gem in itself, which required little embellishment, and is worth producing here in full:

> The piece which Mr. Randal will play for his encore is a hitherto unpublished, unperformed, Hungarian Rhapsody in F, composed by Franz Liszt in January 1840, during his triumphal return to Hungary. Liszt gave the original manuscript of the piece to his host in Pest, Count Leo Festetics, and by some mishap his own copy was lost. The Rhapsodies were composed after Liszt had been reacquainted with the gypsy music of his native land, in which he had a passionate interest. One is immediately aware in this piece of the distinctive and lively elements that have accorded the other Rhapsodies their firm niche in our musical heritage. The manuscript was recently discovered by Mr. Amos Demeter in the former chapel of the Festetics' country house outside of Budapest. Mr. Demeter is a Pulitzer Prize–winning photographer and world traveler. In January, the manuscript will be auctioned off at Sotheby's, with the proviso that music scholars are first permitted three months in which to study it. The proceeds of the auction will be donated to the John M. Randal Wing for Tropical Diseases at New York Hospital.

So the barracudas went away happy.

Knowing I would be busy the next day, packing for the tour and closing up house, I planned to make my first nonstop run-through of the recital program, including the encore, after dinner. I had played the pieces to death that week, but with dozens of interruptions—to turn a phrase differently, to repeat some tangled bars, to mull over an interpretive fork in the road. Now, I wanted to play them through exactly as I would in New York on Friday.

The run-through was technically flawless. I had expected that much. As always, I played from memory. The *Diabelli* took off, the *Waldstein* was solid, the *Hammerklavier* a little flat about the edges, and the Opus 10 and the Liszt fine. I timed it: Willy was right, it would be a marathon. Three hours and five minutes. I listened to bits of the tape I had just made and it was all good, more than adequate, but I was still dissatisfied. Maybe I would always be dissatisfied. If you could divide what I thought missing from my work in the spring into fifths, I had perhaps recovered four-fifths of what I wanted. This through endless mistakes, and more hours of raw practice than I was accustomed to in a year, and sufferings and illuminations and even miracles, all of which I have tried to chronicle. I had come that far, however jagged the path. But now I was after the missing fifth that would make Friday a tour de force, not just a good performance. Perhaps I was getting greedy, for in June I was not even sure I could rise above the rendition of a keyboard mechanic. I should have been grateful. Or perhaps I had lost that fifth for all time, in my twenties, along with a few other things. Now all I could do was wait for Friday night. I knew one thing, though: I didn't want a good performance—I wanted to bring the house down, to knock them dead. My career required it. Mr. Brown that afternoon had kindly reminded me of the "level" I was on, where names like Horowitz and Gould were comfortably mentioned alongside my own. I wasn't used to anything less, and I knew in my bones that I couldn't survive with anything less, professionally or otherwise. It was that or nothing.

The next day, Wednesday, was cluttered with practical considerations. After all, I wasn't the only one leaving. We had to get Daphne packed up, and Greta had all her stuff, and I even had to buy a deluxe carrying-case for Mango, who after some discreet jockeying from Willy's office, was about to break the feline barrier at the Plaza. We were going to drive to New York. I would garage the car there until December. My other possessions would be divided about equally between a Manhattan warehouse and the Boston loft.

I would miss those sunbathers, I thought, as I gazed out the window at them one last time, still in their matching briefs, a shade of ebony by now, the photogenic cat romping over their supine bodies. I wondered what those girls did for a living. I had meant to introduce myself at one point, but it never worked out. Perhaps I had missed yet another set of complications that might have changed my entire summer. I would never know.

When Greta and Daphne went to bed, I ran through the program again. The *Hammerklavier*, that Death Valley of the keyboard, was livelier, and the *Waldstein* strong, but I was still on the threshold, I still hadn't taken the last step. I didn't want to think about it anymore. I was sick of living with the ax over my head. Friday would come and Friday would go.

Greta was still reading when I went in to get ready for bed. All day I had wanted her, and in the evening more than ever. But by the time I showered and emerged in my kimono, she had fallen asleep with a book in her lap. My old copy of Kierkegaard, her fellow Dane, and once again, with his rambling reprises on the musical-erotic and *Don Giovanni*, he had let me down. This time he had put my lover to sleep. I should have learned from him earlier, from his elliptical seducer's logic, that this was the way things really went, and all that operatic sexuality was so much hot air.

It was with a grim foreboding that I climbed into bed with the darkness all to myself. The *Dhammapada* tells us that Mara the Temptress will overthrow him who lives seeking only pleasure, senses uncontrolled, immoderate and weak, just as the wind topples a weak tree. I was no Christian when it came to sin, but I had come to believe one was expected to pay over and over again for his follies. And the true fool always considered the worst payment the denial of further folly. That was why Dante made hell circular. Why the worst punishment of all is the vicious circle, in which we keep coming back on ourselves, each time finding a little less than before, until in the end we are nothing at all.

I didn't sleep a wink that night and I never stirred from my bed, beside Greta, my former wife. I thought of all the nights in the preceding months I had lain sleepless—drunk, sober, meditative, terrified—in that place. Even if it meant giving up my career, I swore I would never live like that again. Ever.

At seven o'clock we all left the loft together for the last time. It was raining hard. The rain continued all the way into Manhattan.

Daphne and I stood in the darkness for a moment and then walked down the aisle. The hall felt cavernous. It always did. Rows of empty seats hold their own kind of silence. Only the stage was lit. My Steinway gleamed as if it were silver-plated. Daphne, who had never been to a concert hall after-hours, was awestruck. She gripped my hand as we went up and around onto the stage. Now the blackness of the house was a wall just beyond the lights. The stage manager joined us with two of his men. I had them move the piano a few feet back, then a few feet to the right. Then another few feet back. We talked about the lighting and how I liked the curtain handled. He shouted up to the lighting men and they made some adjustments. After a few minutes, I had the effect I wanted, at the piano and downstage. I walked to the very last row in the house and Daphne played some bars from a minuet.

"That sounds fine," I called out.

I returned to the stage and played several sets of scales, very slowly—the tuner had done his work well. I made sure the velvet pads had been stuck to the four legs of my chair so it wouldn't scrape. I had them make one more lighting adjustment. Then the stage manager and his men left us.

"Don't you want to play one of your pieces?" Daphne whispered. I was sitting at the piano and she was leaning against my shoulder.

"No. It's in tune and it's placed right, that's all I need to know."

She blinked out toward the house. "Now I know I would be scared," she said hoarsely.

"No you wouldn't. Look, you can't even see anything."

"But it's so big. And the ceiling is so high. Do people sit way up there?" she said, squinting at the upper tiers.

"Sure."

"You must look like a little dot from there."

"But they can hear the music just as well."

"Show me how you're going to come out," she said.

"Well, I'm just going to walk out."

"Come on, show me."

"Okay, when you walk out, you take a small bow, you hope they're clapping hard, you acknowledge both sides of the house, and then you sit down." I stared at the keyboard, looked up into the lights, and played the ringing, opening bars of the *Diabelli* waltz. I felt a little funny. I pushed my chair back and stood up. "Then at the end, you bow again."

"Show me where I'll be sitting," she said, as we returned to the house.

"Third row, near the aisle—right here."

She sat down. "And even here you won't be able to see me?"

"No. But I'll tell you what. At the end, when I take my bow, some of the houselights will come up and I'll look for you."

"You won't forget? Promise?"

"I promise."

She went out into the lobby and I stood at the back of the hall alone. The piano looked smaller now and the light very intense. Except for that brief moment at the piano, I hadn't felt much of anything. It all seemed routine, mechanical. Unreal. Being there seemed to have nothing to do with the fact I would be performing the next night. It was so quiet.

As we walked outside, past the ticket office, someone recognized me and asked for an autograph. Daphne took this in stride. She paused to admire the poster-sized photographs of me flanking the main doors.

"You look pretty young there, Dad."

"Thanks a lot."

"Maybe you just weren't so tired," she said, patting my arm.

She was right. I badly needed some sleep. The rain had tapered off and the sun was breaking through. We strolled alongside the park back to the Plaza. It was strange not having Greta around. Daphne and I had been alone together most of the summer, but after only two weeks with us, Greta left a large void. We had dropped her off downtown before checking into the hotel. We had all been cheerful during the drive from Boston, and she was joining us for dinner, but still it wasn't the same.

Our suite was lovely and we had a good view of the park, which Mango, especially, enjoyed. He planted himself on the windowsill for hours and stared down into the dark expanse of trees. Maybe it was his jungle instinct, reawakened in the big city. Or maybe he sensed the presence, among those trees, of his less fortunate brethren, the raggedy strays foraging in trash cans at that moment while he was ensconced twenty stories up dining on tuna and chopped egg. More probably it was I, his unstable patron, who was inclined to such thoughts, staring down at the bustling hordes, and the hustlers, and the bums sprawled on benches and tormenting myself with the fear that, with my single rarefied talent, like a plank over quicksand, I might be just a few missteps away from joining the most hopeless of them. Was the distance from that suite to one of those benches really so far? What would I do if I ever bombed completely?

After a short nap, I went up to Willy's apartment to use the piano. My last run-through. And it was just that: lukewarm, competent, tired around the edges, no fire. That didn't trouble me; it had always been my pattern. They say a good boxer is careful not to leave his fight in the gym, and I considered this a useful maxim in my trade. I wasn't going to find that missing fifth I so coveted by practicing anymore. The essence of the performance was already alive within me, in my head and my heart, and nothing I did on the outside would make much difference. The run-through was for the benefit of sinews, tendons, bones, and nerves—the ones in the fingertips, not the other kind.

Daphne was in the kitchen, eating lunch and chatting with Willy's housekeeper, Helga. I went into his study and sat at the desk. There were books and papers stacked everywhere. His private correspondence and personal music studies. Mendelssohn's journals, in French, were lying open before me. I got through two lines of the entry for May 16, 1841, before dozing off. My fatigue was catching up with me. Daphne woke me soon afterward, and Helga, whom I had known since I was eighteen, scolded me for not sampling her oyster stew.

"Watch out, Mr. Max, or you will collapse before you reach the stage tomorrow night. Oatmeal again, eh?"

Helga's parting shot was not facetious. Back at our suite, on the coffee table, we found twelve packets of instant oatmeal, provided by Willy's assistant. Oatmeal was my standard fare for the forty-eight hours before a recital. Early in my career, it was all I could hold down, but later, even when I no longer emptied my stomach regularly backstage, I kept to my oatmeal diet. Part superstition, part habit. This time I thought I really needed it again. Daphne was vastly amused when I called room service for a bowl and a pot of hot water.

"And send up a quart of buttermilk, too," I told the clerk. "And the masseuse."

The masseuse was another old habit, essential for staying loose. This one, a lady from St. Lucia named Crystal, sashayed in an hour later with her bag of ointments. I stripped down and she went to work on me. Daphne peeked through my bedroom door (I saw her in the mirror), suspecting some vaguely lewd activity as Crystal's powerful hands smacked liniment onto my shoulders and pummeled my spine. My back was stiff and my arms sore. Or as Crystal informed me: "Your neck is like a spring and your shoulder muscles are fit to jump through your skin."

I grunted.

"I never knew playing the piano was such hard work, Mr. Randal."

I grunted again. I was thinking about Thalberg, "Old Arpeggio." When he retired, he didn't even have a piano in his house. He never played another note. I wondered what that would be like.

After a flurry of karate chops, Crystal went on to a gentler, circular motion. Someone must have given me some wonderful backrubs in infancy, for as a grown man my euphoria was undiminished when I was in capable hands. I was drifting off pleasantly when the telephone rang in my ear. I wedged the receiver between my head and the pillow. It was Willy, in high spirits.

"How are you, Max? Your suite is all right?"

"Great."

"How did the run-through go?"

"Everything's fine, Willy."

He chuckled. "Well, the press releases went out, and our phones have been ringing all day. The barracudas are jumping. This business of the Rhapsody No. 21 is causing a real stir. As I expected, we also heard from our friends at the Hungarian Consulate. They are quite wrought up."

"How did they find out?"

"News travels in this town."

"What did they say?"

He laughed. "Stolen goods, smuggling . . . a protest to the State Department . . . Demeter will never be allowed back into Hungary . . . an international star abetting theft . . . an outrage, a scandal . . . et cetera, et cetera, et cetera."

"I'm glad you find it amusing."

"Why not? They can't do anything. They can't prove anything. If it weren't for your friend Amos, the manuscript would still be in oblivion. Anyway, I told them they could bid for it at Sotheby's like everyone else; it's for a good cause. I offered their ambassador a half-dozen choice seats for tomorrow night. That's the end of it as far as we are concerned."

"Do you think they'll press charges against Amos? He did steal it, you know, by his own admission."

"Not in a million years. This is an embarrassment for them; they won't play it up. A national treasure, rotting away in a nursing home storehouse until an American photographer saves it. At most, our government will send him a stuffy letter. I've already checked it with my lawyers, there's nothing to worry about."

"And you don't think it taints the recital?"

"People don't care how you got the sheet music. They're excited about what they're going to hear. It's causing a sensation. The box office has been inundated—people are begging for standing room. The press attention, the uproar—we couldn't have hoped for a better start to the tour."

Willy, a born worrier, was not given to hyperbole, so I knew things must be humming along.

"Now, tell me," he said, "are you feeling well? Do you have everything you need?"

"I told you, I'm fine. How does the reception look?"

"Fine, fine. It's a private penthouse ballroom at the St. Moritz. Two terraces overlooking the park, sitting rooms, enough champagne for an army, wonderful food. Your Uncle Louie asked for two extra tickets and we sent them. And that man Lancio asked if he could send champagne to your dressing room after the recital. I told him it was fine. So, listen, get plenty of rest. If you need anything, call me."

After my massage, I took a hot bath and sat by the window in my robe smoking a cigar and sipping buttermilk. Mango and I watched the night fall. The lights twinkled on Fifth Avenue and the office buildings glittered like beehives. Daphne, dressed for dinner, was watching a gangster movie on the television in her room. Greta was due at any moment, but I couldn't drag myself inside to get ready. I tried to read my interview with Mr. Brown in the previous day's *Times*. It was a good interview, well-edited, and he had only the most glowing things to say about me, but it didn't hold my interest. I felt a deep inertia. The idea of going out to a restaurant, where I wouldn't eat or drink, wasn't appealing. I amused myself by thinking about Willy's tangle with the Hungarians. The previous week, in Boston, I had seen a piece of graffiti that stuck in my mind: sprayed in purple, above a hammer and sickle, it read, PROPERTY IS THEFT. If the Hungarian authorities should harass Amos about stolen property or ethics, that epigram could serve as a neat rebuttal. In truth, I sympathized with the Hungarians: it seemed more appropriate that the manuscript be displayed in Budapest than, say, San Diego. I wondered if it was Sinonescu, seizing an opportunity to tweak his revisionist comrades, who had gleefully tipped off the Hungarians. I had a hunch that Winters had boasted about the Liszt when he spoke to Sinonescu.

"What did you say?" Greta asked softly from the door.

I jumped up. "I didn't hear you come in. I'm just getting ready."

"The door was open . . ." She glanced around the room. "Who were you talking to, Max?"

"Nobody. I was looking out the window. Why?"

"You were talking when I came in."

I shrugged. "Just thinking out loud, I guess." Things were getting to me, I thought.

"Are you okay?"

"Fine. You and Willy seem to think I'm going to drop dead at any moment."

"I hope not," she said, combing her hair.

She sat on the bed while I dressed. She seemed more relaxed than she had all week in Boston, and this depressed me. A few hours away from me, from my personal pressure cooker, and the clouds had lifted from her brow. She didn't even seem to be forcing it: she was in genuine good spirits. Or a better actress than I thought. In the mirror, I saw her take something from her purse and stuff it under the pillow.

"Planting a bomb?" I said.

"With the press you received today, they would lynch me if I did. You're the hero of the arts page. Haven't you seen the papers?"

"No. I mean, I saw that interview, but I haven't gotten around to today's papers. What did you put there?"

She sighed. "My nightie, of course."

"You're staying here tonight?"

"I told you I was. Unless you don't want me to."

I stopped knotting my tie and looked at her. "I thought you just said that in passing. I didn't know you meant it."

She glanced away. "Of course I meant it."

"My mistake. Yes, of course I would prefer you stay."

She looked beautiful in a white suit with a ruffled shirt and white hat. She was wearing a pendant I had bought her in Rome. I watched her in the mirror while pretending to adjust my tie. Even in the muted lamplight, her hair glowed brightly. We had agreed to discuss our future after the recital, and that's exactly what I planned to do. Sometime, somewhere, between the curtain call and the reception, I would grab a few moments' privacy and put an end to this waiting game.

At dinner, I splurged and ordered pastina in broth (Daphne called it baby food) and a glass of buttermilk, while she and Greta feasted on tortellini and red snapper. Daphne was terribly excited. Friday was a big day for her. She was going to see her mother for the first time in two and a half months, and hear me play in recital for the first time ever. And of course it would also be her first meeting with Uncle Amos in his new role of stepfather. She chatted with Greta about all these things. And though I fought my detachment, I might just as well have been on the moon. I did not feel fatigued or pensive anymore, and my active mind was well removed from my music—it was something less tangible, a kind of deep inner lassitude. I wanted to coil up within myself and sleep. I felt as if my heart were beating painfully slowly, that the flow of impulses to my brain was down to a trickle, that I barely had to breathe—a kind of suspended animation. Perhaps this was due to my odd diet, gruel and milkfats, or to a brutal suppression of nerves. But it continued on the street, where walking seemed effortless, levitating.

There were three good-luck telegrams awaiting me at the hotel desk: from Patty, from Dr. Selzer (a surprise), and from Stella in London. Willy phoned again, and then Kim, who was in town unexpectedly and would attend the recital. Then some big wheel from my record company got through, and after that I told the desk to hold all calls. I changed back into my robe and made another bowl of oatmeal. I called down for the masseuse but it was too late. Daphne was watching another movie in bed, and Greta offered to give me a massage.

"It won't be professional," she said, "but I'll do what I can."

About twenty minutes into her massage, which was quite professional, I picked up where I had left off in the afternoon and drifted off deeply, pleasurably. All sorts of things passed in and out of my head. Finally, languidly, I thought: there are eighty-eight keys on the pianoforte. Fifty-two white and thirty-six black. There are ten digits on the human hands. That's all it is. The rest is talk. And double-talk. There's money and death. And love. And those we love dying. And love dying. And more money. Fame. Death. Eighty-eight keys and ten fingers. What else? Oh yes, there's fucking. Of course. You're playing the piano and fucking your mother. Eighty-eight keys and ten fingers and people watching you fuck your mother. Music and love, death and money. What else?

I flipped onto my back and took Greta by the shoulders. She was startled. I wanted to talk with her. She leaned over and kissed me very hard. I hadn't expected that. She pulled back, then kissed me again, even harder. I began to unbutton her blouse. The buttons were difficult to find amid the ruffles.

"Wait," she whispered. She got up to close the door. Then she began to undress.

"Daphne—"

"She's asleep. The movie put her out."

She removed her skirt and blouse, then her bra. From the side, her eyes looked sad. She stretched out beside me, running her fingertips along my abdomen in an elliptical motion.

"What were you thinking?" she said.

"I was thinking about your breasts and shoulders."

"Before that, before I got up. Tomorrow night?"

"Not exactly."

"Is it the way you want it to be?"

"Almost."

"So, what were you thinking?"

"I was thinking about money and death."

"That's a combination."

"And love. And fucking."

"Even better. And what did you conclude?"

"That we all spend too much time making money, and trying to love and be loved, and not nearly enough time fucking. And in the end we die."

"That's very profound." She grinned.

"I nearly forgot. I was also thinking of something Selzer told me: that when I play the piano, I'm fucking my mother."

"What did she mean?"

"I'm not sure. We never really got around to it."

"Hmmm. You certainly spend a lot of time at it."

"What's worse, I do it for money. Is there a word for that?"

She pursed her lips. "Motherfucker."

We laughed. I pulled her closer and kissed her. "Let's face it, all that's important in life is how you avoid death."

"And how do you do that?"

"Only one way I know of," I said, running my hand down the small of her back.

"But does it always work for you?"

"Not always."

She switched off the lamp and rolled on top of me.

"Greta, tomorrow night . . ."

"I know."

". . . the people, all those people . . ."

"I know, I know." She stroked my cheek. "Don't think about it now. There's no time now to think about it."

Later, when she was asleep, and I was staring out the window, wide awake, I knew she was wrong. I had learned long ago that there was always plenty of time when you didn't want it, and never enough when you really needed it.

On Friday night at six-thirty I sat alone in my dressing room in my formal trousers, bare-chested and barefoot, and looked at myself in the mirror. The room was dead silent. I could have been anywhere. I could have been dreaming. But this time I wasn't.

I had just called in the stage manager to confirm that the wall clock was correct. I never wore a watch when I performed, never carried anything in my pockets. I preferred walking out there without any baggage from my other life. Actually, until I was twenty-four I kept an old St. Christopher medal in my back pocket. It had been my father's, given him by his mother, and he wore it pinned inside the hem of his trunks during his fights. But I lost it in Paris when Daphne was born.

In ninety minutes I would go on. I leaned into the mirror and saw that, despite the bright light, my pupils were dilated. They nearly overran my irises. Otherwise, I looked calm. I felt calm. Cold. So clearheaded my temples ached. I had slept plenty, and that was important. I lay awake beside Greta until four and then slept through until noon. The rest of the day flew by. I had another massage. I ate two bowls of oatmeal. Greta took Daphne out for lunch and I sat by the window again with Mango. I sat there for hours, in my robe. Accepted no phone calls. Talked to no one. At five o'clock I drank a glass of milk with a fistful of vitamins. Suddenly it was time to go. Greta and Daphne stopped by on their way downtown. Greta had to change into her evening dress. Amos and Ellen hadn't shown up. They had a suite awaiting them at the hotel. We would all be staying there that night, like one big cozy family.

The rest of my performing clothes were laid out neatly before me. Two white shirts and a white tie, my pumps and socks, and the new jacket hanging on the rack. I wasn't ready yet to dress. The spare shirt was standard—for emergencies. Some performers get sick at the last minute. I had never been that careless, though I had occasionally changed at intermission during a rigorous evening. But after I had paced the room, from the sofa to the dressing table, back and forth for ten minutes, my stomach felt tight. As if there were a small leaden muscle deep in my fundament. I touched my toes. I drank some water. My temples ached more sharply and my mouth, dry for hours, became clammy. It began to fill with hot saliva. I knew what that meant, but still I didn't feel sick. I didn't even feel queasy, I just had that tightness way down. I went into the toilet and washed my face with cold water and spat into the sink. Then I sat on the john. Then I stood over it and spat some more. Then suddenly my veins turned to ice, my knees buckled, and my stomach exploded. Whatever was down there shot up violently, so that it wrenched my head and chest. After the oatmeal, it was all bile that burned my tongue. Then the tightness went away and my temples stopped aching. I brushed my teeth, gargled with mouthwash, filled the sink with cold water, and stuck my head in. At least that was over, I thought.

I sat down and stubbed out the cigar I had been smoking in snatches for an hour. I pulled on the long silk socks and slipped into the shiny pumps. The socks felt cool up my calves, and I walked around the room to get the squeaks out of the shoes. Greta and Daphne were due to come by at seven. Greta had asked me if I wanted her to stay with me until I went on, the way she used to in the old days, but I said no. I wanted to be alone. I sat staring into the mirror again and waited. My mind was a blank. The day had flown by, but now the seconds were crawling. I didn't have to be alone, but that was the way I had wanted it. I had to follow my instincts: at that point, I didn't have much else to go on.

I heard voices outside, then a hurried knock, and Greta and Daphne walked in. Daphne hugged me tightly.

"Oh, Daddy, there are going to be so many people. The lobby is already full."

Greta glanced at the clock, then at my bare torso and pale face. "Everything okay, Max?" she asked quietly.

I nodded.

She got a towel and draped it around my neck. "It's cold in here, you're going to get chilled."

"Your mother hasn't arrived yet, Daphne?"

"Not yet."

"How was your dinner?"

She told me about it, and I smiled, but I wasn't listening. I was thinking about Stella, how she wore a white dress like Daphne's to my first recital, how afterward, after two encores and staggering applause, she came down that same corridor to the room next door, kissed me, and in a hoarse whisper said, "Never let it go to your head." I promised her I wouldn't.

". . . and I had pistachio ice cream and orange cake for dessert," Daphne concluded.

I patted her stomach. "You're going to get fat if you keep eating that stuff, and Mother will blame me for it."

"But I only eat that way when I'm with you."

"That's what I mean."

As if on cue, we heard a commotion in the corridor. There was a single loud knock and the door flew open.

"Mommy!" Daphne shouted, and shot out of my lap into Ellen's arms. Behind Ellen, I saw Amos and Willy.

"We made it," Amos said, hugging Greta. "It was close, but we made it."

Willy, elegant sharp in his tuxedo, surveyed the scene nervously.

"You son of a bitch," I said to Amos. As he took my arm, I suddenly realized that he and Ellen were dressed for the bush. She was wearing white jeans and a white sweater and he was all in khaki, safari jacket, knee-high boots, and a purple bandana. Their hands and faces were bronzed.

"Where's your tux?" I said.

"Don't you remember—I had to send it back to Athens."

"You drop into my kitchen at dead of night in a tux and you come to my recital in jungle gear."

He grinned. "We were out last night photographing waterfalls in the interior. We barely made our plane, came here straight from the airport."

Ellen had disengaged herself from Daphne and embraced Greta warmly. Then she came up behind Amos and waited for him to finish. Our eyes met.

"I'd like you to meet Mrs. Demeter," he said softly.

"Hello, Max," she said, and hesitated. She even blushed.

"If you think I'm not going to kiss the bride, you're crazy," and I took her in my arms. "Congratulations, Ellen," I whispered. "You look wonderful."

She kissed me and stepped back. Her jet hair gleamed, her eyes were clear, and she was slim and tan. There was nothing dainty about her. She looked as if she'd had a few adventures and they had agreed with her. She and Amos looked so happy, I felt happy with them. I knew she could never have been that way with me.

"Well, you got yourself a bona fide wildman," I said, throwing my arms around both of them.

"You're not kidding. If I told you where I was today at four a.m., you'd never believe it."

"I want to hear about your getaway driving, too."

She rolled her eyes and laughed.

"Better tell us later," Willy piped in discreetly from the door. He looked worried. I glanced at the clock: 7:25.

Amos patted my shoulder. "He's right. We'd better get this circus out of here. We'll have all night to party." He embraced me. "Good luck, Max. It's all yours—just take it." He went out into the corridor.

Ellen took my hands. "You did such a good job," she whispered. "I've never seen Daphne so happy."

"You did the good job, for nine years. She made my summer, Ellen."

She looked surprised. "Good luck to you, Max."

Daphne jumped up into my arms. "Good luck, Daddy. I've got all my fingers crossed. And don't forget to look for me at the end."

She ran out and Willy came up to me.

"Now, don't you embrace me too," I said. "I feel like I'm about to walk the plank."

He clasped my arms. "You feel good?"

I nodded. "I have a good feeling."

He looked into my eyes and squeezed the back of my neck. "So do I," he said, "so do I. *Viel Glück, mein Sohn.*"

I was alone with Greta now. She had been quiet while the others were there, and now, with just the two of us, the little room reverberated with silence. It was seven-thirty exactly.

I let out a long breath. "I didn't expect all that. It's good to see everybody together."

She nodded. She had spent enough time with me in rooms like those when we were married to know how my mind was working.

"Maybe you would like help with your tie before I go," she said.

This was an old ritual, and it sent a jab through my heart.

I picked up a shirt and put it on slowly. A shiver ran up my back. Now, with the shirt against my skin, the room did feel cold, colder than when I was naked. I sat down and she came around behind me. I watched in the mirror as she fastened the white bow tie and adjusted my collar.

"Give me your comb," she murmured, and she combed the back of my head carefully. "You never did pay attention to the back. You know, that's all half of them will see."

I felt restless again.

"Now let me see you in your jacket," she said.

I put it on. "All right?"

She nodded. Her eyes were moist, which surprised me. "You look like what you are, Max. A great musician. A great soloist." She kissed me quickly. "Remember: you are the best and they know it."

"Thanks, Greta."

She turned on her heel and left without another word. I couldn't understand this until I realized that she had a more accurate notion of real time at that point than I did. She knew I should be alone. I took off my jacket and sat down in front of the mirror again. I folded my hands on the table, leaned forward, and closed my eyes. I forced myself to keep them closed, though I saw blue lights flashing on the lids. I could hear the blood in my temples too. And my mouth was dry again—too dry. I opened one eye: it was 7:40. There was a knock at the door. I figured Greta or Willy had come back.

"Come in," I called out, and my voice sounded detached, alien. I didn't open my eyes. The door closed.

"Hello, Max."

I sat up. "Louie! What are you doing here?"

"Hope I'm not busting in. I just wanted to wish you luck."

We shook hands. "I appreciate it." He was all decked out, tuxedo, a flower in his lapel.

He jerked his thumb toward the door. "The girl out there said, only immediate family, and I told her, sister, I'm as immediate as they get."

I smiled, but I must have had a funny look on my face.

"Anyway, I'd better clear out," he said. "I've got the whole family out there. Shirley and I are so proud. The new son-in-law thinks he married into Culture," he chortled.

"Bring them all to the party later."

"I wouldn't miss it." He looked around the room. "The house is buzzing," he laughed uneasily, "and they leave you all alone back here, huh? Almost the way it is before a fight. Well, good luck," he said, opening the door. "And play your ass off, kid."

It was 7:45. I felt utterly calm. They would come for me in fifteen minutes. I drank a glass of water. I closed my eyes and didn't move. For the first time, in my active mind, I thought about the music. I went through the opening bars of the *Diabelli*. Then I shut them out. I thought about crossing the stage, the physical sensations that would wash over me. The lights. The feel of all those eyes. The enormous collective breath. The applause. The sense of the stage itself, at once huge, expansive, yet claustrophobic. Like being out at sea and in a small black room at the same time. There was no other way to describe it. And there must be things, I thought, that I didn't remember. Little things. Like a parachutist who hasn't jumped in four years. I tried not to remember them. It would be just a minute of all that, and then I would play and there would be nothing else. I reminded myself not to look up when I first went out or I would blink into the lights. Nothing looked worse. Just stare straight ahead and walk with a measured step. Follow the old instincts. Let them take over.

There was a knock at the door. It was eight o'clock. A young woman came in.

She said, "Are you ready, Mr. Randal?"

I stood up and put on my jacket. She helped me.

"I've waited a long time to hear you again," she said. "Good luck."

She followed me down the corridor. I was thinking about nothing, about everything. I walked impassively, with my head up high. I was thinking about Orana the first time I visited her in the hospital. Her white hands folded on the sheets. I was thinking about Greta's body the night before. Yielding yet holding back. I was thinking about Ellen our first night in Vienna and how her hair had smelled like jasmine. I was thinking about my father drinking double-whiskies and disappearing on me. I was thinking about Greta's body in the twilit hotel room, yielding yet holding back. I was thinking about Ellen's voice in the darkness the morning Daphne was born, saying it's time, it's time, waking me to the sound of rain in the cool darkness, saying Max it's time now, it's time.

"It's time now," the young woman said into my ear. We were standing in the wings and the houselights were dimming. My temples were ringing. I took a long breath. I let it out slowly, very slowly, and threw back my shoulders.

I walked out into the lights. For an instant the noise was a shock. The applause. Thunder crashing. It was pitch-dark beyond the lights. I could feel the animal out there. Breathing, shifting. Coiled in the darkness. I walked miles to reach center stage. I bowed to each side of the house. I saw nothing. I turned around and for a split second felt a whiff of vertigo. Terror. The piano grew enormous. The floor opened. The darkness yawned. Suddenly I knew what the last fifth was, the essence of what I had been missing: it was Fear. The immediate, enormous, mortal fear that hits you onstage and nowhere else. That lifts and pumps you for the most potent adrenaline. You forget it when you're not onstage. A soloist needs both confidence and fear. I had regained my confidence in Boston, but this fear could only have reemerged at that moment. Four years earlier I had lost it, sidestepped it, cheated on it. I had lost my edge. You need that fear like a slap in the face, a blast in your gut. All of this shot by me in a flash. Then there was a blank. Freud says that in a moment of illumination the ego dissolves. It was that kind of blank.

I sat down. I shook my sleeves back. The applause died. The animal stirred and stiffened in the darkness. I had to keep the animal at bay. To enchant it. To make music for it. Make music. Make music. Amos told me later that I waited fifteen, maybe twenty, seconds longer than usual before I began. I don't remember that. I remember opening my eyes and putting my fingers to the keys, then raising them up, and while it was still absolutely silent hearing faint music in my head and a moment later someone played the opening of the *Diabelli*, the distinctive staccato waltz, *allegretto vivace*, I heard someone playing it into the darkness and then I was playing it, and the animal was gone, the lights were gone, the stage was gone. I was playing. There was no fear, no pleasure, no anticipation. It was all happening from under me. I was swimming down a waterfall and my strokes were perfect, I was regulating the flow, when I slowed it slowed and when I sped up it sped up, until I was the waterfall, living and breathing only the sounds I was creating.

By the tenth variation I was not only lost in it but I knew something special was happening. After Leporello's theme in the twenty-second variation, I felt I had never played so well in my life. I had prayed that the notes would dance off my fingers, but it was better than that: it was the music dancing off my fingers, with a spring and surety that could only be lent from within, from the sounding board of the heart and the abdomen and the spirit. Though you don't think, in the normal sense, when you perform, you still feel amazement. You're humbled and exalted simultaneously. My amazement grew out of the realization that nothing in my life, no sensation, no experience, ever made me feel so complete, so sensually fulfilled, as playing a piece to my own satisfaction at the moment of performance. It was an elemental transcendence, leaving everything else far behind. It meant realizing physically, with flesh and blood, the full and rounded abstraction that is a piece of music. It was becoming the music, the waterfall, and not a man playing that music or riding that waterfall. The body, the hands, became a medium between the spirit and the piano. There were the hammers of the piano and the digits of the hands and the lights of the spirit. And it helped to have the animal out there, even when it was forgotten. It helped to be alone in the lights. It helped to be alone inside. But above all it helped to be lost, having to find the way back to yourself through the music you were making. Each piece, and the recital as a whole, became a small journey, not just for the audience, but for the performer, a journey away from, around, and finally back to the self. That was the way it should be, not just six pieces played powerfully. And that was how I had embarked as I began the Opus 10, the Sonata No. 5 with its crashing chords, its fragile skiff awash in monstrous seas, rising and falling, rollicking, rolling, the second leg of my journey.

If anything, I grew stronger. I flew through the first two sonatas, with their exuberance, Beethoven's exuberance at twenty-eight, before his hearing went, when he was still dedicating pieces to the ladies. Still, he sprang his usual tricks. The key to the No. 6 lies in the little figure at the end of the exposition, where he jumps out of F major to D major and then back to F. In the second movement he fools with minor keys, and there is a tricky canon in the finale. At first it resembles a rondo—then it surprises you. Sonata No. 7 prefigures his later, darker work. It draws the other two, with their quick vitality, into a wider circle, onto higher ground, and it is there, especially in the second movement, the *largo e mesto*, that I hit my stride, culling nuances I had only anticipated in practice, nuances that renewed the piece for me, opened it up, before whirling me into the final *allegro* movements. I finished at a dead run and the animal roared. The applause was deafening. The blood rushed to my head. I stood up and bowed and went off for the intermission.

Time had become meaningless. I felt as if I had been out there just a few minutes. I was running so well that I didn't want to break my momentum. The young woman greeted me in the wings. There were other people beside her. The stage manager sent them away. The young woman was saying something but I couldn't hear her. She followed me down the corridor to my dressing room. She waited at the door when I went in and said something else.

"Just some icewater," I replied, "that's all. Thank you."

She disappeared, returned with a pitcher of icewater, and disappeared again.

I was alone again, really alone. It was as if I had been transported from the Arctic to the Equator in a matter of seconds. From that limitless cavern to this little room. It made me dizzy. I drank a glass of water. I went to the bathroom, wet the corner of a towel, and dabbed my eyelids. I sat down before the mirror again. My face was transfigured. It looked like someone else, no better or worse, no more or less alive, just crucially, integrally different. I sat back and closed my eyes. It was an hour or a few seconds later when the young woman knocked once and said, "Five minutes, Mr. Randal." After another hour or another few seconds, she came back. I had thought about nothing, seen nothing, felt nothing. I was on my way back down that corridor, into the wings, and I was itching to return to the piano. My hands were on fire and I didn't want to lose any ground. I wanted to slip back into that flow, that unity of the piano and the music and me, the animal poised close by, menacing and protective.

The lights dimmed and the young woman touched my arm. I was ready, this was my night and I knew it now. As I crossed again into the enormous-tiny empty darkness, the animal roared at twice the volume. The animal was with me now. For an instant that same fear shot through me, emptied and refilled me, redefined me, and I sat down again terrified in my heart. But ready. And the animal fell silent.

I waited. Then I began to play, and I was daunted for a moment because it was me now playing the *Hammerklavier*, it wasn't someone else, but that sensation ebbed and I fell away from it. There were some rapids this time, snaky and treacherous, and it took me a few measures to accommodate my stroke, to reverse the flow and make it follow me again, but soon I was approaching that waterfall and then I was inside it, it was moving with me and then we were one and I had it back, I felt the music dancing off my fingers again.

Of all the pieces, the *Hammerklavier* was the most rigorous. I had practiced it the least. It had worried me the least, for some perverse reason. And now, performing it taxed me terribly. It was an endurance test, complex and exhausting, right down to that final, exquisite fugue. To maintain the intensity of the first half of the program I had to play my heart out. Performing at that pitch I would need every ounce of my strength to negotiate these two remaining sonatas, to reach the Liszt, that spectacular bit of fireworks to dazzle the animal once and for all. But after the first movement of the *Hammerklavier*—to my ear, the one lull in an otherwise flawless assault—my heart, my gut, something took over and I found a tremendous second wind. There were wings on my wrists as I flew into the latter movements. I got stronger each moment. It was thunderous to my own ears, percussive, sparks flying. I couldn't believe how well I was playing it, again gleaning fine points, subtleties, that I had only glimpsed in practice. The long iron sonata, the killer, took on a life of its own, and this time, truly, I was no more than its instrument. It nearly outraced me in the end, such an extended journey within my larger journey, and I finished hard again, dazed, with a flourish, thinking consciously just that once, during the applause: two to go, two to go.

And I played the *Waldstein*, my father's piece, my concession to my own sentiments. I played it lovingly, for it had been a part of me since my ninth year, those notes I had learned as a boy in my mother's living room. I played them now with the hands and heart of a man. And though it was a piece more familiar to the animal than the others, I played it only for myself, and for my father in that room that long-ago evening. This time he didn't disappear on me, this time I disappeared on myself. I nearly forgot to stand up at the end. And when I did, I had to lean on the piano for an instant, for I was exhausted, yet higher, fuller, lighter-than-air, as I hadn't been in years.

The houselights came up and the animal became an audience and the audience was on its feet and the roar was deafening. Either I had forgotten some along the way, or this was the finest ovation I had ever received. I walked to center stage and bowed. I looked out and saw nothing. A hundred—a million—faces. And the roar. I bowed again and went off.

The young woman, my anonymous Beatrice who had escorted me in and out of hell, was waiting stolidly. "Excuse me," I said, and braced myself on her shoulder. She turned pale, probably afraid I was going to pass out. But I smiled, or thought I did, and then nodded, and she signaled to someone and the houselights dimmed again. The animal was my friend now, my long-lost, dearest, and most faithful friend, and I crossed over and bowed and sat down. This was the last stretch. Now the pins could be heard dropping. I had given them the works but still they were waiting for this, the bit of history snatched from the rats by a madman who was more to me than a brother, ten minutes of music last performed on a pianoforte in a country house by Monsieur Liszt himself. I hoped he was there too, somewhere in the eaves with my father.

The Hungarian Rhapsody No. 21, like music out of a fairy tale, sounded otherworldly after the hard beauty of the Beethoven. The *friska*, the gypsy strains, the icy lilting cadences like magical winter music flew into the air, as if I were erecting geometric abstracts with sound. It carried a linear density, radiating lines and planes, rather than the gigantic waves generated by the *Hammerklavier*. It did not emerge, to my ears, as it had during my few practice sessions. It again carried that luminous intimacy I had experienced the first time I played it. In a hall, the fireworks were subtler than I had imagined. The rest of the program, after all, was familiar to me; I could anticipate, and remember, how those pieces should sound in a concert hall. But I had never heard the rhapsody outside of my studio and Willy's living room. It was virgin. And I was its first interpreter. Two-thirds of the way through, it sounded balletic, angular and delicate, balanced as crystal—then suddenly the dervishes whirled out. The *friska* reannounced itself with a lightning arpeggio run, *allegro presto prestissimo*, flying under my hands, the fingering grew torturous, the pedaling dense, the Roman candles and flares went up, exploding, until the climax when it jerked back to *adagio, diminuendo*, and concluded with a stately repetition of the original theme, carried through a whirlwind and then returned intact—fused and more intense. I played the last note, I held it, and as in Boston that first time I thought I would cry. I had done it.

The place went crazy. I came up and faced the house. I felt hot, flushed, triumphant. They were on their feet again, clapping and stamping. There were more "Bravos" than I had ever heard. And "Encores." I bowed twice. I went off. There were four curtain calls. The second time out I remembered my promise, and though my vision was blurry, I squinted down past the lights, found the third row and, near the aisle, Daphne's bright smiling face. She was standing between Ellen and Greta clapping her heart out. I winked at her and blew a kiss, and she waved to me. I looked back out into the house. At the last curtain call I took a sweeping bow and held my arms outstretched and bowed again, deeply. It was a heady moment. It was worth everything. That last roar put fire into my veins.

I went off and my friend Beatrice was clapping too. I kissed her cheek. She said something. The stage manager shook my hand. Other people came out of the shadows and shook my hand. They were all talking at once. My ears were still ringing from the stage. A crowd was forming. Someone put a program under my nose to sign. Then another. Beatrice pushed them away, took my arm firmly, and led me to the corridor, where there was no one. I thanked her. I think she was still afraid I would pass out. But she did her job well, delivering me back to my dressing room. She was speaking to me again but I still had trouble hearing her.

"What did you say?"

"I said, that was something, Mr. Randal. That was really something. Are you all right?"

I nodded.

In the dressing room, everything was the same except that there were five magnums of champagne in ice buckets and a tray of glittering glasses on the table. I collapsed into a chair. My head was spinning. My gut was on fire. I felt emptied, yet I wanted more. Much more. Beatrice started to leave. "You were just wonderful," she said, as a farewell.

"Where are you going?" My voice was far away to me. I didn't want to be alone just then. Not yet.

She sat across from me pensively. The silence was deathly after the applause. It made me dizzy again. I looked at her.

Just then the door burst open and Daphne ran into my arms. "You remembered," she said, "you remembered."

The dream was over.

"Of course I did, sweetheart." I lifted her up onto my lap and held her close.

[*293*]

Ellen and Greta came in and they had tears in their eyes. Greta was flushed.

"What's all the bawling?" I said. "Was I that bad?"

Greta wrapped her arms around my neck. "Oh, Max, it was beautiful, magical. I died out there. I have never heard you play like that."

Ellen leaned over and kissed me. She had a beautiful face for tears: they shone silver under her jet hair. "Wonderful, just wonderful," and she kissed me again on the mouth.

"Thanks, kid."

"Kiss him again," Daphne whispered, and my eyes locked on Ellen's. She looked away.

"You kiss me, Daphne," I said into her ear. "Mommy's a married woman."

That was the last bit of coherent activity around me for some time. Amos and Louie swarmed in with Louie's entire family, and on their tails was the unlikely duo of Frank Lancio and Willy. I saw Willy's face and he was just busting all over. He winked at me. I would have loved a minute alone with him, but it would have to wait.

Louie bear-hugged me. "Damn it, those people out there think you can walk on water," he shouted into my ear.

Amos, with an ingenious touch for corks, already had all five magnums open and flowing. He and Beatrice were doing the honors, and the brimming glasses were passing overhead, sprinkling Daphne and me, en route to the doorway and beyond.

"That's the sweetest rain I've felt in years," I said to Ellen, but she couldn't hear me.

Everyone was talking at once. The din was terrific. Shirley and her daughters were standing around Daphne and me. My cousin Jeannie had her hand on my shoulder. Louie slipped me some cigars. The stage manager was out in the corridor keeping people away. Willy and Lancio were deep in discussion by the door. When I caught Lancio's eye, I signaled my thanks for the champagne. I couldn't find Greta for a moment, but she was behind me. I still hadn't recovered my bearings. And my arms were rubbery. I wished I had had a few more minutes alone with Beatrice, just until my head stopped pounding, before this deluge hit. I stood up and kissed Shirley and Jeannie again, and Ellen for good measure, and then got Amos in a corner. I embraced him.

"You know you were out there with me, right beside me. How was the Liszt?"

"Incredible. You had the place mesmerized from the start." I smiled. "Something happened. It all just clicked."

"You're not kidding. I've never heard you, or anyone else, play better. And you had one tough house—they were expecting plenty. What the hell did you take before you went on?"

"A mighty dose of terror."

Winters and Sinonescu were in the doorway, introducing themselves to a skeptical Willy. Winters was dressed smartly, replete with black derby, gold-knobbed cane, and a meerschaum pipe carved as a mermaid. Sinonescu, in an ancient boxy tuxedo and white gloves with buttons, was glancing around haughtily. They made an odd pair.

"Be nice to Winters," Amos said.

I made my way across my former cell and greeted them.

"Astonishing performance," Winters announced, then lowered his voice. "I hope you won't press charges, but Emma got it all on tape. Every note."

Sinonescu shook hands and bowed formally. "Mr. Randal, my congratulations and warmest felicitations from His Excellency Mehmet Fallou, United Nations Ambassador from Albania."

Louie, who was beside me, gaped at Sinonescu. He couldn't contain himself. "From where?" he blurted.

"Albania, Louie. This is Mr. Sinonescu, their cultural attaché. This is my uncle, Louis Randal. Please thank the ambassador for me."

"I was honored to be here tonight," Sinonescu said. "You are indeed a great artist."

Amos interceded with two glasses of champagne. We all clinked glasses.

"To neurovisual harmonic phenomena," Amos said. Then he went off with Sinonescu.

There was another commotion at the door and Kim burst in.

"Max, it was magnificent. Welcome back."

I took his sleeve. "Better than Brussels six years ago?"

"Couldn't you hear yourself?"

I saw Greta again, alone, swilling champagne. I worked my way over to her.

Her eyes were funny, a little off, the big swimming-pool-blue irises cloudy around the edges. "To your great triumph, Max," she proclaimed, raising her glass high, "to your victory over the Furies." She said it so loudly that what I had hoped would be a private conversation suddenly became a general toast. Everyone stopped talking, turned around, and raised their glasses.

"Congratulations!" they shouted, not in unison, and Louie thumped me on the back.

The room fell silent and I felt obliged to say something. "Thank you. Every one of you helped make this possible. I toast you all." And I grabbed Greta's glass and downed it in one throw, before she could.

"And now the party!" Willy shouted. "The cars are waiting."

I took Greta aside. Out of the corner of my eye, I saw Ellen intercept Amos, coming over to join us, and steer him outside.

"Are you all right?" I said.

"I am so proud of you, Max. So happy for you. Come, you mustn't miss your own party."

"I want to talk to you first."

"They are all waiting for you. We'll talk later."

"We can talk here."

She touched my cheek. "Please. I want to go to your party."

Daphne ran back to fetch us, and she and Greta went on ahead of me. I paused amid the debris and surveyed my little room. The toilet, the mirror, the table. It was silent again. It was just another green room. I went out. Beatrice escorted me one last time, and after more autographs and other delays, I made it to the street.

My limo was as jammed as the dressing room had been. Daphne was on my lap, and Ellen on Amos's, Greta between us, and Willy in front with the driver. Amos was clutching one of the magnums. Willy was going on about the Liszt. He was very excited.

The party was well in swing. I made my entrance with Greta

on one arm and Daphne on the other, Ellen and Amos preceding us in their bush outfits. When people saw me, they broke into applause. There were more "Bravos" and handshakes while the champagne corks exploded at the bar. Greta disappeared and I was left to fend for myself among a swarm of barracudas. Willy had picked the place well. It was a good-sized ballroom, tables all around, a long bar, and a staggering buffet. Off this room, there was a lounge, and several private rooms with couches and over-stuffed chairs. At either end of the ballroom, glass doors opened onto softly lit terraces overlooking the park. People were already drifting outdoors. The room was packed. It smelled of perfume. Of champagne. Of money. Like Carnegie Hall, the atmosphere was heady, unlike anything I had been accustomed to for some time. The crowd was full of beautiful people and music people. Mr. Brown, from the *Times*, was among the reporters, and we had a nice chat. He was enthusiastic. The recital had moved him deeply, he said. But his colleagues were insatiable, with dozens of questions about my layoff, the Liszt, the tour. . . . I was foun-dering when Willy and his people finally stepped in and allowed me to slip away. I looked for Greta. Party or no party, glory or no glory, I had to speak with her. It was Friday night, the recital was over, the game was up. But I couldn't find her anywhere, and I kept getting waylaid. I was the man of the hour, after all, and I was rusty at this, too, after my years of seclusion.

I saw Amos in the lounge, talking with Sinonescu and Win-ters. Discreetly to one side was the charming Emma in evening dress, puffing a cheroot. I got myself a soda and joined Ellen and Daphne at a table. They were catching up on things. Daphne was talking about Frank Lancio.

". . . and Daddy could have asked for *anything*," she said rue-fully.

"I asked him for Mango," I said, grabbing her from behind. She rolled her eyes. "You see, Mom, he's always teasing."

"I've been hearing all about your adventures." Ellen smiled.

"I was afraid of that."

"You two had quite a summer."

Two women from my record company descended with their own brand of felicitations.

"Max," one of them exclaimed, "your little girl looks just like her mother, doesn't she."

Daphne and I started laughing, and after they were gone, Ellen tugged at my arm. "What was so damn funny about that?"

"I'll let Daphne explain it," I said, for I had just spotted Greta in the crowd. "Excuse me a minute."

I caught up with her near the terrace. She looked preoccupied. She didn't even see me until I was right on top of her. She was holding an empty champagne glass.

"I've been looking for you everywhere," I said, taking her arm. "Come with me." I led her around the corner into one of the private rooms and locked the door behind us.

She sat down on the red plush ottoman by the window. "Yes, I suppose it is time we had our talk," she said. I was hovering by the door. "Aren't you going to sit down with me?"

Her hair was very bright against the black window. She took my hands and studied them.

"Why have you been drinking so much?" I asked.

"Don't tell me you have become a moralist, Max," she said airily. "A few weeks of abstinence, and now you're preaching. My father used to preach."

I sat back slowly. She looked at me.

"I have not had that much to drink," she said softly. "It's not that."

"I know."

We both fell silent. I felt as if I were looking in on us from outside the window. We seemed substanceless, like the shadows the sun casts in shallow water. Only our voices were real to me.

She took my hands in her own again.

"It's not going to work out with us, is it?" I said.

She looked down and shook her head. "No."

"You've known for some time, haven't you. You knew it when you came to Boston."

She nodded.

I let out my breath. "I guess I knew it, too. I'm just a bit thick."

"You're not thick, Max. But it's not right. It was never right. I was wrong in June, I was dreaming. I wanted it to work, but I could not live with you again."

"That stupid incident—"

"It's much more than that." She wet her lips. Her voice was scratchy.

"Well, spill it," I said angrily. "Let it fly."

She bridled. "I don't want to let it fly. I don't have to explain anything to you. I just cannot live the way you do, that's all."

"You make it sound dirty," I said, for I was stung.

"I don't mean to. I know, you think you have changed. That it's a big change. Maybe it is—for you. I don't say this to hurt you, but some people are not made to live with other people in the customary way. Or if they do, it must be with a very special kind of person. I am not that person for you."

"I see. Then there's not much more to say." I stood up.

"Please, don't be angry with me."

"Why the hell not?" I started pacing. My fists were clenched, and my jaw, but I felt strangely listless within my agitation. Powerless. As if I had already witnessed this scene internally, felt its repercussions, and now merely had to endure it in the flesh. "Look, maybe you're right," I muttered. "I don't know anymore."

"I am right," she said.

"Why did you come to Boston, then?"

"I came—and I know this will sound wrong—but it was because I thought you needed me, to help you through tonight. After Orana, and the problems with your music, I did not want to make things even worse. I did not have the heart for that."

"I said you were just playing wet nurse. I knew it. If I'm that delicate, I didn't deserve to get through tonight."

"You needn't be cruel."

"I'm just not good at accepting pity."

"And I was not offering it. I knew how much tonight meant to you. I am still your friend, and I couldn't desert you on the brink of all this. Do you remember the last time we saw Orana? She whispered something to me before we left."

"Don't get dramatic."

Her eyes narrowed. "She asked me to help you. She said you were afraid."

"Great. So she felt sorry for me, too. Even on her deathbed."

"Now you're talking stupidly. Listen, maybe I had selfish reasons for coming to Boston, too. Maybe it was my way of saying goodbye. Maybe I wanted to be along one more time for the ride."

"That's even worse than pity. That's bullshit. I don't believe you."

"Max, I do love you, but I cannot live with you. Please try to understand that. I have no regrets about this summer."

"Well, I don't understand and I do have regrets. So we close the books and move on. Will I see you anymore?"

"Probably not very often," she said slowly. "You see, I am moving out to California. I decided about a month ago. I want to make a fresh start. I had to be here in Manhattan when I was modeling, but now I can do my work anywhere."

"But it's a wasteland out there. You'll go crazy."

"I don't think so. I'll get a place by the ocean. It's just a different kind of life."

"What about the loft—will you rent it?"

"No, I am going to sell it. In fact, I wanted to offer it to you first. I'll give it to you for whatever I require to buy a cottage out there."

My head was throbbing again. For an instant I wanted to throw the lamp through the window. To kick over a chair—anything. But that sort of violence doesn't come naturally to me.

"Max, I—"

"Shut up, Greta, just for a minute. You don't have to be so damn considerate anymore. You can retire that good samaritan stuff." I ran my hand across my eyes. "No, I do not want the loft. I couldn't live there now, for Christ's sake. Anyway, you can get good money for it and buy yourself a big house on the beach instead of a cottage."

"I am not so interested in big houses," she said sharply. "And by the way, I won't need my alimony anymore either come January. My own business will be bringing in more than I need."

"You don't have to do that. I can afford it."

"No, you didn't hear me. I said that I don't need it. I don't want it. I like supporting myself. I did it for years before I met you."

"Fine. And Ellen's married now. I've got plenty of dough and I can spend it all on myself."

"Why does that make you angry?"

I shook my head. "I'm just tired. And I'm not used to people feeling sorry for me."

"Who feels sorry for you, except you yourself?"

"Come on, I can see it in your eyes."

"You may see something, but it's not that."

"Ellen, too," I went on. "The way she looks at me."

"She was once very much in love with you. Don't you think it might have been difficult for her tonight, with you and Amos such close friends?"

"I know that. You all think I live in a vacuum, goddammit."

"Nobody thinks that."

"I had actually conned myself into thinking we might re-marry. Now I feel like a fool."

"You're not a fool. Back in June it was my fault, and I'm sorry. But after a certain point, did you really think that was going to happen? Did you?"

"No, I knew the score weeks ago. Maybe you're right. Maybe you—maybe the past—have helped keep me going lately."

"But you don't need that anymore. Or me. You have your music back now. Your power. I will never forget how you played tonight."

I grunted. "That doesn't make me feel any better."

"It will."

I touched her cheek. I was drained and I didn't want this to go on any longer. "Are you going to stay for the party?"

She shook her head. "I'd like to go home."

We stood up.

"I'll walk you down, you can take my car."

"No, don't come out with me now. Please."

I opened the door. My stomach turned a little. "Good-bye, Greta."

"Oh, Max, I'm so sorry." She embraced me. "Take care of yourself."

She was gone. I sat down and took out a cigar. My hands were like ice. I could still smell her perfume. I studied a vase of irises

across the room which I had not noticed before. And some litho-
graphs of mountains over the mantelpiece. Suddenly I felt
calmer than I had all night. And vaguely relieved, as I had on the
day Orana died. Another ordeal had ended. But I also felt lowdown, dazed there amid the trappings of my great triumph, my
"victory over the Furies," as Greta had proclaimed it. I'm afraid
I would never get the better of my Furies for very long. In the
end, they would always have the last lick.

I returned to the party. Ellen was sitting alone, and I joined
her.

"It means a lot to me," she said, "that you're so happy for
Amos and me." She folded her hands on the table. "You've
changed, you know. I could never talk to you before."

I squirmed. "I haven't changed much. I just found that out
once and for all."

She glanced down. "Greta was looking for Daphne. Then I
saw her leave. I didn't want to ask."

"That's all right. Did Amos tell you what's been going on?"

"A little. I'm sorry, Max. I really am."

"Greta's right. It wouldn't have worked. It didn't work the
first time."

Ellen didn't say anything. I had forgotten how pretty her eyes
were.

"I am happy we'll all be living in the same place for once," I
said. "I'll see Daphne now the way I always should have."

"She adores you. It's all she can talk about."

I signaled a waiter for some champagne. "Let's drink to something. Your health?"

"How about Daphne's first day at Juilliard?"

"Right. Our daughter, the virtuoso."

We clinked glasses. A pack of strangers came up and introduced themselves. One lady invited me to a dinner party. Another had programs for me to autograph. Then Amos and Kim
appeared and pulled up chairs. The strangers disappeared.

"Here you are," Amos boomed. "I've been looking for you.
Where's Greta?"

"She had to go home," Ellen said. "She wasn't feeling well."

"What do you mean?"

"I mean, she wasn't feeling well," she said, and from his blank look I knew she had kicked him under the table.

"Oh. I'm sorry to hear that."

There was an awkward silence.

"You're going to use the Liszt piece throughout the tour, aren't you?" Kim said.

"Sure, I'll trot it out every night."

"You go to Philadelphia next?"

"On Sunday. Then Washington." I hadn't thought much about that in the previous few days, and the long vista of hotel rooms and airports and restaurants stretched out dismally before me. In my mind's eye, it would be raining in all of those places all the time, and it would be dark.

"I'm going to miss Mango," I said lightly.

"Oh, don't worry, we'll take good care of him," Amos said. "Filet mignon in the morning and whipped cream at bedtime."

"I think I'll go find Daphne," I said. "I haven't seen much of her tonight."

I felt Ellen's eyes on me as I walked away.

My heart was heavy. After the party, Daphne would return to the Plaza, but to her mother's suite. Mango was already there, with his bowl, his toys, and his deluxe traveling case. The previous night had been our last together, and it had come upon us so fast, with so much attendant confusion, that I hadn't had time to prepare myself. I had been too preoccupied with the recital and with Greta. And now in two days I would be leaving town. Daphne would start school. Amos and Ellen would set up house. And Mango would have a new window for his reveries.

Daphne was on the smaller terrace, at a table with Louie and Frank Lancio. She was listening wide-eyed while Louie regaled her with stories. There were three empty dessert dishes in front of her.

I shook Lancio's hand. "Thanks again for the champagne, Frank."

"It was nothing. I'm proud to be here. They're cooking up quite a storm in there, huh?"

"Yeah, I'm getting a little tired."

Louie sat up. "What's the matter with you—no spunk?"

"You forget, he worked hard tonight," Lancio said kindly.

"Work! The piano is second nature to Max. Like eating or breathing. It's not work, he loves it."

"He has to practice a lot, Uncle Louie," Daphne said earnestly.

She got her cheek pinched for it. "I know he does, doll. I'm just kidding. I'm taking this kid home with me tonight, Max. Would you like to come live with Uncle Louie, Daphne?"

She nodded slowly. "When I'm not with Mom or Dad, sure."

"You can visit them, but you'll live at my house. I've got so many rooms even your cat can have one. His own bathroom, too."

She laughed. "Anyway, I have to go to school here in the city, so I couldn't do it."

My heart was sinking.

"Isn't the moon beautiful, Daddy?"

"Very beautiful."

It was ringed with blue haloes. The few clouds scudding by were tinged with gold or suffused with that milky glow that El Greco employed to flesh out his saints and martyrs. Below, the lights of the city were blazing. It was a warm, moist night, and the moon was carving sharp shadows all around us. Lancio, with his hard features, cast a cold rigid silhouette against the terrace wall, though in reality he was very relaxed.

"Daphne, would you mind helping me pick a dessert?" I said. "I have a hunch you can tell me which ones are best."

"The chocolate mousse pie is the best. Come on." She took my hand.

We found a table in the back.

"You look so handsome tonight, Daddy."

"Thank you. You really enjoyed the recital, didn't you."

"It was great. All those people hollering for you. But did you get scared this time?"

"Terrified. But just for a minute."

"I was scared for you. Mom told me my hands were shaking."

I took her face in my hands. "I love you so much, Daphne. I want you to know how happy you make me. If it hadn't been for you, things might have been very different tonight."

"I love you, too. I wish I could go along on your tour. We could cook together and go to movies and everything."

"I wish you could, too. But it's not like that. Remember, I'm always in hotels. And there's no time for movies. I'll be back soon and you'll see me all the time."

"I'll miss you, though." She threw her arms around my neck. I couldn't remember ever suffering such separation pains from anyone, even as a boy her age—especially then. Good-byes had never been particularly tough for me.

"You help your mother all you can in her new life."

"I will."

"And work hard at school, but not too hard. Sometimes the kids there forget they're in this world to enjoy themselves."

"I won't forget."

"Now, what would you most like me to bring you back from my trip? Anything you want."

She bit her lip. "Mom brought me clothes from Europe. I don't need any more of those. Can I tell you tomorrow?"

"Of course."

"Dad, I wish you didn't have to go away. You'll be all alone."

It had been a long recital, and it was a long party. They told me it rolled on past four. I left at two, soon after Amos and Ellen took Daphne. I drank a little bourbon with Louie and Amos, and I finally had a few minutes alone with Willy. He was in great spirits, no worries for once, full of talk about the tour. Then, without a word to anyone, I slipped away. I told my driver to wait for Willy, and still in white tie, I turned up my collar and walked across Central Park South to Fifth Avenue. It was good to be out of the party.

I was on my last wind, the currents of adrenaline I had generated onstage finally ebbing. The night air cleared my head. Away from the chaos, I took a deeper satisfaction in the outcome of the recital. I had done what I had to do. Raised the roof, brought the house down. It was a complete triumph musically, beyond even my wildest hopes in the previous weeks. I felt as if I had overreached myself, and yet had still caught the brass ring. And that isn't the way it usually happens.

By the time I reached the Plaza, my spirits had peaked, leveled, and plummeted again. My suite was like a tomb. I had lingered at the party because I so feared the moment I would enter that plush pneumatic darkness—a reproach in itself. The staff had done their usual superlative job. That was why one stayed at the Plaza. There was no trace that Daphne or Mango or Greta had ever been there. Only my bed was turned down. I switched on the lights and took off my jacket. I opened the door to Daphne's room, looked in, and closed it. I sat in my chair by the window. I kicked my shoes aside and pulled off my tie. I thought about Greta. About how she was putting a continent between us, without looking back. I thought about Amos, my best and dearest friend, assuming the stewardship of what should have been my little family. These were the fruits of seeds sown long before that summer. They had been growing beyond my control for some time. They had become simple facts.

And what was that summer to me in the end? Now that I had reached its climax (for I had known all along that the night of this first recital would be both an end and a beginning), could I possibly encapsulate, or distill, all its events? I couldn't, I still can't, or why would I have been impelled to explore them in such detail? That night, sitting until dawn in the cool stillness in my performing outfit, I called one last time on my old friend Byron to help me put things in perspective, in terms to which I could particularly relate. Terms that I have introduced here before. He wrote, in one of his last dispatches before fleeing the Carnival, that "All tragedies end with a death, all comedies with a marriage." In my small but lively sphere of affairs, there had been a death and a marriage, and many things tragic and comic had come to an end, but I was still alive and still single. I had arrived at a different terminus, for more than ever I was alone.